W9-BLF-098

Praise for *The Astonishing Thing*

"*The Astonishing Thing* is a unique and poignant tale of a family's struggle as witnessed by someone who sees everything. A heartfelt homage to the four-legged companions who accompany us through life's toughest times, this is a triumphant debut for Sandi Ward."
—Helen Brown, *New York Times* bestselling author of *Cleo*

"This sweet and insightful book, told from the perspective of the bright and loving cat Boo, follows the story of Boo's family. This tale provides a beautiful and touching look into the intricacies of marriage and family life, all seen through the loving and unique perspective of the family pet."
—*Modern Cat*

"*The Astonishing Thing* is so much more than a debut. Sandi Ward's writing will enrapture you, pull you in by the heart, and insist you become part of her story."
—Karen Sargent, author of *Waiting for Butterflies*

"This is a truly special book, one that captured my heart from the very first line. In Boo the cat, Sandi Ward has worked magic to create an utterly believable narrator with the consciousness and emotions of both a feline and a human member of a close-knit but troubled family, and with the wisdom of—well, the wisdom of a creature who loves deeply and unconditionally those with whom she shares a home. And we trust this wise and yet vulnerable narrative voice as if it were indeed *possible*."
—Holly Chamberlin, author of *Home for the Summer*

Please turn the page for more praise for
***The Astonishing Thing*!**

WITHDRAWN

JAN 1 8 2019

More outstanding praise for *The Astonishing Thing*!

"This charming novel reminds us that love and salvation can come in the most unexpected ways. I suspect all of us will look at our cats differently after reading this book."
—Susan Breen, author of the Maggie Dove mystery series

"Bittersweet, insightful, poignant, and devastatingly original. *The Astonishing Thing* will stay with you for a long time."
—Barbara Bos

SOMETHING WORTH SAVING

Books by Sandi Ward

THE ASTONISHING THING

SOMETHING WORTH SAVING

Published by Kensington Publishing Corporation

SOMETHING WORTH SAVING

SANDI WARD

KENSINGTON BOOKS
www.kensingtonbooks.com

WHITCHURCH-STOUFFVILLE PUBLIC LIBRARY

This book is a work of fiction. Names, characters, places, and incidents either are products of the author's imagination or are used fictitiously. Any resemblance to actual persons, living or dead, events, or locales is entirely coincidental.

KENSINGTON BOOKS are published by

Kensington Publishing Corp.
119 West 40th Street
New York, NY 10018

Copyright © 2019 by Sandra Ward

All rights reserved. No part of this book may be reproduced in any form or by any means without the prior written consent of the Publisher, excepting brief quotes used in reviews.

All Kensington titles, imprints, and distributed lines are available at special quantity discounts for bulk purchases for sales promotion, premiums, fund-raising, educational, or institutional use.

Special book excerpts or customized printings can also be created to fit specific needs. For details, write or phone the office of the Kensington Sales Manager: Kensington Publishing Corp., 119 West 40th Street, New York, NY 10018. Attn. Sales Department. Phone: 1-800-221-2647.

Kensington and the K logo Reg. U.S. Pat. & TM Off.

ISBN-13: 978-1-4967-1114-4 (ebook)
ISBN-10: 1-4967-1114-9 (ebook)
First Kensington Electronic Edition: January 2019

ISBN-13: 978-1-4967-1113-7
ISBN-10: 1-4967-1113-0
First Kensington Trade Paperback Printing: January 2019

10 9 8 7 6 5 4 3 2 1

Printed in the United States of America

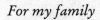

For my family

Chapter 1
A Boy Named Charlie

I worry most of all about the youngest boy.

Bad things have been happening lately. Unpredictable things that I don't see coming.

And someone has been hurting Charlie. I've seen the bruises.

Who would do such a thing?

Charlie arrives home at the same time every afternoon. Usually, I hear his footsteps on the outside stairs, and then the front door swings open. Most days, the doorknob clicks when it shuts behind him, and Charlie is already on the move—flinging his sneakers off, dropping his black backpack in the middle of the hall. He always heads straight for the kitchen to make a snack.

But today, he is early. Charlie opens the door cautiously, looking left to right. He steps into the house and waits on the mat, listening, clutching the strap of his backpack with one hand.

I watch from the middle of the stairs. I startle when I first see him, and scamper back.

He has changed in a most peculiar way, and I hardly recognize him!

This morning, the hair on his head was dark, and he looked very much like Dad. But now his hair is light, reminding me of the snowshoe hare kept in a crate by a girl down the street. What in the world happened to him?

He sees the way I arch my back, whiskers spread in shock. "It's okay, Lil," he whispers. "It's just me."

Why yes, it is. I would know that smooth face and those green eyes anywhere. I feel foolish for scaring so easily. Bending my head, I lick my paws to cover my embarrassment. My feet gather dust from the floors, which the humans rarely sweep. I reflexively clean myself whenever I don't want to be the focus of attention.

When I look up again, Charlie is leaning back against the front door, taking in a deep breath. Okay, so maybe he looks different. But I'll get used to it. Charlie shrugs his backpack off of his shoulder and lets it fall to the floor with a thud.

I hear Gretel, the big family dog, barking in the backyard. She's probably wasting her energy chasing a squirrel, and so Charlie and I will get a nice quiet moment together.

Charlie is such a sweet boy. He comes up a few stairs to sit beside me. His hands always smell like peanuts and pencil lead, although today a strange scent coming from his hair also tickles my nose. Charlie whispers in my sensitive ears: "Lily, Lily, Lil-Lil. Sorry if I scared you." His touch is gentle and soothing, and I lean my head into his fingers. "You're so beautiful," he coos.

I know, I know.

"Look at you. You're gorgeous. All that fluffy fur."

You're not so bad yourself. And I'll learn to love your hair. Just give me time.

Charlie likes to flatter me, but I think Charlie is good-looking too, compared to other humans. I would tell him so if I could. Charlie has grown several inches this past year, and he is getting stronger. He is almost a man. His long legs stretch out over many stairs.

I suspect that this change is something that Charlie did to himself, and it was not a sudden illness or an accident that lightened his hair. He is healthy and has a good appetite. Charlie is at the age when the teenagers start to preen and groom and try to make themselves attractive to other humans. I remember when Kevin and Victoria went through the same change.

Before long, we hear a bus rumbling down the narrow road in front of our house. It is big and yellow, so you can't miss it from our windows. A group of teenage boys ride on the bus in the afternoons to get to the sailing club across the street, and then they go out in boats on the river.

The humans enjoy living on the river, but I stay away from it. When I was younger, I would sneak through the fence across the street and pad my way under the boat trailers to get to the water. But the salt marsh is pungent and wet, not a good place for a cat. One time I accidentally fell into the river. The water was cold and dark, with no bottom. My feet flailed in nothingness and I barely managed to scramble out, my claws sunk into the mud. My fur was so heavy when wet! I still have nightmares about that day.

Another time, there was a red fox hiding in the marsh, and I had to run for my life. It was terrifying. Not that I had a doubt I could outrun that fox, because I'm fast and nimble. But the river doesn't interest me much anymore.

The teenage boys go out in their boats every day, until spring turns to summer. But before they do that, they run. They sprint right past our house. It's part of their routine.

"Here they come," Charlie whispers to me, shifting to get a better view out the big picture window.

Most days, Charlie will make himself a peanut butter sandwich and then watch the boys from the safety of our home. He can be shy, cautious about who he talks to. But maybe it's just curiosity. Perhaps Charlie wants to observe, without being seen.

I would understand that. I know a little something about curiosity.

Two years ago, I think Charlie hardly noticed the boys at all. Last year, he started watching from an upstairs bedroom.

This year, he usually stands behind a sheer curtain in the living room, stuffing his face with his sandwich. And he watches. I suppose that he is now the same age as some of the boys that sail on the river. I wonder if he knows any of them from school or the neighborhood.

The boys run together, like a pack of dogs. For the first couple of weeks, the days are so cold they can see their breath in the air. The boys jog past in sweatshirts and sweatpants, wearing hats that cover their ears. But now that spring is breaking, they wear shorts and thin jackets. There are usually a few big, strong, older boys in the lead. Then comes the middle of the pack, and there are always some stragglers at the end. They run around the block repeatedly, circling three times, before heading to the boats. Charlie is usually done with his sandwich, taking the last bites of the crust, by the time they are on their final round.

Sometimes he frowns, watching them. He occasionally moves away from the curtain, as if afraid someone will see him.

Other times, he looks wistful. As if he wishes he could join them. He seems lonely sometimes.

I have never seen Charlie run in my life. So this may not be the right activity for him. I wonder if he will ever try it.

Today, as soon as we've watched the boys run past, Charlie stands and heads upstairs. "C'mon, Lil!" he calls to me, and I follow.

First he walks into the bathroom. I jump onto the toilet to watch him. When he lifts up his shirt, I see it: faded bruising, turning from purple to green. On his side, by his ribs.

I have seen this kind of thing twice before, both recently. I know it means he has been injured. But I haven't seen Charlie hurt himself here at home.

It's truly terrible. The bruises on his body have convinced me that someone must be hurting him. But I don't know who to blame.

I tip my head to ask: *What happened to you?*

Charlie sighs, and stares at the mirror. I sometimes puzzle over why humans look into the shiny wall, but I have concluded they see a reflection of themselves. And in that reflection, they find the answers they seek.

I don't see anything but a silver sheen when I look at the wall. It's something of a mystery to me.

Charlie takes both hands and messes with his newly lightened hair so it stands up every which way. I blink. I would find it very uncomfortable for someone to push my fur around like that. But it doesn't seem to bother him.

We both flinch at the same time as we hear the front door open again. Charlie straightens out his shirt. I know he won't show anyone that he has been hurt.

When he is injured, he hides it.

"Charlie!" we hear from the front hallway. It's Kevin. He is bigger, older, louder. He gives Charlie all kinds of advice and orders. I think Kevin often feels the need to confirm his place as a dominant human in this house. His voice booms up the stairs. "I know you're here. I see your backpack. What the hell's going on? The principal stopped me in the hallway to say no one could find you. He was about to call the police, but I told him you probably went home, and I'd check." There's a pause. "Hey, Charlie. Answer me."

"SHUT UP," Charlie yells back, not leaving the bathroom. "It's none of your business. You're not Dad. So stay out of it."

Oh dear. Did Charlie leave school in the middle of the day again? I always worry about Charlie getting himself into trouble.

"CHARLIE." The voice gets louder, and we freeze. Heavy footsteps let us know Kevin is coming up the stairs. Charlie's face creases in concern. "Mom and Dad are too busy at work to keep getting calls from the school." There are three hard knocks on the door. "I'm coming in."

Kevin has to push to get the sticky door to open. All of the doors in the house get jammed in their frames. Nothing quite fits as it should.

Charlie and I both take a step back. The bathroom is small, and Charlie is up against the shower curtain. "Stop," he begs. "You're not Dad. Stop shouting at me."

I wish I could say: *I agree.*

I don't like it when humans yell. It makes my fur stand on end.

Kevin's eyes open wide. "Holy hell. What did you do?"

Charlie shakes his head. "I just missed a few classes. Gym. And study hall. No one cares. And maybe math—okay, I missed math too."

"No," Kevin interrupts, "your hair."

Charlie looks over at me, but there is nowhere to hide. Nowhere to go. I don't know what to tell him to do.

Kevin starts to move toward Charlie, with his hand up as if he wants to touch Charlie's hair, and Charlie flinches. I instinctively *hiss!* I spit like a sparking blaze in the fireplace. Just a warning: Stay away from my boy.

Kevin moves back to where he was.

"Kev, please. I went to Karen's house and we dyed my hair. It's not a big deal." Charlie tries to move, but his legs are up against the tub and there's nowhere to go. "Please just leave me alone."

Kevin steps out of the bathroom, hands up in surrender. "Wow. Dad's going to love that. I don't even know what to say, just—wow." He backs up slowly, as if he's afraid I might attack him. "Okay. Good luck when the principal calls Dad. He's gonna love this. Really. Dad will love it. Skipping school for *that*? Man. Good luck, buddy." He turns and heads down the stairs, shaking his head.

Thanks for nothing, I wish I could call after him.

Charlie and I look at each other. I don't think the hair change is so bad. It's already growing on me. I think Charlie looks rather interesting.

I let Charlie pick me up, going limp in his hands. I'm not a small cat. But he places me carefully on his shoulder as if I'm delicate cargo, and carries me to his room. We both lie down on his bed, right on top of the red wool blanket. Charlie and I enjoy lounging in his bedroom upstairs, staying away from activity. The afternoon sun peeks through the slats of the blinds and casts a warm light. We don't have a view of the river since his bedroom faces the backyard, but through his window I can see down into the garden lined with bright pink rugosa and the woods beyond. Charlie sighs and puts his big blue headphones over his ears; I hear a beat playing. I curl up near the bruise on his side.

Poor Charlie. He is the youngest in this family. He often seems sad and I wish I could do more to make him feel better.

Charlie is my favorite human. He's the one who chose me. He walked up and down the long hallway full of hundreds of cats where I was waiting to be adopted, and as soon as he saw me, he pointed me out to Dad. I was the only one left of my litter, and I missed my siblings terribly, living alone in a cage. As soon as our eyes met, I knew I'd found my soul mate. Charlie has the most amazing human eyes, and they lit up when he looked me over.

There is a reason I was the last one chosen in my family. It is something unimportant—something that makes no difference to me—but the humans notice it.

I was injured when I was young. My siblings and I were born in a cold house, and a human who I can hardly remember liked to move us out of his way with a kick. I was only a kitten when I unexpectedly received a hard jolt from a heavy boot one night, and my back leg was broken. The pain was horrible. My siblings were in no position to help me. There was nothing any of us could do but stumble to get out of the way when we heard the human coming. Finally, one day we were put into a bag and the next thing I remember is waking up in a cage.

Humans smile when they see my face, but frown when they first see me walk. My gait is not graceful, because my back leg never healed quite right.

But rest assured it does not slow me down. No—just the opposite. I take pride in my speed. I have worked hard to become as strong as any cat who lives on the river.

When he saw me in the cage, Charlie lifted me carefully with two hands and told Dad, "I want this one. Look at her long fur. Why hasn't anyone adopted her yet? She's so cute." He laughed. "She's practically hugging me. Look at her, Dad. I love her already. She wants to go home with me."

When the woman in charge of the cages put me on the ground and had me demonstrate how I walk, I looked up at Charlie and Dad to watch their reaction. And I tell you this: They did not frown. No.

In fact, Dad gave a small smile and nodded, as if I were exactly what he wanted. Charlie looked up into his father's face, and that was that. Their minds were made up.

"She's a little different," Dad said quietly to Charlie, his hand on the back of his son's head. "I like that. You know, it's okay to be a little different."

Charlie bit his bottom lip, and I knew that he agreed. And I guessed that, perhaps, Charlie was a little different himself in some way.

So they brought me home and named me Lily. Dad found a nice bed for me, which I appreciate and sometimes use during the day. But at night I sleep with Charlie on his bed.

Now that I am older, I appreciate Charlie even more. I know

who looks out for me. I know who loves me best. We are as close as animal and human could ever be. So I wish I could do more for him.

No creature should be mistreated. I did not deserve it, and neither does Charlie. I remember the fear, the constant knot of anxiety in my stomach that I felt when I heard the bad man coming. And I recall how humiliating it was to be too small to fight back. It makes my eyes sting and nose quiver when I think about it.

Believe me, if I knew who was hurting Charlie, I would scratch his eyes out.

I am sound asleep when the doorbell rings. Charlie jumps up, and I scramble to my feet. It is a loud musical chime that always makes my heart leap. We hear Kevin's footsteps clomping down the front hall, and the door creaks open. Gretel's nails click on the wood as she follows Kevin, and she gives a sharp *woof woof woof!* Her bark of warning echoes up the stairs, but Kevin scolds her, telling her to quiet down. Adult voices murmur, and Charlie puts a hand on my back.

There is a long pause. "Charlie," Kevin calls up the stairs, his voice breaking. He does not yell this time, which almost makes it worse. "The police are here to talk to you."

Like I said, bad things keep happening.

Chapter 2
Serious Face

Charlie walks down the stairs slowly, one hand on the railing. I watch from the top of the stairs.

Two young men in blue uniforms stand in the doorway. They don't step inside, but they study Charlie, looking him over from head to toe several times, as if he must be hiding something. As they question Charlie, Kevin folds his arms and says "sorry" quite a few times with a stern glance at Charlie, as if he is Dad.

Which he certainly is not.

"I'm fine. I'm safe," I hear Charlie plead. "My older brother is here. There's nothing wrong. I just didn't feel well, so my friend Karen brought me to her house. Then I came home."

There are many more questions. One of the men, with a shaved head, writes down Charlie's answers on a pad of paper.

"It won't happen again," Kevin promises, putting one hand on the doorframe, as if he's getting weary and needs to hold himself up. Charlie hangs back, as if he's nervous the men might try to snatch him and take him away.

The men warn Charlie that he cannot just leave school anytime he feels like it. Finally they go, getting back into their fancy car in the driveway.

Once they're out of sight, Charlie whirls around to face Kevin. "Why didn't you call the principal back?" He has tears in his eyes, and his bottom lip trembles. "Why didn't you tell him I was home?"

"I did." Kevin shakes his head. "That's what I don't get. I did call him right back, and I told him you were fine." He chews on the inside of his mouth a moment, thinking. "I guess when the principal called Dad, Dad probably told him to send the cops anyway. Just to teach you a lesson."

Charlie puts one hand on his forehead, and takes in a deep, shaky breath. I walk over and throw my body against his ankles to help him calm himself.

"Jesus, Charlie. You deserve it," Kevin mutters as he walks away, moving down the hall. "You bring this stuff on yourself."

Charlie frowns, watching his older brother.

"I don't deserve it," he whispers. But Kevin is already gone.

When she gets home from school, Victoria sees Charlie's hair and gasps in delight. She tells him she loves it. He flashes her a shy smile.

If there's anyone in the family who would appreciate this change in Charlie, it is Victoria. She is interesting to look at, and takes care with her appearance. Victoria has long hair, sleek and dark and shiny. She wears little jewels that sit on her ears and one that she has somehow attached to her nose. Her fingernails are painted striking colors: purple, pink, or blue. And she decorates her collarbone with glittering chains. If she were a bird, I think she would be a graceful blue heron, with a strong back, long neck, and glistening eyes.

As the middle child and the only girl, you might think Victoria was at a disadvantage in this family. But believe me when I tell you: They all get out of her way when they hear her coming.

"Do you really like it?" Charlie asks.

"Yeah," she gushes. "It suits you. It does."

The kitchen is bright and warm, and Kevin rolls his eyes as he sets the table for dinner. "It doesn't suit him. We all have dark hair. He looks crazy."

"What, Kev?" Victoria puts her hands on her hips. "Hey. Jackass. Did you say something?"

"Nope." Kevin adjusts a fork and knife so they are perfectly lined up. I watch him swallow, as if his mouth has gone dry.

We are the babies of the family, Charlie and I, but Kevin is the one with a baby face. He combs his wavy hair and buttons his shirts and keeps himself clean. He has very good grooming habits.

If Kevin were an animal, he might be a sleek black bear. Neat. Solitary. Quiet unless provoked. I saw a bear once in the woods, at a distance. He didn't notice me, and I certainly didn't bother him. I'm not stupid.

Mom arrives home last, rushing in from work. She is surprised at Charlie's hair, but doesn't seem too concerned about it. She starts making dinner, taking a bag of vegetables out of the freezer.

Mom has been a ball of nerves lately. Distracted. And tired. I know she misses Dad, even though she's the one who told him he had to move out.

As the family eats, I lounge on the tile floor, listening to the pleasant sound of silverware clinking and voices murmuring. Gretel, who is black and tan and what they call a "German shepherd," waits on the opposite side of the room. I think "German shepherd" is just a showy name for a big dog. Gretel is Dad's dog, just as I am Charlie's cat. Dad did not take Gretel with him when he moved out, for reasons that aren't clear to me just yet.

Gretel's pink tongue hangs out, panting as she watches the

humans eat. While she has the strength and quickness of a wolf, and probably has the skills to survive in the wild, Gretel spends half her time begging the humans for food.

It's just chicken. Yes, of course it's delicious and the savory scent makes my mouth water. But I would never beg for it. One time, Gretel stole raw chicken from the kitchen counter. Raw chicken—imagine! She got in big trouble and made herself very sick. The humans think she is an intelligent dog, but I'm not always sure about that. Her instincts overcome her common sense sometimes.

Mom sits where she always does, near the window. She pulls her hair back behind her shoulders repeatedly, when it threatens to touch her food. Her eyes flit from Kevin, to Victoria, to Charlie. She doesn't stare at any one child for too long, but it's clear she is studying them.

Mom's skin is pale, and her face seems to reflect a reluctant understanding of everything around her, as if the world disappoints her in some way. Her hair is thin, warm and brown when she is in the shadows, but glinting as red as a maple leaf when strands catch the sunlight just right. Sometimes she will braid it. Her eyes widen slightly when she sees something that interests her, reminding me of a cat in the darkness. Her mouth is small. It pouts when she is listening carefully to someone, and relaxes when she is thinking about something that pleases her.

Gretel turns her head, and her ears perk up. A minute later, a knock at the door makes me jump. Could that be Dad? But the family isn't done eating yet.

Mom glances at the kitchen clock. "He's early."

Kevin immediately stands, and pushes his chair back. "I'll get it."

Gretel takes off, bounding down the hallway. I don't know how she always knows it is Dad. I believe it is something about the sound of his shoes on the walkway. Gretel has amazing hearing. I will admit, it is better than mine.

I follow Kevin and Gretel to the front door. Sure enough, it's Dad! He studies Kevin with a serious face. It's a face that lets you know he's thinking about very important things. "Hey, Kev. Okay if I come in?"

"Yeah, of course." Kevin nods. "We're just finishing up dinner."

Hmm. This is interesting. When Dad comes to the house, sometimes he sounds the car horn, and the children all run out to meet him. Other times, he comes to the front door. But Dad doesn't usually step inside. He waits out on the porch, even in the rain. It seems curious to me.

And oh, how Gretel loves him! She jumps right up on Dad and tries to lick his face and hands. He rubs the thick fur around her neck with two hands in response.

I believe she may be happier to see him than the children are sometimes.

I miss Dad too. When he visits, I can't get enough of him. There are three things I think about the most when I remember Dad:

1. Our naps together. On weekend afternoons, Dad would work outside in the yard, and then he and I would nap together on the big couch. His body smelled like sweat, dead leaves, and rotten marsh grass—absolutely wonderful!
2. The sand. He often had sand in his shoes and socks. On summer days, he would walk barefoot in the house.
3. His thumb. Dad liked to rub his thumb up against the base of my left ear. I loved how it felt. He always put just the right amount of pressure on my skull. Not too hard, not too soft.

When we reach the kitchen, Charlie slumps down in his seat. Victoria glances up, but then resumes eating. "Hi, Dad. We're not ready yet."

"I know," he says, one hand on the back of a wooden chair. He's staring at Charlie. Who won't look back at him. "Hey, Charlie. Your principal called me today. Can we talk for a minute?"

Mom raises an eyebrow. She clears her throat. "Hi, Jeremy. Nice to see you too. What's this about?"

Dad keeps his hair short and neat. He has gentle eyes and a fine face, as far as human faces go. But his expression is often set in a frown, his mouth tight, as if he is trying to tolerate something uncomfortable.

Dad sits. "I got a call that Charlie left school in the middle of the day. The gym teacher reported him missing, and then no one could find him."

"So you had the police come?" Charlie grips his fork tightly. "Dad. That was so stupid and ridiculous."

"The police?" Mother's voice goes weak. "What?"

Dad nods, and looks down at his lap. "When the principal called me, I told him to go right ahead and call the police. Because we have a law that says a fourteen-year-old has to stay in school." He looks up at Charlie. "You're lucky we live in a small town where people know each other."

Charlie snorts. "Yeah. I'm real lucky."

"You *are* lucky. I'm friends with most of those cops, so I knew they'd go easy on you."

Charlie finally lifts his head to squint at his father. "So you told my principal to send the *police*? Isn't that a little dramatic? I mean, where else would I be but home?"

"I DON'T KNOW." Dad's voice takes on a deep, harsh tone. I realize that he is very unhappy. I'm sure Dad wishes he could move back home. "Sometimes, I have no idea what you're thinking. You can't leave school. You have to stay there. If you need to leave for some reason, I'll come get you. You can't just disappear."

My whiskers tingle. Maybe Charlie left school because someone is bullying him there. I bet that's it. I haven't figured out where Charlie is getting his injuries, but this makes sense—it could be happening at school, during the day. I wish Charlie would say something to Dad. If I were Charlie, I would tell my parents that someone was hurting me. I would allow them to tend to my wounds.

I would also tell Kevin. He is the older brother and his job should be to protect Charlie. There might be something he could do to help. It makes me angry and frustrated to think that no one even knows about it.

"You haven't said anything about his hair." Kevin gestures toward Charlie. "Dad. Seriously. I mean, did you even notice that he looks different?"

Dad narrows his eyes and turns toward Kevin. "Can you excuse us, go upstairs, and get your stuff ready?"

Kevin blanches. "Um, yeah. Sure, Dad. Sorry." He glances down at his unfinished food. Reaching across the table, he piles his silverware on his plate and grabs his glass, carrying everything over to the sink. With care, he scrapes and rinses each item and places it in the dishwasher, then heads upstairs without a word.

"We can talk about this more at my apartment," Dad offers. "Why don't you guys finish up and get your bags." He nods toward Victoria. "Okay?"

"I don't want to go," Charlie moans. "Please, can I just stay here this weekend? You're just gonna watch baseball with Kevin. It'll be so boring."

Victoria takes a look at Dad. He looks exhausted, his face ashen. She gets up, taking her glass and plate to the sink. "C'mon, Charlie. We'll find something fun for you to do. Let's go pack."

Hanging his head, Charlie gets up, sticks his hands in his pockets, and follows his sister. He leaves all of his things right where they are on the table, knowing his mother will clean up after him.

"He's having a rough week," Mom says quietly, pushing her food absentmindedly with a fork.

"A rough week?" Dad shakes his head. "*He's* having a rough week? He should see *my* week. Christ. It sounds more like he's choosing to skip school, and then back-sass me when I ask about it. Goddamn it." He pinches the bridge of his nose with one hand, and closes his eyes. "If Kevin hadn't texted me back . . . I swear to God, I would have torn this town apart looking for that kid myself."

"But he did text you back. And Charlie was home safe." Mom stands. "Charlie is okay, Jeremy. You know he's not the kind of kid who gets into trouble."

Dad gets up when he sees Mom moving toward the sink. "Okay. I know. You're right." He is still for a moment, watching Mom start to clean up. She rinses plates and ignores him, as if he's already left. He stares at her back as if there's something he wants to say, but he's unable to say it. "Okay. I'm going to go wait in the car. I'll talk to Charlie tomorrow when I've cooled off."

Once Dad has shut the front door behind him, Mom turns off the sink faucet. She walks to the foot of the stairs. "Are you guys ready?"

Kevin comes jogging down, duffle bag over his shoulder. "Change your T-shirt, will you?" Kevin calls over his shoulder to Charlie. "That one's so bright it hurts my eyes. It's giving me a headache."

Mom hands Kevin his sweatshirt. He leans in toward her.

"Mom," he says quietly. "I think it's okay if Charlie stays home sometimes. Dad and I just want peace and quiet to watch some baseball, you know? But Charlie's being a pain in the ass lately. We wouldn't mind a break from him."

Mom's eyes open wide as she looks up at her son. As the oldest in the family, Kevin says things to Mom that no one else would dare say. He's a good boy, and she listens to him.

"Kevin. Your Dad wants Charlie there. Your Dad loves all of you. And he misses all of you. Very much."

Kevin pulls the sweatshirt over his head, and shoves his hands in the pockets. "Yeah, I know. He loves all of us. That doesn't mean Dad wants to hang out with Charlie. There's a difference, you know? Look, Charlie doesn't want to be there. He complains the whole time. Charlie's going through some stuff right now, a phase where he—"

"Kevin. It's not—"

"But maybe if he just stayed—"

"Shhhhh," Mom says, rubbing his elbow. "Charlie isn't coming with you to *hang out*. It's not a frat house, or a play date. He needs to see his dad."

I understand why Mom doesn't want to hear it. There may be nothing she can do to fix this. The children have to visit their dad sometimes. It seems natural, and right.

I wish I could ask Dad why he hasn't talked to Mom about moving back in. I think he is a little afraid of Mom, and what she might say. Dad moved out after the big winter holidays, under a full moon. Now, the snow has melted, the earth is warming, and a full moon has come and gone several times over. So it has been a while.

Kevin peeks out the window when lights flash against the walls. "He's waiting. I'm gonna go."

"Kevin, you drive, okay?" Mom turns to him and taps his elbow. "Don't let him drive. Your dad has been really tired lately."

"Sure."

As soon as Victoria appears at the top of the stairs, Kevin opens the front door. He runs out, Gretel's leash in hand. They practically race each other to the car.

A minute later, Kevin brings Gretel back.

"Um, Dad said you should keep Gretel." Kevin hands Mom the leash. "He said he thinks you need Gretel for protection when you're alone in the house. He said that's why he got the dog in the first place, for security." Kevin seems annoyed. "I don't get it. It's not like anyone has ever tried to break in here."

Confusion creases Mom's forehead, but only for a moment. "He's just trying to be thoughtful. He's trying to be nice. And having all three of you for the weekend at the apartment is a lot for him. It's all right. I'll take her." Mom unsnaps the leash, and Gretel walks reluctantly down the hall to the kitchen, head hanging low in disappointment.

I feel a little bad for Gretel.

Mom sighs. Her work has been tiring lately, especially now that she works all day, and she is the only one here to cook and clean up after the children at night. Mom works at a preschool, where she is the director. I don't know what this means precisely, but I know she is in charge of many important things and must bear the burden of worrying about many people. I imagine that at work she wears a special hat or perhaps a crown, and her workers listen carefully to her and do her bidding.

That's my best guess, anyway, from the way Dad says she "lords it over her subjects" at the preschool. I have heard him explain it this way at the dinner table, and call her Queen Kate. He says she is very tough. When Dad says she intimidates her subjects with her icy stare and strict tone, the children nod eagerly, and then burst into smiles.

The children find something funny in this, but I do not. It is true that Mom can be strict. No one likes to cross her. She is the voice of authority around here.

Victoria takes her time, coming down the steps while staring at the phone in her hand. Head bowed, back straight. Mom moves just in time to kiss the side of her daughter's head as she passes by.

Charlie is last to come down the stairs, his backpack in his hand. He has changed his shirt. He looks like he is on the verge of tears. Mom hugs him for a good, long minute. Finally, a honking from the driveway startles them both.

Charlie turns to me. "Bye, Lily."

Good-bye, sweet boy. Take care of yourself.

"Bye, Mom."

"Bye, baby." Mom swallows. She watches Charlie for a minute before shutting the door gently behind him.

Mom leans against the door. I go to sit at her feet. When I crane my head up, I see her face is set in a hard frown. I think that Charlie's actions and Kevin's words have upset her.

I wish she wouldn't worry. But I understand. I worry too. I want both Charlie and Dad to be happy—not just in life, but with each other.

The fact is, I might as well forget about them for a while, because now we have a nice evening to look forward to! Mom and I will enjoy fluffy blankets and tasty snacks and the comfy couch and the blaring TV. Mom might let me lick the bowl when she finishes her ice cream. And later, I will snuggle up right by her side, my head near hers, my paw on her arm. We will have the big bed all to ourselves!

Gretel will lie on the bedroom rug and guard us. She does not cuddle. Watching over our family is her calling in life, and I respect that.

As soon as the kitchen is clean, Mom and I both stretch out on the couch. It is lovely. Perhaps it is a little too quiet, but very nice nonetheless.

I wish I could talk to Mom about Charlie. If only there were a way I could tell her about the awful bruises.

Mom and I worry together in spirit, if not in words.

Little do I know that tomorrow someone will enter our lives and change the course of everything.

Chapter 3
The New Man

Mom has a good friend, a man named Vincent. He has been her friend for years, and he has come over quite a bit since Dad left. I know he lives down the street, because I've seen him in his yard during my evening walks. He has his own wife and children. Vincent is very good at fixing things that are broken.

I know all of our neighbors, because I spend a lot of time prowling around the block. The fact is, our house is small and cramped on the inside—but oh! We have a wonderful outside! The river attracts magnificent white swans, green-headed mallards, and long-tailed wood ducks. Behind our house is a small garden, and beyond that there are woods full of deer, voles, daddy longlegs, dragonflies, big black ants, and bats at dusk. The forest floor is covered in dry, spiky pine needles, and beneath that is the cool sand. I go exploring all the time.

Vincent lives five houses down, in a little gray cottage not much different from ours. He will look at whatever it is that is perplexing Mom, and suggest a solution. For example, if a painting needs to be hung, or a pipe is leaking, he will study the problem. He'll push his glasses on tighter and think about it.

Then he goes out and gets what he needs, and comes back to repair it.

If Vincent were a creature, he might be a crafty spider who weaves beautiful webs. He has a talent for his work.

Kevin once suggested to Mom that she "give the poor guy a break." Kevin sometimes scowls when he sees Vincent is over yet again. But Mom knows something that her son is not quite old enough to understand.

I understand it, because I am always watching.

You see, Vincent doesn't mind helping Mom. Not at all. He rather enjoys it. He is a problem solver.

The way he beams when she compliments him makes it clear to me that he feels rewarded by her words. Perhaps his own family does not appreciate his skills. And it probably doesn't hurt that she is genuinely grateful.

"I don't know what I'd do without you," she'll say.

But this Saturday morning, when Vincent comes over, he is not smiling.

We started the day with our usual breakfast—coffee and cereal for Mom, dry food for me and Gretel—and then Mom did her stretches. When she was done, I think Vincent sent her a message, because Mom frowned after checking her phone and made more coffee. She ran upstairs to change into different clothes and brush her hair. Then she came down to pick up the things all over the kitchen counter and throw them into a closet.

Gretel started pacing anxiously. We both wish we could help Mom sometimes.

"It's okay, Gretel. Just give me a bark when he gets here."

Gretel answered: *Roo!*

After Vincent arrives, he and Mom sit at the kitchen table and talk quietly. I flop down on the floor, across the room, catching every other word. Gretel listens too, her pointy ears alert.

I hear that someone's condition is "bad, very bad." Vincent looks grim, adjusting his glasses. I listen more closely, and determine that his wife is sick—or, perhaps, sicker than she used to be. He hunches over his coffee cup as if the news is threatening to swallow him up. He says his wife is being admitted to the hospital to treat her cancer.

Mom winces. "Vincent. I'm so sorry."

When Mom rubs his arm, he just closes his eyes, as if he cannot believe this small kindness. As if it is the only good thing to happen to him in a long time.

Mom looks worried. She stares at Vincent, eyes creased in a frown. She drinks more of her coffee, gulping it down in a hurry.

"I'm really sorry about the timing. I don't want this to delay your project. You've been waiting a long time to get this done." Vincent shakes his head. I am not sure what project he is referring to.

Mom startles. "Don't be silly. Don't worry about it. The project can wait."

"Yeah, maybe some of it can, but it's more than just the bookshelves." He gestures toward the back room, off of the kitchen. "Those window frames are really rotted out, and you can barely see through the windows with the seal broken and all that fog between the panes. And you need more insulation in the walls—you said they're drafty all winter, right? I think we should get it done this spring, so you're ready for the fall. And we'll have to finish with a new coat of paint, but honestly, you need it anyway. The wall above the couch is pretty scuffed up, probably thanks to the kids." Vincent looks at her over his glasses. "I actually have an idea on how we can get started. I've found a friend of a friend who can help us out. Someone I know through church. Someone who needs a small job just like this one. He's a good guy."

I watch Mom's nose wrinkle. Of course, she doesn't want a

"friend of a friend" in this house. I know that. She wants Vincent. Vincent likes Mom, he likes the kids, he likes Gretel, he likes me. It's hard to consider allowing someone else—a stranger, someone with an unfamiliar voice and habits—in this house for any period of time.

"I'll send him over to get a look at the space," Vincent offers. I can see how he hates to disappoint Mom, the way he glances down at his lap. Vincent barely touches his coffee. "Would today be okay?"

Mom nods. "I have to go out this afternoon," she responds, leaning toward him. "But your friend can come by. The key will be here."

I know where Mom hides the key. I have seen it on the rim of a large potted plant by the front door.

Vincent knows where it is too. That's how much Mom trusts him.

"Thank you," Vincent gushes, as if she has done him a great favor.

"Oh, Vincent. This is terrible." Mom envelops him in a hug. "It's not fair. You're such a good person. Why is this happening to you?"

I feel bad that Vincent's wife is sick. He is always so good to Mom. But Mom is wrong to think that the health of Vincent's family has anything to do with him being a good person.

Perhaps it is unfair. But that's just the way the world works.

The world is made up of predators and prey. Some creatures are big and athletic, natural hunters—like myself—and we rule the top of the food chain. I can clear our yard of any bug, bird, or animal that becomes a nuisance. But other creatures are born frail, or they become weak because of age or illness. It is a fact of life. If a human or an animal gets sick, it is no one's fault. It is just the way bodies work. They are susceptible. They break down.

When I was little and the bad man kicked me, my leg broke.

When someone hits or pinches Charlie, he bruises. He feels pain.

I know all about it. Many creatures are vulnerable.

Eventually it's time for my morning nap. Charlie's bed is my favorite spot, so I gallop up the stairs. I love the abrasive texture of his blanket. His bed is unmade, just the way I like it, and I find a comfy spot to rest.

I'm only half-listening as Mom shows Vincent out. Soon after, I hear the shower running and water draining through the pipes of the house, and I nod off. I wake when I hear the door to the garage open and close as Mom goes out to do her errands.

The only sound left is Gretel panting. I know Gretel is sitting in the hallway, waiting to see if Mom comes back because she forgot something.

Like a big black-and-tan dog, perhaps?

But Gretel has no such luck. Mom must have other plans that don't involve driving around a giant dog with a long snout and a slobbery tongue.

Time floats by. I stir when I hear the sound of a key rattling in the lock to the front door. My head immediately picks up.

Ah! The friend of a friend.

I hear the creak of the heavy front door swinging open, and then Gretel's low growl.

Hmmmm. This could be interesting.

I have seen Gretel chase men before. I have witnessed a man who was trimming the bushes in our yard scramble up on top of a car to get away from her. First he jumped onto the hood of the car, and then realizing he was not high enough, he climbed right onto the roof! The poor man was just doing his job, but Gretel didn't seem to understand that.

When humans first see Gretel, their eyes light up with fear. Gretel is certainly strong and fast, and the humans say she is smart. As I've mentioned, I haven't quite seen the evidence to convince me one way or the other regarding her intelligence. But there is no doubt Gretel is a physical force to be reckoned with.

So it remains to be seen how Gretel will react to this intruder.

I need to see this!

I jump up, stretch my back, and then leap down to Charlie's rug. I pad over into the hallway to take a peek from between the slats of the balcony, and look down to see who has come in.

At first, the sun coming in the picture window blinds me. I blink, and then my eyes adjust.

Oh.

Oh!

Tall and broad and younger than Vincent. Pale skin and black hair that twists in waves, looking like it's never seen a brush. It covers his forehead and almost hangs in his eyes. A faded T-shirt, more threadbare than the smart way Vincent usually dresses.

I don't know what I was expecting. But not this.

The man freezes when he sees Gretel crouched in the hallway, and slowly shuts the door behind him. He puts out a hand.

"Hey, boy. It's okay. It's alright."

Gretel cocks her head. For goodness sake. She's not a boy. But I'm sure it makes no difference to Gretel. She waits to see if this is friend or foe.

The man's voice is soothing, but his rigid posture gives away the fact that he's nervous. He stands completely still. I'm sure Gretel senses it too.

I assume that Vincent, in his grief, forgot to mention to this man the wolflike creature that guards this house. So now I get to watch, to see if Gretel will make a sport of chasing this man.

He has a bag over his shoulder, which he finally slips off, taking his time and not making any sudden movements. He sets the bag on the floor. Crouching down to Gretel's level, he murmurs to her. Gretel just watches him for a moment.

"C'mere, boy," he calls. "It's okay. Hey, you're a good boy."

This guy is never going to get anywhere. Gretel doesn't like any man who is not Dad. She doesn't even like Vincent that much, and he's lovely.

I also suspect Gretel doesn't like being called "good." I enjoy being called a "good girl" because I try to be just that: sweet and loving, greedy for cuddles.

But for a warrior like Gretel, it's just condescending. She'd probably prefer—yes, I think this works—"brave dog."

Finally, Gretel walks over, head down. She sniffs the man's hand and his knees. She allows him to pet her head, then her back. I'm impressed to see the man actually kneel down on the floor and let her smell him all over. She jumps up and sticks her wet snout in his ear. He flinches, but lets her do it.

Most humans aren't so patient. They're usually in a rush. And afraid of Gretel's sharp teeth.

Gretel is intimidating. But this human is not in a hurry, and he forces himself to be still. It makes him a little different from most other humans. He has a calm energy.

When he finally stands, the man takes a long look around. I'm surprised all over again when he looks up and sees me. I thought I was fairly well hidden, on the balcony. But we make eye contact, and his mouth turns up into a crooked smile.

"Hey, sweetheart," he says to me.

My goodness. My ears twitch.

Hello, sir.

I suppose I'm hard to miss. With all this buttery fur, fluffed just so.

I get up and decide to go right down the stairs and see what project this man is going to work on. Each paw sinks silently into the musty carpet that covers our stairs as I sneak after him.

By the time I reach the bottom stair, he has disappeared, taking long strides to go straight back to the kitchen and around the corner to the study. Vincent must have told him where to go. Gretel follows him, and I take up the rear. I stop at the doorway to observe.

The man places his bag on the floor and hunts around for this and that. He studies the back wall and pulls some kind of tape out of a little box and runs it over the wall before typing things into his phone. Then he does the same to the three windows. I watch as he takes his time with this task. Gretel stands right behind him, watching him with curious eyes.

I think I have figured out what this project is. Mom has talked before about wanting bookshelves built into the wall, surrounding the fireplace. She has a lot of books, and nowhere to put them. They pile up on the floor of her bedroom. And Vincent also mentioned he is going to replace the rotting old windows. So I think the whole room is going to be fixed up.

I finally feel comfortable enough with this new man to wander in and brush my head against Gretel's shoulder. She moves away from me.

Gretel loves me, but she does not like to get too close. I believe she prefers to think of herself as fierce and independent.

Believe me, I am independent too, but at least I'm capable of showing affection to those I love. Sometimes I resent Gretel for being so standoffish.

Gretel's priorities in life are:

1. Dad.
2. Guarding the family.
3. Food. Preferably meat. But anything she can sink her teeth into will do in a pinch.

The man watches me walk and frowns. "Are you okay, sweetie?"

It's an old injury to my leg. Just ignore it.

When he is satisfied that I am not in pain, he turns and looks over some photos of our family that sit on a side table. He studies each one carefully. There is one of Mom and Dad and all of the children from many years ago that he stops to study. In this photo, the children are younger, all either squinting or squirmy or distracted. But Mom is smiling up at Dad and he has his arm around her with a grin on his face. They look very happy.

The man shakes his head. I don't think he is very focused on his job at all.

He finally unfolds a big piece of paper. He reads it carefully. The man looks up at the wall, then back at the paper. His eyes turn again to the wall, and then down to the paper. He sighs, taking in a deep breath. There is clearly something he doesn't understand. He looks around the room almost wistfully, as if this room calls memories to mind.

But, of course, he's never been here before.

It's puzzling.

Finally, the man packs up his things. Gretel allows him to pet her again, and she follows him to the door. I can see that something about him attracts her. We both move to the picture window to watch him go down the walkway in the front yard, and then get into his truck and drive away.

Truth be told, I have mixed feelings about this. I am happy and excited that Mom is finally getting bookshelves and new windows. She and Dad talked about this project many times.

But I'm sorry that Dad won't be here to enjoy it. And I'm concerned this new man may not be able to make Mom's dreams into a reality, because he is not Vincent. I don't know if he has the talent to pull it off. I sincerely hope he does, because Mom has been sad lately and this might make her feel better.

If Mom starts to feel better, she might have more energy to devote to my sweet Charlie, and she may discover that he is being bullied and take action. So I will welcome this man, and try to make him feel at home.

I would like to be Charlie's hero. I need a plan. It's one thing to chase down a cricket, or scare off a squirrel. I've even faced off against two huge, wild turkeys and sent them running into the woods.

But dealing with a human bully? That will require a little more thought.

I remember the pain when that human kicked me. I don't recall much about the man himself, but his hands were always cold and smelled sour, like the tomato sauce he ate every day. He took our mom from us and left us in a dark kitchen for hours at a time with no food or water. And there was nothing we could do. We were just kittens. I wonder if this is how Charlie feels, as if there is nothing he can do about it because he isn't strong enough to fight back.

But why hasn't he told anyone?

I feel sick about it, because after my siblings and I were abused, we were moved to a shelter. Is that what Charlie fears? It is hard to imagine, but would that be Mom's solution, to send him away in order to keep him safe?

What would my life become without my sweet Charlie? I can't imagine my days without our quiet hours napping in his lovely warm room, lying on our favorite scratchy wool blanket. It breaks my heart to even think about it.

Chapter 4
Powerful Medicine

When Mom comes home later, there is no trace of a man having been here, although I can still smell him. The back room retains the faint odors of pepper and cheese, which might reflect what he ate for a recent meal. But Mom doesn't notice it, because she doesn't have my exquisitely sensitive nose.

Mom fries flounder for dinner, and I get leftovers in my bowl. The white slivers of fish are buttery and flaky, melting on my tongue.

Gretel has some fish too. She will eat just about anything— and I mean anything. She once ate paper money off a side table. Mom was angry, but perhaps more than that, she was shocked. Because what creature on earth eats paper money?

Gretel's hunger gets the best of her.

After dinner, Dad calls Mom on the phone, I suppose to tell her how the children are doing. Mom listens patiently, but I can tell she is exhausted. She closes her eyes and holds a hand to the side of her head. And, later that night, we sleep soundly in the quiet cottage.

* * *

When the kids get home on Sunday night, I'm excited to see them. I'm waiting on the front step, and I hear Gretel give a *woof!* from inside the house at the sound of the car engine. Dad gets out of the car to hug Victoria and Kevin good-bye, and the two oldest children jog past me to get inside. Charlie starts to follow them.

"Charlie. Wait." Dad puts his hands in the pockets of his jeans.

Charlie stops in his tracks.

"No more leaving school, okay? We need to know where you are at all times."

"Why?" Charlie's voice quavers. "Why are you so paranoid? What do you think I'm going to do?"

Dad shrugs, and kicks at a stone on the driveway. "Nothing bad. But we still need to know where you are. It's not *you* I'm worried about so much as *other people*. You're only fourteen." Dad looks over his shoulder, out at the river, toward the dock where the boys launch their sailboats. "I don't get it. Kevin never gave me a hard time when he was your age."

Charlie rolls his eyes. "I'm not Kevin. I'll never be like Kevin." The sun is setting, and the temperature dropping. Our small patch of lawn is deep green, darkened by the shadows of the pine trees. I want Charlie to come inside so we can get ready for bed.

"I know. I just worry about you, all the time," Dad goes on. "You know that I—"

"Maybe you shouldn't have gotten kicked out of the house, then." Charlie whirls around to face his father. "Maybe if you still lived here, you'd know where I was."

Dad's face darkens. "Charlie. Please don't turn this around on me. We're talking about you."

"Not anymore." Charlie resumes his walk up the driveway and sees me on the stairs. "C'mon, Lil," he coos to me, and I stand up to follow him. Before we go inside, I look back at Dad. He and I stare at each other a moment.

I'm sorry, I wish I could say to him. *I know you want to come home. I can see the longing on your face. I wish you still lived here. Gretel does too.*

Last spring, *something* happened to Dad. Something that made everyone very worried and upset. I know Dad was injured and had to be rushed to the hospital, which is a place where humans go when they need care, like Vincent's wife. When Dad came home, he was stuck in bed for a week and Grandpa came to help out. Father brought home with him some powerful medicine—pills that he took every day.

But by the time summer arrived and Dad was back to work, Mom said enough was enough and he needed to stop taking those pills. Dad said no. Absolutely not. He was sure he still needed his pills. He told Mom he needed those pills for three reasons:

1. For the pain.
2. To forget.
3. In order to get through every day without fear.

But Mom didn't buy it. She flushed the pills down the toilet.

Dad was stunned. I will never forget the look on his face as he watched her do this, eyes wide. He started to shudder, standing there, realizing what she had done.

He soon found a new medicine, a special water he poured every day from a large glass bottle. My eyes stung when I sniffed the bottle, and there was something strange about it. One time, Dad spilled it on the floor, and Gretel took a lick of it. But she hacked and coughed it back up, unable to stand the harsh, bitter taste. Clearly, this water had powerful healing powers.

Mom did not like his new medicine either, and insisted he

needed to stop drinking it. She would make demands and then stare at Dad, waiting for him to answer. But he only dropped his gaze, unable to look at her.

We could all see he was still in pain. He craved silence sometimes. He would go sit on the deck, even when it was bitter cold outside. Sometimes he forgot his hat and gloves. It was as though he couldn't sense the cold until it was almost too late, and he would hustle back inside with hands turned purple. I think it contributed to his overall fatigue.

It seemed that Mom always wanted Dad to *do* or *not do* something. Finish his chores. Stop going out at night with his friends. See the doctor about his stomachaches. Think about finding a new job, something not so stressful.

Mom suggested all of these things at one point or another. Sometimes he'd hang his head and promise to try. But the most important thing she asked him to do, the one thing she always asked, was: stop drinking.

Yet this is the one thing he would never agree to do.

When we get in the house, Charlie runs straight up to his bedroom, and I follow him. He lays on the bed and stares at the ceiling for a long time.

"Hi, sweet baby." He rubs my head.

How was your weekend? I want to ask him. *What's the matter?*

Sometimes I cannot reconcile the dad I know with the way Charlie reacts to these weekends away. Charlie does not seem to enjoy himself, and I'm not sure why. Dad is not mean to Charlie.

Perhaps Dad has not always understood Charlie. It is true that sometimes he seems confused by his youngest son.

There's a knock at the door, and Mom peeks in. "Charlie? Are you okay?"

Charlie sits up and we make room for Mom to sit on the bed. "Yeah."

She puts a hand on Charlie's arm. "Everything go okay this weekend?"

He shrugs. "Yeah. I guess so. But Dad's on top of me all the time. He won't let me do anything. He doesn't trust me. He thinks I'm like . . ." Charlie wipes his nose with the back of his hand. "He thinks I'm a bad person."

"That's not true." She gives him a small smile. "He just wants to protect you. You know that's your dad's calling in life. He watches over people. He saves people when they need saving. Don't you remember how we met?"

Charlie looks up at her. We've heard this story before, many times. But Charlie still chews on his lip and asks, "Something about your bike, right?"

"Yes. My bike broke on the side of the road—the chain came off. And I had no idea how to fix it. I got grease on my hands and I was so upset I was practically crying. It was your dad's very first day of work, and he was running late, but he still stopped his car to help me out." She reaches up to tuck a strand of his hair behind Charlie's ear. "Your dad is the type who likes to come to the rescue, you know. He's just overprotective."

Charlie smiles. He enjoys a good dramatic story. "He was your hero. He said he saw your red hair in a ponytail and had to pull over. He said it was love at first sight."

Mother laughs. "Well . . . maybe it was. I don't know." She pats Charlie's elbow. "Right now, your dad wants to take care of you. The problem is, he's having trouble taking care of himself."

Charlie's smile fades. He nods.

I suppose that the changes going on in the family are making Charlie sad. And Charlie himself has been changing. Growing. Becoming a young man. That must be difficult to deal with too.

I wish Charlie would be honest with Dad, show him the bruises, and let Dad get involved. I think Dad would be very effective at finding and punishing Charlie's bully. After all, Dad hunts down bad people at work. So he is probably the right person to help Charlie.

After Mom leaves the room, Charlie grabs his backpack off the floor. He does work on his laptop, plays with his phone, and listens to music. We stay holed up for hours, and no one bothers us. Charlie doesn't talk to me, but he doesn't need to. Just the touch of his hand on my back makes me happy.

When Charlie changes into his nightclothes, I scrutinize his body. I look for new injuries.

But I don't see any at this time. That, at least, is a relief.

We head to the bathroom so Charlie can brush his teeth. He gazes into the mirror, pulling strands of his blond hair this way and that. I jump up to the counter to bump my head against his tummy, and he runs a hand down my silky fur.

"How do we look, sweet girl? Is my hair really okay? Did I make a mistake?"

I blink at him. *No. We look amazing.*

After Charlie gets into bed and checks his phone one last time, I knock my head into his hand over and over, until he scratches between my ears and fluffs up the fur under his chin. When I look into his sad eyes, I tell him: *You're a good boy. Don't worry. I'm going to help you.*

When I start to lick his salty hand, Charlie whispers, "What am I gonna do, Lil?"

I don't know, but I'll help you. I promise. No one has the right to hurt you. And I won't let anyone send you away. We'll figure this out.

I'm not sure how much he understands, but he gives me a kiss before turning out the light.

Chapter 5
Rifle Range Poker Run

Later in the week, Charlie and I are relaxing after school in his bedroom when I hear the front door open and slam shut. Charlie has his headphones on, and he doesn't move. I jump down off of the bed and walk to the hallway so I can peek over the balcony.

It's Victoria and Aidan.

Aidan is a young man who is interested in Victoria. He has been to the house a lot lately, especially in the afternoons. There is a gap between the time the children get home from school and Mother arrives from work. Aidan drives Victoria here in a small red car.

Aidan sneers at everything, and I avoid him. He is an outsider, with shifty eyes. I run from him, because I don't want him to even know I am here.

Don't get me wrong—I'm not afraid of him. I just don't like him. I suspect he might be the type of human who thinks cats are pests.

Charlie and Kevin feel the same way I do about Aidan. They

stay away from him, as far as possible. Victoria knows how we all feel about him.

But the fact that we don't like Aidan doesn't seem to worry Victoria. She is fond of him. She focuses on him in a way I've never seen her act before around another human. Her face takes on a radiant tone when he is near, her eyes bright and satisfied.

I'm really not sure what she sees in him. He smells strange to me.

I watch as Victoria slips off her light coat and hangs it on the stair railing. She takes off her shoes and places them neatly on the mat by the front door.

Dad used to yell at the children all the time to keep their things neat. Kevin and Victoria took this advice to heart. Perhaps they were sick of the nagging and decided it would be easier to just follow orders.

Charlie, on the other hand, does not always remember to put his things where they belong. I see his black sneakers lying in the middle of the hallway downstairs.

"Take off your sneakers," Victoria says.

Aidan hesitates, and rolls his eyes, but then does it.

Victoria and Aidan are involved in a complex mating ritual. I know something about mating, having seen it up close in nature every spring.

Birds. Squirrels. Neighborhood cats. You name it, I've seen it.

Mating is not something I have any interest in personally. I'm not sure why. But I recognize the instinct in others.

Although I don't like Aidan at all, I've been watching him from a distance, fascinated. I am trying to pinpoint why and how Aidan makes Victoria happy, but I haven't quite figured it out yet.

Often, the two of them sit at opposite ends of the living room couch, as if trying not to get too close. It's an old green couch, and the material is frayed on the armrests. But the cushions are soft and comfortable. Victoria studies, a textbook open on her lap. Aidan plays with his phone. And he drinks the family soda, draining can after can.

Aidan will watch Victoria with a stealthy patience, his face turning pink with the damp warmth of the room now that it is spring. He'll strip off his sweatshirt and push the sleeves of his T-shirt up over his shoulders. But when Victoria glances at him, his face is already turning away, as if he doesn't want to get caught looking at her.

Sometimes Victoria will slide across the couch to get closer to him. She tugs at the rope cord tied around his wrist, or glides two fingers over the hair on his lower arm. Aidan turns his head slightly toward her, and pretends to be distracted by the noises coming from his phone. "What?" he'll demand, as if she's interrupting something important.

But I know he listens to her every word. I watch him closely, tracking his eye movements, the flush of his cheek, the pace of his breath.

Everything about Victoria interests him. I look at her to see what he sees.

The way the rings on Victoria's fingers, all silver, flash when a beam of sunlight hits them through the window. The way she gracefully moves her hands to adjust the textbook on her lap, nails painted blue and perfectly round. The way her necklace falls just so, against the soft part of her neck. The color of her lipstick, dark red like a bruise.

I know Aidan notices all of these things, the way I do, and is mystified by them. Sometimes he bites his thumb, or taps his foot, and I can almost feel his anxiety traveling through the wooden floorboards.

Victoria knows she has an effect on him. But I suspect she does not understand the extent of it.

I believe from what I've seen that Aidan is in love. But he

tries to hide it. He snaps at her, and ignores her sometimes. Perhaps he is nervous about the way he feels. I'm sure it is scary when a young human falls in love. It must feel sharp and unfamiliar.

It is as if Aidan is holding his breath, trapping his love tight inside him. Maybe he is afraid it will suddenly spill out into the open, and become a thing not easily controlled.

Once the two of them are settled in the living room and seated on their favorite couch, I feel a pang of thirst and make my way down to the kitchen for a drink of water from my bowl. The water is cool and soothing on my throat.

On my way back to Charlie, I peek into the living room and glance over at Aidan and Victoria for a moment. I sit right in the doorway. Aidan sees me and scowls. As I've mentioned, I don't think he likes me. But I'm not afraid. I wish he and Victoria would end this nonsense and he would just leave, once and for all.

Victoria has always been kind to me. While her exterior may look tough, and she likes to be in charge, I know her heart is in the right place. Maybe this is why she likes Aidan—she wants to take care of him. He is like a scruffy dog she picked up at the kennel. Perhaps she thinks she can fix whatever is wrong with him.

Aidan reaches up to run his fingers over Victoria's ear. I have never seen him kiss her, but he sometimes works up his courage and touches her when she sits close enough for him to do so. Victoria has several pieces of metal attached to her earlobe. I'm often tempted to bat at them with my paw. So I can't blame Aidan for wanting to play with her ear. But Victoria swats his hand away. So instead he takes one of the little braids she has woven into her long dark hair in his hand, and runs his fingers down that instead.

Today, Victoria is busy reading and typing things into her

laptop. She ignores Aidan, who looks around the room, bored.

I hear someone coming down the stairs, and as he rounds the corner, I see it is Kevin in his uniform. It is a special kind of clothing he sometimes wears, tan with little patches all over it.

Kevin startles when he sees Aidan, and freezes. But he manages to collect himself and stand up straight.

Aidan screws up his mouth and takes a quick glance at Victoria, seeming to weigh his options. I think sometimes he views Kevin and Charlie as entertainment. They are lesser creatures he can torment.

Aidan runs his tongue over his teeth. "Nice uniform," he mumbles. But from the tone of his voice, I can tell he means the opposite. Kevin knows it too, from the way his face falls.

"I'm going rifle shooting," Kevin announces, a little too loud.

"Good for you." Aidan's voice is even and slow. "Going to kill some furry small animals?"

Victoria finally picks her head up, pulling her attention away from her phone, and shoots Aidan a dirty look. "Shut up." She smacks Aidan on the arm.

Kevin hesitates. "Um, no. We don't shoot animals. We just aim at cards, like out of a deck of cards? It's a competition, called the Rifle Range Poker Run."

Aidan nods eagerly, as if this is just what he expected. "Wow. Shooting *and* gambling. Doesn't sound very Scout-like."

Aidan has Victoria's full attention now. Her body turns toward him, and she gives him an icy stare. "SHUT UP."

"It's not gamb—Never mind. You wouldn't understand." Kevin walks to the front window and looks out.

"Why wouldn't I understand? Because I'm not Scout material?" Aidan sounds very amused at this point. "I wanna shoot things too. You think I should apply?"

Kevin opens his mouth and shuts it, as if he is going to answer, but thinks better of it. "My ride's here," he says with relief, as he yanks open the door and practically runs out.

I don't blame Kevin for running away. I'd run away from
Aidan too.

"Why do you have to be such an ass?" Victoria sits up
straight and slaps his hand as she waits for her answer.

Aidan just looks away. He has heavy-lidded eyes and often
looks sleepy. But I can tell he's calculating what to say to her
next.

"So." He turns back to Victoria and starts playing with one
of her braids again. "You're going with me to Dave's party on
Friday night?"

Now it's Victoria's turn to look uncomfortable. "I can't. You
know I can't. My dad's got me, and Friday nights we always go
out to this diner in Ipswich for supper. It's our tradition."

Aidan scoffs. "It's your tradition? Your dad just moved out
a couple of months ago. That's hardly a *tradition*."

Victoria has no answer to this. She just shrugs.

"Okay. Whatever." Aidan removes his hand from her hair.
"Blow me off. But I'm not going by myself." He slides his own
phone out of his pocket and starts pressing buttons. "Maybe
Jen will go with me. Or Bunny."

Victoria grits her teeth. "Are you serious?"

"Hell yeah, I'm serious." Aidan concentrates on his phone.
"I told you, I'm not going by myself. Dave's party is go big or
go home. I'm not going alone, like a loser."

The old grandfather clock in the hall chimes four times. I
wish it would chime five times, because then Aidan would go
home, and we could eat dinner. I lean forward to lick my front
paws. I prefer my fur clean and bright, like butter right out of
the wrapper. And, to be honest, Aidan is making me nervous.

When I look up, Victoria is reaching forward to gently push

Aidan's phone away from him. "Alright. Just . . . just wait. Let me talk to my mom. Let me see what I can do."

Aidan smirks. He's won. Again.

I have noticed that he usually wins arguments.

"I'm going to the bathroom." Victoria scowls and gets up.

"Bring me back a soda," Aidan calls after her. He watches her go. "Something with caffeine. And ice too."

"Get it yourself," she yells back at him.

When she leaves the room, I study Aidan. I can't figure it out: Why does Victoria like him?

He has wide-set eyes, a broad forehead, and dark hair. There is something in his face that is essentially unhappy, no matter what day of the week he visits. Sometimes I'll catch him staring at nothing, and he will flinch with a memory. I wonder what else is happening in his life to cause him such torment.

When he sees me staring at him, and we make eye contact, I think that Aidan looks very dark. What I mean is: as if he thinks evil thoughts. He is a creature that could turn on you, like a mouse that you think you have caught and killed, but then suddenly turns and sinks his sharp teeth into your paw.

Aidan and I get into a staring contest. I finally blink first.

Humans staring at me make me uncomfortable.

I hear a rustling upstairs, and my ears prick up. It's Charlie, moving around. He probably has his headphones on again, and doesn't know Aidan is here.

I don't want Charlie to come down. Aidan isn't very nice to Charlie.

Aidan comes over a lot lately, so perhaps Charlie should assume he's here. But Aidan is a new visitor, and this is Charlie's home. I can't blame Charlie if he forgets to be careful in his own home.

I hear the bed creaking, and the sink running, and then footsteps coming down the stairs.

My heart starts beating faster.

Oh, Charlie—

No, no, Charlie, I think, my whiskers tingling. *Don't come down the stairs. Go back.*

But it is too late. Charlie appears on the bottom stair. He is studying his nails, which I see he has painted black. The scent of the polish is faint, but I have a powerful sense of scent, and it stings my nose. Charlie smiles absentmindedly at his work.

I stand up on all four paws, to get his attention. I prance toward him.

Go back, Charlie. Quickly.

Charlie sees me out of the corner of his eye, and I think he is going to talk to me. But he freezes when he sees Aidan. His face goes pale.

I follow his gaze, and we both see Aidan has his head down and he is playing with his phone again. Perhaps he has not seen Charlie.

Charlie begins to move very slowly, turning toward the kitchen. I realize he is trying to get by without Aidan noticing him. Charlie moves with the stealth of a cat, and I think he will get away with it.

I decide to create a distraction. I run and leap up onto the coffee table next to Aidan, crying out a loud *rowr!* so he's forced to look at me.

Aidan does look, and he is startled. But he quickly turns back to Charlie.

And only then do I realize he knew Charlie was there all along.

"Hey, fruitcake," Aidan greets him, just as Charlie is about to disappear, out of sight, down the hall. "Where are you sneaking off to?"

Charlie stops, and turns. I watch him force his chin up.

"I'm just getting a glass of water," Charlie says, keeping his voice even.

Aidan looks Charlie over, from head to toe. "What did you do to your nails?" Aidan makes a *tsk*ing sound with his tongue. "Does your sister know you used her nail polish? I hate to be a tattletale, but . . ."

Charlie glances down at his hands. "She doesn't care," Charlie blurts out. "I mean, she lets me use it. She knows I borrowed it." He turns to go.

"Wow. What a great sister you have. She lets you be you. Weird, wonderful you." Aidan's voice drips with sarcasm.

Charlie pauses. He presses his lips together and then turns to go again.

"Hey, wait," Aidan calls out, as Charlie disappears down the hall. "Can you get me a soda while you're in the kitchen? Thanks, buddy."

I leap down from the coffee table and run to catch up with Charlie. He stands in the middle of the kitchen with tears in his eyes. I throw my body up against his ankles. When he doesn't respond, I stand on my back legs with my front paws on his legs, stretch upwards, and gaze at him until he reaches down to stroke my soft fur. I hope it calms him down.

Charlie looks at the back screen door, and I know what he's thinking.

Should he walk out to avoid having to talk to Aidan again? Flee from his own home?

Charlie shouldn't have to fetch Aidan drinks. Nor should he have to suffer being tormented in his own house. Someone is already hurting him at school.

How many places are there where he can go and feel safe?

Charlie takes a deep breath, and with a last glance at me, goes out the back. He pulls the door shut quietly behind him. I wish I knew where he was going, but I don't follow him. I give him some space.

I wish I could tell someone Charlie's secret. Someone is

hurting him at school, and Aidan is causing him pain here at home, where he should be able to relax. This isn't fair, and it isn't right.

I've decided: Aidan has to go. And if I have to, I'm going to be the one to get rid of him.

Chapter 6
Rock Star

Before he visited the hospital last spring, Dad could be very focused. Every autumn he would sit on the floor for a long time with Victoria, carving a pumpkin. They used a big sharp knife to slice off the top. Sleeves rolled up, they reached into the bowels of the pumpkin and pulled out long, stringy pumpkin meat, throwing it down on a newspaper where it landed with a *splat!* The slimy guts of the pumpkin were disgusting, but I could see from the gleam in Victoria's eye that she was having fun. Victoria sketched a frightening face, and Dad cut out the shapes. They worked quietly and with a tremendous effort, stopping to laugh a few times when it got too messy or Dad cut the wrong way. They laughed until they cried, wiping their tears away.

I watched from under the stairs, and fell asleep there. I woke later to the warm scent of roasting pumpkin seeds and a glowing pumpkin with a frowning face staring right at me.

Scary! My fur stood on end.

Dad also liked choosing old movies to watch with Charlie. They used to make popcorn or grab a whole package of cookies to eat while watching. Sometimes they'd laugh together. Other times, Charlie would get weepy, and Dad always comforted him, one hand on Charlie's shoulder. "Sorry, kid," Dad would say, "I didn't remember this movie was so sad." Charlie would nod, grabbing a tissue.

After the children went to bed, Mom liked to light candles in the study. The candlelight made the room glow. Dad and Mom would relax, get cozy, and talk. Mom liked to lie down on the couch and rest her head on his leg. Dad told Mom all kinds of stories about his day, and she would laugh at his jokes or squeeze his knee with worry when his stories got suspenseful.

Now that he has moved out, Dad seems to make everyone unhappy. Sometimes, on Fridays, Charlie will get home from school and I can sense the stress radiating from him. It builds through the afternoon in a slow and steady manner, like the way the river rises and floods with a high tide during the full moon. Charlie lies on his bed, very still, his arms wrapped around himself.

Even though his time with Dad makes Charlie upset, Mom usually insists that he go. She says it is important that Charlie spend time with his dad.

But this weekend, Charlie is not going to see Dad.

After a family negotiation, it was decided that Charlie and Victoria could stay home. Charlie wanted to have his friends over, and Victoria wanted to attend the party with Aidan. So Kevin is the only one who is going to stay with Dad.

Kevin agreed that Mom shouldn't make the others go if they didn't want to. He was loyal to everyone involved. He seemed happy at the thought of having Dad all to himself.

Mom made the call to Dad. I could see it was not easy for her. She held her phone in her lap a long time, sitting in a kitchen chair and practicing what she would say. I don't think her children understand the position they put her in when they make these demands, that much is clear to me.

Yet I don't think Dad protested very hard. I could hear the relief in Mom's voice with her every "thank you," holding one hand to her forehead.

So now it is Friday afternoon, and Charlie has a relaxed smile on his face. His best friend Karen is here.

Karen is tall and thin, and often wears her long dark hair in a ponytail. She comes to the house about once a week, which interrupts my private time with Charlie. But I don't mind. Karen is kind. I'm glad Charlie has a good friend.

Mom seems to like Karen too. She watches her son and this girl from a respectful distance. Sometimes she offers snacks, or asks Karen if she'd like to stay for dinner.

The two of them sit outside on the front step after school, each with a can of brown soda, the kind of drink that hits the pavement with a *fizz!* if it gets spilled. It is a fine spring day. This morning, the air was so cold that the children could see their breath in the air when they walked to the bus stop. But now, if I sit still, the sun feels warm and strong.

I lie down between the humans, my paws just at the edge of the step. I gaze out on the river. The water is smooth and gray and glassy today beyond the marsh grass. No waves, no chop. My ears twitch at every bird cry, my eyes distracted by every beating wing. Nature is waking up after a long, tedious winter.

The yellow bus rumbles by and pulls into the parking lot across the street, rolling to a halt. It's not long before the boys spill out of the bus, stretching their arms and reaching down to touch their toes. They peel off layers down to their T-shirts and shorts.

The group exits the sailing club gates and turns. About ten minutes later, they appear at the end of the street to complete their first lap of the long block.

When they jog by, Charlie and Karen talk quietly amongst themselves, but they both watch the boys. I come to realize that perhaps Charlie doesn't need to hide when he is with Karen because, like a dog who is part of a pack, he is stronger with another human beside him.

Humans can be doglike in that regard. It's a concept that doesn't apply to cats. I am very territorial, and would never allow another cat in this yard.

Never!

There are three boys who are usually the last in the pack, and today is no exception. One of them glances over, and happens to see Charlie and Karen. He's a little out of breath, and his cheeks are pink from the effort he's making. He smiles and nods at them. "Enjoying the view?" he calls out, spreading his arms out in front of him.

Charlie's mouth drops open, and Karen giggles. It is the first time Charlie has sat out in the open while the boys run past. I doubt he expected any of them to address him from the street. Charlie's eyes sparkle with surprise, but he clearly has no idea what to say.

Of course, we do have a lovely view of the river from our steps. But I get the impression this young man is making a joke of some kind.

The boy just keeps smiling, and continues running.

They watch him go, keeping their eyes on him until the moment he is out of sight.

Karen grins. "He's funny, isn't he?"

"You know that kid?" Charlie asks. "He's new."

"Yeah." Karen plays with her ponytail. "He's in my math class, and he's hilarious. Everyone loves him. He's a year older than us. Maybe at his old school they had a different order of math courses."

"You've talked to him?" Charlie persists. "What's his name?"

"I think it's Raul, or something like that. It's Spanish, maybe . . . ?"

"Does . . . Do you think Raul likes you?"

"Me?" Karen leans in and put her hand on Charlie's arm. "Do

I think he likes *me*?" She shakes her head. "He wasn't talking to me. He was looking at *you*, Charlie."

Charlie opens his eyes very wide and shakes his head. "Nah."

"Yes, he was," she says, singing the words. "Yes, yes, yes."

The birds in the trees around us seem to agree with her. They chatter excitedly. I turn my head left and right, but they are all out of my reach. What a bunch of babbling fools. I feel like they're mocking my human friends. I could catch and kill every one of those birds before days' end if I wanted to.

Stupid birds.

Karen continues to tease Charlie, but he isn't mad. He just laughs. Although he does take a quick look around.

"Don't worry." Karen adjusts her ponytail. "Aidan's definitely not here. I saw him and your sister drive off in his car after school. They headed downtown."

Ah. So even Karen knows about Aidan! He's trouble.

Charlie and Karen talk for a long time, until the sun begins to dip low in the sky. They are eventually joined by another girl who comes walking up the street. I don't recognize her. I wander off to stalk birds, and do not return to the house until dusk.

I scratch at the back door until Mom lets me in. I first grab a drink at my water bowl, and then go to find Charlie. I gallop up the stairs and find him in the upstairs bathroom. Charlie sits patiently on the toilet and lets the girls assemble tools on the counter by the sink.

"We're gonna make you look like a rock star, okay?"

Charlie looks back and forth from one girl to the other. He swallows nervously. But then he smiles and agrees, and the girls squeal with happiness.

Karen hovers over Charlie with a focused gleam in her eye. She orders him to close his eyes so she can draw with a pencil on his eyelids, and then she tells him to open his eyes so she can feather out his eyelashes with a brush. Then she powders his nose.

This is curious! I watch them closely.

I figure out that the new girl is named Candice. Candice is short with brown curls. She teases up Charlie's hair, spraying it this way and that. She works with many brushes and tools that she plugs into the wall. Brush. Spray. Brush some more.

Okay, now this is boring. And the spray makes me sneeze.

I stroll over to the thin paper on a roll. I've seen this work many times before. I wonder if I can make it go.

I reach up, pawing and scratching, until I get more and more paper to spool out onto the floor.

Woo-hoo!

This is fun. Paper is everywhere.

"Lily J. Potter, *stop*," Charlie begs, waving a hand at me.

I scamper back to my corner. Charlie calls me by my full name when I'm causing trouble.

"Your cat is beautiful, Charlie," Candice says. "Her fur is so long and lush. But she walks funny. Is she okay?"

Charlie shakes his head. "She doesn't walk funny. She's fine."

Looking up at her, I notice for the first time that Candice has metal on her teeth. Metal! And elastic bands. I think it must be some kind of human jewelry that I've never seen before. Bizarre.

I learn new things about the humans all the time.

The girls continue their task, laughing and poking at Charlie, and work on him for a long time. There is a lot of back-and-forth, with the three of them talking loudly. Finally, the girls decide that their job is done.

"Oooh," Karen coos, tipping her head so her ponytail falls to one side. "You're so cute, Charlie."

Hmm. "Cute" is not the word I had in mind.

Fearsome, perhaps. Charlie looks ready to scare off predators. Like a deranged human. Or a fierce raccoon.

"Wow," Candice gushes, taking a photo with her phone. "You look hot. I'm putting this online."

"Wait," Charlie jumps in. "I haven't even seen it yet."

He is too nervous to look into the mirror. The girls push and prod him until he finally does. When he looks at his reflection, Charlie turns his head left and right, and laughs heartily. He tells them he loves it, that they did a great job, and the girls beam with pride.

"Do you really like it?"

"Yeah. Thanks." He reaches up and gently moves a strand of his hair out of his eyes. "It's cool."

Candice unplugs a cord from the wall. "Now you owe us big time. I want snacks."

"Can we order a pizza?" Karen asks.

"Sure. You guys got any money with you? Maybe we could all chip in. Or maybe my mom will buy it for us. I'll ask her."

The three leave everything where it is, tools strewn about the bathroom. A burning smell hovers in the air from the small machines they've been using, but they don't seem worried about it, and hustle down the stairs. I decide to follow.

I can tell Charlie feels carefree tonight. He offers his friends a drink and they start to make popcorn in the microwave. It makes a terrible racket as it cooks. The scent of butter soon fills the kitchen.

There is a knock at the front door, and I run to see who it is. Gretel has beat me to the door, her tail wagging forcefully.

Dad enters, wiping his feet on the mat. He wears a light coat. It has cooled off a little since the sun has started to set. He seems distracted, his eyes moving although he doesn't focus on anything. Even when he reaches down to pet Gretel, he doesn't say anything, and barely looks at her.

When Mom appears at the top of the stairs, he slowly turns his head toward her. Dad's eyes relax, as if he suddenly recognizes an old friend.

"I'm sorry about the confusion this weekend," she says. "Everyone is just so busy."

"It's okay." Dad shrugs. "I like it when everyone can come, but . . ." He looks away, down at the floor.

Mom lingers at the bottom of the stairs, her hand on the bannister. "Kevin will be down in a minute."

"Did Victoria already leave?"

"Yes. Aidan drove her to a party. I guess they probably went to get a bite to eat first."

Dad's eyes narrow. "That kid has his driver's license now?"

Mom nods.

"Great." His mouth screws up in frustration. Aidan started coming around the house right about the time Dad moved out. I don't think Dad likes Aidan very much, although I have never heard him say so out loud.

There is a pause. We hear laughter from the kitchen.

"Charlie has some friends over," Mom explains.

Dad takes in a deep breath. "You doing okay?"

But there is no time for Mom to respond, because Charlie's friend Karen suddenly appears at the end of the hall and walks toward them. I can see the curiosity on her face. Although Karen has been Charlie's best friend for a few years, I don't think she has ever met Dad before. Dad has always worked long hours, and he keeps to himself. When Dad looks up, he freezes.

"Hi," he says tentatively. "I'm Mr. Anderson. Are you one of Charlie's friends?"

"Yes, I'm Karen," she answers brightly. There is a pause where no one speaks, and Karen's smile fades a bit. "We were going to order pizza."

When Karen glances back to see what is holding up her friends, I watch Dad give Karen the once-over, checking her out from head to toe. Karen turns back, and his face softens. "So, you guys are hanging out tonight?" He sounds hopeful.

I suppose Dad might think that Karen could be why Charlie

decided not to go with him this weekend. Dad might think that hanging out with Karen is a very good excuse for his son to stay home. Charlie is, after all, at the age where he might want to attract a mate, and perhaps Dad thinks Karen would be a good choice.

I agree with Dad. Karen makes Charlie very happy. They are only friends at this point, but Charlie is still very young. I think that soon he will start to look at her in a different way.

It hasn't happened yet. But it will, any day now. I am sure of it.

Just then Charlie comes down the hall with Candice, both talking loudly. Candice holds a big red bowl, full of the popcorn they made.

I watch, hoping they spill a few kernels. I love playing with popcorn that people drop on the floor. It's so light and fluffy and fun.

"Dad," Charlie exclaims. His eyes open wide. The two make eye contact.

Dad does a double take. And then squints, as if he has no idea who this young man is.

"What . . . ?" Dad stops himself. And then seems to have no idea what to say.

Why are you surprised? They were just playing around. You know Charlie likes to dress up. The girls had fun drawing on Charlie. It's not a big deal.

Charlie has clear green eyes. Just like his dad. They flutter when he blinks.

"Uhhh, Dad." I can almost feel Charlie's heart start racing from where I sit. His face goes pale, and he puts his head down. But there is nowhere to hide. "We were just going up to my room."

It seems unfair. Just moments ago, Charlie was happy. And now, he's miserable again.

"Hi," Candice says, with a friendly smile. "Nice to meet

you." She holds the bowl with one arm and sticks out her other to shake Dad's hand.

It's enough of a diversion that Charlie slips past his parents and starts climbing the stairs to where Karen is waiting. "Bye, Dad," Charlie calls quickly over his shoulder. He sounds tense. Karen puts a hand on Charlie's back and they keep walking up the stairs.

Candice smiles at Dad again, and follows her friends.

Dad doesn't say a word. Or smile back. He just watches.

He keeps his eyes on the stairs long after the kids are gone. Looking worried. "Is Charlie doing okay?" he whispers to Mom.

Mom nods. "Yes. He had a better week." She sighs. "He stayed in school every day, as far as I know."

Dad puts his hands in the pockets of his jacket and bites his lip, as if trying to solve a puzzle. "He's hanging around with good kids, though, right? These girls seem okay."

"Well, it's usually just Karen. But she's always great with him."

Gretel gets up on all four paws, turns around, and then sits back down. She's aching for attention. But she will have to wait.

Mom puts her hand on Dad's arm. "How are you doing?" The way her eyes search his face, I know she really wants to know.

Dad is just about to answer her, but then Kevin comes hustling down the stairs, duffel bag slung over his back. "Oh my God," he gushes. "I just saw Charlie." When he reaches the bottom of the stairs, he looks from parent to parent. "What is that crap all over his face? I didn't know he was doing that. I can talk to him about it. I mean, I guess as long as he's just staying in the house tonight it's okay, but can you imagine if he went out like that—?"

"Don't." Mom reaches out to hug Kevin, and gives him a squeeze. "Leave him alone. It's fine. He's fine."

"Go put your stuff in the car," Dad says. "Say good-bye to Gretel."

Once Kevin has pet Gretel and gone out the door, Dad looks down at Mom, and takes the tips of her fingers in his hand. She lets him do this for a moment. Her eyes close briefly, and she looks tired.

"Kate. I don't know if Charlie . . ." He takes a quick glance up at the top of the stairs, but the kids have disappeared into Charlie's bedroom and shut the door. "I should've said something when he came down the hall. I should have told him it's okay. He needs me here. I want to come home."

Dad does not sound like he is begging. He is just stating a simple fact.

And I realize, once the words come out of his mouth, that I want Dad to come home too. I believe it's the right time.

I know that Dad and Charlie might not be getting along as well as they should. But that is not a good enough reason to hope that Dad never returns. I have always felt, in my heart, that Dad and Charlie will reconcile one day.

I think they will say quiet words of peace. And they will embrace.

It will be a satisfying day. No one will be happier than me!

Mom looks away, down at the floor, and I imagine there are things she could reply to Dad's request, but she is biting her tongue. There is a long pause, too long perhaps, and Dad pulls his hand away.

Mom crosses her arms, and hugs herself tightly. "You know what needs to happen if you want to come home."

I walk over to Mom and rub hard against her leg. *No, no, no,* I try to communicate to her. I smash my face into her calf to try and get her attention. *Just tell him it's okay for him to come home. Don't make demands.*

I know what "needs to happen." Dad must promise to stop drinking. I tip my head to look up at Dad. I guess he must also know what Mom is talking about, because he doesn't ask what she means. He only stares down at his shoes. Then he closes his eyes and rubs his forehead, as if she's giving him a headache.

"I can't—" He stops himself. Apparently, that's all he can say. "Kate. You know I can't."

"Jeremy," she says quietly. She scrunches up her nose, and I know she is fighting off tears. "You mean you don't want to. I thought that once you'd moved out, and saw how serious I was, you'd change your mind. But obviously your mind is made up, which I find very sad."

Dad opens his mouth, but then shuts it.

He nods and walks out the door. Dad doesn't bother to look back.

I feel more and more disappointed every time Dad comes and goes. It makes my heart hurt. And I suspect it makes Mom's heart hurt too. I slink off to hide under a chair and think about it.

Chapter 7
Making a Terrible Mess

On the day Dad is supposed to bring Kevin home, Mom gets up early and goes for a long walk. She takes Gretel with her, since Gretel needs the exercise. I wait for Mom under my favorite holly bush, near the driveway. The day warms up as the sun moves higher in the sky.

I don't "walk" with humans. I'm never on a leash. I don't understand why Gretel enjoys it so much. It seems like torture.

I suppose Gretel is proud to be paraded around with her human. She trots alongside Mom, growling at other dogs and keeping a close eye on cars and people. I don't know what the point is of getting so worked up.

Dogs are strange.

There is a dense fog rolling in off the river. It makes it hard for me to watch the birds. Our spring can be cold and wet, not my favorite type of weather. But I enjoy the tremendous explosion of birds returning to the area. They are hungry, which makes them foolish. The birds take unnecessary risks, which makes them easier to catch.

I kill a small bird and leave it at the back door. I don't wait around for praise. An experienced hunter does her job and doesn't require thanks. I just leave it as a surprise for my humans to stumble upon later. I hope they know it is a token of my devotion.

When Mom gets back, the salty aroma of the river has seeped into her skin. I smell it when she bends to pet me in the driveway. "Hi, Lily," she coos, her mouth puckered as she makes kissing sounds at me.

Kiss, kiss to you too!

I follow her inside. I settle down for a nap as Mom runs out to do her errands and takes Charlie and Victoria with her.

When I hear a key in the lock of the front door and Gretel lifts her head, I realize we're going to get a chance to see the new man again. How unexpected! I had no idea he was coming over today.

There is something about him that I like. It's hard to pin down what it is exactly. Maybe it's because he is relaxed, and everyone in our house seems tense most of the time.

Vincent and the new man let themselves in the house, already in conversation, laughing at something. I watch from upstairs, through the rails of the balcony. I keep one ear open and listen as they go to study at the back of the house, talking the whole time.

But almost immediately I hear Vincent's phone jingle, and after he takes the call, he hurries back out the front door. I run down the stairs so I can look out the big picture window. I see Vincent walking down the street, headed toward home. I hope it is not more bad news.

The new man stays behind. I hear him go out to the garage through the kitchen.

A little while later, I hear a horrific grinding sound. I head back toward the kitchen to see if I can figure out what's going on. I'm puzzled.

The high-pitched buzzing continues, coming from the garage. It makes Gretel pace with anxiety. Finally, the man comes in from the garage and stands there, his head tipped, staring at the back wall of the study. Gretel sits right behind him, as if she's waiting to assist him in some way. I jump up to the couch, and the man turns his head.

"Hey, gorgeous," he says to me.

I stare at him. Gorgeous? I know what that means.

Hello, yourself.

I flick my big bushy tail because I love praise. And I can be a bit of a show-off sometimes.

He folds his arms and frowns. "Don't look at me like that, sweetheart. I'm doing the best I can. I'll figure it out. Eventually."

Does he think I look skeptical?

Hmm. Perhaps I am skeptical. I don't see any evidence of work being done, and this man always seems slightly confused.

This time, when the man goes out to the garage, I follow. Ah! The fine dust in the air and on the floor smells sharp, and makes me sneeze. It feels strange and soft under my paw pads. What a huge mess the man has made already!

There are two sawhorses set up in the garage, supporting a long board that has been set across them. More boards, of uneven lengths, lie on the floor. I see a machine with a long cord sitting on the cement floor. The man picks this up with both hands.

He sighs when he sees me. "I know what you're thinking. I'll get the hang of it."

Will you, though? This doesn't seem to be going very well, my friend.

The droning of the saw is piercing to my ears when he turns it on. Since the garage doors are wide open, I scamper out into the yard. I duck under my favorite bush as the machine whirs on and off.

He works for a few minutes, and I watch the birds flying in flocks overhead. But then—a strange noise catches my attention. I know that sound. It is a human sound. The man has growled in pain.

I look to see he is holding his hand and inspecting it. Perhaps he has cut himself on the blade. I step silently forward to take a look.

Sure enough, when he lifts his hand, I see a bright red scar across the palm of his hand. He is injured. The cut is bleeding.

The man looks around our garage and shakes his head. He glances at the door to the house, perhaps unsure if he should try to clean his wound in our kitchen. But, of course, he doesn't know where we keep our bandages.

He finally decides to leave, I assume to take care of his injury at home. When he lets go of his hand to punch buttons on the side of the garage and lower the doors, I see drops of blood roll down the side of his hand and fall onto the driveway. The palm of his opposite hand is smeared red from trying to stop the bleeding. He gets in his truck, wincing, and drives away.

Finally I see Mom's car coming down the street. I sit under my bush and wait.

Mom parks in the driveway. The garage doors glide up as she approaches, as if the doors know she is coming.

I've never figured out how those doors know when to open as she drives up.

It's a mystery.

She slams the car door shut, staring at the inside of the garage. Her jaw drops as she surveys the scene: tools everywhere. And, of course, there is the sawdust. It has settled like a fine powder on the rake, the bikes, the snow sleds, the trash can—on everything.

Charlie looks around. Victoria appears confused.

Mom turns, as there is the roar of another car pulling into the driveway. It lurches to a stop, and the engine turns off. Kevin gets out of the driver's seat, dragging his duffel bag after him. Dad climbs out of the passenger side, and he walks right up to the garage, hands on his hips.

Dad surveys the scene. "Jesus. There is shit everywhere."

Mom frowns. I don't know if she is angry at the mess or at Dad's cursing. Probably both.

Mom doesn't like it when Dad "uses the Lord's name in vain" and "swears like a Gloucester fisherman." Both of which I believe he has just done.

Mom doesn't approve of cursing. She once said that swearing means the speaker is too lazy to find better words. Mom makes the children put a coin in a jar in the kitchen if she hears them say certain words. She doesn't demand that Dad do the same, although he swears more than anyone else.

I suppose that also makes him the laziest, in Mom's eyes.

Kevin stands right next to his Dad, and also puts his hands on his hips, mimicking his father's body language. "This is Vincent's stuff," he says slowly, as if trying to solve a puzzle.

"Who's Vincent?" Dad demands, eyes narrowing. He never did pay much attention to Mom's friends.

"He's the guy . . ." Kevin trails off. His eyes dart right and left. I'm not sure he knows how to define Vincent. I also suspect he's trying to figure out how to explain it in a way that will not upset Dad. "You know, the guy who fixes and builds stuff for us. The construction guy."

"Well, he's doing a crap job of it." Dad turns to Mom. "Do you want me to talk to him for you?"

"No. He's a friend of mine." She is firm about this. "Don't you remember? He's our neighbor. No. Just—Please, no."

Dad throws his hand out toward the tools, glaring at Mom like he's about to explode. "THIS IS A MESS."

Kevin takes a step forward so he's standing between his parents. He's the same height as Dad, and stares him down, eye to eye. "Dad. Shut the hell up. Just knock it off."

"What?" Dad flinches. "What did you just say?"

"You heard me. I said knock it off. This isn't your mess to clean up. This is our house now. You moved out, remember? We'll deal with it."

Dad gawks at his oldest son, just for a moment, and then his face relaxes. "That was not my idea. To move out. That was not what I wanted." He shakes his head. "I'm sorry. I just—I just worry about you guys. I don't want you to have to deal with any problems. That's all. I'll go." Yanking open the car door, he climbs in and pulls his door shut. The car immediately starts to back out of the driveway.

Charlie and Victoria stand there. They half-heartedly wave good-bye to their dad, who nods back. Charlie finally walks through the garage and goes into the house. Victoria bites her lower lip, waiting for a moment to see what her mom and brother have to say.

Mom grabs Kevin's elbow. "What was that about?"

"He's in a bad mood," Kevin grumbles. "He had a few beers. Whatever. He's not your problem anymore. Isn't that what you wanted?"

Kevin yanks his arm away from his mom, picks up his duffel bag, and heads inside.

"Kevin," she tries one last time. But it's too late. He's gone. Victoria shrugs, and follows her brother inside.

Mom's eyes water up as she looks over the garage, high and low. She hesitates, and then pulls her phone out of her back pocket. She puts one hand over her stomach, as if she doesn't feel well.

"Vincent," she says, voice trembling, hand gripping the phone too tight. "I'm really sorry to bother you, but were you here today? What? What's his name? Mark? Well, he left a terrible mess. It's a disaster. Yes? It's really not . . . Okay, you'll call him? Right now? Okay. Thank you. Sorry again."

Mom is always saying sorry about something.

She finds a broom, shakes the dust off it, and props it against the side of the garage. Then she turns back to the car and takes in a load of groceries. She makes three trips, back and forth. Usually Kevin helps her, but not today.

The whole time, Mom's lips move as she talks silently to herself. I think she is preparing what she is going to say to the man to express her disapproval.

Oh dear. I wait outside. I want to see the man when he arrives. I wish I could warn him!

Eventually, a black truck pulls up and parks at the curb. Yes, it's him. He gets out and comes up the driveway cautiously. From the look on his face, I suppose he knows he has done something wrong and Mom is mad about it. He looks into the garage. Both doors are wide open. I watch his eyes light up as he looks around, thumbs in his jeans pockets. His left hand is wrapped in a bandage. Finally, he nods in understanding. Seeing the broom, he grabs it and starts sweeping the floor.

I wander out and sit in the driveway, careful not to get in the way of the clouds of dust he creates as he sweeps. He works quietly, head down.

When he stops for a moment, he rests his head against his hands on the broom. He looks exhausted, and I assume it's not from sweeping. His eyes flicker up, and he sees me.

"Hey, sweetheart," he says again, in a weary voice.

I think I must remind him of someone or something. Crouching down, he extends a hand to me.

I'm not as desperate for human attention as Gretel is. Normally, I'd walk away. But in this case, I make an exception. I feel bad for the man. He did make a terrible mess, but he also seems very unskilled at building. I'm not sure why Vincent hired him.

I get up on all fours and walk over to him. The sawdust makes me sneeze again. I shake my head and then continue my approach. I put my wet nose up to his fingers, carefully. They are dusty, but it is a pleasant scent. I go ahead and rub my head and body against his knee, looking up to study him. When he crouches down, I put two paws right up on his leg and stretch to get closer.

Here is one thing I like about the man: his posture. Unlike Charlie and Kevin, who often walk hunched over as if they are hoping no one notices them, this man holds his head up and his back straight.

If he were an animal, I can see this man would be a stag. Fearless, alert, and curious. I can almost imagine the antlers sprouting up from atop his head.

He is just picking me up with two hands when Mom swings the door open, hard and with purpose. She stands in the doorway to the house, her forehead creased and mouth half-open as if ready to address him.

The man is already in the motion of lifting me to his chest, and he holds me there. But he does a very funny thing. Usually when Charlie carries me, he hoists me up onto his shoulder. And when Mom needs to move me, she puts a hand under my chest and one under my haunches, so I can face forward and look around at where we are going. But this man does it differently.

He flips me upside down, so we are face-to-face. He is holding me the way a human holds his baby.

Seriously. He is cradling me as if I were a baby!

How strange. I've never had a person hold me like this before. It's not bad. The man has a firm grip, and I feel secure.

I sense the man's heart beating through my fur. I look up at his hair, at the way it waves, and a few strands stick out here and there, and I have half a mind to bat at it with my paw. But I decide to leave it alone. I'm cozy right where I am, and if I get too squirmy he might put me down.

Here is another thing I like about the man: He holds me with ease, as if he's done it a million times before, as if his arms were made for holding someone just my size. I feel comfortable in his hands, not skittish. I am sure he will never drop me.

I wait for Mom to say something. But she just frowns when she sees the man has me nestled against his chest.

Well! This is awkward for me. I don't usually allow a stranger to hold me like this.

I wait another moment. Mom's eyes soften. Her mouth quivers, and whatever she was planning to say dies on her lips.

Ah. It is the same reaction I had. I can see this man is not at all what she was expecting. Perhaps it is that he's not like Vincent, weary with responsibilities. There is something innocent and expressive in this man's face.

Mom takes four steps down into the garage, and now instead of looking down at the man, she must look up at him. She stops suddenly, as if there is an invisible wall between them. "You're Mark . . . ?"

"Yeah. I'm really sorry about the sawdust on everything. I wasn't really thinking about it, and I should have cleaned up. I'm taking care of it now." He pauses, and bends to gently place me back down on the cold cement floor.

When he straightens back up, Mom is still standing there staring at him, as if there is something she was meaning to say but can't remember what it is. Mark reaches for the broom to show he's ready to get back to work.

Mom glances down at me, puzzled, then back at Mark. "It's okay. It's fine." She seems suddenly flustered. "I'm sorry to make you hurry back here. It's not really a big deal—"

"No, it's okay," he interrupts. "I'm the one who's sorry. I shouldn't have left a mess."

The man seems genuine in his concern. I turn to look at Mom. She is pale, and her hair needs brushing. To me, she appears fragile. Mom is easily upset, and not the kind of person you want to see suffering, because it is so plain on her face.

"Still. I didn't mean you had to hurry back here right now, on a Sunday. I don't know why—I mean, I did tell Vincent I needed it cleaned up, but—I'm sorry you had to rush back here just to sweep up. It seems so silly and pointless, now that you're here."

Her eyes go right back to his face. Perhaps she is as surprised as I was to see that he has so many freckles with such dark hair.

"It's fine." I notice he does not mention that he hurt himself. Perhaps he does not want Mom to know that he's not very good with the saw.

Mom gives him a nervous nod. "Thank you for coming, anyway."

"No worries. I'll leave it like I found it."

Enough already, I want to say to Mom, *you're talking in circles now. He feels bad. He's fixing the problem. Your job is done.*

It is unfortunate that humans feel the need to talk so much, to fill every silence. They should hear themselves talk sometimes. They would realize how much energy they waste.

Mom's mouth opens, but no words come out, almost as if she has read my thoughts. She reaches down and snatches me up, as if she's afraid Mark is going to steal me away. I relax in her arms as she turns to head back into the house. But she spins at the door, making me dizzy. "I'm Kate, by the way. Sorry I didn't introduce myself."

"Kate," he repeats.

Okay, I think, *he's got it under control now. Let's go inside.*

It still takes her a moment. Finally, she reaches over, and misses the doorknob on her first try, probably because my big furry body prevents her from seeing what she's trying to grab. On the second try, she opens the door.

And in we go.

Chapter 8
Rocking Chair

The next time Vincent comes over, he has a brown bag in his hand. Mom greets Vincent with a pat on his shoulder, and he hands her the bag.

"What's this?"

"We brought you breakfast."

Mom places one hand on her heart. "Thank you so much, Vincent," she says. Looking in the bag, she reaches in and pulls out a plump muffin topped with crumbs.

"Don't thank me," Vincent says, his cheeks rosy from the cool morning air. "It was Mark's idea. He felt bad about the mess."

"Oh." Mom frowns at the memory. "I'm sorry I overreacted. I felt terrible about making him hurry over here."

"Nah, you kidding me?" Vincent shakes his head. "He shouldn't have left without cleaning up. His head is in the clouds sometimes, as they say."

Vincent goes back out to the garage and I hear him talking to Mark. The two of them are probably setting up their sawhorses. Mom goes upstairs and I hear her start the washing machine. I lie down on the kitchen floor. I find the sound of the water running in the pipes upstairs very relaxing.

When Gretel suddenly trots into the room, I look around to see what she has sensed that I do not. She has such good hearing that she seemingly anticipates things before they happen.

Sure enough, I hear a door swing open and Mark comes into the kitchen from the garage. He looks around to see if anyone is in sight.

When he realizes that it is just Gretel and I who greet him, Mark approaches the kitchen sink and refills his water bottle. On the way back out to the garage, he stops at the entrance to the study and surveys the wall where the bookshelves will go. Gretel moves past him into the room and he follows her, stopping in front of our family photos. I remember he looked at these photos before. He gives Gretel a scratch between her ears when she looks up at him with her big brown eyes.

There is something about the way Gretel looks at humans that makes them respond. She always looks a little bit sad, I think. Like she needs them to acknowledge her. But I don't think that's how she actually feels. I think she's just interested and perhaps suspicious. Always trying to determine who is a friend and who is not.

Feeling a little jealous, I run forward and push my wet nose into Mark's leg to put my scent onto him. I'm not surprised when he reaches down with two hands and scoops me up.

Look, this is not a competitive thing, but—no one can pick up Gretel. She's huge. I'm the right size for a cuddle.

Taking a few steps backward, Mark sinks into a rocking chair, taking care not to jostle me. As he did before, he flips me over so he can rest me in the crook of his arm and look me in the eye.

"Sweetheart," he says, and his voice is a deep rumble. I like it. I can feel the vibrations in his chest when he speaks. "Aren't you a good girl? Yes. You're a good girl. You have big eyes."

He rubs my tummy gently, swirling around my fur, and I blink with gratitude.

I feel incredibly secure. Mark holds me tight, and I can tell he will not put me down until he is good and ready.

He speaks slowly, as if I don't understand English very well. "Your eyes are so big. You're a pretty baby and so soft. You're a very good kitty."

Why yes, I am.

I love the scent of him. I carefully poke my nose forward so it bumps against his T-shirt. It's very soft and smells like the cinnamon Mom shakes into her coffee. It is not something I would eat, but it is familiar, and therefore pleasing to me.

There is a slight sound—an almost imperceptible hum—and it causes my ear to twitch. I watch Mark raise his head, mouth open. I turn my head to see what he's looking at.

It's Mom. She stands in the open doorway, arms crossed, leaning her head against the doorframe. A smirk twitches at the corner of her mouth, and I can see she finds this very entertaining.

Goodness! I've been caught cuddling again. With the same man.

I check back with Mark to see if he is as embarrassed as I am. But I don't think he is. Instead, a smile grows on his face, the same wide, lopsided smile I saw before. It lights up his entire face, opening it up like the sun coming out from behind a cloud. He looks happy. Almost glowing.

His smile is an amazing thing to see, and it intrigues me. No one in my family smiles quite like that.

Not one of them.

Ever.

"You like cats?"

Mark chuckles. "Sure." He shrugs. "Who doesn't?"

Mom hums again. Just a little "mmmm." It's a funny sound. Almost as if she wants to purr.

I start purring myself, at that silly thought. I just can't help it.

Gretel turns in a circle and sits back down, looking from human to human. I suspect she's a little jealous.

Too bad. Get over it.

Mom stares and rubs her elbow with one hand absentmindedly. I suppose she thinks it is funny to see someone sitting in the old wooden rocking chair. Grandpa gave it to our family a few years ago, when Grandma died. No one in our family actually ever uses the chair. I have tried to jump up on the seat, but I find the polished wood slippery and uncomfortable. Yet Mark seems perfectly fine in the chair, possibly because he is sitting up straight and leaning back into it. He has found the right balance to make the chair work.

"Do you have kids?" Mom suddenly blurts out. "I can tell you do. You have a baby at home, right?"

And with these words, his smile diminishes. Mark's eyes are still friendly, but the cheerfulness fades. He looks a little confused.

"Me? No." He clears his throat. "No kids."

"Kate!" Vincent bursts into the room. "Did I tell you they said Caroline could come home from the hospital this weekend? I can't believe I forgot to tell you."

Mom spins to face Vincent, pushing off from the door frame. "Oh, that's great news," she gushes. "I'm so glad. Tell me what the doctors said."

She and Vincent talk excitedly in the kitchen. I am glad Vincent has some good news to share.

Mark looks down at me, and I back at him. I give him a quick wink. I think we have a bond.

"You're a very lucky cat," he murmurs to me, relaxing and lowering his arms so I can settle myself on his lap. "You have a nice home." I sense that he wants to get up from the chair. I can usually tell when a human needs me to jump down because I feel their leg muscles tense. So I oblige, and hop to the rug.

Sure enough, the next thing I know Mark is on the move and

headed back out to the garage. I slink over to Mom in the kitchen, and rub my face on her ankles. I can't believe she caught me with Mark again. I hope she understands that my interest in him does not diminish my love for her.

"Is Jeremy doing okay?" I hear Vincent say in a low voice.

It takes me a moment to realize that Vincent is not talking about his wife anymore. Now he is asking about Dad.

"Sure," Mom says. "You know. As well as ever." She shrugs. "Same as always. No change. But it's okay." She tucks her hair behind her ears.

Vincent looks at her over his glasses, which slip down a bit on his nose. "All right."

"He's fine. And I'm fine. Honestly."

"Okay, Kate. If you say so. Just thought I'd ask."

She pats his arm. "Thanks for asking."

Mark steps back into the kitchen, the red toolbox in his hand. "Thought I'd bring this in, just in case you need it."

"So . . ." Mom leans against the kitchen counter and looks Mark up and down. "I'm glad you found an assistant."

Vincent smiles. "Well, I needed the help, and Mark happened to be available."

Vincent and Mark start talking about the plans for the new bookshelves, and Mom makes coffee. Vincent outlines some of the details of the project to Mark, who nods and asks a few questions. Mom brings a cup of coffee over to the kitchen table, where she sits and cuts her muffin in half.

Gretel sits patiently but watches Mom's every movement. She knows that food is being prepared.

"Oh, Gretel, it's just a muffin." Mom sighs. "It's not really for dogs."

I remember when Dad first asked Mom about bringing a dog home. I was the only family pet at the time. Dad talked to Mom several times about a working dog who had been injured. He said she was a beautiful, loyal dog who was still young and deserved to retire early with a nice family. Dad had worked with this dog himself for over two years, and he loved her and wanted to bring her home.

Mom was nervous about it. She was afraid the big dog would hurt someone accidentally. She wondered if the dog might turn vicious when she got excited.

Mom asked many questions, including:

1. Doesn't this dog attack people at work? Isn't that what you trained her to do?
2. What if she attacked someone here?
3. What about Lily? Will this dog be good with a cat? Has she ever even met a cat?

These questions got my attention, believe me.

I see dogs around the neighborhood, and I avoid them without a problem. For the most part, they are stuck on leashes. And the two times I've been chased, I managed to outrun and outsmart those dogs. Despite my limp, I have long powerful legs and an ability to dart through small spaces. I don't say this to brag. It's just a fact.

But now Dad was talking about bringing a large, adult dog into the house. Mom was so upset that I started to get anxious too. I listened carefully when Dad talked about the dog.

Dad reassured Mom over and over that this dog was not usually asked to attack or hurt people. Most of the time, she was used to search for drugs. And she didn't even know she was searching for drugs—no, she had been trained to find her toy, which had the scent of drugs on it. He told Mom that Gretel was a smart dog, and there was no reason to worry. Once in a while she disarmed a threatening person, but she was overall very loving.

Once I heard Dad explain all this, I started to relax. After all, Dad had been there when Charlie picked me out. He was the one who drove Charlie to the animal shelter, and he knows how much Charlie loves me. I had to believe Dad wouldn't take any risks with my life.

Mom looked at me. I blinked back at her.

Let's give this dog a chance. She was hurt, and she needs a home. I understand. I was in that position once myself.

I have heard Dad say that Gretel is a hero. Dad admires her, and I think he is drawn to her because he has done great things himself. I have seen two medals hanging from the dresser in his bedroom. They are gold, like my fur. Kevin and his best friend Phil once went into Dad's room and tried on the medals. They handled them with great care, so I know they are special.

Sure enough, Gretel has turned out to be a fine dog for our family. Big? Yes. Strong? Yes. Smart? Well . . . I'm not sure. But she is not vicious. We get along fine. She will bark at and chase outsiders, but she does not bite them. Usually.

She has snapped at one or two people, perhaps, in the past year.

No one should expect perfect behavior all the time. Even I accidentally scratch Charlie once in a while.

Gretel sits very still and watches Mom take a bite of the muffin. I can tell Mom thinks her treat is very good from the way her eyes close slightly as she tastes it. She glances back at Gretel.

"Oh, all right." She breaks off a chunk and tosses it on the floor.

Gretel has lapped it up and gulped it down in two seconds. For goodness sake. Ridiculous. She doesn't even take the time to taste her food.

Mark enters the kitchen. "Okay if I use the sink?"

Mom nods. She watches him walk over to the sink and wash his hands. He is careful not to get the bandage on his hand wet. It's funny, but Mom's whole face lights up when he turns.

She raises an eyebrow. "How did you know blueberry was my favorite?"

"I didn't. But now I know." He dries his hands on a white towel. "I'll bring you one next time too."

"You don't have to do that," she protests.

"It's no problem."

Mark just stands there, drying his hands on that towel for a long time. Certainly his hands must be dry, but he keeps running the towel over one hand and then the other. Mom gazes at him and he smiles back.

Mom is acting a little strange, it seems to me.

"Please don't feel you need to always bring me food or something. I'm sure you've got better things to do than bring me snacks."

"Not really." He laughs. "I work at a restaurant on the breakfast and lunch shift. So that was free. I can take whatever I want." He nods at the muffin. "I bake everything myself. Using organic ingredients. I've been trying to cut down on the sugar, and use healthier foods, like applesauce."

"Oh." Mom squints at the muffin, as if suddenly suspicious about it.

"Besides, I do feel bad about leaving such a mess in your garage. The truth is, I cut myself on the saw." He holds up his hand and shows her the bandage. "The gloves were right in the toolbox, but . . . I forgot to put them on. And I didn't want to bleed all over your garage. So I went home to wrap up my hand. But I should have come right back to clean up."

Mom is alarmed. "Oh my goodness." She stands up. "Are you all right?"

"Yeah." He shrugs. "Fine."

"I'm sorry. That's terrible." She stands and walks right up to him and takes a closer look at his hand, as if he still needs tending to. "I'm so sorry that happened."

When Mom looks up and they are face-to-face, she seems to realize how close she is standing to him, because she quickly takes a step back.

"It's okay," he says, glancing down at the floor a moment. "I'm fine."

At that moment, Vincent walks into the kitchen and taps Mark on the elbow. "Where'd you go?" he asks Mark. "C'mon, buddy. We've got things to do."

As soon as Vincent turns to head back to the garage, Mark steals one last glance at Mom. And then he's off, hustling to catch up to Vincent.

Gretel walks over to the entrance to the garage, listening to the men work through the door. She sits, and I know she is waiting for them to come back in so she can follow Mark around.

I trust Gretel. We are friends. And if she has decided that the new man is okay, it's fine for me to think he is okay too.

Of course, it also occurs to me to wonder what Dad thinks of these people working in our house. The project sounds like a big one, and I heard Vincent say it may take a while.

Dad didn't like the mess Mark left in the garage, and he didn't remember who Vincent was when Kevin mentioned his name. A small churning in my stomach warns me that Dad may not approve of these men being here for so long. If Dad feels there are too many outsiders here, then he might get upset, because he is always suspicious of strangers. Or he might decide not to visit us so much, if he feels unneeded. And if that happens, who will catch and punish Charlie's bully?

Chapter 9
The Clever Fox

You wouldn't know it if you saw him lately, but Dad loves to laugh. He has a big smile and an infectious laugh, and once he starts he cannot stop. I would not generally describe him as a silly person, but sometimes when he bursts into a grin, you can see the fun-loving child he probably was. I imagine him pulling pranks on his mother and laughing even while she yelled at him.

His mother is dead now. There are old photos of her around the house. No one talks much about her. But I'll bet Dad drove her crazy.

Dad laughs when Victoria puts on silly accents, or crosses her eyes.

He laughs when Kevin makes fun of how Grandpa hates to spend money. The two of them tell stories about Grandpa until Kevin is laughing so hard he has to put his head down on the table, and Dad doubles over and hides his face with his hands because he has tears in his eyes.

Grandpa doesn't come over much anymore, even though he lives close by. He and Dad had a tremendous argument in the driveway, right around the winter holidays, which I witnessed from the picture window. They stood in the snow and there was yelling. It was about Dad's medicine. Dad needed to drink a lot around that time, and Grandpa didn't like Dad's drinking any more than Mom did. But Dad could be fierce when defending himself and the need to have his special water.

Dad does love to laugh. He used to smile at Mom's sly comments, the ones she would say under her breath, as if only to him. Dad would laugh even when the children couldn't follow the joke. He would pat Mom's knee or grab her hand under the kitchen table, and she would smile.

I haven't seen Dad laugh in a while though.

There was one time Dad cried too.

It wasn't in front of the other humans. But one night when he was still living here and the family was out, he wept. His whole body shook as he lay on the couch, and he yelled and he cried and shivered all over. He had to wipe away the tears with the sleeve of his shirt. He had his bottle of medicine with him, and he pushed it away but then grabbed it back. I think perhaps he did want to stop drinking, but he just could not do it. Once he quieted down, Gretel lay on the floor next to him, and I snuggled up behind his knees.

We helped him get to sleep. Sometimes, for humans and for animals, sleep is the best thing.

Dad stops by the house early one evening to drop something off for Mom. I know she is expecting him from the way she cleans the kitchen over and over, moving little things from counter to shelf, and then back again.

When the doorbell rings, I chase Gretel to the front door. Sightings of Dad interest me enormously. I heard Dad when he asked if he should "come home." I wonder if there is anything I could do to help him make this happen.

I believe he must now not only stop drinking, but also win Mom over, as he did when they first met. He has lost her trust.

Dad always took good care of this family. He was productive, working long hours. There were flowers for Mom. Gifts on everyone's birthday. Ice cream every Friday night, in two flavors. And bacon for Gretel and I, handed right to our mouths under the table where no one could see it.

I never doubted his love for Mom. His devotion may have wavered on the surface sometimes, the way the river gets choppy to the eye on a windy day, but deep down there are reserves of concern and commitment.

But I worry that Mom has given up on him. She realizes that she cannot help him. He will not allow it.

He is a hero, someone who has received gold medals for good works! Yet now he seems lost, and can't find his way back.

It is clear Gretel is suffering too. I see the way she is completely devoted to Dad. Following him around. Begging to be noticed at all times. She worries about him even more than I do, and she doesn't know how to help him.

Dad lets himself in. After he wipes his feet on the mat, I smell his boots. Gretel sniffs his hands. We are eager to see him. He bends down and gives Gretel a good rub around the neck with both hands, and then a hug. She licks his ear and he coos at her.

I get out of their way. I don't want to get slobbered on. Gross.

Gretel and I know that Aidan is here in the house too, visiting Victoria. Usually he comes by after school and leaves at dinnertime. But today he came late, and he is still here.

Dad doesn't see Aidan at first. The living room to the left of the hallway is dark, and Dad doesn't glance in that direction. Victoria and Aidan were talking on the couch, but at the moment Dad enters, Victoria is upstairs fetching a notebook. So Aidan stands by the window, alone. He does not say anything to alert Dad to his presence.

Dad has been oddly preoccupied lately. He does not seem to

be aware of his surroundings. He was always that type of person, prone to daydreaming, and it is one of the things he and Charlie have in common. But lately he has seemed even more sluggish than usual.

Dad pats down his pockets. He has a tool he carries in a belt under his jacket, and it is called a gun. I don't know what it does exactly, as I have never seen him use it. He takes the tool out, examines it, and puts it away again.

Aidan stands in the corner, watching Dad. He reminds me of the red fox that stalks the marsh. He has sharp eyes, and the ability to stay perfectly still.

Clever, that fox.

Clever, this young human.

Dad is just lifting his head when he notices Aidan, and jumps slightly.

"Christ, you scared me, Aidan," he growls. "What the hell are you doing lurking in the corner?"

Aidan doesn't move any part of his body, although he studies Dad while running his tongue over his teeth. Aidan clears his throat and stands up straighter.

Dad squints, as if he can't fathom how Aidan got into the house, as if he's a squirrel who fell down the chimney. Aidan is not his favorite person.

"Going hunting?" Aidan finally asks.

"What?" Dad's eyes furrow. Sometimes it's as if the other humans are speaking a language he doesn't recognize.

"With the Scouts. You going hunting?" Aidan shifts his weight from one foot to the other. He hesitates, but then plunges ahead: "Kevin told me about the rifle shooting competition or whatever. Fun and games." The way Aidan says this, it's clear that he thinks this is neither fun, nor a game. He shoves his hands in his pants pockets. "Cool gun. My dad used to have a gun."

Dad's face clouds over. "No, I'm not going hunting, for

Chrissake. Does this look like a rifle to you? I carry a gun for work. And tell your dad he shouldn't have a gun in a house with kids. It's not safe."

Aidan folds his arms. "Yep. You're probably right. It's not safe."

Dad runs his hands over his pants, as if drying them. "I know what you're thinking. This is for work. And I live alone now. It's different."

Just then, Mom's voice calls out from the kitchen. "Jeremy. Jeremy, come on in."

Dad heads down the hall without another glance at Aidan.

"Yep. It's different," Aidan mutters when Dad is out of sight. "You're different, all right."

Victoria comes bouncing down the stairs carrying the notebook, and approaches Aidan. She squeezes his hand. But he barely seems to feel it. He looks upset.

"Your dad hates me," he says quietly, "And he's carrying a freaking gun."

Victoria shakes her head. "He doesn't hate you."

"He's wound up so tight. You ever notice that your dad talks like a robot?"

"What?" Victoria's head jerks back. "No. Just the opposite. He feels things too deeply, and then has anxiety about it. That's why he's taking Valium. You just don't know him."

Aidan winces. "Nope. I think I do know him. I've talked to him a few times now. And I say: robot. He has no empathy. That's why they hired him to bust drug dealers. You ever think about how funny it is that he works for the DEA? I mean, think about it." He squeezes her elbow. "The Drug Enforcement Agency."

Victoria's face stays blank. "No, I don't get it. It's not funny. What's funny about that?"

Aidan seems like he is on the verge of saying something, but then stops himself and sighs instead. "Vic. I'm just saying. He scares me a little bit."

"I don't dispute there's something wrong with him lately. But robot? That's so off. Way, way, way off."

Aidan thinks it over. He pushes a strand of hair out of his face, and studies Victoria. Something in her face seems to help him relax. "Never mind. It's okay." He puts his hands on his hips. "I know you'll protect me against the robot invasion."

Victoria leans in. "I will," she whispers. "Just stand behind me when the robots get here, and I'll take care of you."

He opens his eyes wide and nods vigorously, and she laughs.

My tail swishes back and forth. I'm not sure what they mean by "robot." I don't understand the joke.

When I arrive in the kitchen, Dad and Mom are looking over some papers that are spread out on the counter. Dad stands so that his shoulder touches hers. He talks and points to the papers. Something about *bills* and *the total*. His voice is low and patient, as he points *here*, and then *there*. And then also *here* again.

He watches her to make sure she is following, and when she glances at him, he gives her a small smile. She gives him a cautious smile back.

Then Mom explains something else to him, about *the bank* and *the accounts*. He nods and listens carefully.

They both turn when they hear footsteps going upstairs.

Mom asks Dad whether or not he thinks Aidan should be allowed upstairs. In the end, they agree the answer is definitely no. So together they walk over to the foot of the stairs and yell for the kids.

Victoria and Aidan listen from the top of the stairs, faces grim and sullen, as Mom and Dad explain the new rule. But they don't argue, and come back down to the living room.

I'm not exactly sure what Mom is so worried about. But I'm glad Aidan is not allowed upstairs. Now there's one less place where he can bother Charlie.

Mom and Dad end up having lemonade on the back deck. They sneak out while I'm getting a bite to eat at my bowl, so I miss my chance to slip outside. Although I sit and stare out the sliding glass door at them, Mom and Dad are deep in conversation and don't notice me.

However, I see that Gretel has somehow managed to get outside. Lucky! She sits proudly by Dad's feet, head held high. Her giant ears stand alert, listening to the intonation of his voice.

I feel bad. She admires Dad so much. And she really misses him.

Since I'm stuck inside, I decide to go find Charlie. I pad my way past Victoria and Aidan, who have camped out again on the green couch. I see they have put down the blinds for privacy, so the adults on the deck can't see them.

I watch as Aidan leans over Victoria's shoulder to glance at what she is looking at on her phone. She smiles and moves farther away. "Stop spying on me." Aidan slides closer to her, and reaches as if to grab her phone. Victoria squeaks like a field mouse, but she also has a wide grin on her face as she holds the phone too far away for him to reach. "Stop."

He moves to reach out again, and in doing so, his hand brushes her arm and lands on her knee to steady himself. Victoria laughs.

Aidan knows how to play this game. She reels him in, and he obligingly gets closer—but not too close. He respects her space.

These young humans have the strangest mating rituals. It seems like torture. Why do they make it so complicated?

"I can't believe your mom and dad are out on the deck," Aidan says quietly to her. "Having a normal conversation."

"Why?"

"Because." Aidan takes a strand of her long hair in his hand, twirling it in his fingers. "She kicked him out. I thought she was mad. But she's being really nice to him."

Victoria frowns. "Yeah. Well. He's still my dad. I think they're just taking a break. She's starting to cool down, so . . . Maybe he'll be moving back in soon."

Aidan snorts. "That's not how it works, Vic. Once someone moves out, that's usually it. They don't come back. People don't really change."

I'm afraid I agree with Aidan, for once. It is hard to imagine Dad changing much. He is set in his ways.

I move along and down the hall, turning to spring my way upstairs. My claws sink into the carpeting to propel me along.

My good boy Charlie is spread out on his bed, big blue headphones covering his ears, humming along to music. I jump up and snuggle down in the dirty laundry at the foot of his bed. It smells so much like Charlie in this room. It is my favorite scent in the world, even better than fresh tuna. It makes me feel content and secure.

I doze. At one point, Charlie wakes me as he turns over. He yawns, stretching his arms over his head. I peek with one eye to watch him flop onto his right side. His eyes slowly close.

He is so much like a cat sometimes. It is highly satisfying.

I think Charlie would make a wonderful cat. His movements are graceful for the most part, with the occasional awkward gesture. Like me, he scampers away when embarrassed. He loves to rest, and nestles his head against his pillow when he rolls over, smushing his face back and forth into the softness of it. He enjoys his food, but doesn't beg and worry about it like Gretel does. He's also highly nocturnal, staying up late in the night typing into his phone.

Yes, I can imagine him with ears and paws and lovely fur and claws to sharpen. I think he'd quite enjoy it.

It's just a little fantasy of mine. No harm in it.

I wonder if he ever wishes I could be changed into a human.

The sun has gone down, and Charlie eventually gets up to change for bed. He strips off his jeans and pulls on striped pajama pants. He slips on an old T-shirt and heads out to the bathroom to brush his teeth. I follow, as I do every night, because Charlie lets me sit on the counter and play with the water coming out of the faucet.

I bat the water with my paw, and—spray! Bat, spray! Bat, spray!

"Stop, Lily J. Potter," Charlie says with a laugh. "Whoever heard of a cat who likes water? You're a cat, not a dog."

I know that, silly.

As Charlie brushes his teeth, the sound of the trickling water echoes off the ceiling. My tail twitches as I watch him swish the water around in his mouth.

Charlie walks over to push the bathroom door almost closed, and sighs. He peels off his T-shirt, leaving the water at a steady drip, so I can continue to bat it with my paw. But now, I glance up at Charlie. He looks in the mirror and sees what I see: the bruise on his side is fading to a greenish tint. His face doesn't give anything away. He has more dark spots on his arm.

Charlie and I both jump when Victoria suddenly bursts into the room.

"Oh. Sorry. I didn't know anyone was . . ." Victoria pauses. "In here."

Charlie looks around to figure out where on the floor he dropped his shirt, but it's too late. Victoria walks up to Charlie and stares at his arm.

"What happened?" She points, accusatory. "You have a bruise. No, wait—you have . . . three bruises. They look like fingerprints." Her face creases in confusion. "Charlie. Did someone grab you so hard that you bruised?"

Her eyes jump up to meet his, piercing in intensity. Charlie looks over her shoulder like he wants to make a run for it, but there's no room for him to get around her. She grabs his wrist as if to hold him there.

"No," he states. "No. It's no big deal. I was just horsing around with a friend. In gym class."

I tip my head. I don't think that's true.

"What *friend* would do that? And you never play rough." Victoria sounds angry, as if Charlie has done something wrong. "You know it, Charlie."

Victoria finally lets go of his arm as he yanks himself away. Charlie grabs his shirt from where it sits on the tiles near the bathtub. "Seriously. Vic. It's nothing."

"It's not nothing," she spits out. "Jesus. And what—is your side bruised too? What's that?"

A dark shadow appears in the doorway. Charlie shrinks back, and scrambles to get his shirt on as fast as he can, pulling it over his head.

"Hey," Aidan greets Charlie, and he couldn't sound less interested. "What's up, little man?"

"Guys. Get out. I'm not done in here. I'm getting ready for bed."

Victoria whirls to face Aidan. "He's got bruises on his arm. And his side." She turns back. "Are you being bullied by some jackass at school?"

"No," Charlie groans, exasperated. "I told you. It was . . . I was just trying a trick on Karen's skateboard and I started to fall, and she grabbed me."

"That . . ." Victoria's face suddenly crumples. Her tough demeanor seems to melt away in an instant. "That's not what you said a minute ago." She stamps her foot, and her eyes start to water. "That's not the explanation you gave me just a second ago, Charlie. You said you were horsing around with a friend in gym class."

Charlie bites his lip. He glances at Aidan. "Can you please

just go away? I want my privacy." When Victoria doesn't move, Charlie's hands clench into fists at his side. "GET THE HELL OUT, VIC."

Victoria whirls to face Aidan. "Did you see his bruises?"

He shrugs. "C'mon, Vicky. Give the kid a break. I've seen worse. Let's go."

"You've seen worse?" She leans toward Aidan, grinding her teeth for a moment as she pierces him with her stare. "You've seen worse? Where? On your rounds at the emergency department?"

Aidan opens his mouth, then closes it. "No, I'm just saying . . ." Looking uneasy, he shrugs. "No, I just meant: Guys do stuff. Accidents happen."

Victoria storms past him, out of the bathroom. Aidan doesn't follow immediately. He and Charlie look each other over warily.

"It's no big deal. I've seen worse," Aidan mutters again. Directly to Charlie.

My whiskers twitch.

Leave, clever fox, I demand silently. *This is our home. Our bathroom. You're not wanted.*

I'm sure anyone would sense what I do. Aidan has the potential to inflict pain. Maybe it's because someone has been cruel to him, in his short life.

Charlie, to his credit, lifts his head defiantly. "Good for you," he replies, a little too loudly. "Now GET OUT before I yell for my dad. I know you're not allowed up here. You're not supposed to be upstairs. He just told you that an hour ago."

Aidan shrugs again. "Whatever, dude. Your parents aren't really paying attention. And you know it." He smirks. "Besides, your sister wouldn't take no for an answer. She's a demanding woman."

He exits to the hallway, and we hear his footsteps as he

heads straight to Victoria's room. Charlie steps over to slam the bathroom door shut.

"It's not fair, Lil," he says to me. "They drive me crazy."

I'm so sorry. They drive me crazy too.

I stand, and push my nose into his hand. Charlie picks me up and strokes my fur. I feel his heart beating, his body shaking, and realize how anxious he is. Again I think about how unfair it is that Charlie has to be distressed in his own home. I wish Victoria would break up with Aidan, and this could be over.

For the first time, something occurs to me. I have been under the assumption that someone is hurting Charlie at school, while Aidan teases Charlie here at home.

But maybe Aidan is the one hurting Charlie. Could he be the bully himself, one and the same?

It seems unlikely. But also possible.

It doesn't make sense that Aidan would do anything that would seriously upset Victoria. Does it?

I see the way he looks at her. Like a dog whose owner kicks him, Aidan fears rejection, and he doubts Victoria's love, but he is too devoted to stay away. Although he ignores her wishes sometimes, he is also desperate to please her. He wants her attention, and hurting Charlie would certainly achieve that, but not in a good way.

No, I find it hard to believe he'd hurt Charlie and risk losing Victoria.

At the same time, he has a cold look in his eyes sometimes.

I will continue to be vigilant. Aidan must be considered a suspect at this point.

I am so completely engrossed with thinking about Aidan that I almost don't hear Dad come storming in from the back deck, where he was talking with Mom. As soon as Charlie opens the bathroom door, I sprint out, and I barely get to the balcony in time to see Dad striding down the hallway. Gretel trails after Dad, tail and tongue both wagging, but it's no use. He doesn't even notice her.

Dad rips open the front door. Mom is following him, and he turns back around to face her. He speaks quietly, I assume so the children won't hear. "I drink too much, okay? Kate, I know. I've admitted it. That's the first step, right? Admitting it? But it's not as bad as you make it out to be. I don't have a *problem*. You're making this into a problem that doesn't exist. I can stop when I want to. I just don't want to right now, because of the pain. You're the one who flushed my pills—and that's okay. Really. I don't want the pills. I don't. They're illegal. Drug addiction is . . . completely different. I just need a drink sometimes."

She just shakes her head. Mom has heard this before.

"Kate," he begs, tears in his eyes. "I need to come home. I don't want a divorce. I can't do this anymore."

She closes her eyes, and wraps her arms around herself tight, as she does when she is upset. "No," she says in a shaky voice. "I've already said no. Not unless you get help."

"Kate. I don't need help." He cringes when he says *help*, like it's a terrible word. "You know I want to come home, don't you?"

"Yes. I know that. But you're not well. You say you know it, but you don't. I'm sorry, Jeremy, but you don't get it. I talked to Dr. Lodge about it. You have a cross addiction. You just substituted one thing for another."

Dad's mouth twitches. "You talked to our doctor about it?" he whispers, unbelieving. "But I don't want people to know about this, Kate." His eyes are wild and desperate. But he and I can both see that Mom has her mind made up.

"Too late," she replies, her voice fading. "It's too late. I'm getting help for myself, even if you won't."

"But you don't need—" Dad shakes his head. He takes a

step back, rubbing his forehead with one hand. "Ah, Kate. For-get it." And then he lets himself out.

Gretel watches the door, but Dad does not come back.

Gretel finally lays down on the hall rug, head on her paws. She will wait. She will wait there all night if necessary, waiting to see if Dad returns. But I know he will not.

Chapter 10
Faking It

Vincent comes and cleans out our entire garage. I suppose he felt bad when Mom complained about the mess Mark left.

He lets himself in the front door one morning when everyone is out, waking me from my nap. When he walks through the house, and I hear his boots on the kitchen floor, I jump up to scamper after him. Very polite, he holds the door open for me as we both go out to the garage.

"Ladies first."

Why, thank you!

Raising both overhead doors so that light pours in, Vincent gives our garage the thorough cleaning that Mark did not quite achieve. In fact, he does much more than his fair share. He moves the bikes and other sports equipment out to the driveway before sweeping. He straightens the garbage and recycling cans. He piles his building tools and equipment carefully in one corner, so a car can once again park in the empty space.

I watch Vincent from the stairs that lead from the garage to the house. It is my favorite perch. I can see the green of the pine trees outside and breathe in the humid spring air, all while remaining in the cool shadows.

When he is done, a bead of sweat runs down Vincent's face. He pushes his glasses more securely on his nose when they slip down. His face is red and his breathing uneven.

My! I hope he is not having heart trouble of some kind.

I walk outside, stretch my legs, and sit under my favorite bush. Vincent wipes his brow, and closes the garage doors as he heads back into the house. Once the grinding noise of the doors stops, all is quiet. I am able to hear the rustle of marsh grasses across the street, and the chatter of the birds in the woods behind us. A seagull swoops overhead with a loud cry.

I hunt for mice as the sun rises high in the sky. I wasn't expecting to get outside today. Usually after Mom leaves for work in the morning, I go back to sleep. So this is a nice change of pace.

I do believe this is the cleanest our garage has ever been. Once in a while, Mom asks Kevin to sweep it out. But the family rarely straightens up the way Vincent just did.

When he lived here, Dad sometimes spent time in the garage. He has a special cabinet that he keeps locked. He did not let anyone in his cabinet, not even Mom. He would only open it when other humans were not around.

There was one day last spring when Mom asked aloud if Kevin knew where the key was. Kevin just shrugged. He said he had no idea.

Dad had his secrets. But everyone has a right to privacy. I firmly believe that. When I am cleaning myself, I prefer to do it alone, in an otherwise empty room.

That same day, Mom asked Dad about the cabinet. He was drinking a cup of coffee at the kitchen table and looked surprised, caught off guard. He just shrugged, saying he'd lost the key, and would look for it later. Snapping the newspaper open in front of him, he made it clear the conversation was over.

But I knew the key was not lost. Dad opened the cabinet frequently enough for me to know better.

*　*　*

About an hour later, I hear voices, far away. I take a look in the direction of the noise. Charlie and Victoria are walking up the street, coming home from the bus stop.

Victoria approaches the garage and presses some buttons to lift the doors. Her mouth drops open in surprise. "Who cleaned up?"

"Maybe Vincent was here," Charlie says. "Wow. It looks amazing." He bends to slip his backpack off. It's stuffed full and Charlie lets it slide from his shoulder with a groan. He straightens back up. "Maybe we should hang here and enjoy the nice weather for a while before we go in."

"Yeah," Victoria says with a shrug. "It's actually pretty decent out. The sun feels warm."

Charlie sniffs. Sometimes I think he is allergic to the outdoors, the way the sun makes him sneeze. "Did you ever have Mr. Carver for science? I'm so glad I got him for biology."

They get into a conversation about Charlie's science class. Victoria tells him a few stories about her own teacher.

Eventually, a group of boys appear as they round the corner. As they get closer, my siblings stop and watch. Victoria slowly slides her own yellow backpack off, dropping it at her feet on the driveway. Charlie and Victoria face each other and continue their conversation. But I can see: They're watching the boys.

"Hey, Vicky," one of the lead boys calls to Victoria as they run past. He is an athletic young man. It's a warm day, and his T-shirt is off and tucked into the waistband of his shorts. She waves back.

When the next group comes by, another boy yells, from the middle of the pack. "Hi, Vic!"

This time she smiles. "Pete, run faster! You're falling behind," she teases him.

Finally, the last stragglers jog down the street, including the boy who spoke to Charlie before.

"Hey again," he says to Charlie, when he gets close. "You live here, huh? Cool. You're so close to the beach."

"Yeah," Charlie says, glancing down at his sneakers.

"Hi, I'm Vicky," Victoria says brightly.

Charlie gives her a quick glance of panic before turning back to the boy. "I'm Charlie."

"Yeah, I know." The boy smiles and nods, his face friendly and open. He slows down and then stops, allowing the other boys to sprint ahead. His face is pink, but he is not sweating yet, as they have just started running. "My name's Ronaldo."

"It is?" Charlie meets his eyes for the first time. "My friend Karen told me it was Raul."

"Ah, so you've been talking about me?" Ronaldo teases him.

Charlie's lips part, but no words come out. He shoves his hands in his jeans pockets.

Something about Ronaldo's voice sounds interesting. He pronounces words a little differently than my humans. His skin is darker, and his hair is cut very short. Ronaldo couldn't look more different from Charlie, in the same way my long creamy fur is very different from that of a short-haired tabby.

He continues, talking very fast. "It's Ronaldo, like the footballer from Brazil. Or soccer player, as you say. That's how you can remember it. You've heard of him, right?"

Once again, Charlie seems at a loss for words. He can barely look at the boy, never mind keep the conversation going.

The boy gestures toward the open road. "Okay, well . . . I've gotta run. Literally."

Victoria laughs, sounding delighted. "Yeah, you better get going," she says. "They're going to think you're slacking off."

Charlie just squints and studies the pavement. "Okay," he says quietly. "See you tomorrow, maybe."

"Definitely." Ronaldo smiles, and heads off.

Victoria gives her brother a disgusted look. As if to say: *Really?*

My nose twitches. I'm not sure why she is so dissatisfied.

Charlie stares down toward the end of the street. Once

Ronaldo is out of sight, he exhales. "Oh my God," he moans. "Oh my God. That was so painful."

"Do you like that kid?"

"Do I like him?" Charlie turns back to his sister. "Are you kidding? Did you see him?" He sounds like he is in agony. "Oh my God."

She smirks. "Yeah. I saw him." She shakes her head at the look of misery on her brother's face. "C'mon, Charlie. You couldn't laugh when he was trying to be funny? You didn't even crack a smile. You looked like you were going to throw up. You can do better than that."

"I can? I really don't think I can. I can't."

"Yeah, you can. It sounds like he follows soccer. Maybe you should look it up and learn something."

Charlie leans over and lifts his backpack, wincing as he heaves it onto his back. He sighs. "I don't know, Vic. I already have to study baseball to talk to Dad. I don't want to fake it with Ronaldo too. It's too exhausting."

Victoria tips her head, considering this. I approach her, and rub against her ankles.

Go easy on him. He seems uncomfortable.

"Okay," she finally says. "I guess you're right. Never mind what I said. But you could be a little more chatty."

"I couldn't think of what to say."

"How about: Where are you from? Where'd you go to school before? How do you like the sailing team? What team do you follow in soccer? Blah-blah-blah-blah-blah?"

Charlie kicks a small rock. "He didn't have time for all that." I watch the rock roll away.

Victoria reaches out to give Charlie's shoulder a gentle push. "I think he'd make time for you. He completely stopped running. He stood there in the middle of the street. He couldn't wipe the stupid smile off his face. C'mon, Charlie."

"I don't know about that," Charlie objects, but he's looking away now. Thinking about it.

I'm a little confused. Is Victoria suggesting that Charlie needs to be more aggressive about making new friends? I suppose that must be it.

Charlie has always been tentative with other people. He watches and waits. He is careful. I think he feels safer keeping to himself sometimes.

"Hey, Vic," Charlie says, wincing, "Don't say anything to Kevin, okay? I mean . . ." He glances down the street. "Don't mention Ronaldo."

Victoria opens her mouth, as if to object, but then shuts it tight. She swallows and makes a face like she has a sore throat. "Sure. Yeah, okay. I won't. He doesn't need to know. He's been kind of a jerk lately. He thinks he's the boss now that Dad's gone."

Aidan too, I remind her. *Don't leave him off your list of idiots.*

Charlie gets his backpack centered on his back, and reaches down to pick me up. I explode in a purr at the touch of his hands. It reminds me of lying on Dad's chest. Dad and Charlie have the same strong but gentle hands. They have the same eyes. The same scent.

Dad and Charlie. Both sensitive in their own ways.

I'm determined to help my sweet boy, if I can just figure out how. I think if Dad is not moving back home, then Mom must be the key. She has been tired, and sad, and miserable. There must be a way to help her feel better, so she can focus more energy on Charlie.

I hate seeing Charlie's bruises, and I don't like to think that what happened to me as a kitten is now happening to Charlie as a young man. It is forcing me to think about those days when I was young and helpless, and I can't stand thinking about it. I've worked hard and come a long way, to the point where I forget about my injury most of the time. It is usually only the reaction of new humans when they see my limp that reminds me. But now I'm forced to think about it.

I don't want Charlie to be badly hurt, which is what could eventually happen. If he were permanently scarred in some way, the way I am, I would blame myself.

But soon I come to realize that this task of getting Mom to concentrate on Charlie will be harder than I anticipated. There are other distractions brewing.

Chapter 11
Wedding Photo

"Vincent and I had a vision for this room," Mom announces, moving her hands back and forth in the air.

Mark nods. "Yes. Right. He gave me the plans."

"No, I mean more than just the *plans*." Mom pouts, staring at the blank wall. "I mean we had a *vision*."

Mark looks around the room, as if he's missing something that's floating in the air around him. "Right. I've got all the measurements. I'm not winging it. He gave me a detailed sketch."

Mom sighs, and I would sigh right along with her if I could. Mark clearly doesn't understand her at all.

Mark can see Mom is frustrated. He reaches into the back pocket of his jeans and pulls out a piece of paper. Mom watches him unfold it. Mark frowns at the paper, as if trying to decipher a mysterious message.

While he's distracted, Mom studies his face. I watch her gaze move, tracing the outline of his shoulder. She then looks at his arm, and her eyes stop at his hands on the paper.

Hmm. I feel like Mom is trying to learn the outline of his body. She is sizing him up, but for what purpose, I cannot guess.

She cannot doubt that he is strong enough to build this book-case. He is tall and sturdy. But from the hard time she is giving him, I think perhaps she doubts his mental ability to put it together correctly.

"Look. Mark. Forget the sketch for a minute." She marches over to the wall, breezing past him, and spreads out her arms. "Just think about the big picture. We've got the fireplace in the middle. We want to build a new hearth around it. The shelving will go on either side of it. But the problem is . . ."

I tune Mom out and pivot to study Mark. He listens about as long as I do, but as soon as her back is to him, his head tips to one side as he takes in her hair. Then his eyes trail down to her waist. He watches her with eyes glazed over, and I realize he is seeing but not hearing. I imagine he is dreaming of something. A small smile comes to his mouth, and I can see he is pleased by his own thoughts.

Perhaps he is impressed with how red Mom's hair is when the sunlight catches it at the right angle. I have never seen another human with hair quite that color.

Between Mom's grand "vision" and Mark's daydreaming, I'm afraid the two of them may be far apart in terms of getting this project done in a timely way.

They end up talking for a long time. Mom finally relaxes and sits on the couch, and I jump up and lie next to her. Mark slouches on the other side of the couch, so I am between them. The three of us are quite comfortable, sunk down into the old cushions.

Mark listens carefully, and talks a lot, using his hands and arms to illustrate his ideas. Mom sometimes frowns at his comments, cautious, as if afraid he is leading her into a trap. But I can see he is a natural storyteller, and she is intrigued.

I have watched and listened to enough humans to see who feels awkward about making conversation and for whom it is very easy. Mark belongs with those humans who find talking easy.

I realize at that moment that Mark is the polar opposite of Aidan.

Aidan always appears gloomy, like he finds the world around him depressing and annoying. As if he assumes others will not want to talk to him or listen to him. As if the sound of other voices grates on him.

Mark, on the other hand, is relaxed at all times, breaking into a wide smile at the smallest provocation. Mark smiles even when Mom does not smile back. He looks Mom in the eye, always has a reply, and eventually makes her comfortable. As if he is used to people agreeing with what he says. And—even more impressive—he listens as if what others have to say is very interesting.

At one point, I realize that Mom has her hand on my neck, her fingers gently scratching under my ear. At the same time, Mark has his hand on my tail and he occasionally strokes my back.

I'm amused to be the center of attention for two humans at once!

At the same time, I realize they're not really focused on me at all.

When I hear the refrigerator open, my ears spring to attention. I get up, and scamper into the kitchen to see who is preparing food.

Victoria and Aidan are in constant motion, hustling back and forth from refrigerator to stove. From the scent and the heat and the sound of butter sizzling in a pan, I realize they are making something good. Gretel paces around their legs, eager and excited, until Kevin enters the room and points at her.

"Sit."

She sits. Kevin, in her eyes, is second-in-command to Dad. Kevin spends a lot of time walking and playing with Gretel.

So she obeys. But her big brown eyes are still melting, pleading, begging.

I turn, and flop down on the tile floor away from the action. I know well enough to stay out of the way. Perhaps I'll get a scrap of cheese in my bowl at some point, but I don't beg. I'm not *that* hungry, for goodness sake.

Aidan makes a *tsk*ing sound with his tongue, and shakes his head. "Man," he says quietly to Kevin, who pours himself a drink of lemonade. "It's only been a few months and your mom has a boyfriend already. Who would have guessed."

Victoria turns sharply and smacks Aidan's arm. "Shut up."

"They can't hear me," he argues. "The door is closed."

Kevin turns to look. There is a door with glass panels between the kitchen and the study. It is, in fact, almost closed. Not quite. It was open just wide enough for me to slink out. We can hear Mom and Mark talking, but it is muted. We can also see them, but Mom's back is to us. They aren't paying any attention to the children.

"What the hell are you talking about?" Kevin asks. He doesn't take his eyes off Mom, and looks genuinely concerned.

Aidan comes up behind Kevin and puts a hand on his shoulder. "Sorry to break it to you. But the new guy is obviously enjoying your mom's company. Trust me. I've got a sixth sense about these things. I've seen enough guys with my mom to know what I'm talking about."

"What?" Kevin sounds disgusted.

"Dude. If he didn't care about impressing her, he'd still be working. Or maybe he'd talk while working, to be polite to the customer. But he's literally sitting there, entertaining her, like he has all the time in the world. He has a captive audience."

"Gross," Victoria mumbles, flipping a sandwich in the pan. "My mom's not interested. You don't know my mom at all. She's not like that."

Aidan turns back to Victoria. "Oh, yeah?" He pokes her shoulder. "She doesn't seem to be in any hurry to get up off that couch. If she's not interested, then why did she schedule him to start coming three afternoons a week, and tell you she's going to be leaving work early to meet him? We're not going to have any privacy anymore."

Victoria shrugs. "He works in a kitchen all morning, so the only time he can come is in the afternoon. And my mom prefers to be here so she can keep an eye on his work and so there's not a total stranger working in the house when she's not here. Besides, who cares? I don't," she grumbles, sounding like she does in fact care very much. "They won't bother us."

"Um, yeah. That's my point." Aidan crosses his arms across his chest triumphantly. "They're not going to bother us, because they're into each other. Point made. Case closed. Mission accomplished."

Kevin's brows furrow. "No. No, no, no. My mom and dad are going to work things out." He taps Aidan on the arm. "Hey. Listen. My dad said they were taking a break. That means he's probably going to move back in soon." Kevin reaches behind Aidan to grab a loaf of bread. He rips open the plastic bag, pulling out two slices and putting them on a plate. "That guy just has no idea what he's doing, so my mom has to supervise his every move. He practically *cut his hand off* the first day he started working here. He's an idiot. I don't know why Vincent hired him." Kevin's voice cracks, and he clears his throat. "He's too young for my mom anyway. Seriously. Look at him. How old is he, do you think? In his thirties?"

Aidan runs his thumb over his bottom lip. His gaze shifts away, then slides back to Kevin.

Well! This is interesting.

Kevin has never asked Aidan for advice before. In fact, Kevin usually avoids Aidan like he's a garden snake.

I can almost see the wheels turning in Aidan's mind as he makes a few quick calculations. Deciding how to react. As I mentioned, Aidan is keenly aware of human dynamics.

He can sense power shifting in a room. I can feel it too.

"Why don't we find out?" Aidan suggests, with a nod toward the counter. "There's the guy's wallet and phone."

Kevin draws in a sharp breath. "Um. We shouldn't touch his stuff." He freezes, a piece of bread still in his hand. "I mean, he's right there. He might see us."

Aidan takes a few steps closer to the wallet. I can't quite see what he's doing from my angle on the floor, but I watch him rearrange some papers on the counter, move a stack of mail, and shuffle items around. "Nah. He's deep in conversation." Aidan glances toward the doorway, and seems satisfied.

Tracking Kevin's eyes, I assume Aidan has moved the wallet close to the sink, out of Mark's line of sight. Kevin just stares at the counter, unable to move.

Aidan sighs when he sees Kevin can't—or won't—touch the wallet. "Okay. Fine. I'll look." Aidan picks up the wallet, his back to the glass door, and rifles through it quickly. "His license says he's . . . yeah, he's gotta be ten years younger than your mom." He flips something over. "Awwww. Bad news, guys. Sorry to disappoint your mom."

"What?" Victoria asks, curious. She turns, spatula in hand.

Aidan holds up what appears to be a small square picture. "Wedding photo."

"Oh." Victoria puts a hand on her hip. "Well, that's okay. I guess."

Kevin's eyes open wide, in relief. "Good. He's married. That's good. Really good." His whole body seems to relax. "So, okay. Put that back where you found it."

Aidan peeks up from the wallet. "They're still talking?"

Kevin checks. "Yeah." He sounds frustrated to have to admit that. He unscrews the lid from a jar of peanut butter and stabs his knife down into it.

Aidan pulls a piece of green paper out of the wallet, and stuffs it in his back pocket. I assume that he is taking money. I don't know what money is for exactly, but I know it holds value.

Aidan puts the wallet back down on the counter, and slides it to its original position.

When Aidan glances up, Kevin is staring at him.

Kevin the Scout.

Kevin the baby-faced oldest child.

The two young men seem to communicate something with no words.

Maybe there are no words for this.

Perhaps Aidan feels he has earned something by his actions. And Kevin seems to decide, in that moment, that he is not going to challenge Aidan. I'm not sure it's a wise decision, but I understand. After all, Aidan did just help him out.

There is also the fact that Kevin has no love for Mark. He can't stand that Mark is here eating up Mom's attention. What does Kevin care if Aidan takes Mark's money?

Kevin just turns away and jabs the knife into the jar of peanut butter again, with even more force. Gretel senses the anxiety in the room, and starts pacing.

"Your grilled cheese is ready," Victoria calls out. Aidan turns and starts walking toward her.

"Awesome. You're the best. I'm starving."

Now I know for sure that Aidan is capable of theft. I have seen it with my own eyes. Kevin is my witness.

It makes me wonder once again if Aidan is capable of hurting Charlie. I cannot believe I ever considered giving him the benefit of the doubt.

Crook!

I give a loud *meow!* Just to let Aidan know I saw what he did.

All of the children turn their heads to look at me, surprised. Victoria laughs. "You hungry, Lil? You want a grilled cheese too?"

I just stare at her. I love my humans, but sometimes they can be foolish.

I slink away before they try to put food in my bowl. I've lost my appetite once again.

Aidan is a thief, and Victoria doesn't know it. Mom seems distracted by Mark. Dad won't stop drinking, so he is not welcome at home. How can I get anyone to help Charlie when my humans keep making things more complicated?

Chapter 12
Soap

A few days later, Aidan comes over after school. I hear the hum of the television and pad downstairs to see what's going on. I find Victoria in the kitchen preparing snacks, and I watch her set out cheese and crackers on a big red plate. Gretel paces and then sits very still, hoping that if she's good she will receive a chunk of cheese thrown her way, which she does. Victoria joins Aidan on the couch, placing the food on the little table in the middle of the room. It looks like there is something on the TV they both want to see, something important.

When they're done eating, Victoria snuggles closer to Aidan and rests her head on his shoulder. He supports her, a hand around her back, holding her close.

"Jeez. Another school shooting," she murmurs, turning her head toward his chest. "It's so sad."

"Yeah," he answers, although he doesn't sound sad. Rather, he sounds frustrated. "Crazy people with guns."

"It's sad, isn't it?" she asks, as if she might be wrong about it.

"Of course." He sits up straighter. "It's ridiculous. Ludicrous. People shooting and killing each other for stupid reasons. I don't get it. I don't know why your dad and brother are so hot on guns."

My tail twitches. Is that what people do with guns?

Humans shoot and kill each other?

I had no idea. The very thought of it is shocking. I have never seen a human kill another human. Does it happen often?

I suppose it makes sense. I know that sometimes animals attack their own kind over food or a mate.

Humans must attack each other too sometimes, although I rarely see it. In my experience, humans talk things out. And sometimes yell. Or even throw things. But I've never seen two humans have a physical fight.

Is that why humans kill each other with guns, I wonder? Lack of food? Or to compete for a mate?

It boggles my mind.

Victoria reaches up and runs her fingers gently through Aidan's hair, and he leans into it. She strokes his head over and over. His eyes flutter closed and he sits very still.

When he finally stirs and opens his eyes, they are wet. He takes Victoria's open palm and presses it to his cheek, which is not the intimate kind of gesture I usually see him make.

She sits up. "What's wrong? Are you okay?"

"Yeah." His voice is scratchy. "It's just that no one ever . . ."

"What?"

He breathes out heavily, like he's needed to exhale for a full minute. "That just feels really good. No one ever touches my hair like that. What I mean is, no one ever touches me at all. No one but you has touched me in probably . . ." He thinks about it. "Maybe a year."

"What?" Victoria spits out. "Like, not even your mom? Doesn't she run her fingers through your hair?"

Aidan chuckles. "My mom? No. Jesus." He rolls his eyes, like this is the craziest thing he's ever heard. "No, Vic." His eyes are still moist, his heart silently pleading with her. "My mom doesn't do that. That's not her style."

"I want to meet your mom," Victoria suggests lightly.

Aidan winces. "No. You really don't want to." It doesn't sound like the matter is up for discussion.

My whiskers stand at attention. What fantastical tale is Aidan weaving now? No one has touched him in a year? Surely he's joking. I can hardly go a day without a human's touch. I absolutely insist upon it. I will jump into any lap, rub against any ankle, and walk across any sleeping body to get the attention of my humans.

What he is saying has implications that are so astounding I cannot even fathom it. No wonder he is so cautious and desperate around Victoria. His heart is probably not sure if he should trust her or not.

Slowly, carefully, Victoria drags the palm of her hand across Aidan's cheek. She breaks into a wide grin.

He raises an eyebrow. "What?"

"Do you mean to tell me . . ." She pauses, making him wait a beat. "Are you admitting to me that you've never kissed a girl? You just said no one but me has touched you in a year."

He tilts his head, just a bit. He is amused by how excited she is to realize this, that he's never kissed a girl. And the look that he gives her forces me to see it, to understand what she likes about him.

I don't want to see it. Believe me. I don't want her to like him. He's a thief and a sneak and a manipulative human.

However.

What I see is this.

It's not that Aidan smiles at Victoria. No, he rarely smiles.

The look that he gives her is guarded, but it's also: Warm. Inclusive. A little naughty. As if they are in on a secret together.

"No. I actually haven't." He shrugs, like it's no big deal. "No point in trying to fake it at this point, right?"

"Good." Her face is very near his. "I'm going to kiss you right now."

I see him almost flinch, fear crossing his face. But the next thing I know, Victoria leans forward and presses her mouth into his. He freezes for a moment. Finally his whole body relaxes, and he pushes back, eager to please her.

Their first kiss. And I am witness to it.

When they part, Victoria is all glorious smiles. Triumphant.

Aidan, to me, looks a bit dazed. I think I am witnessing him slowly coming into his own as a young man.

He must also be realizing his weaknesses. He is going to have to submit to Victoria's whims if he wants to keep her as his mate.

"I suppose . . ." he falters. "I guess you've kissed a few guys before."

Victoria reaches up and plays with her necklace, twirling it in her fingers. "Maybe. Just a few. It doesn't matter. You're a good kisser." She turns back toward the TV.

Aidan puts his arm around her again and draws her close. He looks smug and proud of himself.

Well! Victoria has certainly made her feelings clear.

I don't approve.

Victoria turns suddenly to face Aidan and make eye contact. "You know, you smell really good. Do you—?"

He looks down, watching her mouth. I can see he wants to kiss her again. "It's just some soap my aunt bought me for Christmas."

She laughs. "Are you sure you're not wearing some kind of cologne or—?"

"No. Vicky, I told you. It's just soap," he repeats, interrupting her. But he's not angry. He looks happy, about as happy as he ever gets.

I feel a little squeeze of satisfaction in my heart. I do love to see humans happy. Even bad creatures deserve love. I believe that.

But then I hear the big clock chiming in the hall. And Charlie's footsteps on the floor above us. My ears flatten. I don't feel so well all of a sudden, because I remember how Aidan is not nice to my Charlie.

How am I so easily swayed? The humans confound me. I have to remind myself that Aidan is not worthy of Victoria. He shouldn't be taking up space in our house.

This partnering will not work in my favor. Victoria is getting close to a bully, and I must act with more urgency to expose him, before it's too late. It is time to make plans. I slink away to think it over.

Chapter 13
Bees

It is late afternoon and Mom is standing in the kitchen with a cup of coffee when Mark comes bursting in. He is wearing a dark T-shirt coated in wood dust because he's been working in the garage, and he comes straight at Mom almost in a run. She is so startled that a splash of her coffee sloshes onto the tile floor.

He stands in front of her, right by the kitchen sink. His eyes are open wide and he is almost panting, red in the face. "Bees," is all he manages to say. "Garage gutter. A nest. Or—hornets. A swarm of them."

When she looks down at his arms as he holds them out in front of her, I see them. Red welts. A few of them. On his right hand and arm. And one on his cheek.

Mom hurries to put her cup on the counter. "Oh my God. Are you allergic?"

His face is quickly turning from red to white. "Um, no. I mean, I don't think so. I don't know." He takes in a shaky breath. "But . . . I feel kind of. You know. Like I might. Pass out."

"Oh God. Don't faint. I could never catch you if you did. Just sit."

Mark looks around wildly. He takes one step toward the kitchen table but instead staggers into the counter, hitting it hard with his hip.

"No, no, no." Mom puts both of her hands on his arms. "Just sit right down. On the floor." She helps him as he sinks to the floor, and makes sure he is leaning securely against the cabinets. "KEVIN," she shouts. "COME HELP ME."

Mom goes flying to the drawer where she keeps medicine and starts ripping boxes out and throwing them on the counter. She finds a red box and shakes out the contents.

Kevin comes sauntering in. He sees Mark on the floor, and stares at him, hands on his hips. "Yeah?"

"Ice!" Mom yells. "Get ice."

"Oh. Sorry. Okay." Kevin jumps into action and takes a glass bowl out from a low shelf. He begins dispensing ice from the icemaker into the bowl, where it lands with a *clink, clink, clink, clink.* When a cube misses the bowl and hits the tile floor with a *smash!* I bat it with my paw and it slides toward Mark.

I love playing with ice even more than I love playing with popcorn. The way it glides across the floor—amazing! But I'm just trying to be helpful.

Mom fills a glass with water, and kneels down on the floor. "Here. Take an antihistamine." She helps Mark take a little red pill and swallow it down. "Just in case you're having a reaction."

Kevin wraps ice in a white towel, and crouches down on the other side of Mark. "Are you okay? Can you breathe? Your arm is swelling up."

Mark fills his lungs with a deep breath. "Yeah. I'm okay. It just really hurts. I'm surprised how much it hurts. And it kinda itches." He puts the ice on the wrist of his right arm. Looking from Kevin to Mom, who are both hovering over him, he suddenly seems embarrassed. "When they started to swarm me, I didn't know what to do."

Mom takes the phone out of her back pocket and shakes her head. "There's nothing you could do. This is my fault. Vicky told me about that nest weeks ago, and I forgot to do anything about it. I'm going to look up bee stings."

"You're not allergic, are you?" Kevin asks.

Mark leans his head back against the cabinets and shakes his head. "Nah, your mom asked me. Not that I know of."

"I'm going to check your pulse," Mom announces, and then places two fingers on the side of his neck. "You're supposed to check for a weak, rapid pulse." Mark closes his eyes. I think he is trying his best to relax.

"Is he okay?" Kevin demands. "Should we call 911?"

Mom sees Mark has his eyes closed, and shrugs at her son. She mouths: *I don't know.*

"I'm fine," Mark says, without opening his eyes. "Do not call 911. My medical insurance is shit. Don't bother."

What's that—?

Ah. Mark has said a bad word! One for which the children would have to put a coin in the swear jar. That's one of Mom's rules. I wonder if Mom will be angry or upset.

But no. She says nothing. I suppose she lets Mark get away with it because he is new here. He may not know all the rules yet.

Instead, Mom leans forward and puts her head right on Mark's chest, I suppose to listen to his heart. I know where the human heart is. I feel it beating when I lay on Charlie's chest. I felt Mark's heart when he held me in his arms.

I believe this catches Mark by surprise, because his eyes open with alarm. He takes in a quick, deep breath and some color comes back into his cheeks.

Well! If his pulse was weak, I believe Mom has straightened it out now.

When Mom backs away, she holds onto Mark's arm to keep the ice securely in place. "You're breathing okay? You can swallow?"

"I think so," he says, speaking softly, and not taking his eyes off of Mom.

"Okay. That's good." Kevin stands up. "Excellent. He's okay, then. I think he'll live." He pushes up his sleeves. "I was nervous there for a minute. I learned First Aid in Scouts. In case of emergency. You're supposed to call 911 for an anaphylactic event. But I guess you'd probably be gasping for air right now if you were having a severe reaction."

A few wood shavings stick to the dark blue of Kevin's shirt. Kevin brushes himself off.

With a sigh, he turns to go. When his back is to his Mom, I see his face darken.

He doesn't look too happy about the fact that Mark is okay.

At the foot of the stairs, Kevin turns. He shuffles his feet and scratches the back of his head. "You know, you should call your wife," he yells a little too loudly from the end of the hallway.

Mom's head turns up sharply. She squints, as if she may not have heard him right. "What, Kevin?"

"His wife. He should call her. So she can pick him up and drive him home."

We listen to Kevin's footsteps as he goes up the stairs. At first he climbs slowly, but then he runs up the final few steps.

I suppose Mom and Mark are considering Kevin's suggestion. But Mom looks a little surprised. And Mark doesn't reach for his phone.

The kitchen is quiet once Kevin leaves. I can hear clothes tumbling in the dryer, a low rumble. It's a nice sound. I'm sure Mom will put everything in the basket, and I will get to snuggle into a nice warm pile of clothes before the day is out.

But in the meantime, I contemplate my options. I'd like to climb into Mom's lap to reassure her, but she is on her knees. So I step between Mark's legs, which are splayed across the floor. I settle down, nesting comfortably.

Mark is still a stranger to us. I don't know if we would consider him a family friend quite yet. Sitting on a stranger's lap isn't something I would normally do.

But they're just legs. They're warm. Who cares who they belong to?

Besides, I'm starting to get used to Mark's peppery scent. It's not bad. I rather like it. And maybe I can help his recovery from the bee stings by comforting him with my big warm body.

Mom and Mark both stare at different points on the floor. I think they are comfortable enough together to have a quiet moment without talking.

"I didn't know you were married. Do you want . . . do you want me to call your wife?"

Mark looks down at me, and we make eye contact. Using the hand with no bee stings, he caresses the very top of my head, and I lean into it. His fingers circle around and scratch under my chin, so I tip my head back. It feels great, and I start to purr.

Out of the corner of my eye, I see Mom waiting for a reply. She chews on her lower lip. I believe she might be holding her breath.

"No," he finally says.

Mom nods. She studies his bowed head and her eyes relax. I don't think she wants him to go anywhere. I think she'd rather take care of him herself.

Mark drags his hand down my back. With a sigh, he goes on: "My wife's not here. She moved back to California. She's living with her parents." His voice is calm, but he glances over at Mom, as if unsure how she'll react to this news.

Mom waits, as if Mark is going to say more, but he doesn't.

There is a long pause. And in that space and time, I know in my heart that things are being said that I cannot hear.

This happens sometimes between humans. They don't speak out loud, but I can sense that something is going on. I'm no dummy.

"Oh." Mom sinks down farther onto the floor, but her hands

never leave the ice pack that rests on Mark's forearm. "I'm sorry. How long ago did she move away?"

"About nine months."

The big clock in the hall starts to chime. The sound echoes down the hall.

Mark looks down at Mom's hands, at the way she holds the towel full of ice on his arm. Mom has pale hands, with a silver wedding band on one finger. She wears red nail polish, but it is chipped up. Her knees nearly touch his thigh.

"How long were you married?"

Mark's face softens, and suddenly he looks younger to me. "Um, maybe five years? Not quite five years." He must realize Mom wants more information, because he takes in a deep breath before going on: "We're getting divorced. It's just taking a while."

Mom nods vigorously. "Yes. That's what I've heard. It takes a long time."

I lift my head when I hear loud music. Kevin has turned on the radio upstairs.

I suspect he wants nothing to do with what the adults are talking about down here.

Mark closes his eyes again, and Mom frowns. "Keep talking," she insists. "I want to make sure you're okay." Somewhere upstairs, I hear the sink running. "What happened?"

I'm not sure if Mom wants Mark to keep talking simply to make sure he's okay. From the focused look in her eye, I'd say she also genuinely wants to know what happened with Mark and his wife.

He clears his throat. "You mean—why are we getting divorced? Well. You know. I don't usually go into it." His voice gets deeper and quieter. "Nobody really wants to hear the whole horrible story. Once I start explaining it, people regret asking."

Mom looks away, disappointed. "That's okay." She leans back against the counter and exhales. "You don't have to tell me.

I understand. Believe me, I get it. You don't have to say anything. Sometimes you just can't make it work, no matter how hard you try."

Mom lifts the ice to look at the bee stings. Mark's arm still seems slightly swollen. She pulls his arm so his hand rests on her lap, and shifts the position of the ice. Mark watches her, his eyes flickering from her hands to her face, and back again.

"We didn't try very hard to make it work," he suddenly blurts out. "The thing is, we . . ." He swallows, as if his mouth is getting dry. "It was too much. We wore each other down. We both moved out and put the house up for sale. We couldn't keep living in that house. I don't know what else to tell you."

"Oh. Look—you don't have to—" Mom's hands cling to the ice pack on his arm, as if the pressure she's applying is the only thing keeping Mark alive. The heat of her hands is probably making the ice melt, as I see a drop of water run down his arm and onto her leg. "What's her name?"

"Hannah," he says.

And then, just as I thought he was getting the color back in his face, Mark goes pale again. From the way his eyes dart back and forth but see nothing, I imagine he is thinking about something important. Perhaps it's a memory that floods his mind.

He turns to look at Mom with horror. "Oh my God. No. No. No, I mean—our baby was Hannah. She lived for six months. But you're asking for my wife's name. I don't know why I said Hannah." Mark hangs his head. "Felicia. My wife. Her name is Felicia. After Hannah died, we didn't try very hard to make it work. We just couldn't do it again."

Mom's eyes widen, just slightly. I watch her pupils dilate.

My goodness. A baby. Who would have guessed? I can see Mom is as surprised as I am.

"I was so tired," Mark goes on, "Just tired of everything. I quit my job. I barely had the energy to leave the house. I couldn't even get out of bed. Felicia had no use for me in the end."

Mom is so close to Mark that for a moment I think she's

going to lean her head right against his shoulder. But she just closes her eyes. "I had no idea," she says. "Mark. I am very sorry to hear—" She shifts her weight and puts one hand under his elbow, adjusting the ice pack so it rests higher up on his arm. "I am very sorry to hear you lost your baby."

He chews the inside of his mouth for a moment. "Thanks." He frowns. "It's funny, I never tell this story to people. I've learned not to. People find it too upsetting. I don't know why I just said her name. I've been trying really hard to forget."

"Mark." Mom sits up a little straighter. "Maybe you're thinking about Hannah because you're lightheaded. You had a scare."

"Maybe it's because I'm talking to you," he adds. "I just mean—you're a mom. So you understand."

"I do," she agrees. "And of course you didn't want to go through that again. You suffered a terrible shock. But I don't know if you should try to forget Hannah. I'm sure you have some happy memories of her." When he doesn't reply, she goes on: "I don't think you should avoid talking about her, even if it's painful. You're going to encounter a few tragedies in life no matter what you do, even if you do everything right. At least you're living. You're trying to live."

Hmm. Do all humans encounter a few tragedies in life?

Has our family ever experienced a tragedy?

Perhaps by a "tragedy" Mom means something like Charlie getting bullied. That must be it. Mom will certainly snap to attention when she finally sees how Charlie has been getting hurt.

I look up at Mom. Her eyes are red and she looks upset, but confident in her advice.

Mark rests his head back on the cabinet and blinks. Twice. Thinking about it.

I glance up to see Mom's cup of coffee on the edge of the counter. It must be cold by now.

Mark bites his bottom lip, and I think he's afraid he's said something wrong. I sense his body temperature going up, even through his jeans and my fur. His eyes start to water up, and he opens his mouth to speak, but hesitates for a moment.

"I didn't know what to do, Kate," he finally blurts out.

"Of course you didn't—"

"I mean—when they swarmed me. I felt the first sting as soon as I saw them, and suddenly they were all over me. They were everywhere. It happened so fast." His eyes fill with tears, but he doesn't cry. He just swallows, taking a deep breath. "I still don't know what I'm supposed to do." He shivers, and I sense his body is still trying to adjust. "I hope no bees followed me in here or got in the house."

Mom glances around the kitchen, as if suddenly remembering where she is. Sitting on the kitchen floor. On a nice spring afternoon. With a man we hardly know. "In here? I haven't seen any buzzing around."

Mark tells her that his arm is frozen and getting numb. She removes the ice pack and massages his lower arm and hand to bring the circulation back. I can tell it makes him feel better by the way he tips his head back and closes his eyes. His breathing becomes more steady and even.

"Kate," he says softly. "You're a good nurse."

She smiles.

Eventually the ice melts and soaks the towel. Mom gets up to put the wet towel in the sink, and then sits back down again next to Mark, right on the floor. He hasn't moved. When she looks on her phone again, I can tell from her face that something is troubling her.

"I should have called 911." She presses the phone again. "It says here you should always call for an ambulance when you have an allergic reaction. Just like Kevin said."

"I'm not allergic," Mark says. "I just got dizzy."

Mom leans over him and studies the welts on his arm. She gently touches the sting on his cheek. "I'm not so sure. You should go get checked out by a doctor."

Mark smiles at her. "You're funny, you know that? Seriously. I am A-okay. I am in perfect health."

"I'll call the exterminator tonight," she promises. "We'll get rid of the nest."

While this afternoon has been very exciting, I'm concerned.

Something about this new man is distracting Mom from the real problem, the most serious issue, which is Charlie and his injuries. I need to stay on Mom's case until we get to the bottom of things.

The problem is, Mark seems to be working his magic on me too. Here I am, warm and cozy and nestled between his legs, like a loaf of bread in the oven. We've been sitting here for the longest time.

I am getting sidetracked, which happens sometimes in life. I'm not going to beat myself up about it. But I do feel a little guilty.

It's time for me to begin my efforts to rid our house of the clever fox.

Chapter 14
The Kissing Problem

Now, when Aidan comes over after school, there is less talking and more kissing.

Aidan and Victoria sit side by side in the middle of the living room couch, glued together at the mouth for long stretches of time. Not much else happens. They hardly change positions or move their hands, other than Aidan reaching up to twirl a strand of Victoria's hair in his fingers. It seems terribly boring to me.

At least they are quiet. And Aidan is too busy to cause any trouble.

I expected this development to go over well with the boys. After all, Aidan is less focused on Kevin and Charlie than ever before. He has no time, energy, or incentive to bother them. He has found something much more interesting to do! And he has Victoria's undivided attention.

But on the contrary, Kevin isn't happy. Although mating is a natural part of life, he seems to find their behavior disgusting. When he has to pass by the front room, he holds his hands out in front of him like he cannot stand the sight.

"Please. STOP. So gross. I shouldn't have to watch that."

Victoria lazily turns her head. "What?"

"Can't you do that somewhere else?" he begs.

"We're not allowed upstairs, dude," Aidan offers.

"Go outside to the deck, can't you?" Kevin sulks and walks away.

"It's more comfortable here." Victoria shrugs, and puts her head down on Aidan's shoulder, her arms around him.

When Charlie witnesses the same behavior, he makes noises like he's gagging, hand at his throat. At first, I think he is actually getting sick or choking, and hurry to his side. But then I realize he is just voicing his displeasure.

Victoria doesn't argue with Charlie. She just laughs. "Sorry, buddy," she calls out after him as he leaves the room.

Poor Charlie. He doesn't have Kevin's size or strength, so he doesn't say anything in front of Aidan. But he is uncomfortable with this development too. He goes upstairs to his room and when I get to the top of the stairs, I see he has closed the door so I cannot go and comfort him.

He has shut me out! My goodness! This has never happened before.

I can see that the boys are right. It is wrong to assume that just because the fox is not causing trouble *right now* that it is okay for him to be in our house. It's time to put a plan into action and do something to try and help Victoria see the real Aidan. But what?

After a few days of stewing, I get myself worked up. I've had enough.

I want to be a hero. Just like Dad and Gretel "fight bad guys," I want to scare off a bad guy.

I cannot allow myself to forget about what I've seen in Aidan. The theft. The underhanded comments. The potential for more serious crimes. He might turn on Victoria one day, and break her heart.

This isn't acceptable.

So one afternoon I wait under a chair in the living room. When Victoria goes to the kitchen to get a snack and Aidan stands up to stretch, I sneak quietly over to the couch and position myself on the rug very close to his feet.

I wait for my chance. Watching. Nose twitching in anticipation.

As soon as Victoria turns the corner, I *meow!* and jump. Then I turn toward Aidan and *hiss!* as viciously as I can, pawing and scratching the air.

"Whoa. Whoa. Whoa." Victoria almost drops the glasses of water she's carrying. "What the hell?"

Aidan has moved several feet away from me. His eyes open wide. "You're asking me? Your psycho cat just flipped out."

"Did you step on her tail?" Victoria snaps at him. She has a hot temper, like Dad. She goes from calm to furious in a quick moment.

"No. Definitely no." Aidan glares at me, angry. "I didn't even move. I swear. Vic. Your cat is insane."

I *hiss!* again, crouching and forcing my fur to stand on end for effect.

Aidan's eyes open wider. He is confused.

Rowr! I accuse.

He points at me. "She's a mouthy little bitch."

What? What did he just say? I know human curse words when I hear them!

Victoria's head tips to the side. "Did you kick her? Did you throw her off the couch?"

"No. And NO. C'mon, why would I do that?" He is quickly getting worked up. I can hear it in his voice. "I didn't do a goddamn thing."

Victoria glares at him, and doesn't offer him the water. "What kind of person hurts an innocent animal?"

Aidan's mouth drops open in shock. "What? What are you talking about? Oh my God. I promise you. Seriously. I did not do anything. Either on purpose or by accident."

"Sure you didn't. Then why is she so mad?" Victoria shakes her head in disappointment. Putting the water down on the little table, she turns to me. "What's the matter, Lily? Are you okay?"

I come out of my defensive stance and walk toward her. Victoria reaches down to pet my head, then picks me up and holds me to her chest. She murmurs reassurance into my ear.

Over her shoulder I give Aidan a *look*. Ha ha. He thinks he is the clever one? We'll see about that. He scowls back at me.

I have outwitted a fox before. When that red fox chased me in the marsh, I ducked under a fence and ran for cover under the deck of our house. I'm sure I can beat Aidan in any game he wants to play.

I intend to expose him for all he's worth. Once Victoria sees that Aidan is capable of hurting me, she'll soon realize that it's possible he's doing the same to Charlie.

Chapter 15
Strawberry Fields Forever

After the incident with the bees, things change between Mark and Mom.

The two of them are always aware of where the other is in a room. Closing in, then pulling away.

I hear how the tone of Mom's voice changes when she speaks to Mark. With Vincent, her old friend, Mom's voice is bright and confident. With Mark, her tone is still friendly, but more playful by a notch. I would say there is a more suggestive quality to it. She is very interested in his replies. And she is starting to smile at him—with her mouth, and her eyes, and in the way she slightly tips her head.

It makes me realize that it has been a while since I've seen her smile.

She has been so weary. I almost forgot what her smile looked like.

Mark must hear the change in her voice too. He stops whatever he is doing to listen when she talks. He turns his body toward her when he answers her questions, squaring his shoulders and standing still.

Mark has also started to bring over food every time he is here. He brings things that everyone likes to eat: scones, muffins, or a loaf of bread.

One day, there is a knock on the front door in the middle of the afternoon. Victoria goes to answer the door, and Mark is standing there.

"Hey," Victoria says. "Are you working here this afternoon? I don't think we were expecting you."

"No," Mark says, "Is your mom home?" He squints, as the sun is in his eyes.

"No."

Victoria shifts her weight from foot to foot. She's wearing fuzzy purple socks. I look from one to the other. It seems to be one of those unusual moments when Mark is at a loss for words.

Mark finally nods. "I just had an extra cake I made at the restaurant this morning, and I didn't know what to do with it. It's carrot cake." He hands Victoria a white bag, which she takes.

"Okay." Victoria holds the bag with one hand a little bit away from her body. "Yeah. Okay."

"Give it to your mom," Mark finally says, shoving his hands in his pants pockets. "Maybe it will cheer her up."

"Cheer her up?" Victoria looks confused.

"Yeah." He shrugs. "I've gotta go." He heads back down the path toward his truck. Victoria and I watch him for a moment before she shuts the door.

It reminds me of when I hunt down a mouse and deposit it on the doorstep. It is instinctive to me, to take care of my loved ones by awarding them my spoils, sharing my bounty. It is a possessive gesture and a protective one.

So I see how Mark's behavior reflects how he feels about Mom. He often comes into the kitchen to check on her, stalking back and forth to make sure he knows exactly where she is. It reminds me of the way Gretel paces around Dad when she is keeping an eye on him.

It's almost as if . . .

Well, I'll have to see how it plays out.

Vincent starts bringing his own dog with him sometimes when he comes over to work, to "get him some fresh air." I don't know why Vincent thinks the air in our damp old cottage is any fresher than the air at his own home.

Vincent's dog is squat, with a smashed in face that I think looks very smug. His fur is black, and his round eyes are too. His name is George. George is a wobbly thing who walks around with his nose in the air.

I think he's a bit ridiculous. I'm not sure Gretel knows what to make of him. When Gretel sniffs him all over, her long nose prodding his belly, George just stands there with a superior look on his face.

But Vincent loves George, so he can't be all bad. Mark seems fond of George too. When George can't climb up on the couch because his legs are too short, Mark lifts his heavy body up and plops him down on a cushion.

The men are funny together when they are both here. Even though Vincent is the one who has known Mom for years, he and Mark both tease Mom in equal measure. She especially likes to complain about them tracking in sawdust on their work boots and jeans.

"It just clings to us, Kate," Vincent says, his eyes twinkling behind his glasses. "What can we do about it? I'm sorry. We'll vacuum when we're done. We promise."

"Maybe she expects us to strip off our boots and pants and leave them in the garage every time we come in here," Mark suggests, as he carries in a piece of wood, which he has hoisted up on his shoulder.

"Me, building in my underwear. Oh, sure." Vincent laughs

heartily. "That's the last thing anyone wants to see. Trust me." It's nice to hear Vincent laugh, after seeing him so upset about his wife. I can see why he likes working with Mark. Mark entertains him.

Mom smiles at both of them. But her gaze gravitates toward Mark.

Vincent heads back out to the garage and Mark starts to follow, but then stops to linger in the doorway. He places his hands on either side of the doorframe, leaning in toward Mom. He fills the space so that Mom and I can't help but stare at him. "Katie, do you think Vincent wears boxers or briefs?"

This is another thing Mark has started doing: calling Mom "Katie."

I don't get it. Katie is not her name. No one calls her that.

She rolls her eyes and sighs loudly for his benefit, her arms wrapped around herself. "Honestly, I don't want to know."

Mark says nothing, but raises an eyebrow. I think he has other things he could say, perhaps a joke he could tell, but he is being careful. He keeps his mouth shut.

Vincent appears back in the kitchen, holding his hammer. "What are you doing? I thought you were right behind me."

"I was," Mark says. "But then I stopped to ask Katie if she thinks you wear boxers or briefs. I'm going to guess you probably wear boxer shorts with little black pug dogs on them. You know, that look like George."

George looks up, tongue hanging out stupidly, when he hears his name.

"Little pug dogs on them?" Vincent laughs again. "Uh, yeah, I love pugs. But on my boxer shorts? I guess that would be cute. I suppose." His face has turned pink, and he adjusts his glasses.

It's clear to me why Vincent hired Mark. What Mark lacks in carpentry skills, he makes up for in amusing chatter. For Vincent, Mark brings a lightness to work at a time when everything is serious and awful at home.

There are other days when Mark comes over by himself, and on these days Mom does not limit herself to the kitchen. She goes right into the living room and curls up with a cookbook on the couch. I can see that she likes to look at Mark, and watch him work. Although, frankly, he never seems to get much work done.

The two of them chat, about everything and nothing. Mark plays music while he works, something Mom never does, but she doesn't seem to mind.

One day, something out of the ordinary happens. It starts as Mark stands by the window. He seems to have made some progress on the bookshelves at this point, but I am not sure exactly how much, because I don't know what the plans look like. Mark stops what he's doing to listen. Music is playing softly from speakers that I cannot locate. "I love this song," he says. The music almost seems to come out of nowhere. "Living is easy with eyes closed."

Mom turns her head. "What?"

"It's the Beatles. You a fan? 'Strawberry Fields Forever.' "

"Oh." Mom seems disconcerted. I'm not sure she knows much about music. "Is this one of their psychedelic songs? One you're supposed to listen to while you're taking drugs?"

Mark smirks. "I guess we could, if you want," he jokes, but when he sees the serious look on her face, he stops smiling. "Maybe you're thinking of 'Lucy in the Sky with Diamonds.' "

She looks Mark over. "Are you one of those people who wishes he lived in the 1960s? You know, a hippie at heart?"

He snorts. "No. I'm happy to live now. With modern appliances and civil rights and all that. I have no interest in going back in time." The tempo of the song seems to change, and Mark tips his head. "This is a classic." He nods his head, as if his mind is made up about something. "Hey, do you dance? Felicia had this idea we'd learn to ballroom dance for our wedding."

Before she can object, Mark has stepped up to Mom, and reaches toward her. She lets him pull her up to a standing position, right in front of him. He holds one of her hands in his, and tucks his other hand around to rest on the small of her back.

Well! This is new.

"I can't—" She tries to move her feet with him. "Mark, I don't know—"

"Sure, it's easy." He doesn't stop smiling at her. Again, I note his perfect posture. Hips forward, shoulders straight, head up. So different from Charlie and Kevin, who stumble and slouch through the day.

"Why do I get the feeling you'd rather do anything else than build my bookshelf?" Mom says with a sigh.

"On the contrary." He turns her with an easy move. "I love this project. Getting my hands dirty and all that."

"You do?"

He stops moving for a moment, but doesn't take his hand off her back. "Sure. First, I nearly cut my fingers off with the saw. And then I almost went into anaphylactic shock from the bee attack. It's been awesome. Plus, Vincent is teaching me a lot. I can't wait to see how we frame out the windows. I'll probably lose an eye at some point. But it'll be worth it."

Mom smiles, at first tentatively, but then completely.

I suppose it is their eye contact that interests me the most. Mom often glares at Dad when she talks to him, but he averts his eyes. As if he is trying to make himself invisible. Or as if the sound of Mom's voice is painful to him. I think everything about their relationship affects Dad deeply, and sometimes it hurts. It hurts more than he can bear.

But when Mom and Mark are together, neither one looks away. She smiles, and then tries to quiet her face, but ends up smiling again even wider. I think it must be nice for Mom to have someone look and listen so attentively.

I watch them from under the kitchen table, but now turn to

make my escape. Music hurts my ears sometimes, and people moving unpredictably spooks me.

Kevin is just entering the kitchen, and I almost bump into his feet. I was so distracted by the music that I didn't hear him coming.

Through the half-closed glass door, Kevin sees Mark showing Mom how to dance in the study. He freezes in shock, as if he's just seen a raccoon in the house. So many emotions cross his face at the same time it's impossible for me to guess what he's thinking.

His hand goes to his stomach, and he turns to leave the kitchen as fast as he can. I follow him.

He pads up the stairs, and ends up in the bathroom. At first, I'm not sure what he's doing when he falls to his knees on the cold tile floor. But then he starts retching into the toilet.

It sounds terrible. I wince, but I don't leave. I sit and watch. I'm worried about him.

I think all of the changes around here have caught up to Kevin. They are making him physically sick. He heaves again and again, and my whiskers twitch with the awful sound of it.

When he's done, Kevin stands by the sink. He splashes water on his face and peers into the looking glass. His eyes are red and his face is pale.

I'm not sure what he sees there that upsets him, but Kevin goes into his bedroom and ends up facedown on his bed, weeping quietly. It reminds me so much of the time Dad cried that my little heart melts.

He is usually such a good, strong boy. It's hard for me to see him like this. I settle down at his side and give him the most comforting purr I can muster.

I wish I had a way to tell Kevin that I think Mark is okay. Mark is making Mom happy even though he is not very skilled at building. But this may not be what Kevin wants to hear. I realize that Kevin wants things to stay the same. He wants Mark to leave and Dad to come back.

But the fact is, in life, this is one thing we can all count on: Things will not stay the same. No matter how much we might want them to. I settle in with my back up against Kevin's side until he tires himself out and falls asleep.

I agree with Kevin on one thing: Mark being here is forcing another change upon us. And I don't know yet if it will be a development that works in Charlie's favor.

I soon discover that Mark might be of more help than I realized.

Chapter 16
The Lawyer

Dad was steadfast when he wanted to help someone out.

I remember when Charlie had an accident in the backyard. He fell down the deck stairs, his foot twisting in an unnatural way, and he cried out in pain. Dad ran to help. He was there to hold Charlie, to ask him where it hurt, to comfort him and tell Victoria to fetch ice. He carried a sobbing Charlie out to the car and they left for the hospital.

When someone was in trouble, Dad was always the first to offer help. He would get medicine or prepare a wet towel or call the doctor. He was in tune with suffering, and actively tried to end it.

But I'm not sure he understands his own pain quite so well.

I ponder these things as I lay on top of the back of the couch, watching Mark trying to fit a board into place. I think about how Mark has suffered in his life, and the baby he lost. I wonder if being here with our family, helping us out, makes him feel a little better.

I'm still puzzling over these things when Victoria walks in. I think this would be a good time for her to talk to Mom, as Aidan is not here today.

I notice that Charlie has left his blue headphones on the couch. I jump up and bat at the wire with my paw until they fall on the floor. Victoria takes a step forward and picks them up, and then looks at them a long moment.

Remember Charlie! Go talk to Mom about Charlie.

Victoria and I make eye contact. I think she understands.

"Where's my mom?"

Mark peers over his shoulder. "She's in the kitchen."

Victoria exits, and I follow her. I'm curious to see what she wants. I hope it's to talk about Charlie, and I soon find out I am right.

Victoria finds her mother in the pantry. "Mom," she says softly, "I'm worried about Charlie." She holds herself tight, arms wrapped around her torso, the sleeves of her black sweatshirt pulled over her hands. She still grips the headphones tight in her fist.

Mom turns off the light and shuts the pantry door. "You are?"

"Yeah. He has . . . I saw he has bruises on his arm. And his side. I think someone is bullying him in school. Or playing too rough with him. Or whatever. I don't know. I don't know what I'm saying."

From the way Mom's face falls, I can tell she's worried. "Bruises? Did you ask him about it?"

Victoria nods vigorously. "Yeah. He just told me not to worry about it. But seriously. It's been bugging me. I started asking around school. The seniors sometimes haze the eighth graders anyway. It's hard having six grades in one school. And Charlie . . . Well, you know. He's just such an easy target. I mean, you know how kids are. They say stuff to him. But this is different."

Mom's eyes are intense as she scrutinizes her daughter. "You're right. I'm glad you told me."

Victoria, in turn, just stares at the floor. "Yeah. Okay."

Mom goes to the foot of the stairs and calls for the boys.

Kevin comes down immediately, and Charlie follows a minute later. They all stand around the kitchen table.

"Yeah, Mom?"

Charlie's face is so smooth, so clear, so innocent. I feel for him. Because as soon as Mom opens her mouth, I know he's going to be depressed.

At the same time, my heart soars. Because maybe now we will have some answers! And then my boy won't suffer anymore, once we catch the culprit.

Right?

"Charlie. Have a seat." Mom sits down in a kitchen chair opposite him and rests a hand on his knee, maybe thinking this will soften the blow of the conversation. "Victoria tells me she saw bruises on you. Charlie. Why didn't you tell me? Who is hurting you?"

Charlie goes pale.

Kevin turns to look at Charlie, eyebrows raised.

"What?" Charlie asks quietly, as if he didn't quite hear the questions.

"Is it those boys on the bus who gave you a hard time last year? I've got half a mind to call the bus company and give them a piece of my mind."

"No." Charlie looks like he just wants to melt into the floor.

"Is it that kid who harassed you in seventh grade—what was his name, Colin?—the one who stole your backpack and kept taking your gym clothes. The one who kept calling you . . . mean things."

"No." Charlie speaks more forcefully now. "No. Nothing like that. I told Vicky: It's nothing. I fell off the skateboard." He glares at Victoria. "I told you that." He grinds his teeth. "Why are you telling Mom, like it's some big thing?"

There's a moment where Mom just stares at Charlie with pity. I'm sure he hates when she looks at him like that. I know I would.

"Guys. Please." Charlie presses his lips together, and stands up. He starts pacing in a circle. "I'm fine. I'm okay. I hate it when . . ." He stops, resting his hands behind his head. "Just don't worry about it."

A deeper voice cuts in. "Maybe you should call the school."

The whole family turns to see Mark standing in the doorway, resting with his shoulder against the doorframe. Even Gretel tips her head, confused at this interruption. Mark takes up the whole space of the open doorway. His calm energy makes me relax. I watch him with interest.

"Sorry to interrupt. It's just that . . . Katie, since you work in a preschool, I'm sure you know that schools have very strict anti-bullying laws. Start by reporting it to the high school. Call the principal over there. See what they offer to do about it."

Kevin's face contorts with disbelief. "What?" he spits out, as if Mark has suggested something crazy.

Mark's face doesn't change in expression. He stares down Kevin briefly, but turns back to Mom. "If they don't respond adequately, we could threaten to sue. That's the last thing they want."

Victoria and Mom look interested and grateful. They both glance up at Mark from their seats, faces wide open with hope.

But Kevin explodes.

"What do you mean WE?" His hands tighten into fists and he leans forward. "YOU'RE NOT PART OF THIS. No one asked you to get involved. We're having a family discussion, and you weren't invited to join in. WHY ARE YOU ALWAYS HERE? You're not part of this family."

For a moment, Kevin reminds me tremendously of Dad. The way Dad simmers until he boils, and then "all hell breaks loose," as Mom has described it.

But Kevin almost never raises his voice. This is something brand new.

Mom's eyes open wide. "Kevin. That's uncalled for. Mark is trying to help, and he has a good idea."

Mark holds a hand out toward Kevin, as if to say: *hold on*. "I don't mean to imply that I'm part of your family. Sorry. What I meant was, I'm a lawyer. When I say we could sue, what I mean is just that I could help out. I could put you in touch with the right people, who have handled cases like this before. But the school needs to be notified first, and given a chance to respond." He turns his gaze from Kevin to Mom, and for the first time he looks a little hesitant. "I mean, I'm obviously not with a law firm right now. But I was. I mean, I am still. A lawyer."

Mom opens her mouth, but no words come out. I think Mark has utterly confused her.

I don't think she expected him to be a *lawyer*, whatever that is.

Kevin takes a step back. His face is starting to flush. I think he is surprised. But not deterred. "Great. That's great. Good for you. How awesome for you."

"We don't need to do any of that," Charlie insists. "Please, please, please don't call the school."

Kevin clears his throat. "Mark, maybe you should go home. It's dinnertime."

"Kevin," Mom warns.

"I'm sure *your wife* has a hot meal waiting for you, and *your kids* can't wait to see you. So instead of hanging out around here, inserting yourself into *our family* where you don't belong, why don't you pack up your crap and let us have our private family discuss—"

"KEVIN." Mom stands up. She looks bewildered.

Mark goes pale. He stands up straighter. I can see that something about what Kevin said has caught him off guard.

Victoria's chair screeches across the tile floor as she violently pushes back from the table. "Shut up, Kev. He's just trying to help. What the hell is wrong with you?"

Kevin shakes his head. "I'm done." He storms out of the kitchen, and Gretel jumps to get out of his way. "I'm done, I'm done, I'm done." We hear him tromp to the back of the house. He opens the sliding glass door and goes out to the back deck.

"Victoria," Mom asks, her voice shaky. "Why don't you go upstairs and give us a minute, honey."

Victoria nods, and gives her mom a pat on the arm as she passes by. She also touches Charlie lightly on the shoulder. "It's okay, Charlie," she whispers.

Once she's gone, Mark sticks his hands in his back pockets. He bows his head. "I'm really sorry. I should go. So you guys can talk."

"Actually . . ." Mom taps her fingernails on the table. She gives Charlie a look. "I can see Charlie doesn't want to talk to me. But maybe he'll talk confidentially to his lawyer." Mom raises an eyebrow.

Charlie gives her a shrug back, as if to say: *maybe*.

"Why don't I start dinner. The two of you can go into the study. I won't listen. And maybe you could give Charlie some advice on what to do."

Mark looks pleased to receive this offer. He seems to weigh it over in his mind. "Well, sure. Okay. Good. My client and I will retire to my office." He gestures toward Charlie. "Want to talk?"

Charlie hesitates, glancing back at where Kevin exited the room.

"It's okay," Mark says. "I know I'm not Kevin's favorite person right now. But this is important. Maybe I can help."

It takes just one look at Mom's anxious face to get Charlie to turn and follow Mark into the study. He seems reluctant to upset Kevin, but even less so to disappoint Mom.

I follow, naturally.

Charlie slows down when he sees me trailing him. "You coming, Lil?"

Of course!

We go into the back room and they sit down on the couch. I watch from the floor. Mark perches on the edge of his seat, as if ready to jump up into action at any moment.

"It sounds like you've been bullied in school before. It sounds like this isn't the first time."

Charlie sighs, and leans back against the soft cushions. His blond hair is spiked up in all directions, and he has outlined his eyes in black. I've become used to his new look. In fact, he looks a little like me, with my tan fur and dark eyes, now that I think about it. "Yeah. Of course. But this is different."

"How so?"

"I don't want my mom to call the school. I just . . ." He turns his head away.

"I agree that this is different. This is more than teasing. You have bruises. Someone grabbed you, hit you, or pinched you. On purpose. Am I correct so far?"

Charlie shrugs. "I guess so."

"So you were physically harmed. Now, if the reason . . ." Mark leans forward a little and stares off at the bookcase, I think so he won't make Charlie nervous. "If someone is hurting you because of . . . certain reasons, that makes it more serious. For example, your race. Or religion. Or a disability. Or your gender or sexual orientation. That sort of thing. The school is supposed to protect you from that type of harassment. Do you want to talk more about that?"

Charlie's eyes dart over to Mark for just a moment, and then he stares down at his lap. "Um . . . noooo. Nope. I'd rather not."

Mark nods, as if he expected this answer. "Okay." He doesn't move his head, but he lets his eyes slide over to Charlie for a moment. "You don't talk about it much around here, huh?"

Charlie rolls his eyes. "I don't want to talk about it."

"Okay. That's fine."

They sit in silence.

I hope Charlie understands that he is safe here. I think he can trust Mark.

I haven't understood all of the words Mark has used in this conversation. But he sounds like he knows a few things. Maybe he really could help. I wasn't expecting this development, but I'm grateful for it.

When Charlie doesn't respond, Mark turns his head. "Charlie. If you're not ready to talk about it right now, that's okay. We can pick up this conversation later. But I want to ask one more question. There is something I'd like to understand right now."

Charlie's face lights up, as he realizes he's almost done here. I suspect this conversation wasn't nearly as bad as he thought it was going to be.

"Yeah? Okay. Go ahead." Charlie's hands, which were nervously drumming on his legs, fall still.

"Is the reason you don't want your mom to call the school based on the fact that someone will brand you a tattletale, and make your life worse? Or is it that the assaults are not actually happening in school?"

Ah. This is interesting. Mark has guessed at a few things that didn't even occur to me.

But his second question confounds me. Because if the assaults are not happening in school, when are they happening? I never see anyone hurt Charlie.

I watch Charlie. He pulls his feet up onto the couch, as if he's now trying to make himself fit into a smaller space. His hand absentmindedly plays with his shoelace. He tips his head back, as if there is something fascinating to look at on the ceiling.

"Um . . . they're not assaults. I mean, someone grabbing or pinching me isn't that bad. I'm always fine."

"Charlie. No one should be touching you at all if you don't

want them to. No one has the right to inflict pain on you. Don't you agree?"

Charlie squirms a little in his seat, frowning down at his knees. "Yeah. I guess so."

When Charlie doesn't say anything else, Mark nods. "Okay." He looks at a spot across the room again. "I'll think about what our next move should be. I'll help you, whatever you need. We can talk about this more later."

Charlie turns his head away. "You won't say anything to my mom, right? I mean . . . if we talk, you won't tell her everything, right?"

"No. I won't. Unless I think you're in danger. But you need to know that sometimes when someone is getting hurt, it gets worse. It doesn't always resolve itself. Even if you think it's not that bad right now, you need to tell someone if you realize you've come to that point where things are escalating, where you're really in danger."

Charlie lets out the deep breath he's been holding. "I'm not *in danger*. I'm just . . . frustrated." Slowly, Charlie gets up and heads over to me. With two hands, he picks me up off the floor, slings me over his shoulder, and we head upstairs.

I don't know why Charlie is making things seem better than they are. They are not okay. I've had to comfort him more than once at night, as he sheds a few tears and pushes his face into my fur. But he hasn't told me what's wrong. He just hugs me and whispers nice things in my ear. He's keeping this secret, even from me.

Once we get up to his bedroom, Charlie stops and looks out his window, perhaps wondering what happened to Kevin. I understand. I'm a little worried about Kevin too. He doesn't seem quite himself lately.

Once Charlie drops me on his wool blanket, I purr in relief. I'm so glad Mom knows about Charlie's injuries, and Mark is helping out. Now we're finally getting somewhere! This is tremendous!

But I can see now this won't get resolved as quickly as I'd hoped. So I need to stay focused. And keep things moving forward.

Chapter 17
Walking Disaster

It is not long before Mark has another accident. Luckily, he does not get injured this time.

Unluckily, he smashes a vase when he backs up while holding a hammer in one hand. The vase gets knocked to the floor, where it shatters.

I saw it happen. Mark got distracted when Mom entered the study. Mark always turns to face her when she speaks.

"Ugh. Katie, I'm really sorry," he says, putting the hammer down on the wood floor and bending to pick up the pieces.

"It's fine," Mom says. "Honestly, I was sick of that vase anyway. You're doing me a favor. Don't try to pick up anything sharp with your hands. Let me get a broom."

Well! I thought Mom liked that vase, but perhaps she did not.

I think about the fact that there are two fat, fresh blueberry muffins sitting on a plate in the kitchen. I could smell them from the kitchen floor when Mom took them out of the bag. I wonder if Mark's gifts are influencing Mom's attitude about that vase.

They are cleaning up the mess when Vincent walks in. He looks distressed to see the shards all over the floor.

"Again?" He crouches and holds a bag open so Mom can empty her dustpan. "Mark. Seriously. You are a walking disaster, aren't you? A living occupational hazard."

"Yeah," he agrees. "It's funny. I swear, I don't have these kinds of accidents in the kitchen at the restaurant."

"Never burned your hand on a pan, huh?" Vincent looks skeptical.

Mark grins. "Okay. Maybe once or twice."

Vincent sends Mark to take out the trash. "You're banished to the garage for the rest of the day!" Vincent calls out behind him, winking at Mom. Then, in an aside: "I'll reimburse you for the vase."

"Oh, you don't have to do that. I was going to get rid of it anyway." Mom stands and wipes her hands off on her hips. "Vincent, you said you met Mark at church . . . ? I know I haven't been to church in a few months, but I've never seen him there before."

Vincent looks sheepish. "I know what you're thinking. He's obviously new to construction. He's a little green."

Mom nods.

He continues: "The truth is, he needed a second job to keep himself busy, and I thought I'd give him a shot. We didn't actually meet at church. I met him in the chapel at the hospital. I was praying, but I don't know why he was there. He might have just needed somewhere quiet to sit down. Honestly, I don't even know if he's Episcopalian." Vincent chuckles. "Sorry. I wasn't trying to put anything over on you. I just don't know how much he tells people. He and his wife lost their baby. I think he fell out with his old friends too, because he doesn't seem to hang out with anyone. It's a sad story. That's why I wanted to help."

Mom listens to the story intently. "Yes. It is sad. He told me about the baby."

"He did?" Vincent is surprised. "I've never heard him talk about it, outside of the chapel that day."

"He also mentioned he's a lawyer."

"Really?" Again, Vincent does a double take. "Oh. Well. Yeah. I guess after the baby . . . Maybe he needed a break. Or he got fired. I don't actually know. I don't like to pry, so I haven't asked."

Mom frowns. "He's been through a lot."

"He seems to be doing pretty well, all things considered." Vincent shrugs. "I mean, it's been a year now since the baby died. I think he's recovered okay."

"I don't know about that." Mom twists her mouth into a pout for a moment.

Vincent blinks, thinking about it. "I don't know, maybe this job is helping a little. He seems to like our company. Having someone to talk to. He sure seems happy to come and work here at your house. He always offers to come with me or take my shift." Vincent gestures toward the bookshelves. "So. Anyway. Let me show you something I was thinking about. I want to get your opinion."

Vincent starts describing different kinds of doors for some of the shelves. He explains glass-paneled doors versus solid wood. Then he talks about hinges on the side versus hinges on the top. Finally they discuss different colors of stain. Even when he has already made a plan, Vincent often has new and creative ideas that he gets excited about. He loves to throw out last-minute suggestions.

"What do you think, Lily?" he asks, when he sees me watching him.

A shelf is a shelf is a shelf. What's there to think about?

When Mark comes back into the study, Vincent has finished his explanation. He and Mom have made some decisions, and Mom is standing near the window, looking out absentmindedly. The blinds are only halfway up. Vincent asks her to pull the shades all the way up so they can go over how the new windows are going to look.

"I'll get it," Mark offers and walks right over to Mom. He puts two hands gently on her waist to move her body slightly to the left. And when he leans to pull the cord, he leaves one hand on her back to steady himself. His hip nearly brushes up against hers. Mom turns to watch Mark, as if he's doing something fascinating. I suppose it is intriguing to her: the way his shoulder rolls as he lifts his arm, the way his fingers wrap around the cord in a fist and hold it tight, the way the vein in his arm pulses against his skin as he pulls the cord.

Mark smiles broadly when he sees Mom is looking at him. "That's better. Now you can see everything," he says. "The whole window." It is obvious to me that he is talking only to Mom, not to Vincent. It's as if Vincent is not even in the room.

And the way Mom gazes back at him, beaming in a way that I never see her light up for anyone else, it is as if he never broke that vase. It's already forgotten.

And that's when I glance over at Vincent. His brows furrow. I think he is realizing something he was not aware of before.

This confirms it for me. It is exactly as I suspected. There is something going on with Mom and Mark.

Mom and Vincent have been friends a very long time. Years. As long as I can remember.

Here is one thing I know for sure: Vincent has never put his hands anywhere near Mom's waist, the way Mark just did.

Vincent looks down at his boots, looking a little disheartened. He rubs the back of his neck and tries to compose himself.

Hmm.

Mom is acting like she wants . . . But how could this be? It isn't just that she wants Mark to be her friend. She may be considering him as a potential new mate. And he looks at her the same way. Which makes this a dangerous situation.

Dad left not long ago. And Kevin seems to think Dad might come back. I have heard Dad say that's what he wants.

For now, I consider Vincent's strange reaction. Is it a bad thing that Mom likes the new man? Wasn't Vincent hoping she'd like him? Does Vincent not approve? He's always wanted the best for Mom.

My goodness! This concerns me.

Kevin doesn't like Mom's attachment to Mark at all. And now Vincent doesn't seem too thrilled.

I have to imagine it won't be long before Dad knows—and I expect he won't like it either. Not one bit.

It is dawning on me that Charlie's injuries are not the only problem this family is facing right now. They may not even be the worst of it. I have a terrible hunch that there may be more dangerous things coming around the corner.

Chapter 18
The Gun

The afternoons grow longer as spring emerges, bright and insistent. I find windows cracked open in odd rooms. The world smells fresh and salty. The silence of winter has given forth to chirping birds and clanging wind chimes from the neighbors' porch. Mom serves the children dinner later in the day. The schedule loosens, and my heart expands with the increasing light and warmth of each day.

One afternoon, Mom is in the back room with Vincent and Mark. They are laughing about something. Vincent is telling a story, with much animation and waving of his arms. It is as if Mark has infused him with a shot of energy, because Vincent seems more talkative than usual. I sit on the cool of the kitchen tiles, eyes closed but listening to the drone of their voices. My stomach is very full because Charlie gave me not one, not two, but *three* cat treats today.

I am spoiled. I do not deny it.

Charlie and Kevin are upstairs, and Victoria is not home. So no one hears the front door open.

Gretel, who lies beside me, immediately jumps to attention. My ears twitch.

From the heavy sound of the footsteps, I know it is Dad. He comes down the hallway uninvited, which is unusual. Gretel stands tall on all four legs, but does not run to Dad, which is also strange.

She senses something I cannot.

When Dad rounds the corner, he stops and stares at Gretel with eyes that are red and seem devoid of comprehension. "C'mere, girl," he says softly, perhaps out of habit. She goes right to him, and I sense how worried she is as she sniffs his hands and legs.

Just then, Mom laughs again, and Dad freezes. He slowly turns his head and sees the people in the back room.

And then there is silence. I check, and sure enough, they have all turned toward Dad, having seen someone moving in the kitchen. A frown settles on Mom's face. Her expression goes from glowing to dark immediately, like a light being switched off.

Dad stumbles into the room toward Mom and her visitors. "Hi," he says cautiously. "Still working on this project, huh?"

"Yes," Mom says, gesturing at the bookshelves. "It's coming along really well. I didn't know you were coming over, Jeremy. Do you need something?"

Dad tips his head and pauses, as if trying to translate what she is saying. It takes him a moment. "Yes."

I wait.

We all wait.

While Mark and Vincent wear short-sleeved shirts because it is a warm day, Dad has on a long-sleeve button-down flannel shirt and a down vest. He seems to be dressed too warm for a lovely spring day. Yet he does not look sweaty or hot. If anything, he looks ashen and cold, like he needs to lie down. He has not shaved, so a dark shadow covers his face.

Mark crosses his arms and stares Dad down. This must be his first time meeting Dad. Vincent adjusts his glasses, looking sheepish, as if he's been caught doing something wrong.

Dad puts his hands on his hips, and everyone's eyes flicker, as do mine: When he pushes his vest aside, we see the shiny metal at his waist. The gun.

Dad licks his lips. "Kate. Is there a reason there seem to be people here all the time? People not in our family? Every time I turn around Aidan is jumping out of a corner, scaring the hell out of me. And Vincent—that's you, correct? The guy who leaves his shit everywhere? He's always here. And now, this other guy, whose truck is parked in my spot in the driveway— he has to be here all the time too?" Dad makes a gesture toward the men. "I'm confused who lives here now. Why are there always people here, Kate?"

Vincent backs up a step or two. "Sorry, Jeremy. We just—"

"Do I know you? Why are you talking to me like we know each other?"

Vincent swallows, and puts a hand up. "We've met. I live down the street."

"Jeremy, you've met Vincent," Mom interrupts. "More than once. MORE THAN ONCE."

"Jeremy, I'm a friend of—" Vincent stops himself, and shakes his head. "We go to the same church. Anyway. We're just building the bookcase. It's taken a little longer than we expected—"

"NO KIDDING." Dad's face is starting to flush red, his hands clenched in fists. He turns to Mom. "I hope they're not charging you by the hour, for Chrissake. You've got to be careful or people will take advantage of you. I mean, if you don't care about your own money, that's one thing. But keep in mind it's the kids' college fund. That you're throwing away."

"Throwing away?" Mom bristles. "Are you serious? We've been planning this project for years. You promised we'd get this done ten years ago. Who's the one who throws away money on a regular basis every time you go down to the liquor store to—"

"Kate," Vincent interjects. "We should go."

Mom's face falls. "Go?" She seems stunned.

"We'll let you guys talk. We shouldn't be here now. For this."
He turns to Mark. "Come on," he says quietly.

Vincent walks away, head hanging down. Mark pauses, and
tries to catch Mom's eye, but she is glaring at Dad. Mark finally
follows Vincent, who is waiting by the open door that leads to
the kitchen. I listen to their footsteps as they cut through the
laundry room to the garage, and shut the door. I hear a truck
outside start up and drive away.

Gretel walks them to the door, but then comes back to sit at
Dad's feet. Ears alert. Eyes wet and concerned.

Dad sticks a hand out toward the garage. "Is that why,
Kate?"

"What?"

"Is *that* why? Is it Vincent?"

Mom scoffs. "Are you crazy? No. No, Jeremy. *That* is not
why." She gestures toward Dad with both arms. "THIS IS WHY."

Gretel starts a low whine. She doesn't like conflict. It gets
her agitated.

"I have asked you to choose," Mom continues. "Over and
over. And you've made your choice. You obviously are not capable of choosing anything else. And I don't appreciate you
storming in here and scaring people. With your gun."

Dad scowls at her. "My gun? Jesus. I didn't take out my gun.
What are you talking about?"

"You're wearing your gun. Don't you even know that? You
don't even know what you're saying. You don't even realize
what you're doing. You—"

Mom freezes and looks over at the doorway. She squints,
and it takes her a moment to register who it is, the dark shadow
that has appeared. Perhaps she thought it might be one of the
children.

"Vincent had to go," Mark says. "I'm going to clean up our
stuff." He enters the room and breezes right past Mom and Dad

as if they haven't just been arguing. There are tools on a drop cloth, and he gets down on the floor and starts putting them into a pile.

Mom clears her throat. "Okay. So." She crosses her arms over her chest and turns back to Dad. "Did you come by because you need something?"

Dad breathes out heavily, a long sigh, the fight drained out of him. "Yes. There is something I need. But damn-it-all if I can't remember what the hell it was."

When his eyes finally find Mom's, he notices she is tearing up. And that affects Dad tremendously, I can see, because his mouth sets in a hard line and he steps toward her. Gretel stands and moves closer to Dad, perhaps not wanting him to forget about her. If I were her, I'd move closer too, to get in on any hugging or cuddling that might take place.

But Dad doesn't hug Mom. He knows he should not. Even I can see that is not what she wants from the way her arms are wrapped tightly around herself.

"I'm sorry," he says very softly, as if Mark is not in the room. "I'm really, really sorry, Kate. You know that, right? I never wanted it to be like this. Why would I? I wish it were different." He reaches over and strokes her shoulder, and she allows it. Finally, she nods to show she has heard him.

"I'm sorry too, Jeremy." She looks him in the eye, and he instinctively lowers his head. "Believe me. I don't want this. I am so, so, so sorry."

The grandfather clock in the hall chimes. As she looks Dad over, Mom's face softens, and perhaps her heart does also. She reaches out and rubs his elbow.

I feel bad about this. I know they love each other. So why can't Dad move back in? If he is really still sick or in pain, why can't Mom nurse him back to health, like she did when Mark was stung by the bees? Why can't Dad just go back to the hospital to get better like Vincent's wife? And why isn't his special medicine working? I have many questions with no answers.

Dad walks out, never glancing back at Mark. I think he has forgotten all about the visitors, at least temporarily.

Once we hear Dad shut the front door, Mom moves to sit on the couch. One tear falls from her eye and runs down her pale cheek. It makes a trail down her face that glistens, and she makes no move to wipe it away.

Mark stands several feet away. He stares at Mom, but she does not look at him.

He clears his throat. "I didn't go anywhere." His voice is hard and angry. But I know he is not mad at her. Energy vibrates from his body, dispersing into the room. "I'm sorry Vincent left, Katie. I'm not going anywhere."

Mom doesn't move. I'm not even sure she hears him.

I jump when Mark moves forward, taking a few steps to kneel—right on the floor—at her feet. There is a small blue rug in front of the couch, and this is where he positions himself. And then he does the most curious thing.

He takes her hand, and places it on his shoulder. He holds it there. Mom doesn't pull her hand away.

Rather, Mom's mouth opens, just a bit, and she watches him. Amazed.

I think she was so distracted by Dad that she forgot about Mark for a moment. But he is determined to reclaim her attention.

His chest presses into her knees as he leans forward. "I don't think you should allow him to come in here and scare you like that."

Was Dad acting *scary*? Mom doesn't scare easily. But maybe, just maybe, Mom has felt scared, and I wasn't completely aware of it. It's puzzling.

Mark now lifts her hand, the one he put on his shoulder, and places it on the side of his head. Mom startles, confused.

But then, sure enough, she slowly starts to stroke the black, silky waves of Mark's hair, just above his ear. Mom runs her fingers through his hair with great care and tenderness, although his hair is a mess as always. She licks her dry lips, and takes in a deep breath. This action, caressing his hair, seems to soothe her.

Perhaps Mark knew it would.

She is a mom, after all. It is natural for her to show affection. There's nothing wrong with that.

Mom stares at him, her breathing continuing to slow. I can see she is fascinated by Mark, and the strange things he does.

"Mark," she whispers. "It's okay. It's fine. Jeremy might . . . I don't know what he was planning to do, honestly, but he just doesn't like other people being here. So you should go."

"I don't think so."

Honestly, I'm not sure Mom is listening very carefully to what Mark is saying, and the tone of his voice. I've never heard anyone so sure of anything in my life. Mark is certainly not going to leave.

"We're still married," she says, all in a rush, "And Jeremy doesn't understand why all these people are in the house. You heard him. He's going through a rough time. And he . . ."

"He had a gun." Mark states this as simply as possible, as if it might have somehow escaped Mom that Dad had a gun. But in my experience, when Dad reveals his gun, it is all anyone can think about or remember.

Mom searches for the words. "I know. And he's not feeling well. That's all. He would never—But I don't know about . . ." It is so, so hard for Mom to say these words. She nearly chokes with the effort. "I think you should go. I mean, you saw how fast Vincent ran out of here, didn't you?" Mom's voice sounds strained all of a sudden. Upset. "And he's been friends with me a long time. A very, very long time." She swallows back her words, but another tear comes. She rips her hand away, so she can gesture toward the door, and Mark lets go of her wrist. "Vincent has been a very good friend to me. And he RAN out of here. Don't you understand? HE RAN."

Mark blinks, staring at her. He leans forward, so his abdomen presses tighter against her knees. "I'm not going anywhere." He tips his head, as if not sure if he should go on, but then plunges ahead: "Jeremy was so drunk I'm surprised he could stand up in front of you without falling over."

So drunk? My ears twitch.

I'm not exactly sure what this means. Dad sometimes drinks so much medicine that it makes him sleepy and cranky. So I guess this is what Mark means.

"Shhhhhh," Mom waves her hands frantically, with a glance toward the doorway.

Mark's face crumples in a frown. "What, the kids? Don't they know? You don't think they already know? Katie . . . seriously?"

"They don't. At least—not the extent of it." She whispers now, face flushed pink. A trembling hand wipes a tear from her cheek. "I didn't understand at first. He hides it well. I mean, he's been a big drinker for years, but he's not a . . . He doesn't drink in front of the kids. It's just that—things changed a year ago. Something terrible happened to him. And everything got worse."

I blink. I remember when Dad came home from the hospital.

A year ago. It was a dark time. But I didn't understand that it would affect us for so long. I didn't realize it would change things forever.

Mark's shoulders slump. He finally relaxes a bit. I can see he understands something that he didn't know before, from the way his gaze drops away from Mom and he stares down at her knees. But whatever it is that he is processing at the moment, I have to admit I don't share his understanding.

They are in agreement that *something* is wrong with Dad. I can see it too. But I still don't know exactly what it is that needs fixing.

"I'm starting to get the picture. You don't talk about anything around here."

Mom just shrugs.

"I'm going to stay here tonight," Mark says quietly. "Just—on the couch. In case he comes back."

"No. Mark, the kids will—"

"We'll tell them my truck broke down. Or I'm having some rooms painted in my apartment, so I can't sleep there. Or something." He reaches for her hand again, wrapping his palm around her delicate fingers and gripping them tightly. I imagine he is warming her up.

It is Mom who finally unwinds now, nodding and letting her head fall ever so slightly. "Okay."

I think there is something about a human who has his mind made up that makes other humans simply give in sometimes. When someone is certain he is right, beyond all reasoning, why argue?

These are things humans do that cats never do: Talk in circles. Quarrel. Reason. Insist that they know best.

It's exhausting to listen to. But I'm glad Mom is giving in to Mark and his persistent heart. Maybe this is just what Mom needs: someone to give her his full attention.

Perhaps . . . perhaps it is true, that Mom needs a new mate. Maybe Dad does scare Mom sometimes. He certainly upsets her. It would hurt my heart to learn that Dad really isn't coming back. But I do want Mom to be happy. I don't know if it is good timing for this sort of thing, but Mark is here now. Right now. And I like him very much.

Later, when Mom explains to the children that Mark is staying overnight because his sister is visiting from out of town and she needs his bed, they are surprised. Kevin grumbles about it, suspicious. But Mom orders in food, more than they can possibly eat, and they seem to come to terms with it.

Mom and Mark have the study to themselves for a while. They talk, and eat, and listen to music. Kevin takes his plate of food and disappears upstairs to his bedroom. Charlie and Victoria sit in the living room at the front of the house, eating in front of the TV. Gretel paces, hungry and waiting for leftovers.

When Charlie finishes eating and puts his tray of food on the coffee table, I snuggle down on his lap. "Hi, baby doll," he coos at me, tickling my ears.

Hello, sweet boy.

Charlie and Victoria watch a show that interests them greatly. They frequently comment on and shout at the screen. Yet sometimes Mark's laughter and Mom's voice can be heard, even over the noise of the TV. It is a small house, and noises travel.

"Oh my God," Charlie groans, turning to his sister to speak to her in a hushed tone. I lift my head as he leans over me. "What is going on back there? What could possibly be so funny?"

Victoria gives him a look. "I think it's good," she decides aloud. "It's good for Mom. To have a friend. An admirer. She deserves to be happy. Right?"

Charlie raises an eyebrow. "I guess so. I mean, yeah, of course she should be happy. It's still a little weird. No, it's a lot weird. But yeah, I guess it's okay." He looks skeptical, but nods. I know Charlie respects his older sister's opinion. "What's Mark's deal, though? Isn't he younger than Mom? And he's a lawyer, but he's here all the time building bookshelves."

"I don't know." Victoria shrugs. "Does it matter? I mean, if Mom's happy, maybe those things aren't important." She pulls at one of the small braids she has woven into her long dark hair. "You talked to him, right? And you said you liked him." She reaches under her thigh to scratch the back of her knee. "What's going on with that, by the way? Have you given Mark some information he can act on? Like, the name of the kid who's bully-ing you?"

Charlie sighs, and turns away. "No. No, I don't want to do that."

Victoria's nostrils flare. "Are you kidding me?" She reaches out to shove his leg. "How is Mark supposed to help you when you won't tell him anything?"

Charlie moves to lean back on the other end of the couch when he sees his sister start to get frustrated. He pulls me up onto his chest with two hands. His shirt is soft under my paws.

"Vic, leave me alone. I'll talk to him when I'm ready. You think this is front page news? Oooh, someone grabbed me. Big deal. You think no one has ever given me a hard time before? You think I don't know how much worse everything will get when I tell someone? Jesus. Just watch the goddamn show."

Victoria frowns and shifts in her seat. I'm sure she doesn't like to hear this from Charlie any more than I do.

She bites her lip for a moment, and then her face relaxes. "Charlie," she says in a teasing voice, "Don't curse. You're only fourteen. Do you think it makes you sound cool, or some-thing?"

Charlie responds with a bunch of phrases I've never heard him say before. I won't try to repeat them. There are several bad words mixed in there.

I feel my eyes widening and ears flattening. *Charlie!* I'm sur-prised. As I've mentioned, Mom doesn't like cursing. But it's nothing worse than what I've heard Dad say.

Victoria gasps in mock surprise, and Charlie laughs. He grabs a handful of popcorn from a big bowl at his feet and throws it at her. She ducks her head, but several kernels land in her hair. He shelters me when she throws some back at him.

Our heads all turn as Kevin comes down the stairs with his dinner plate to bring it to the kitchen. He's a good boy, always completing his chores. He comes over to talk to us.

"Don't talk to that guy," he warns Charlie in a low voice. "I don't trust him. Dad wouldn't like him."

"Kevin, knock it off." Victoria clucks her tongue. "Mark's okay."

Kevin continues to stand there, and Charlie shifts in his seat. His whole body tenses up. "Leave me alone," Charlie says, but in a quiet voice. "I'll talk to whoever I want to."

"Don't talk to him. Dad would agree with me. Are you listening to me?"

"Kevin." Victoria gasps in exasperation. "Get out of here. We're watching our show."

I can hear Charlie's heart beating hard from my seat on his lap. Even after Kevin has gone to the kitchen, Charlie's hands shake as he strokes my back.

Kevin's not making this any easier. I scowl in frustration.

Later, after the children say good night to Mom, she loads the dishwasher and turns out most of the lights. She goes upstairs for a few minutes to put her pajamas on. Then she comes back down and sits next to Mark on the couch.

It looks cozy! I jump up to sit with her.

While they watch TV, Mom slumps down with her head very close to Mark's shoulder. He takes a sideways glance at her, but otherwise sits very still. He reminds me of myself, when I'm watching Gretel out of the corner of my eye, wondering what her next move will be.

I glance up at Mom. She is wearing a thin gray sweater wrapped tight around her body, even though it's a nice spring evening. Usually, she cinches the belt in a double knot so it stays closed. But tonight the belt is tied in a bow that could be undone with a quick pull.

I wonder if Mark has noticed that. Of course, he hasn't seen her wear the sweater before, so he doesn't know the difference.

But I find it a little amusing. To me, it is a clue that she likes him. As if she is ready to be unwrapped. But I am the only creature on earth who is in a position to notice this particular evidence.

Mark is very alert. I can sense, for the first time, the strong pheromones he is giving off in the darkness of the quiet room. The scent I sense rising from his skin makes my whiskers tingle. In contrast, Mom gets sleepier, her eyes starting to close, and she contently rests the weight of her entire body back into the couch.

"I'm sorry," she says, not taking her eyes off of the TV. "I didn't mean for all this to happen."

"It's fine." His arm is thrown up across the back of the couch behind her, but he glances down as if he's trying to figure out how to get his arm over her shoulder and can't quite figure out how to do it. "I've been trying to get you to invite me to stay for dinner for a while now, but you've never taken the bait before."

"Hmmmm." Mom makes that sound she's made before, where it sounds a little like she's purring. She runs her tongue over her upper lip. "You're the chef, not me. But you've never offered to cook."

Mark shakes his head. "I don't cook. I just bake. You know, cake and bread and stuff like that. But I'm pretty good at picking out meat and cheese and crackers from the store, if you ever want that for dinner. And I'm pretty good at making breakfast." His face starts to flush, as if he realizes that he has said something embarrassing.

Mom smiles. She nods and closes her eyes briefly, as if imagining the dinner he might bring, or the breakfast he might make. Her eyes snap open again, and she glances around the study. She sighs. "Sometimes I wonder how my life ended up this way. How I got here."

Mark makes a sound of agreement. "You and me both." He pauses. "But you have a nice life, a cute house. Great kids."

"I know." Mom sounds weary. "That's all true. I'm lucky." Her voice fades. "Very lucky."

Mom lays her free hand on her thigh, open and palm-side up. I think this is an invitation to hold her hand, but a subtle one. She has made a move where if Mark doesn't respond, it will be okay for everyone. No one's feelings will be bruised. After all, Mark is her friend, and he has declared his intention to stay over, so that part of it is already settled. But Mark immediately notices and reaches over to take her hand with his free hand, closing his fingers around hers.

Mom's eyes flick up toward Mark, and then back to the TV. She suddenly looks more awake.

I see a change in Mark's face, the way his eyes brighten. "I'm sorry, Katie. Everyone will take care of you," he says in a softer voice.

"Thank you."

I am surprised at Mom. She has never needed anyone to "take care" of her. But she does not protest.

They keep watching the TV for several more minutes, but I can see neither one is actually paying much attention. Mom's cheeks are turning pink. Mark fidgets a little bit, as if he has an itch somewhere but is afraid to scratch it.

Mark suddenly straightens up, and Mom turns to face him. The glow from the television in the dark room flickers bright and then dim. When Mom gives him a sleepy smile, he doesn't smile back, for once. Instead he nods, as if to acknowledge that he understands why she's happy. But he looks very serious about it.

Hmm. I think that if anything is going to happen between them, it must take place now. I don't believe this can wait any longer.

He hesitates for a moment, and then leans forward to kiss her on the mouth. He moves slowly, as if he doesn't want to startle her. As if he might bruise her if he presses too hard.

Ah! I knew it. I'm so smart.

Pulling back, he searches Mom's face to check her reaction. I think this kiss is a question, as much as it is a statement.

That was a good move. Mom is entranced, her eyes locked on his. She is so focused on Mark that if the paintings were to fall off the walls around her right now, I don't think she would notice.

I anticipate Mom will say yes. There are many reasons she might say no. But I believe she truly wants to say yes.

She reaches up with one hand and sinks her fingers into Mark's hair—right where he put her hand earlier, just above his ear—and pulls him back to her with fierce intensity. Her body almost comes up out of her seat as she throws herself into a new kiss. He rocks backward with the force of her assault.

Well!

If he is surprised, it only takes him a moment to recover. If he wasn't exactly sure how Mom felt before, there can be no doubt about it now. He redoubles his effort, pushing back against her.

This much is true: Mark doesn't need to treat Mom as if she's made of eggshell. She's made of flesh and blood.

Mark holds her with one hand on her waist and puts his other hand on her back, pulling her into him. Mom reaches for his shoulder. She grabs the material of his shirt in her fist and pulls hard, as if she might tear it right off him.

This is a little surprising! Mom is not usually impulsive. But I have to assume she knows what she's doing.

Mom unties the belt of her sweater in one move and shrugs it off of her shoulders. Mark helps her peel it from her arms and throws it on the floor.

Mom's nice soft sweater. On the floor! Is that what we do with clothes around here? No, it is not.

It is shocking that Mom permits him to toss her sweater on the dirty floor. But Mom does not get angry. She resumes kissing him, with energy. It is as if he just told her he must leave immediately for some faraway land and she cannot bear to let him go.

And—goodness. Under her sweater, Mom does not have on her usual pajama shirt. No, she is wearing a new top. It is small. And lacy. And black.

Black? That's not a color Mom wears. Not ever.

Victoria? Yes, she wears black. Mom? No. Never.

Mark grabs one of the stringy straps that holds up her top and pulls it right down off her shoulder. He bows his head to kiss her bare collarbone.

Okay, this is not what I expected at all. Have they had a conversation that I was not aware of? When was all this decided? Is this completely normal human behavior?

It is only when Mom's hands move to his belt that Mark stops, glassy-eyed, and stills her hand. "Sweetheart, I don't think—"

Mom's eyes widen. She doesn't let go of his belt.

His face is just a few inches from hers. "Katie," he whispers. "We should wait."

"Wait? What?" She purses her lips, thinking. Slowly, her shoulders relax. "Oh." She swallows.

"I don't mean for a long time. Just a few days. Until we have the house to ourselves."

"Are you afraid Jeremy will come back and find us together?" Mom sounds like she is struggling to keep her voice light. But I know she is concerned.

"No. No. Definitely no. It's not that at all." Mark pulls his hair off his forehead, but it just falls back where it was. "I mean . . . yeah, maybe it's that, too." He nods. "But mostly I was thinking that one of your kids could come down here anytime, for a drink of water or something. We'd both be distracted, worrying about being interrupted."

Mom lets go of his belt and puts her hands on his arms. When I glance at her face, I can see her desperation. "I don't think they'll come down here. They're all in bed."

"Katie. Listen." He tucks a strand of her hair behind her ear. He has very expressive eyes, and they watch her carefully, making sure she understands. "Let's wait. Because when we really do this, I'm going to want your complete and undivided attention." He relaxes, resting his forehead against hers and closing his eyes. "I think about you all the time. All the time, every day. It's making me crazy. This is the first thing I've wanted in a long time. So I want it to be good. I don't want it to be quick. And I don't want it to be quiet. I want to have all night with you."

Well! Okay, then. I turn to see Mom's reaction. When he pulls away to look at her, I can still see her expression.

What I think I see in her face is: disappointment. Maybe: a flash of anger. But mostly: desire. Whether by design or just from his sheer honesty, he has whipped Mom up into a frenzy. She doesn't want to wait. She wants to pounce on him.

Mom struggles to compose herself. "Should I go, then?" She squeezes his arm, waiting for his answer. It's clear to me that leaving is the last thing she wants to do.

"You don't have to go just yet," he offers, stroking her hair. "Stay a while."

"I'm sorry. I don't know what's gotten into me."

"Don't be sorry."

Humans exhaust me with their strange behavior. Sometimes they are quite fragile and vulnerable. And then other times, they are unexpectedly strong. And, often, unpredictable. I can't always figure it out.

I decide it's a good time to go for my evening walk around the perimeter of the house, checking each room for spiders. I've had enough of this. I'll let them talk in private.

Later I hear Mom walking around, and I go to see what she's up to. Mom has tiptoed upstairs to fetch blankets and a pillow, and is now on her way back down. She looks flushed and happy. So I suppose that even though she didn't want to "wait," Mark has said the right things to hold her over in the meantime.

When we reach the back room, he is standing by the couch. Mom hands him what he needs, and even has an extra toothbrush at the ready, which makes him laugh.

"Thank you," she says, standing in front of him and handing him the pile of blankets. "I'm sorry I'm such a mess. The whole family is a mess. I'm sorry you feel like you need to stay."

"Oh, no," he quickly interjects. "I want to. My empty apartment won't miss me one bit, trust me. It's fine."

I'm not sure Mark feels that way at all. What I mean is: I don't think he believes everything is "fine." But humans will do that: At times, they say one thing when I am convinced they believe something else entirely.

The clock in the hall chimes many times. Mom floats up to bed.

It is so strange to me that Mark is afraid of Dad and his gun. I wish Mark knew Dad a little better. If he knew the Dad that I know, he would understand that we have nothing to fear.

I remember the man who kicked me when I was a kitten. That was a cruel man. He cared nothing for how others felt.

Dad is not a cruel man. He has been sick. He has been distracted, and in pain, and at times he has needed his medicine more than anything else in the world. But he is also loving, and he has taken good care of this family for a long time. He's a hero, for goodness sake! Mark has him all wrong.

There is something very personal about the act of sleeping. For instance, Gretel will not cuddle and nap with me, because it puts us physically too close, and she does not feel that way about me. She protects the humans, and I am her friend who just happens to inhabit the same house.

Gretel loves me, but she does not want that level of intimacy with me. I understand.

But tonight, I decide to sleep awhile with Mark. Once Mom is gone, I jump up to the couch and curl into a ball by his chest. He puts his arm protectively over me.

"Hello, baby," he whispers to me. "Aren't you pretty? So soft too." I settle into a purr.

I imagine that Mark and I are on a raft together in the middle of the river, adrift from the rest of the world. Our souls are safe here. I am glad Mark insisted on staying. And it's not because I am afraid of Dad, or what he might do.

I just rather like Mark. He has been a welcome presence here. I enjoy his company. I think everyone does.

Everyone except Kevin, of course.

Eventually I hear Mark breathing slow and steady, and I know he is almost asleep. I sit up for a moment. I am almost ready to go see Charlie. Charlie will worry if he wakes up and I am not there by his feet. Mark's eyes click open, however, and he studies the ceiling. Looking at him, I see him turn his head back and forth, as if frustrated and looking for an answer.

"There's no rush," he whispers, so quietly that I almost don't hear it. Maybe he is talking to me. He is also reassuring himself.

No rush? No rush to do what? To finish the bookcases?

And then I think—

And it occurs to me that—

Oh! Well, of course.

When he sees me looking at him, Mark raises an eyebrow. He pets my head, running his knuckles over my ears.

"Sweetheart, you're spying on me," he says. "Do you spy on everyone around here?"

Why yes, I do.

I want Mark to stop thinking about Mom for a minute and help us with Charlie. I notice Charlie's blue headphones on the side table next to the couch—he has, once again, forgotten to put them away. I walk over and bat at the wire with my paw.

Forget about Mom for a minute. What are you going to do to help Charlie?

When my claw gets stuck on the wire, Mark is forced to sit up and help me get loose. "What are you doing?"

Charlie. Remember Charlie?

"You're all tangled up."

No—let's think about Charlie.

"I'm sorry, sweet girl, I can't play with you now. It's too late."

Ugh! I give up.

Mark lies back down and moves his arm to scoop me in closer. "You're a good baby," he tells me, nestling me to his chest. "Such a pretty baby. You're a sweet, soft baby." He turns onto his side, and pulls me in tight. It is very warm with his arm around me, nestled between his body and the back of the couch. And then, quietly: "I miss my baby. She was nice and warm. She was a good baby, just like you."

Ohhhhhh. Now I see.

I come to realize how lonely Mark really is. How much he wants someone in his life who will accept his love. I can sense it because I have felt it many times with Charlie.

Charlie has friends and family, but he is still lonely sometimes. He has often whispered to me that I am his best friend. He has nothing to fear from me. I never disappoint my humans.

Humans have a very strong need to love someone. I understand why they love me. I never hurt humans with my words. I am loyal and my needs are simple. I enjoy the feel of a hand on my head and the warmth of a body against my soft fur.

Grief is a funny thing. I believe Mark's heartache is driving him into Mom's arms, because he needs someone, desperately. He clings to me and I start to purr.

Soon Mark is breathing heavily. He has fallen asleep.

At times like this, I wish I could talk to Gretel. I think she would be able to give me more insight into Dad and his words and actions. And she might have ideas on how to help and protect Charlie. The next thing I know, I fall asleep too.

Chapter 19
Stupid Little Twerp Brother

One day, Mom tells the children in the morning that she has something important to do at the school and must work late that night. Charlie sighs to hear this news. I know he prefers it when Mom comes home and Mark is around.

He has been opening up more to Mark lately, but they only discuss small matters. They chat about things like:

1. Cooking. Charlie asks Mark if he can teach him how to make French toast. Charlie loves breakfast foods. Anything with maple syrup.
2. Charlie's science teacher. He admires Mr. Carver! Charlie says Mr. Carver makes the world sound interesting.
3. Songs on the radio. Mark likes old stuff, and Charlie likes bands Mark has never heard of.

I think it is progress. A little at a time.

Charlie, Victoria, and Aidan all arrive home from school at the same time. Charlie hooks Gretel up to her leash and immediately takes her for a walk. He is probably trying to avoid Aidan, but perhaps he is also hoping to run into his new friend Ronaldo on the street.

Gretel is considered a striking dog. She is large and impressive. Humans like to show her off.

That's all it is.

It's no problem. I'm not jealous one bit. I know who Charlie loves best.

I heard Victoria tease Charlie at the kitchen table one night as they were doing their homework. She said she'd seen him with Ronaldo in the lunchroom at school. He shrugged it off. She then said she'd also seen Charlie with Ronaldo at his locker, laughing about something. So it sounds like Charlie really does have a new friend. He smiled when Victoria mentioned it, shaking his head as if it was not important. But Charlie can be quiet and shy, so I know that this is a big deal. I'm proud of him!

After Charlie leaves, Victoria and Aidan shrug off their spring coats and grab a drink in the kitchen. Aidan chugs down half a can of soda as if he's dying of thirst.

Victoria tells Aidan that Kevin had to stay after school for math team. And then she asks Aidan if he wants to go up to her bedroom.

I watch him hesitate. And then say okay.

I follow, my heart contracting in anger. My long fur stands on end. Aidan is not allowed upstairs! For goodness sake! I cannot believe Victoria is breaking the rules again.

I skitter into the bedroom just as Victoria is closing the door. She waits for my long tail to float behind me and out of harm's way before shutting the door with a click.

"You're letting your psycho cat in here with us?" Aidan asks, sitting on her pink bedspread. "Your cat hates me. Just like your dad hates me." He pauses, staring out at the light gray of the sky beyond the treetops. "I guess your brothers hate me too. Wow. I hadn't really realized how much your entire family hates me until this moment."

Well! Whose fault is that?

I give him a scowl. He sees me and frowns.

Victoria stands across the room, looking absentmindedly at the knickknacks on her bureau. Picking one up. Putting it down. "You know, if you ever invited me to your house, we could hang out there instead." I hear a tinge of frustration in her voice.

"Vicky." He turns to look at her. "You don't want to go to my house. I know you don't believe me. But trust me, you don't. It's not nice, like your house."

Well. I wasn't under the impression that our cottage was anything special. There's dust in the corners, mold in the bathroom, and rugs that sometimes feel damp under my paws.

I suppose, however, we do have plenty of cozy spots. Aidan seems to think the green couch downstairs is his special place, the same way I think of Charlie's bed as my favorite place to curl up. But he shouldn't feel that way. This isn't his house to lay claim to.

I rub up against Victoria's leg, and then turn and give a sharp *hiss!* at Aidan. I don't want Victoria to forget what he did.

That is, I don't want her to forget that I pretended he hurt me.

His eyes open wide. "You see?" He points at me. "I didn't do anything to her. That thing is evil."

"She's not evil." Victoria spins and takes a step closer to him. "But maybe she's scared of you. You did hurt her the other day. You probably stepped on her tail. Maybe you didn't realize it, but you did." When Aidan makes a face at her, she gasps. "Why are you such an asshole? I also asked you to talk to people at school and find out who is bullying Charlie. You want to know what Tasha said when I talked to her about it? Do you seriously want to know?"

"No," he says, "But I can see you're going to tell me anyway."

"She said—she said maybe *you're* the one bullying Charlie.

And you know what? I realized you've never been that nice to him. It kinda makes sense." She shakes her head. "It's not you, is it?"

At first, Aidan doesn't move as her question sinks in. Apparently he didn't see this question coming, because he truly seems to have no idea how to respond.

He springs up off the bed and starts pacing in a circle around Victoria's small room. His sneakers barely make a sound on the rug.

"You're serious?" He doesn't stop moving, shaking out his hands by his sides. "You're serious. You are seriously asking me that. Wow."

"Aidan . . ." One of Victoria's small braids falls across her cheek, and she grabs it and pulls on it. Her voice softens a bit as she sees his reaction, the way he has suddenly become agitated. "I just don't know what to think. You're not very nice to Charlie."

Aidan shakes his head violently, as if he doesn't want to hear it. "I'm not nice to my little sister either. Just like my older brother isn't nice to me. That's how it works, isn't it? The circle of life? What goes around, comes around?"

Victoria watches him, eyes wide.

Back and forth he walks, from window to wall, and back again. "If you haven't noticed, I'm not nice to anyone. Except to you." Now he finally stops and turns on her, his voice shaking with anger. "I love you. Do you hear me? Do you?" His voice gets louder and more passionate as he goes on: "JESUS CHRIST, Vicky. How can you even think I would do that to Charlie? I would crawl on my hands and knees on broken glass for you. And you know it. YOU KNOW IT." He balls his hands into fists by his sides.

Victoria tips her head to one side, watching him. She reminds me of myself, when I'm perched on the bookcase and I'm fascinated by a strange bird I see outside the window. Just taking it all in.

"You're one of the few people on earth who can stand me, Vic. Not many people can. This works. *We* work. Why would I mess that up? Why would I hurt Charlie? What in the hell would I do that for? What would my motivation be, exactly?"

Victoria turns away from the intensity of his outburst, and breezes past him to take a seat on her bed. I jump up and climb into Victoria's lap. I want to shield her from Aidan, but she doesn't seem scared. Her hand is steady as she scratches my head. "Aidan. Don't get so worked up. Come on. I was just asking you a question."

He stares at her, looking wounded. "Yeah. So now I realize you don't trust me."

"Aidan."

"What?" He throws up his hands. "You don't, Vicky. You obviously don't." He takes in a deep, shaky breath. "Wow. You're the one person I thought who . . ."

"Who what?"

"Never mind." He chews on his lip, and walks over to the window. The clouds lay low out over the river. The whole day is washed in a wet haze. His eyes, half-open, scan the marsh. Voice quieter, Aidan goes on: "You're the one person in the world who I thought actually liked me, that's all." He turns his head slightly toward Victoria, but looks down at the pink shaggy rug under his feet. Waiting for her reply. Needing to hear it.

"I do like you." She puts the end of one of her little braids in her mouth again and starts chewing on it. "I've always liked you."

"I hope that's true. I don't know what I'd do if that wasn't true." Aidan raises his hand and runs it through his hair. He suddenly looks tired. "Why though? Why do you like me?"

"What?"

"It's a serious question, Vic. Why do you like me? I mean . . . when exactly did it suddenly occur to you that you liked me?"

Hmmph! I would like to hear the answer to this question too.

Victoria takes her braid and throws it behind her shoulder. "I dunno." She rubs her hands together as if wiping off sand. "Maybe it was when I noticed you're the only one who laughs at all of my stupid jokes in history class, no matter how bad they are. Or maybe it was because you always write goofy little drawings on my notebooks." She leans back on her hands. "Or maybe I noticed you when you started wearing your bathing suit to gym class—you know, the board shorts? It was kinda quirky. And cute."

Aidan rolls his eyes. "Oh my God. That's pathetic." He snorts. "As if that was by choice. I had nothing else to wear because our washing machine died."

"I guess it's a good thing it did. Because that caught my eye. Your amazingly hot blue bathing suit."

I glance up at Victoria, as I am still sitting in her lap. When I wink at her, she winks back and grins.

Lifting his head to look at her, Aidan sighs. Her smile seems to calm him down. I watch as his shoulders relax a little, and he tips his head back for a moment and breathes in again. I can almost see his anger wash off him, melting away.

"Vicky. Listen. It's not me. I'm not the one hurting your brother. But I have a suggestion for who it might be. I'm sorry to bring this up. There's only one person who ever bruised me like that. Like the way you see with Charlie. I didn't want to say anything before. But if I were you, I'd know who did that to Charlie."

Victoria's hand, which was gently combing my fur with her fingers, stops suddenly. "What?"

"You heard me." Aidan shoves his hands in his pockets. "There's only one person who would do that in my family. Maybe you should take a closer look at yours."

Her eyes light up, as she realizes what he is implying.

"I'm sorry, Vic. But you know your dad is as high as a kite most of the time, right? I mean, you never talk about it. But you're aware of that, aren't you? He's either drinking a lot or taking too much of that Valium." He shakes his head. "Possibly both. Or maybe he's hooked on something stronger."

"Aidan." Her voice is suddenly hard and angry. "That's not true. I know you don't like him but—"

"I can't believe you don't see it."

"See what? There's nothing to see. He's tired. And really stressed out." Her hands sink deeper into my fur, and she clutches at my sides. I tense up, prepared for her to move or stand.

With a sudden move, Aidan swiftly turns and sits down right next to Victoria on the bed. I jump up, frightened.

I've never liked to get too close to Aidan. And his movements today are startling me.

He slips his arms around Victoria's waist, and she immediately turns to him and puts her hands on his neck. He pulls her down onto the bed so they are lying down.

"Forget it. Forget I said anything. Oh God," he mumbles into her hair. "I wouldn't hurt you, Vic. Or your stupid little twerp brother."

"Okay." She strokes his head. "Okay. Chill out. I believe you." She kisses his cheek. "But you need to be nicer to Charlie. Promise me you will be."

"Yeah, yeah. I promise. I told you. I love you."

I watch the two of them nestle together and comfort each other, from the edge of the bed. My little heart squeezes in my chest. I jump down onto the rug and walk to the opposite side of the room.

What Aidan is saying makes sense to me. I hate to admit this, but I believe him when he says he is not the bully.

I don't want to believe him. In a way, I wish Aidan *were* the bully. Because then we could get rid of him, and the solution would be easy. But Aidan is upset, and I think he speaks from the heart. He has not been nice to Charlie, but now that I've heard him out, I also don't think he's the one who has been physically hurting him.

What I cannot accept is what Aidan is implying. Who he is implicating.

That is not the Dad I know.

Maybe Aidan is not the bully, but he is dead wrong about this. Wrong, wrong, wrong.

I stick my nose into my paw, cleaning it furiously. I must wash this entire idea away. I feel as if I've walked in a sticky jam, and want to get it off of me as quickly as possible.

Chapter 20
Mistaken

When Dad comes on Friday night to pick up the kids, Kevin is waiting for him by the door. I watch from the balcony.

"Hey, Kev." Dad jingles his car keys in his hand. He stands on the doorstep, looking at his oldest son. "You're ready, huh?"

"Yeah. Almost. Come in." Kevin kicks the wooden floor with the toe of his sneaker. "I can't get out of here fast enough."

Dad frowns as he steps inside. "What's the matter?"

Kevin tips his head to one side, and stares down at his feet. "I don't know. I just can't stand it here anymore," he mumbles. "I wish you'd move back already."

Dad's face falls—just for a moment—before he catches himself. "It's okay, buddy. We'll have a fun weekend."

Kevin glances around. His eyes dart up the stairs toward me and then down the hall toward the kitchen. Talking fast and low, he says: "I guess you've heard about Mom's new boyfriend, or whatever he is." Kevin puts his hands on his hips, like Dad often does. "I hate that guy. He's here all the time, and he messes everything up. He'll probably be here this weekend. I bet he's coming over. He's already stayed over once. When we were all here. I mean, he slept on the couch, but it was so awkward in the morning, can you imagine?"

Something turns in my stomach. I have never heard Kevin say anything bad about his mother before.

I don't feel good about this.

Dad squints at the ground. He squeezes the keys he's holding in his fist. "Who, that guy who made the mess in the garage? The one building the bookshelves?"

"Yeah. Mom's being a total freaking crazy nut."

Dad tips his head, as if trying to focus on a very difficult problem. "Don't talk about your mom like that," he insists. "Don't—don't do that. And don't worry about her. That's none of your business. Where's your bag? I thought you were ready. Go get your stuff together. C'mon. Hurry up."

Kevin shrugs, and turns to walk up the stairs.

From my point of view on the stairs, I glance up to see Charlie and Victoria scurrying around from bedroom to bathroom, packing their backpacks, searching for underwear and phones and chargers. Mom appears behind me, emerging from her bedroom, and walks down the stairs, carefully stepping over me. She says a mild hello to Dad but walks past him to absentmindedly stare at the river out the front picture window. Dad never takes his eyes off her.

"You have any plans for this weekend?" he asks.

She shrugs with one shoulder. "The usual. Errands. Food shopping. Paying the bills." Mom crosses her arms, wrapping them around herself as if she is cold.

"Nothing special, then? Just staying in all weekend?"

Dad's stare is intense, but Mom doesn't meet his gaze. "Maybe I'll have Jane over for a drink, or we'll go out for dinner. I haven't decided yet."

He frowns. "Jane might come over?"

"I don't know." Mom moves quickly to the bottom of the stairs and yells: "KIDS. Come on. Your dad's waiting."

The truth is, Mom often seems lost on the weekends when the house is empty. I think she doesn't know what to do with herself.

I have watched her spend every minute—for years—doing things for other people. She goes out and works all day. Then she comes home and cooks, and cleans, and drives the children where they need to go. She is constantly running errands, and caring for me and Gretel. So now when Dad has the kids for the weekend, I suspect she doesn't know what to do with herself. Perhaps she doesn't even know what it is that she *likes* to do. She has never had any hobbies, I assume because there was never any time for it.

But I know she does think about the kids when they're gone. She and I both worry, together. Sure, we cuddle and try to rest. But I suspect Mom is never truly relaxed.

Dad clears his throat. He sticks his hands into the pockets of his light jacket. "Kevin seemed to think you had some special plans. Maybe he was mistaken."

Mom picks her head up and looks at Dad for the first time. "I don't know. I don't know what he's talking about." She stops short. "Sorry—I have to check on something. I'll be right back."

Dad watches her go down the hallway, toward the kitchen.

I slink halfway down the stairs to get a closer look at Dad. He is bent over, giving Gretel a good rub down of the fur around her neck. Gretel looks at me with those big brown eyes, and she seems sad. She worries about Dad. I know she senses the changes in him, and it concerns her.

Dad's face is gentle and relaxed when he gives Gretel a rub down. He is not a bad person. I know that.

I know it!

"Hey, Lil," he says to me, once he sees me. He walks over and gently strokes my head. He feels good and smells even better. I miss the touch of his warm hands. "Look at those big green eyes. I miss you, Lil."

I miss you too.

"You're the real boss around here, aren't you?"

No, Mom is the boss. But she feeds me, brushes me, cleans up after me, and takes care of me, so . . . maybe I am the boss.

He chuckles, as if he can read my mind by looking at my face. But I have a serious question for him.

Is it you? I want to ask Dad, looking up into his eyes. *You would never hurt our Charlie, would you?*

I have to examine the facts.

Fact 1: Dad and Charlie do not always get along.

Fact 2: Dad does not have the potential for cruelty that I have sensed in Aidan. I just don't see it.

Fact 3: Dad hasn't been himself lately. Mark and Mom agree that *something* is wrong with him.

Fact 4: Just because Aidan isn't the bully doesn't mean he knows who is.

Charlie and Victoria break up my chain of thought when they come hustling down the stairs with their bags, and carry them right out the front door. I must scamper to get out of the way. "Bye, Lil!" Charlie coos to me as he dashes out.

Kevin follows, taking his time. Mom reappears from the kitchen just in time to remind Kevin he must drive.

"Your dad is taking Valium to relax, and I don't want him driving," she says to Kevin. "Right?" she asks Dad directly.

Dad looks weary. "Yup. That's right." He hands the keys over to Kevin. "Go start the car."

Kevin seems surprised that his dad has dismissed him so quickly. But he recovers and walks out the door. "Bye Mom," he calls out over his shoulder.

Dad stands there and waits while the children load the car. He shakes his head. "Kate." He keeps one hand on Gretel's head as he talks. He gently runs his fingers through her fur. "Kevin just told me that you had—" He stops and winces, unable to say it. "Sorry. I still don't understand why you can't let me figure this out on my own time. I don't get what the rush is. You know that it's not a good time at work for me to be making changes. If I need a drink once in a while, it's not the end of the world. I want to come home. Let's just—"

"Jeremy." Mom folds her arms across her chest. "It's never a good time with you."

"It's not as bad as you make it out to be. And I do so much for this family. Don't you get that?"

"Of course I get that, but—"

"So this is how you thank me? By throwing me out, for good?" He glances up at Mom, but then drops his gaze again to look into the friendlier face of Gretel. "I thought maybe at some point I could come back."

Mom presses her mouth together tightly before responding. "Jeremy. I wish—Look. Please don't do this. We can't keep having this same conversation. You haven't done the one thing I asked you to do: stop drinking. And I've asked you so many times I lost count. If you won't do it, then . . . What do you want me to say?"

Dad nods. "Okay, okay, okay. I'm sorry." Mom hands him Gretel's red leash, and he snaps it on her collar.

He hesitates, straightening up. "But you understand why I can't do it right now, don't you?"

"Jeremy . . ." Mom closes her eyes. "Don't—"

"Because when I stop drinking, Kate, I start to think too much, and worry too much, and it . . . It just feels like it's going to kill me, you know? I think I'm going to die." Dad shivers, as if a cold breeze has come down the hall. "Literally die. Do you know what that's like? No, you don't. It's overwhelming."

Mom frowns. "People feel bad sometimes, Jeremy." She licks her dry lips. "But they find other ways to deal with it."

"You knew who I was," he blurts out. "You knew." He finally lifts his head and makes eye contact, challenging her.

Mom nods, and swallows. "Yes." Finally, she adds in a quiet voice: "But you know, at one time, you were happy. You drank too much from the start, but you were fun to be with. You were optimistic. You wanted to make the world a better place. Do you remember all that? Do you ever think about that?"

"Sure." Dad nods, as if he understands what Mom is saying, but I don't think he does. "Yeah, sure. I was *optimistic*." He spits out the word as if it is foreign to him. "But that was a long time ago. I was young and stupid. I can't go back now. I can't forget what I've seen now."

What he has seen?

What exactly has Dad seen? I wonder.

"I'm sorry about that." Mom straightens up. "I really am. But it doesn't just affect you. I have the right to say enough already. I have that right."

I see that Dad is stuck at a point where he just can't give Mom what she wants. He once again can't look directly at her. He looks down at her hand instead, as if he might want to hold it, but he does not.

Dad opens the front door and walks down the front porch steps. When he reaches the walkway, Dad spins around. "I guess if Jane is coming over, you won't be alone. But if you want Gretel, I'll leave her here. Are you going to be alone?" His voice suddenly sounds desperate.

I squint against the late afternoon sun. We're greeted by the excited call of birds, boasting about the worms and seeds they have eaten on this fine spring day. Nature is thriving. The world is new again. The outdoors is green and lush and the air smells heavy, like rain is coming.

"No, Jeremy, you take her. I'll be fine with Lily." She gives him a small smile, which he returns. But they are empty smiles. I do not believe for a minute that either one really means it. They are both sad beyond words that could possibly explain it.

Mom and I don't step outside. We shrink back, and Mom slowly closes the door.

Chapter 21
Temporary Amusement

I hear the front door open and close. Heavy feet stomping and scraping mud onto the mat. "Katie?"

I recognize Mark's voice.

But it is not the afternoon. It is Saturday evening, and already dark out. I wonder what he is doing here.

"I'm up here," Mom calls. She opens her mouth and I think she is about to remind Mark to take off his shoes, but changes her mind. She is a mom, after all. And she is the director of a preschool. She is used to giving orders.

A moment goes by. From the sounds of shuffling, I think Mark has remembered to take off his shoes anyway.

I listen to Mark run up the stairs, two at a time. But then his footsteps slow down, and he hesitates at the doorway. He stands there, a dark shadow in the entrance, looking at Mom. She sits on the bed.

"It's raining," he tells her.

Mom nods. "I can hear it on the windows."

There is a soft, peaceful sound when the wind blows the rain against the skylight in the bedroom. I always feel like our lamps cast a more golden glow indoors when the skies are gray outside.

Mark is wearing a T-shirt and shorts with a stripe on the side. It occurs to me that he looks like Kevin when he's getting ready for one of his basketball games at the school. I have only ever seen Mark wearing jeans and work boots, and, staring at his white socks, I realize he probably had sneakers on.

Seeing the way Mom and I are studying him, he explains. "I just came from the gym. Sorry." He smiles. "When I said just tell me *when* and *where*, I didn't realize the answer would be *right now*."

Mom laughs. She motions for him to come over.

Mark walks in and sits next to Mom on the bed, as if it is the most natural place in the world for him to sit. It is as if he's been here in Mom's room before. Which, of course, he has not.

I'm impressed that Mark only hesitated a moment before approaching her. This is Mom's private space. I suppose sometimes in life it is better to act than to think too much. And I suspect he is eager to see Mom.

It is so curious! Mark has a confidence that I don't recognize. It makes me realize how uncomfortable Charlie and Kevin are in many situations. Dad too.

I am nestled into a nice spot on Dad's pillow, as comfortable as can be, but I still get up and walk over to ram my head into Mark's elbow. He is my friend, and I want to ask: *Why are you here?* But I know Mom can get messages to people through her phone. She must have told Mark this was a good time for a visit.

I can sense how alert he is and how interested he is in Mom. He strokes my back, but barely glances at me. He's not really here to see me.

I bat at his arm with my paw and *meow!* until he makes eye contact with me. "Okay, sweetheart," he says to me. "Take it easy. Go easy now. You know you're my baby." He runs his fingers through the fur on my head, and I feel better.

When Mark looks back up at Mom, she lights up. It strikes me that Mom feels something from his gaze alone. I think he must sense it too, because he is the type of human who seems to be in tune with other humans. Mark takes her hand in his.

"If we do this," Mom suddenly says, "it has to be just for us. I don't want Vincent to know about it. He's been my friend a long time, and he wouldn't understand."

Mark shakes his head. "I won't say anything to Vincent."

"Jeremy and the kids can't know anything about it either," she implores. "Things aren't sorted out yet. With the family. Everything is up in the air."

"Okay."

"I don't want you to tell your friends either. Or confess this to your priest. Or write about it online. I mean, you're an adult. I can't stop you if you do. But I would appreciate it if you didn't."

I tip my head. Mom is perplexing me. She is now just talking and talking and talking, much too quickly.

The way Mark is watching her so intently, holding her hand in his, I am quite sure he has no intention of dishonoring her wishes. He waits patiently for her to look up at him.

"All right."

Mom swallows. She looks as nervous as a bird who has landed on the deck and senses the presence of a cat in the shadows. But Mark has no intention of hurting Mom. He is not going to attack. I can tell by the still way he holds his body, the way his mouth hangs open just a bit, as if he wants to speak but isn't sure if he should.

Mom moves closer to him and puts her hand on his upper arm, as I've seen her do before. "I'm glad you came right over." She takes in a deep breath and lets it out, and I think she is willing herself to relax. Her hand glides over his skin, just at the edge of his sleeve. Her voice sounds detached, but dreamy. "I like all the freckles."

Mark smiles again. And then he grabs the hem of his T-shirt and pulls it off, over his head.

Mom startles, and I can see she wasn't expecting him to do that. She takes him in for a moment as he shakes his head so his messy black hair settles a bit. Mom's hand flutters up to touch his face, and gently run her fingers over his cheek. She then moves her hand very slowly to his chest, but she barely touches it, as if she's afraid it will be hot like the stove. I watch her skim her hand up to his shoulder. "More freckles." She sighs.

The freckles on his skin remind me of the heat of the summer. For a moment I imagine Mark and Mom are not sitting on the bed. In my mind, they are sitting on the dock across the street at the boat club, like two teenagers soaking up the sun and dipping their feet in the water. Nervously fidgeting. Full of anticipation. Dreaming about what might be.

Mark shrugs. "These freckles are just crazy. My skin isn't perfect, like yours."

Mom's face creases with confusion, and she laughs. "What? I'm as pale as a ghost."

"Nah, you look perfect, like marble. And that hair. It's not really fair you have hair like that."

I'm not exactly sure what he means by that. How is her hair unfair to him?

Mark leans forward and kisses Mom. As before, he is very tender with her.

I have made up my mind about this human: He wants someone to love. He has a lot of love to give, and he has been searching for the right person. And Mom wants desperately to *be* loved. So it is a good fit.

There are so many nights I have watched Mom and known she was in pain. The way she grips her lower back while working at the stove. The way she rubs her forehead too hard while sitting in front of her computer. The way she kneads a shoulder while lying in bed. It is about time for another human to make Mom feel better.

I think this just might work.

"I'm sweaty from the gym. I should take a shower," Mark blurts out. "I mean, we both should. Together."

"We should?" Mom asks anxiously, as if coming out of a dream. She grabs the edge of the blanket on the bed as if she's ready to pull it up over her head and hide herself under it.

"Yeah." Mark's eyes light up. "I want to shampoo your hair. I think it would be romantic."

Mom looks positively alarmed.

I, on the other hand, am amused. I look from one to the other.

I know what "romantic" means. Sort of. When Victoria uses that word, her eyes flutter upward and she sighs.

I have never heard Mom use that word. Not once.

"Look," she says, swallowing. "Just wait a minute. Here's the thing."

"Yes?"

"It's just that . . ." Mom frowns and tips her head. "I'm not really . . . You know . . ." She seems genuinely perplexed. "So my hair will get wet?"

Mark raises his eyebrows. "Yes, it will. That is exactly how I want to do it. By getting your hair wet. That is, in fact, essential to the process of shampooing." He leans forward so he can put both hands on her hips. "Please don't say no."

I can see Mom is still not sure about this, but she starts to relax again, her shoulders dropping. Mark leans forward to kiss her ear, and she tips her head to the side to give him access to her neck. Mom's eyes close when he presses his fingers into her hip bone.

She reminds me of when someone scratches at the base of my tail. I always stop moving, arch my backbone, and lean into it.

"C'mon, please. Now." He kisses her again. Her cheek. Her mouth. "Please. Now. Shower. Don't make me beg. Okay, never mind, too late. Please. I'm begging you. Right now."

Mom smiles and nods, and then she gets up, and they go into her bathroom. I can see she is finally over her nerves.

After all, it's just Mark. He is our friend.

I hear the water running, and my humans talking and laughing. It is nice to have a minute to stretch out on the scratchy wool blanket on the bed before they come kick me off. I watch the ceiling fan turn in a slow circle.

When they finally emerge from the shower, Mom comes first, wrapped in a towel. Mark wears nothing at all, and while it looks like he has dried himself, his body is still pink from the heat of the water.

Mom approaches me and pets my back absentmindedly; for good luck, perhaps. I blink at her.

It's fine, I want to tell her. *This will be easier than you think.*

Mating is easy. Every creature in nature must do it.

But I know why she is nervous. Humans have all kinds of quirks, and who knows what this man wants exactly? First, the shower. What could be next?

Mark walks up behind her and wraps his arms around her. He buries his face in her neck, and she shivers when his wet hair skims her shoulder.

Mom clears her throat. "Maybe we should talk this through one more time." I understand that she is teasing from her tone.

"This first," Mark insists. "Talk later."

"But are you sure you're ready this time?"

He slides his hands up over the towel that still hides her body. "Yes. Definitely, yes. I would say that I could not possibly be more ready."

Mom's hand lingers on my back just a moment more, and I give her a nod. She allows Mark to turn her around.

He is young—at least, younger than Dad. I imagine that to him this feels important, and urgent. Mom lets him steer her onto the bed. I get to my feet and jump down to the rug. The wet towel comes flying onto the floor and lands beside me with a *thwump*.

I close my eyes to wait. This could take a while.

Or, maybe not. As I said, he is young.

One way Mark is different from Dad is that he talks to Mom the whole time. Dad approached mating with quiet intensity, and sometimes he had trouble with it, unable to focus. But Mark speaks to Mom, as if they are still having a conversation, even though Mom does not join in except to encourage him quietly. I imagine Mark is saying things she wants to hear, because soon she is nodding and practically purring.

I wonder how long this will take. I hate it when anything delays my bedtime. I tune them out for a while, cleaning my paws with my tongue. When I am done with that I let myself nod off, until something catches my ear and jolts me awake.

When I glance up, I notice that Mark moves around a lot, shifting Mom this way and that, changing positions. It is unlike anything I ever saw Dad do, and it seems completely unnecessary, if you ask me. Mark is certainly enthusiastic.

I'm rather glad Gretel isn't here for this. She'd probably just catnap on the rug with me, but it might make her anxious.

A little later—and it seems so strange, but—I hear, loud and clear, Mom take the Lord's name in vain. This is something she never, ever does.

My ears quiver at that! My goodness!

Has she hurt herself?

Mark laughs, and Mom says something quietly to him. But I can't hear what it is, and it makes me anxious. I want this to go well for Mom.

I jump up on the bed again to check on her, to see if she is mad at Mark. But when I land lightly at the foot of the bed, I see he crouches above her, and she is pushing the hair from his eyes, looking at him so fondly that I think she has lost her mind.

She smiles broadly when he beams down at her. Mark has waited and gone through an elaborate mating ritual to get to this point. And now: triumph. He has made Mom happy. Mom reaches up and wraps both arms around his shoulders and pulls him down so he will lie on top of her.

Well!

I turn right around and jump back down. Mom isn't even done with him yet. She doesn't need my help at all.

I lay on the rug and purr. There's almost nothing I enjoy more than seeing my humans happy.

I finally get up, stretch, and go out of the room. The house is dark and still, and it is time for me to make my rounds downstairs. Near the fireplace, I watch a daddy longlegs spider crawl along the floorboards before I toy with it, batting it with my paw. The spider finally escapes through a crack just as I'm about to eat him. I look out the sliding glass door into the woods and peer at the big fat owl that perches in a nearby evergreen tree. He's beautiful. He stares at me, wide-eyed, but otherwise does not move.

Hoo hoo! I wish I could call to him.

The house is so still that I can hear Mom and Mark talking to each other for a long time. The words pour out of them. I get the impression that they have saved up a lot to say. And then I hear Mom drying her hair with a hair dryer. Finally, all is quiet other than the patter of light rain on the roof, and I know they are finally sleeping.

In the early hours of the morning, just before the sun rises, I hear a strange moaning sound. It worries me. I decide to go back and check on Mom. As I slink up the stairs, I realize that it is definitely Mom who is making the noise. I think she may be crying.

My heart starts pounding in my chest. Mom was so happy. Whatever could have gone wrong?

Did Mark do something he should not have done? I hurry into her bedroom.

I dash across the rug and leap right up onto the bed. But I freeze when I see they are sitting up, Mom wrapped in Mark's arms. She looks very vulnerable, and I don't just mean because she is undressed. She has collapsed into him, and he cradles her with a look of worry and surprise.

"I'm sorry," she sobs. "I'm sorry. I've been with Jeremy for so long. It's just that I never thought . . ." She squeezes Mark's arm so hard I think that she must be hurting him. But he is strong, so I think the pain that registers on his face is caused by her words. "I feel like I'm betraying him."

She smashes her face against Mark's chest, and he tries to shush her. "It's okay. Katie. It's okay, sweetheart. This was going to happen. No matter what. You couldn't have done anything differently. I've wanted you for a long time. There was nothing that was going to keep up apart. I love you and—"

"No. DON'T." She rips herself out of his arms and lies down, turning over and away from him. "Oh God. I'm so sorry. This is my fault. This is all my fault. Please don't tell Jeremy."

Mark's face goes pale. "But you didn't do anything wrong. From the minute I saw you, I knew we were going to be together. I just knew. It was fate. I don't think you could have changed the course of events."

"Don't be stupid." She reaches over for a tissue and blows her nose. "We always have a choice." Her face is splotchy and swollen from the tears. "And you don't know how things will turn out. No one ever knows. You don't know everything. I still love Jeremy. He's just not well."

Oh.

Oh!

I don't know who is more shocked. Me or Mark.

Mark watches her. But she does not turn back to him or say anything else. She lies still, eyes shut, clutching the tissue.

He and I make eye contact. It hurts, and I wince. His eyes are wide with disbelief. I hardly know this man, but we have bonded. And now I think I am witnessing something I have not seen before.

I think Mom is breaking his heart.

"Mark. I'm sorry. What I mean is this," Mom clarifies all in a rush, speaking over her shoulder. "We are definitely getting divorced. For sure. I cannot live with him anymore. But it still hurts. That's all."

Mark stares at the back of her head for a long time. He finally retreats, lying down and pulling the covers over himself. He stares up at the ceiling and chews on the inside of his mouth. I think he is stunned by what Mom has said.

Maybe Mark was right when he told Mom they should wait. Perhaps, even now, it was too soon. Maybe they both weren't really ready for this.

The problem might be that for Mark, this is: *love*. That's what I heard him say.

And just maybe, for Mom, this is: *something else*. I'm not sure what. But if not love, then what is it? I'm as confused as Mark is.

And while my loyalties are with Mom, I climb right over her, pushing off of her leg to get to Mark. I curl up next to him, my backbone pressing into his side, and he strokes my fur. As I knew he would. I have figured out that he is desperate to care for someone, to express love, and to have it rejected must be painful.

I don't understand what darkness drives humans to hurt each other when they are so close to some kind of connection. I can't fathom what causes humans to act in ways that are harmful to those they love.

It is extremely baffling.

Maybe Mom can't return Mark's affections right now, but I can. And I do. I purr as loud as I can.

In the early morning, I wake at the foot of the bed to see Mark curled up behind Mom, who is still turned away from him. The movement of his foot causes me to jump up, and I look to see he is awake. When Mom begins to move, he rolls her over onto her back, so his face will be the first thing she sees.

It's funny, but Dad's face has never been very expressive. He looks as smooth as a river rock much of the time. You cannot tell what he is thinking. Mark's face, in contrast, is completely open and easy to read. I can tell it affects Mom from the way she rests her hand gently on his cheek.

Mark looks very tired. He is not excited the way he was last night.

"I'm not a way station you can visit between the time Jeremy leaves and the day you welcome him back here with open arms."

"I know," Mom says, running her fingers through his glossy black hair. "I'm sorry about last night." Her face is pink from crying in the early morning.

"I'm not a toy for you to play with while waiting for your husband to come home."

"I know. I understand." She tugs at a wave of hair that falls over his ear, and gives him a sleepy smile. "I didn't mean what I said. I mean—I did, but I'm sorry I fell apart."

"I'm not here for your temporary amusement. I have a heart."

"I have a heart too." Mom runs her thumb over his mouth. "Listen. I told you. We're definitely getting divorced. This is just new. And scary."

Mark winces, as if in pain. "Ah, Katie. It's scary for me too." He lays his head down on her chest, and she cradles his head in both hands. His hand moves across her stomach, and she draws in a deep breath.

Last night, I thought they were both having fun. But now, they are very careful and gentle with each other.

"If you want me to just leave, okay. That's okay. I'll give Vincent some excuse about why I have to quit. I don't want to be here if this is just some kind of experiment for you, or whatever. I'm not interested in being—"

"Shhh, Mark. Stop. Stop." She glances down at the top of his head, and then back up at the ceiling. "That's not what this is."

Mom pulls him up until she can turn his head to hers. She kisses him, and easily gets him started all over again. He melts right into her advances, with no further protests. His desire is right at the surface, quickly ignited.

Dad's love, in contrast, runs deep. I think Dad's love runs so deep, it has perhaps been buried under mountains of worry and despair, the care of three children, and a difficult job, and a house that needs repairing, and a yard that needs constant tending. Dad has suffered in ways that I don't understand.

But perhaps I am being unfair to Mark. I am not trying to compare him to Dad. He is my friend, and he has suffered too. He needs love as much as the next person.

Mark fulfills Mom's every need. Whatever she asks him to do, he does. However her body moves, he responds. But he doesn't talk like he did the night before. Which worries me.

I don't fully understand. I thought Mom wanted Mark as her

mate. If that is true, she has gotten what she wants. So what's the matter?

I jump down from the bed when Mom accidentally bumps me with her leg. There are still things that puzzle me about the humans, and it is possible I don't know everything going on in Mom's head and heart.

The only human I know completely is my sweet Charlie. And Mark is going to help Charlie, isn't he? So we need Mark.

We need him! Oh, Mom.

Mom does not have to love Mark. But I also think we cannot afford for her to cast him aside.

It's important that Mark stay. I think of all the things I could do to win him over and keep him interested in me, and demonstrate to Mom how much we need him. I have noticed that he likes to cuddle me like a baby. Something about me is comforting to him.

The day is coming when Charlie's bully will be exposed and caught. I hope Mark will help us get that done.

Soon after, Charlie will reconcile with Dad. And I believe Charlie will realize that he is in love with his best friend Karen. Everything will be wonderful!

I'm not sure why it's taking Charlie so long to express his love to Karen in the same way I've watched Aidan fall for Victoria. But I'm not worried.

I remember last summer there was a girl Kevin would bring home sometimes to have dinner with the family. He kissed this girl a few times on the back deck when no one was looking. He was always putting his arm around her and leaning in close. The girl did seem to like Kevin very much, but she also sometimes fended him off with her hand on his chest. I thought he was a bit rude. I could see it was too much for that nice girl.

Charlie is a sweet boy. He would never be so pushy. He is

what Mom would call a "gentleman," polite and kind. So naturally I think it is just fine that Charlie is taking his time with Karen. When he is ready, he will declare his devotion in a respectful way.

I know this day is coming. I know it in my heart. If only I could help it get here sooner.

Chapter 22
Bright Yellow Gloves

Some time later, the sun streams in through the slats, bright and intense. It's going to be a lovely day.

Mark has fallen back to sleep and Mom is lazily rolling over in bed when she and I both hear her phone chirp. She reaches over toward her bedside table and fumbles for the phone.

Staring at the screen, she sits up, one hand holding the bed-sheet up over her chest. It takes her a moment to register whatever it is she sees there.

Mom reaches over and puts a hand on Mark's arm. "Get dressed." She climbs out of the bed, reaching to grab her bath towel off the floor. Walking over to the dresser, she flings open a drawer and pulls out clean clothes.

Mark wipes his eyes, and props himself up on one elbow. Once he sees how urgently Mom is getting dressed, and the worried look on her face, he gets up out of bed.

By the time Dad and the kids come in through the front door, Mark is in the back room near the bookshelves. Mom has taken many bottles out of the refrigerator, and they are all over the counter. She has bright yellow gloves on her hands, and her hair is in a bun up on top of her head.

"Hey, Vicky," Mom calls out. "Once you get unpacked, can you come help me a minute? I'm cleaning out the fridge, and I want to check the expiration dates on everything."

Victoria walks in, backpack slung on her back. She takes a quick glance over at the study, and sees Mark measuring a shelf. He does not turn from his work to say hello. Victoria surveys the mess on the counter. "Sure, Mom."

As Victoria exits, she passes Dad, who is just entering the kitchen. Gretel follows his every step, sniffing his hand.

"What are you doing?"

"I'm just cleaning. You guys are back earlier than I expected."

"Yeah. They asked me to take a late shift today in Boston. So I've got to get going."

Dad turns, and finally sees Mark. He must have seen the black truck parked outside. But I can tell from the way Dad's eyes light up for a moment in astonishment that he was not expecting to see Mark.

Dad seems genuinely shocked. I can only assume he thought it was Vincent who was here.

But Mark is different from Vincent. Vincent is a neighbor with a wife who has cancer, and a construction business, and neat hair and glasses, and three children.

In contrast, Mark is an unknown factor, at least to Dad. All Dad can probably see is that he is younger and taller and wears casual clothes and has black hair that he does not brush. He is a stranger taking up room in the family house.

Dad's look changes. Slowly. It darkens into an expression that is hard for me to interpret. But it is not friendly.

Mark must feel Dad's icy stare on his back, because he makes a partial turn and nods at Dad. Mark's black hair is even more of a mess than usual, falling long to skirt his eyebrows.

"Hey." His voice is flat. I think Mark is trying to sound casual, but to me, he sounds angry. Mark turns back to the bookshelf.

At first, the tone in his voice catches me off guard. I have never heard Mark sound cross before. But of course, it makes sense. It is as natural a reaction as anything else on this earth.

Mark has claimed Mom for his own, spending the night immersing himself in her touch and the sound of her voice. He has put his scent all over her. And now, here is her former mate. Naturally, he bristles at the sight of Dad.

I even heard Mark tell Mom he loved her. But then she said she still loves Dad. No wonder Mark feels threatened, and not in the way he did when he was worried about Dad's gun.

There are many things here that Dad, being a perceptive person, must have noticed by now.

1. It is a Sunday morning. When most humans do not work.
2. I believe the garage doors are not open, as I never heard them go up or down.
3. Mark is wearing a T-shirt and shorts and sneakers, not his usual jeans and work boots. He does not have wood shavings on his clothes.
4. Nor does he have tools in his hands. Just a measuring tape, which may be useless considering the doors to the shelves have already been cut and are ready to be installed.
5. Vincent is nowhere to be seen.

"Hi, Mark!" Charlie's cheerful voice pierces the silence. He smiles and waves with a grin. "Mom, are there any donuts left?"

Mom points to a box sitting by the toaster. Charlie walks over to pull a powdered donut out of the box. He grabs a paper napkin on his way back out of the kitchen.

Gretel, who has been circling Dad, finally trots over to Mark, her tail wagging. Mark glances at her, but does not extend his hand, as if he is afraid to show her affection. But Gretel is not deterred. She sits next to him, looking up at Mark with sad eyes, waiting for a hello.

Dad's brow furrows for a moment, and then his face goes blank. All expression drains from him, and he almost looks calm.

Almost.

"You know, Kate, I don't have to be in Boston for two hours. So I have a little time. Why don't we go out and grab some brunch? We could all go. And your contractor could keep working in peace."

Charlie comes running back into the kitchen, his sneakers squeaking as he comes to a halt. "Really, Dad? Oooh, yeah. Blueberry pancakes. I could go for that."

Mom and Victoria exchange a quick, awkward glance.

And suddenly, I realize: It was Victoria. Victoria must have sent a message to Mom to let her know they were coming.

"Yeah," Kevin chimes in, rubbing his hands together. "Sounds awesome. I'm starving. C'mon, Mom. You've gotta come too."

Victoria clears her throat. "No. No, that won't work. Mom promised to take me to get my hair cut. I need to go now, because I have dance squad later. You promised, Mom. Please. I've been begging you for weeks."

Dad is suspicious. "Since when do you have dance squad? I thought you quit last year."

"Yes," Mom says matter-of-factly. "You're right. I promised Vicky we'd go. Just let me put these things back in the refrigerator. But you boys can go to breakfast."

"It's all or nothing," Dad threatens. "Everyone or no one. We're not going to go without you guys."

"Fine," Mom says with a sigh.

But she doesn't mean: *Fine, I'll go.*

What she means is: *Fine, I accept that the plans are falling through*.

She turns her back to Dad and starts rearranging jars on the counter.

"Okay." Dad clears his throat. He looks over the mess: two tomatoes here, a bottle of mustard there, a carton of eggs on top. He watches Mom's hands, constantly moving. For a moment, his eyes soften, and he looks like he is going to say something more. But then he takes a quick glance at the back room, where Mark is still working, and bites his tongue. "I'm gonna get going." His voice has gone very quiet. "Bye, guys."

Mom stands up and watches Dad walk down the hall. The front door closes with an almost imperceptible *whoosh* behind him.

As soon as the kids are upstairs unpacking their bags, stomping from room to room, Mom strips off the yellow gloves and throws them in the sink. She walks over to the study and leans in the doorway. Mark glances back at her. They stare at each other, as if unsure of their next move.

I am almost expecting Mom to apologize for Dad's behavior. But instead, she sighs.

"Mark," she says, "Look. I'm sorry. This is my mistake. I have three children here. Three older children. And so I can't . . . I can't bring any instability into this house right now. I can't take things one day at a time. I can't wait and see where this goes. I can't have men stay over just because I feel like it. It's not going to work that way."

Mark's face gets red, and it takes me a moment to realize he is annoyed. Maybe more than annoyed. I think he is angry. He straightens up, hands on his hips, the way I have seen Dad do before when he's about to start yelling. He gives her a look of frustration. "Where the hell is *this* coming from? Are you kidding me right now?"

Mom reaches over, and closes the glass door behind her so

206 / Sandi Ward

they will have some privacy. I scamper under the rocking chair to get out of the way. Mom makes a grand gesture with her arm. "Why didn't you leave when Jeremy got here?"

"You told me to pretend I was working. I just did what you told me to do. You wanted to make it even more obvious that I slept over? Why would I leave, if I just got here?" He looks incredulous, and puts his hands out in front of him to plead with her. "Besides, I'm not leaving you alone with him. There's something . . . not right with him. Don't you sense that?"

"He's fine. I've told you before. He's not happy about the divorce, but we're perfectly safe with him."

"No, Katie," he interjects, leaning toward her, "No, I don't think you are. And I didn't want to leave. I just got done telling you this morning that I'm not a toy you can play with and put down at your convenience. And here's another thing: I don't appreciate being treated like a big secret around here. I know you have three children. I'm an adult. And I remember what I agreed to last night. But I think Kevin and Victoria know perfectly well what's going on. And, frankly, Jeremy did too. By not talking about it, by not talking about *anything*, you're just creating a situation where the kids think it's not okay to—"

Mom's forehead creases with anger. "This is *my family*, and these are *my* kids. *Not* yours. You aren't a parent, so you don't understand. Don't tell me—"

Mark freezes and glances behind Mom, startled. He suddenly cannot look her in the eye. "No. I'm not." He swallows, and looks frantically around the room, as if he's lost something and can't find it. "You're right. I'm not."

Mom takes a small step forward. "I'm sorry. I didn't mean . . . I didn't mean anything by it. That is, I didn't mean to remind you." She swallows. "You are a parent. You're Hannah's dad. You remember what it feels like to worry about her. I just meant that—"

"No, no, no, you're right. You need to put your family first.

For a minute I forgot where I was. I forgot what the hell I was doing." He raises a hand and drags it across his mouth, and then wipes down his wrists too, where the bee stings once were. He starts pacing the room, like he's trapped.

"Mark." Mom hurries to him and puts her hands on his arms, forcing him to look at her. "Mark, I'm sorry."

He lets her drag him over to the couch. "It's okay," she goes on, "It will be okay."

She pushes Mark down so he sits on the couch, and she climbs right into his lap, as if the weight of her will comfort him and keep him grounded. Her hand flies to his head and she runs her fingers through his hair until his body relaxes.

I get the feeling Mom has been through this before, calming a man down. I wonder if Dad was the same way when he was younger.

"I don't want to take it one day at a time, Katie," he explains, sounding tired. "This isn't a trial run, or whatever you think it is for me. I want to be with you. For real."

She shakes her head. "You're younger than me. You need to start a family of your own. You need to start over."

"Maybe I don't." He puts his arms around her and his eyes soften. "I don't want to go through that again. I don't want to start over with a new family. I mean it." He glances up at the way she is wearing her hair on top of her head. I can see he is incapable of staying angry at her for very long. I think Mom knew exactly what she was doing when she climbed in his lap. "Don't you think I know what I want?"

She studies his face. "I'm not sure." She hasn't taken her hands out of his hair. "I know what you want right now. But you might feel differently tomorrow." With another sigh, she says, "We can talk to the kids today if you want to. We can tell them that we're seeing each other."

"Okay, good," he says, "That's good." He nods, as if everything has been settled. "We should start with Charlie. He's the only one who doesn't really know. And I think he'll be okay with it. He seems to like me." And with that he pulls her toward him, burying his face in the crook of her neck and holding her tight.

Yes! My heart soars. *Charlie, Charlie, Charlie. Talk to Charlie. And don't stop talking to him until you get some answers.*

I hope Mom knows what she's doing. Because if she decides she doesn't really want Mark, I don't think he's the type who will find it very easy to let go. He doesn't seem to be the kind of person who could just walk away.

And I realize: Dad is the same way.

Just then I turn to see Gretel watching us from the other side of the glass door. She isn't begging to come in. She's just watching, curious. I feel a little sorry for her, because she must be confused.

I walk up to the door, my tail high in the air, and stare back at Gretel through the glass.

What do you think about all this? Do we need to worry?

And in the way Gretel cocks her head, I could almost swear she understands me. Almost.

Chapter 23
Impressionable Teenager

It is very late in the night, and Gretel is driving me absolutely crazy.

I watch her from the edge of Mom's bed. She has not slept a wink.

Sometimes, when our neighbors have a party, Gretel will listen to the unusual sounds and get very agitated. Tonight, she is the same way, but I don't hear anything, so I'm not sure why she's worried. She occasionally jumps to her feet, listening. Sometimes she whimpers, and turns in a circle. There is something making her very uneasy.

Mom scolded Gretel and told her to settle down. So she is trying to lie still. But her eyes are wide-open and her ears are straight up and alert.

I give up on trying to sleep on Mom's bed and go out to the dark hall to sit overlooking the balcony. It's quiet and peaceful. I am lying on the hardwood floor, half-asleep, when Victoria's door opens.

Two eyes look out from the darkness and then a face emerges, pale as the moon. My heart skips a beat when I see it is Aidan.

He is wearing a T-shirt and his jeans. He tiptoes over to the bathroom and shuts the door. I notice that he does not turn on the light. A moment later I hear a flush and Aidan once again makes his way across the hall, his socks gliding on the hardwood floor.

I get up, shocked, and follow him into Victoria's bedroom. He closes the door behind me. Pulling up the blanket, he climbs into her single bed beside her.

"Anyone see you?" Victoria whispers.

"Nah. Just the psycho cat."

"Aw." She giggles. "Lily caught you."

Aidan is still sitting up. "Vicky, I should go home. I should sneak out now. Someone's going to see me in the morning. I'm going to have to pee again."

"Noooo." She grabs a handful of his T-shirt. "Stay. Please. Stay."

"But, Vic." He brushes his hair back from his forehead. "I don't know. I mean, I feel like we're taking advantage of your mom."

Victoria now sits up. "So my mom gets to have her boyfriend stay over, and I don't? Who's comforting *me*?"

Aidan stares at her, mouth slightly open. More and more, I have noticed that Victoria is asserting herself. And starting to win arguments.

I start to realize that since Dad has moved out, Victoria has become increasingly interested in getting Aidan to come over, to stay here, to pledge his loyalty to her. Although I don't know enough about human behavior to say for sure, perhaps she feels Aidan can take the place of Dad as a man who is devoted in whole to her best interests. Aidan is hardly a man yet, but that is what he will be very soon. While he acts contrary and difficult much of the time, that may be exactly what she likes about him—Aidan rejects other people, but not her. Never her. Aidan's constant attention might be preferable to Dad's increasingly distracted manner.

"Yeah . . ." Aidan squints, and rubs his jaw. "I guess that's true."

Victoria slides her arm around his waist, and leans into him. "Lie back down. You're fine. Nobody knows and nobody cares."

"Okay," he whispers. But even when he lies down, Victoria's head on his shoulder and a smile on her face, I can see him staring at the ceiling in the darkness. I get the impression he's uncomfortable being here.

When she squeezes his arm, his eyes finally relax.

"You're bad," he finally says. "You're a bad influence on me."

"Yes, I'm a bad influence. Look, all we're doing is sleeping. Nothing's going on. You're being an angel."

"Yeah, but your mom doesn't know that." He turns toward her. "Vic, are you sure you can sneak me out of here tomorrow if I stay?"

"Mmm-hmm. Sure." She runs her fingers through his hair the way that he said he likes. He takes in a deep breath. By the time he has exhaled, it is clear he cannot leave. He will not.

Something in my little heart jiggers and loosens and breaks off from the hardness that has encased it for so long when it comes to Aidan. I realize it is time for me to accept him. I think Victoria really loves him, and he's not going anywhere. He's not Charlie's bully. There may be hope for him yet. He's just very lucky that my sweet Victoria has taken a liking to him.

I am now stuck in Victoria's bedroom because the door is closed. So I plop down on the floor for a while. But I can't relax. Finally I climb up into the beanbag chair and knead my claws into it, which calms me. I nap on and off until the first rays of dawn start to lighten the room.

At one point, Aidan stirs. He curses and rubs his eyes. "Jesus," he whispers, although Victoria is sound asleep. "I told you I'd have to pee again. Goddamn it."

He forces himself up and clumsily climbs out of bed. Staggering across the room, he hesitates before leaving the room. His hand on the doorknob, he listens for movement.

Nothing.

I pad across the room to watch him slide in his white socks across the hallway to the bathroom. He barely makes a sound.

I find myself rooting for him. I hope Aidan makes it. Because if anyone does see him, I think he will be in very big trouble. Mom will be furious. And she will tell Dad, who will be even angrier.

And then—just when I think he is home free—Charlie emerges from his bedroom, eyes sleepy and hair askew. It is very early, and the hallway is still dark. Charlie is wearing his striped pajama pants and no shirt, and he yawns. When he hears the toilet flush, he folds his arms across his body and waits.

When Aidan emerges, Charlie startles something fierce. He puts a hand right over his own mouth. But he makes no sound.

Aidan sees his opening and puts a finger over his lips to shush him. Charlie nods, wide-eyed. Aidan points his thumb toward the bathroom to indicate that Charlie can go in. Charlie scurries in and closes the door behind him.

I watch Aidan disappear back into Victoria's room, shaking his head.

When Charlie comes out of the bathroom, Victoria is there waiting for him in her oversized white robe. She throws an arm around Charlie and steers him right over to her bedroom. I am quick to follow, and she shuts the door behind us again.

Aidan is sitting on the bed, looking worried.

"Charlie," Victoria whispers. "Look. Aidan just stayed over and it's no big deal, okay? I'm sorry if he scared you."

Charlie's forehead creases. "Vicky. He's not even supposed to be upstairs, never mind stay here all night. Mom is going to kill you."

"She doesn't know."

"And she never will, if you don't say anything," Aidan chimes in.

Charlie looks from one to other. I imagine he is weighing his options.

Charlie! Use this opportunity to get something out of these two. They are going to owe you.

But my innocent Charlie doesn't say anything. His mouth hangs open. He's shocked. "Are you crazy?"

Victoria sits on the bed right next to Aidan. "No. Charlie. Look. Nothing is going on. Aidan's got his clothes on. We're not *doing* anything. He's just sleeping here."

Charlie makes an expressive face to show he doubts this is true.

"Look," Aidan says. "Buddy. Thursday nights are my mom's night off, and she had a few friends over. They're partying. I knew they'd be there all night. And I didn't think it was a healthy atmosphere for an impressionable teenager like myself." His face remains expressionless, but I think he is making a joke. "So I got out of there. I was going to go to my friend Mike's house for the night, but then I was already here, so . . ."

"C'mon, Charlie. Please. Just give us a break. Just give me this one thing. Don't say anything to Mom."

Charlie folds his arms across his bare chest. "Wow. Okay. All right." He looks down at his feet before glancing back up at Aidan. "Your mom had some friends over, huh? I guess I understand. I mean, I get why you'd want to leave."

Well. This is interesting. Aidan is the reason Charlie has fled from our house in the past. Yet now he's giving permission for Aidan to take shelter here.

I hope Aidan sees how generous Charlie is. But that may be too much to ask for.

Victoria reaches out and grabs Charlie's hand. She pulls him so he sits down beside her on the bed. "Charlie. Come talk to us." She points to a red mark by his collarbone, barely visible in the glow from her nightlight. "Who is doing this to you? Can you please just tell us, so we can help you? It's making me sick. And angry."

"Vicky. It's nothing. It's not important. I'm fine."

"Buddy." Aidan leans forward to make eye contact with Charlie. "Is it your dad? It's really okay to tell us if it's your dad. I know he gets drunk sometimes. My dad used to hit me once in a while, before he moved out. I am totally judgment-free on this one. I didn't tell anyone either. I would understand."

Charlie's bottom lip starts to quiver. "Dad?" he asks in a small voice. His eyes fill with tears and he doesn't look at Aidan. Instead, he searches Victoria's face. "You really think it might be Dad? Our dad?"

"I don't know, Charlie," she answers, all in a rush. "No. Definitely no. That is, I don't know. I'm just trying to figure it out. I mean, I don't know if Dad likes . . ." She stops short. "I wasn't sure how he felt about your hair, and the clothes, and whatever. He just hasn't said anything to me. I mean, he never talks about it."

Charlie bows his head. "It's not Dad," he says as quietly as I've ever heard him speak, his eyes glassy.

And then he tells a story. It's one I've never heard before.

Chapter 24
Snow Day

Just a few moons ago, before the holidays, we had a tremendous amount of snow fall to the ground all in one day. It came down hard from the time the sun came up in the morning until long past when the sun set in the early afternoon.

Where we live, it snows often enough that a little bit of snow is not a big deal. But sometimes, heavy snow makes it difficult for humans to get around on foot or by car. On this particular day, Mom and Dad did not go to work, and the children did not go to school. Mom worried aloud that the storm might cause us to lose our lights and heat.

After lunch, Kevin put on his snow pants and went out sledding. Victoria trudged through the snow to a friend's house on the block to watch a movie on TV. Mom ran out to the store to stock up on milk and bread before the snow got too deep.

Charlie tells Victoria and Aidan that he was in his room with me, as usual, curled up on the bed. I have only a vague recollection of that day. I could see out the window that it was snowing hard, so I knew my family wouldn't allow me to go outside. So I relaxed with Charlie—stretching, napping, and staying cozy.

Charlie said it was just by chance, because he was hungry, that he got up and went for a walk around the house. This is where he and I parted ways, as I believe I stayed sleeping on his bed all afternoon.

The way he tells the story, he wandered into Victoria's room, and out the window he saw a solitary figure on the dock of the sailing club. Standing there in the snowstorm. The snow was coming down so hard he couldn't see much of the river or the marsh, as the landscape faded into a whitewash. But he could see the person on the dock, and it was a man who didn't look like he was bundled up properly for a squall. He was just wearing jeans, and a flannel shirt with a down vest. And sneakers—sneakers of all things!

This was what made Charlie really stop and stare. And then he realized: It was Dad.

I imagine that in that moment, Charlie felt a pang of cold. I have always sensed that Charlie is in tune with Dad. When his dad is suffering, he feels it too.

He made his way downstairs, at first slowly. He found his snow pants, pulled them on, and tucked them into his boots. That's when he realized he was alone in the house. He thought he had heard Dad walk with Kevin out to the garage to find the sleds, but it was only then for the first time that Charlie realized he hadn't heard Dad come back in. Charlie began to hurry, to get his winter coat on, put on a hat, pull up the hood of his coat over the hat and fasten it, and find two matching gloves. He tied a big black scarf around his neck.

He hurried out the front door, down the steps, and ran across the street. The road had only been plowed once that morning, so Charlie had to stomp down to the sailing club entrance in snow that came up over his ankles.

The gate was unlocked. Charlie ran across the empty parking lot the best he could in thick boots and snow pants.

He was out of breath by the time he reached the river, his

lungs aching from the cold. "DAD," he called out, once he was absolutely sure it was Dad.

There was no response.

"JEREMY ANDERSON," Charlie tried. But Dad still didn't turn around. He stood on the edge of the dock, looking out at the heavy snow pouring from the sky. It melted when it fell into the river, but accumulated on the marsh grass.

Charlie trudged down the dock carefully, afraid he might slip. The day was quiet, Charlie says, the way it always is when it snows hard. He heard no bird calls; he saw no movement at all. Dad should have been able to hear his youngest son calling to him.

"Dad, what are you doing out here?" Charlie asked when he got close.

It was only then that Dad turned. Charlie recognized the green eyes, the vacant stare, the hollow angles of his face. "Charlie."

"Aren't you freezing? The thermometer says it's, like, ten degrees out."

Charlie hadn't actually looked at the thermometer. He tells Victoria and Aidan that he was making this up. But his toes were already getting cold. Ten degrees would have been a good guess.

Dad had his hands stuffed in the pockets of his pants. "Charlie," he croaked out, "I was just thinking. We found a kid last week. He overdosed."

"Oh. Yeah?"

"He was in an abandoned building and he wasn't much older than you." Charlie watched his dad's face fall as he spoke. "He reminded me of you. He was so young. He looked so fragile. He had a young face, like yours, if you know what I mean." Dad winced with the memory. "People aren't always nice, Charlie, out there in the world. They're not always nice to people who are a little different, people who feel things deeply.

People like you. You might not know it yet. But it makes me feel like I don't want you to ever leave the house again."

"What, Dad?" Charlie was confused. And getting scared. Dad was rambling. "Dad, I know all about it. You don't need to worry so much. Let's go inside. Aren't your feet cold? My feet are freezing. I can't feel my toes."

"Jesus, Charlie. I wish . . ." Dad turned away. "I wish you . . . Christ. That kid looked horrible. He probably ran away from home. I bet he had nowhere to go. And the people he hooked up with treated him very badly." Then he turned to Charlie abruptly, stepped forward, and took him in his arms.

"Dad? It's okay, Dad." Charlie let Dad hug him.

"Please don't get hurt, Charlie. Don't go with people you don't know. Don't meet people over the Internet. Don't—"

"Dad. DAD. I'm not stupid. And I'm not a street urchin." He squirmed to get out of his dad's grip and push him away. "I'm not a runaway or an abandoned orphan. At least, not yet. I think I'll be okay." Charlie laughed uncomfortably. "I get it, Dad. Strangers are bad. Drugs are bad. Okay, I get it. Whatever. C'mon. I'll be fine. I think I hear a hot chocolate calling my name. We can get some candy canes and—"

And this is when it happened. Dad fell on his knees. He didn't slip, Charlie said. He just sunk down, as if ready to pray. And he held Charlie's gloves tight in his bare hands.

"Charlie," Dad said, looking up at his son, his eyes filling with tears. "Listen to me. The world isn't a great place all the time. Not everyone is going to be nice to you. I worry about you. So much. Every day." He gulped in a deep, shaky breath. "Don't get discouraged. Don't end up like me. I can't seem to get better. I can't stop thinking bad thoughts. I can't stop drinking when I feel bad. And then I do and say stupid things. I'm sorry. It's just so heavy. It's hard carrying it around all the time. You have to be very careful. Be safe. And take care of yourself."

Charlie frowned, looking down at his dad kneeling in the snow. He decided his dad had drunk one too many beers in the garage, which happened from time to time.

Here he pauses the story to tell Victoria that he is sick of Dad drinking. And now that Dad lets Kevin drink beer with him while they watch baseball at his apartment, he finds their weekends together very depressing. While Dad just gets tired and numb when he drinks, Charlie explains, Kevin gets angry and irritable.

"I know," Victoria says. "I agree. Kevin's been an asshole lately. But there's no point in us arguing with Dad about his drinking. I don't think we're going to get him to change his mind if Mom can't."

Charlie nods, and goes back to his story:

Standing in the snow, Charlie promised, "Okay, Dad." The tips of his fingers felt numb. "I'll be super careful. But we have to go in. We might get blown off the dock and into the river, or something. Or we might get trapped in here by the snowplow that's going around the neighborhood."

Charlie glanced back at the house. And that's when he realized he could barely see the house because the wind had picked up and the snow was coming down hard in big flakes. Visibility was dropping fast.

Dad shook his head. "You go in. I don't want to go in."

"What?"

"I've still got some things to think about, Charlie. You're going to get frostbite out here. You shouldn't be out here, buddy. I'll meet you inside. You go ahead. Be safe."

Charlie felt a pang of pain in his stomach, a warm pit of anxiety starting to boil up toward his chest. "Dad," he pleaded, starting to panic. "NO. Come in with me now, or Kevin or Mom are gonna have to come out here, and it won't be safe for them." He cleared his throat and started to shout. "It's not safe for us either. We have to go in. YOU'RE DRIVING ME CRAZY. You're driving

Mom crazy too." He yelled over the sound of the wind starting to howl. All of his anger bubbled up and he felt his heart clench. Charlie's head was pounding and his eyes watered and nose started to run. He wiped at his wet face with a glove, and he never had felt so crazy hot and freezing cold at the same time. "Stop acting like this, like a baby. Just COME INSIDE. And lie down. Goddamm it, I'm not going in without you. So you'd better GET THE HELL UP."

Something in Dad seemed to snap to attention, because he opened his eyes wide. And then he stood.

"I'm sorry," Dad said. "Go ahead. I'll follow you."

And that's when Charlie got the strangest feeling of all. He got the impression that if he went first, he would be returning home alone. That he'd start down the dock, and when he reached land he would look back, and there would be nothing left but the white storm swirling behind him.

"No," Charlie announced, feeling his cheeks burn. Ice was starting to form on the ends of his hair. "No. You go first." He gritted his teeth to growl at Dad. "I'll follow you. GO."

Dad looked down at his youngest son. And he finally caved in. He turned and started to walk back down the dock, toward home. Head hanging down, eyes blinking against the stinging gusts of wintry air.

Charlie said that when they got back, Dad started a fire. Dad kept dropping the wood because his hands were blue and numb. His whole body was shivering uncontrollably. Once they got the fire started, he brought his dad many blankets and a hot coffee and told him to lie on the couch. The snow in Dad's hair melted and dripped down his neck as if he was sweating on a hot day. Dad was feverish and didn't seem to know where he was at times.

When Mom got home, ranting about how bad the roads were, Charlie didn't say anything about what had happened. Dad did not either. He lay comatose on the couch all afternoon, wrapped in his blanket, looking sick and shaking and unable to warm up for a long time.

"My point is, I promise you, it's not Dad," Charlie says to Victoria to end his story. "Dad would never hurt me. Please just stop bugging me about it, okay?"

"Charlie." Victoria frowns. "Okay. I believe you."

"Yeah, buddy," Aidan says, resting his head on one hand. "Sorry. I didn't know your dad was . . . like that."

I'm sorry too. I stare at Charlie. *You shouldn't have to take care of your own Dad.*

We hear Gretel breathing and bumping her head against the door. Victoria gets up and lets her in, closing the door once more. Gretel trots right over to the bed, so everyone can pet her.

"If it's someone at school, you know, you could tell me," Aidan goes on. "Maybe I know the kid. Maybe I could tell him to back off. At least I'd know what we're dealing with. What the angles are. How we could approach it."

"Okay, thanks," Charlie states, but he's looking down at his knees. "Look, let's forget about it, okay? Just drop it. My mom is getting really worried, and that's the last thing she needs right now."

"We're all worried, Charlie. But okay. For now." Victoria stands up next to Gretel, who is wagging her tail. She looks at the boys, from one to the other. "I could use a little help getting Aidan out of here unnoticed. Think you could help us? I'm going to go into Mom's bedroom and get into bed with her to make sure she's sleeping. You stand guard and distract Kevin if he comes out of his room."

Charlie grimaces. I don't think he loves that idea.

But when Charlie sees their eager faces, it must occur to him: They are offering to help him, and they need his help in return. And maybe this would be beneficial for everyone.

Go ahead, Charlie. Help them now, and maybe they will help you later.

I search Aidan's face. At one point I thought he was Charlie's bully. Now I wonder: Could he be Charlie's savior? Could he find the bully in school, confront him, and make it all stop? Could it really work? Could it possibly be that easy?

I'm not entirely sure.

But I do think Aidan could be intimidating if he wanted to be. I'm sure I am not the only one who sees that potential in him.

"All right." Charlie shrugs. He rubs his arms with both hands, and I think he must be getting cold from having no shirt on. I get up and rub against his feet, so he picks me up and holds me to his chest. I have a lot of body fat, which on top of the fur makes me a nice warming device.

"Thanks," Victoria whispers. "I'll go first." She leaves the room.

"Hey," Aidan says to Charlie as he stands up and stretches. "You did a good job. With your dad. Getting him to come inside." Aidan grabs his sweatshirt off the floor and pulls it over his head. "I probably would have given up."

Charlie nods cautiously.

I am impressed too! I didn't know Charlie made Dad come inside during that snowstorm. He's a smart, courageous boy.

And I am terrifically relieved. I knew Dad wouldn't hurt Charlie. This time, I was right.

While carrying me, Charlie follows Aidan out to the hallway. We watch Aidan make his way down the stairs in the dark as quietly as he can. And then we go back to bed.

I am fairly sure Kevin did not hear anything. I certainly hope he did not. I know he would never approve.

Chapter 25
Gorgeous

Later that week, Charlie comes home and he is not alone. I am very surprised, but it is not Karen who walks up the front steps with him.

No, it is Ronaldo! I am surprised.

I suppose Ronaldo must have the day off from sailing. Sure enough, I never hear the yellow bus rolling into the parking lot across the street.

It's funny, but to see Charlie and Ronaldo together makes me realize that all of Charlie's friends are girls. Kevin has several male friends who come over from time to time, to play video games or watch TV or eat Mom's spaghetti. But Charlie has never had a boy over that I remember.

"Kevin?" Charlie calls out, from the foot of the stairs. But Kevin is not here. Charlie lets out the breath he's been holding, and then shows Ronaldo where to put his sneakers, on the mat.

On the mat! Charlie lines his sneakers up too, nice and straight. Well, well, well. I've never seen *that* before. I think Charlie is acting very grown-up.

Charlie and Ronaldo make themselves a snack and then settle onto the green couch in the living room at the front of the house. They look very cozy, with a bowl of corn chips and a plate of peanut butter sandwiches between them. I jump up to sit behind Charlie on the back of the couch. His hand absent-mindedly reaches up to scratch between my ears, and I look down at the boys.

"What's your cat's name?" Ronaldo asks.

"Lily. Isn't she gorgeous?"

"Very much so."

Well! I like this Ronaldo already. He has good taste.

"She has pretty eyes, doesn't she?" Charlie smiles up at me.

"Oh, sure." Ronaldo picks a pillow up off the floor and sticks it in the corner of the couch so he can lean back and face Charlie. "Although her eyes aren't as nice as yours, Charlie."

Charlie's eyes flicker to the side, but he doesn't turn his head. He just shrugs, acting like it's every day of the week that a boy sits next to him on this couch in the living room and compliments his looks.

He doesn't respond at all. I think he is frozen with Not-Knowing-What-To-Say.

But honestly, it is true. Charlie's eyes are clear and kind.

They might—*might*—be even more attractive than mine. I can't really say one way or the other, because I've never seen my own eyes.

Minutes go by. The faces of the boys glow, and I don't think either one of them is really watching the TV, although they study it intently, as if they are learning something important and must listen very carefully.

The noise from the TV is quiet at times, and blaringly loud at others. I start to drift off to sleep.

Eventually I am startled awake by the *whoosh* of the front door. I look up to see Victoria and Aidan entering the house and taking off their shoes on the front mat. They stop short at the entrance to the living room.

This is their couch, their spot. The kissing spot.

"Are you kidding me?" Aidan whispers, sounding both annoyed and surprised.

Victoria smacks his arm. "Hi, Ronaldo," she calls out. "Did Charlie offer you a drink?"

"Oh, yes," Ronaldo answers. "Thanks. I have some iced tea. I'm all set."

Aidan scratches his chin and nods at Ronaldo. "Hey, buddy. I'm Aidan. I've seen you around. You're new, huh?"

"Yes."

"You moved here from Mexico, or something?"

Ronaldo glances at Charlie, and they both crack a smile. "Noooo. No. I'm from Uruguay. My dad got transferred here for work."

"Oh." Aidan frowns. He looks like he has no idea where Uruguay might be.

Honestly, I have no idea either. It must be somewhere across the river.

When Victoria and Aidan have left the room to get their own snacks from the kitchen, Charlie breaks out into a big smile. I can tell he is trying not to burst out laughing. He probably finds Aidan's reaction funny. Aidan thought he would have the couch all to himself forever? He thought wrong. Charlie turns to bury his face in the couch cushion until he can control himself.

"Sorry," Charlie finally says. He clears his throat and sits up straighter.

"Charlie." Ronaldo sits up and leans over the bowl of chips to put his hand gently on Charlie's elbow. "Are you going to the dance at school next week?"

Charlie stares down at his arm, where Ronaldo is touching him. I see the shock in his eyes, the sheer terror. He doesn't move. I don't think he even breathes.

"What?"

Why is Charlie so nervous?

And it is only then that my nose twitches, and I realize I detect pheromones coming off of Charlie in waves. That never happens when Karen is here. It is almost as if maybe he wants—

I look up at Charlie. He has frozen at Ronaldo's touch, his cheeks reddening.

Oh! I realize that I have missed something all along.

And—how strange that it never occurred to me before! This just gets curiouser and curiouser. But, of course. I see now that Charlie is interested in Ronaldo as a potential mate. It explains why Charlie has not showed any interest in Karen, other than as a friend.

Finally, Charlie takes a quick glance back up at Ronaldo. "I guess so. I went to the dance in the fall, and it was okay. So I mean, maybe." He shrugs, and tries to smile. But he's overwhelmed, and looks pained. "I hadn't really thought about it."

Ronaldo quickly pulls his hand back. "I was just wondering. It might be fun." He quickly turns his face back toward the TV and settles again into the corner of the couch.

Charlie looks like he's going to pass out. His face has gone pale. He's too nervous to even respond.

C'mon, Charlie, I plead to him. *You can do a little better than that. Come on!* I get up and nudge my wet nose into his ear. But he doesn't react. He's as stiff as a board.

However, he does keep checking. Glancing over at Ronaldo sitting on our couch. As if he might be dreaming it.

Victoria and Aidan come down the hallway with their hands full of sodas and small bags of chips. They stop before turning to go up the stairs. "Charlie would love to go to the dance, Ronaldo," Victoria says in a singsong voice. She grins at the boys. "Aidan is driving. You should come. We could pick you up. But I have to warn you: My brother's a terrible dancer."

She hops up the stairs on light feet. Charlie watches his sister. His mouth hangs open, but no words come out.

Aidan shakes his head before following her. "I can't believe you stole my couch, man." He raises an eyebrow and gives Charlie a *look*.

Charlie finally smiles.

Well! This is surprising, but at the same time, the humans continually impress me. It is a beautiful thing about humans, how advanced and complex they are. It seems I learn something new about them all the time.

It isn't long before the front door swings open one more time. Kevin enters and drops his backpack on the floor. He reaches down to unlace his sneakers.

When he lifts his head and sees Charlie and Ronaldo on the couch, he freezes. Charlie and Kevin stare at each other for a long moment. Charlie is the first to look away.

Kevin stands up straight. "Charlie. Why are you sitting there watching TV? What about your homework?" He glances down the hall toward the kitchen. "And please don't tell me you forgot to take out Gretel. Where is she? You knew I was going to be late getting home—have you walked Gretel yet?" Kevin makes his voice louder than it needs to be. He puts his hands on his hips and grinds his teeth.

"No," Charlie mutters, eyes searching the floor. "I haven't taken her out. I was just—"

"THEN WHY ARE YOU SITTING THERE? You're so irresponsible. Don't you care about your own dog?" Kevin's hands clench into fists.

"C'mon," Charlie says to Ronaldo, his voice breaking, "let's walk Gretel."

Ronaldo's eyebrow arches up. "Right now?" He gestures toward the TV. I suppose their show is not over.

"Yeah." Charlie stands and reaches out a hand to pull Ronaldo to his feet.

Ronaldo looks over at Kevin, puzzled. But Kevin doesn't

move or introduce himself. He just shakes his head, as if sickened at Charlie's behavior.

The two boys walk down the hall to the kitchen, not talking. I hear the rattling of Gretel's leash clicking onto her harness. Then the back door creaks open and slams shut.

I feel my eyes widen as I glare accusingly at Kevin. Just when we finally have a truce with the clever fox, now it is *Kevin* who sends Charlie fleeing from his own home?

I imagine Kevin as a black bear. Quiet until provoked. But then: fierce and unforgiving, roaring out orders.

No. No, no, no, no, no.

I don't even know what I'm doing until I'm in action, leaping toward Kevin, my claws drawn. He is wearing shorts in this warm weather, and I draw blood as I slash his leg.

"HEY," he howls, reaching a hand forward to swat me.

He catches only my fur as I run for my life, nails scraping on the wood floor. I manage to sprint to the study and hide under the couch. I hear Kevin's heavy footsteps as he tromps around looking for me, but I'm squeezed up against the wall behind the sagging couch springs, where I am not reachable.

I stay there for hours. Angry. Seething. I am sick and tired of Charlie being mistreated. I'm glad I scratched Kevin. I've had enough! I refuse to apologize.

Chapter 26
Obviously Completely

I'm hiding out in my favorite spot, under the large, overgrown holly bush by the garage. The leaves are sharp and perhaps this is not the kind of spot most creatures would find welcoming. But the leaves are also thick and hard and still. They do not quiver in the breeze. So once I am hidden, I am confident I will remain out of sight.

A bird calls from a hiding spot in the tall grass. He's shouting out a warning to his friends. It's the time of night when predators emerge, knowing they will not have to expend too much energy chasing their prey, thanks to the cool air.

Just as the sun is hitting the horizon of the river, I am surprised to see Mark's black truck pull into the driveway. He usually comes earlier in the day. The truck tires crunching the gravel sound a little like when Charlie makes popcorn in the microwave.

Pop, snap, click.

One of the garage doors starts to glide up, so I guess Mom is expecting him. A light clicks on, emitting a golden glow from the garage. It casts a warm light, in contrast to the cold pink and gray sky as the sun sets over the marsh.

Mark gets out of his truck and comes up the driveway. He walks into the garage just as Mom comes out from the kitchen, shutting the door behind her. She hurries to him, and falls immediately into his arms.

Grabbing his hair with two hands, she pulls him down to her eager, waiting mouth. He can't help smiling when she kisses him. He put his hands on her waist to hold her steady. Mark is as focused as Mom is frantic.

Ah! I think she loves him, for whatever that's worth. Although I have not heard her admit it, I think it must be true. For all that Mom fought Mark's demands to tell the children about their relationship, and stated that she still loves Dad, she has a big heart. And I imagine that a love for Mark has grown there, making room for itself in a warm pocket, where it thrives.

As I have seen, once the head and heart have gone, it is easy for the body to follow. Mom presses against him as if she hasn't seen him in ages.

"Mark." Mom sighs.

Pausing, Mark looks sad, almost mournful. But he is also so, so happy to be with Mom. "Sweetheart." He gently runs a hand over her hair. "The kids are home?" he asks, with an anxious glance at the garage door.

Mom nods. Her little hand is curled into a fist and she pulls at the material of his shirt, up by his shoulder. "Your truck. Come on. We can come back in twenty minutes."

"Okay." He takes her hand and they run to the truck. He helps her into the passenger seat before walking around to his side of the truck, jangling the keys in his hand. As soon as the engine roars to life, the truck starts backing urgently out of the driveway. And then it drives away.

Well! Mom has obviously completely lost her mind.

But it's satisfying, being right most of the time. I think she is crazy about him.

I turn when I hear different humans talking. The sound is coming from the back of the house. The voices get louder as they get closer.

I hear a sharp laugh, and I see it is Kevin and one of his best friends, Phil. I am no longer angry at Kevin, but I have been avoiding him. I'm a little embarrassed about my outburst.

Phil is a nice boy, like Kevin. He has very short hair and a wide smile. The boys have been friends for many years. They share a love of fast cars and loud TV shows, and sometimes they go camping. Once in a while they will have an expansive debate about big, important things that I don't understand— the workings of the universe or something like that—and Victoria will just laugh at them if she hears them and tell them they're "nuts."

I am surprised to see Kevin walk right up to Dad's private cabinet. Kevin slips something small from the front pocket of his jeans, and I see it is a key.

Interesting! I didn't know Kevin had a key.

Phil talks about something funny that happened in school while Kevin opens the cabinet. He pulls out a big heavy bottle. It is almost full of a clear liquid.

"Whoa," Phil says, his mouth hanging open. "That's your dad's?"

"Yeah." Kevin screws off the cap and sniffs at the bottle opening. His head jerks back.

"I bet it's harsh."

"You wanna try it?"

Try it? Are the boys going to drink Dad's special medicine?

"Me?" Phil takes a step back and laughs. "No, man. You can, if you want."

"No thanks." Kevin grins and closes the bottle back up. "It's gross. There's plenty of beer in here, but it's not cold."

"That's okay. Gimme one."

Both boys soon have a green bottle in their hands. Phil pulls a knife out of his back pocket, snaps it open, and applies pressure to flip off the caps, one bottle at a time.

"Cheers." Phil takes a long drink, and Kevin does too.

Kevin sits his bottle down on the concrete floor, and reaches into the cabinet. He pulls out a gun.

A gun?

"That's your dad's too?"

"Yeah. He has a few. For work. And whatever."

Phil tips his head and studies the gun. "It's not loaded, is it?"

Kevin's eyes open wide. "Nah. It can't be, right? I mean, it shouldn't be. I doubt it. My dad's totally into gun safety. I'd be really surprised if it were."

Kevin stands up very straight, stretches his arm out, and points at an imaginary target in the street.

"Dude, put it down," Phil says, with a hearty laugh. "What if someone drives by and sees you?"

"Okay." Kevin puts the gun back.

"I mean, I realize I'm talking to the two-time winner of the Rifle Range Poker Run, but seriously. You could get in trouble if the cops drive by."

"Yeah," says Kevin, smiling. "Don't forget who you're talking to. Two-time winner. And four-time laser tag champion."

"Oh! Here we go." Phil rolls his eyes. "You have to keep rubbing that in, huh?"

The boys stand in the garage and finish their drinks, talking about this and that. Kevin throws the empty bottles in the big bin where Dad puts his own bottles.

"Where'd your mom go?" Phil asks before they go back in the house.

Kevin shrugs. "She said she was running out and she'd be right back." He sighs. "I guess she went out with her loser boyfriend." He turns to stare mindlessly into the distance. "I hate him."

"Aw, he can't be that bad, can he?"

"Sure he could. He quit his job as a lawyer and had no backup plan. He's not responsible, like my dad." Kevin shakes his head. He shuts the cabinet and locks it. "Come on. Let's get something to eat."

I watch them go. I'm not really surprised Kevin is hungry. He's always hungry, my black bear. He is obsessed with food, much like Gretel.

By the time Mark's truck comes back, driving at a normal speed this time, the sky is dark. The frogs have started to croak out a song with no tune. Mark parks in the driveway once again, and this time he leaves the engine running and Mom doesn't get out right away. I can see them talking. Mark is telling her a story and laughing, reaching out to touch her hair as he talks, and she leans her head back and smiles. She listens to him a good while before kissing him good-bye once, and then twice, and then there's more nonsense that doesn't need repeating.

Oh, but believe me—I understand. This man held me before too, remember.

Once he cradled me, I was in no hurry to leave. His arms are just right for holding someone in a way that I felt safe and secure. I don't know how else to explain it.

Okay, and there it is, a final good-bye kiss. Mom slides out of the truck and floats up the driveway. She waves again at Mark. He makes sure she is all the way inside the house before leaving again.

I am happy for Mom. But there is something not right here that is bothering me.

When and how did Kevin get a key to Dad's cabinet? Dad never lets anyone near his cabinet. I've never seen Kevin open it before and drink Dad's beer. And I have not seen Kevin take out Dad's gun in the past. I didn't know that Kevin even realized where it was.

I remember what Victoria and Aidan said about guns. About humans using them to kill other people.

No, I will say it again: Something is not right here. Something is not right at all.

I go for a walk in the darkness to clear my head. I must warn Mom about Kevin's behavior. I wonder if Gretel knows about this.

I have been mostly focused on my sweet Charlie.

And, slowly, I start to wonder if I've been worrying about the wrong boy all along.

Chapter 27
Purple Headband

Days later, Aidan lies across Victoria's bedspread, head on her pillow. She is playing the radio softly, and he sings along.

Aidan. Singing! This is something I never expected to hear.

Mom does not enforce the "Aidan cannot go upstairs" rule anymore. I think she has given up. And Aidan's behavior has been acceptable.

Not perfect, no. He still eats too much of the family food and drinks all of the soda. He curses, which Mom does not like. And there is too much kissing, even for Mom. But overall, he has been doing okay.

I am lying on the floor near the window. I don't like music very much. It hurts my sensitive ears. But this is a sad song and not too loud. Truth be told, Aidan has a decent singing voice.

He sings something about love.

Victoria stops what she is doing, rifling through the clothes in her closet. "Wow." She turns toward Aidan, holding a black dress on a hanger in her hand, and rolls her eyes. "You're so sentimental and deep. Who knew?"

He ignores her and keeps singing. I turn to see Charlie appear in the doorway. He looks mystified.

"Wow. You know the words to this song?"

Aidan doesn't move, but his eyes pan over to where Charlie stands. "Of course I know it. You don't need to be so impressed. You'd better be careful. I'll tell Ronaldo you were complimenting me, and he'll get jealous."

At first, Charlie's face flushes pink. "Shut up." But then he can't help but smile. He bites his lip to try and stop himself, but he can't.

"Ha ha," Victoria says, pulling out a purple dress. "Charlie. You're so busted. Everyone in school knows Ronaldo likes you."

"We're not . . ." Charlie comes into the room and leans on a tall bookcase. "We're not together. I mean, we *are* going to the dance together, but just as friends." He looks over at Aidan again. "You know, your voice isn't too bad."

Aidan suddenly rolls over to face Charlie, leaning on one elbow. "I know, right?" he asks, excited. "I mean, it's not good. But it's not terrible either." His eyes shine and I can tell he is pleased.

Aidan is starting to get comfortable here in our house.

Victoria sighs. "What am I going to wear to the Winter Ball? I hate all of these old dresses." She whirls on her brother. "What are *you* going to wear?"

"Vicky," Aidan interrupts, while playing with a stuffed dog that sits on her bed. "We're not going to that school dance. I told you. It's lame."

"No, we're going." She opens her closet door wider. "I have a handsome young man taking me." Reaching in, she pulls out a sparkly gold skirt. "Maybe I can mix and match."

Charlie makes a gagging noise. Victoria quickly sticks the skirt back in her closet.

Charlie tosses his head to get the hair out of his eyes. "I think I'm going to wear my white T-shirt, ripped black jeans, and high-top sneakers," he announces with confidence. "Or maybe my purple T-shirt. But I need another accessory. I mean, they do call it a *ball*. So I need something a little fancy." He walks over to her bureau and opens a drawer. "Can I borrow a headband?"

Victoria shrugs. "Sure. I haven't worn any of those since fifth grade."

He pulls out a thin silver headband and places it on his head. "What do you think?"

"I can barely see it against your hair. Try the purple one. It would match your purple shirt."

He pulls out a dark headband. It is thicker than the last one, smooth and shiny, and has a small flower on one side.

"What do you think?"

"Oooh," she gushes. "That's nice with your hair color. Honestly. That's the right one."

Charlie tentatively glances back at Aidan. And waits for a response.

"No comment, dude. Your sister's got me on a short leash. But . . ." Aidan puts the stuffed dog aside and sticks his hands behind his head. "Okay, honestly? You look like a girl. But what else is new? Ronaldo will probably love it."

Charlie makes a face at Aidan, then turns back to Victoria. "Let me wear it a little and see if it grows on me. I guess when I wake up on the day of the ball I'll see if it feels like a *boy day* or a *girl day*."

Aidan cocks his head. He asks, "Is that all you do? Just wake up, and you feel one way or the other?"

Hmm. I'm curious about this too. Is that how Charlie feels sometimes? I didn't know he felt that way. I mean, not exactly.

"Well, yeah," Charlie answers, as if it's the most obvious thing in the world.

Aidan's mouth hangs open as he pauses to consider his next comment. "You know . . . they do have surgery for stuff like that. If you want."

Charlie scowls. "I never said I wanted to be a girl all the

time, did I? I like being a boy sometimes." He puts his hands on his hips. "I like my boy parts."

Victoria snorts and keeps rearranging clothes in her closet.

"Yeah, but . . ." Aidan sits up a little, leaning on one elbow, "Don't you want to make a choice, one or the other? I mean, how is that going to work long-term?" Aidan doesn't break eye contact. He seems to be challenging Charlie, but not in a threatening way. He just wants to know.

Charlie blinks, his clear green eyes never wavering from Aidan's gaze. "It works fine. You don't really need to worry about it."

Aidan nods and lays back down, seeming finally satisfied. "Okay. Yeah, you're right."

Charlie touches his sister's arm. "Thanks." When she nods, he turns and leaves the room.

Aidan sighs. "Vic. Stop worrying about dresses. We're not going to the school dance. It's going to suck."

"I'm going," Victoria states. "You can make up your mind to come or not, but I'll be there." She scours her closet, pushing aside one outfit and then another. The noise of the hanger scraping along the bar hurts my ears. I escape to the hallway.

I see Kevin is just coming up the stairs, dragging his feet as if they're too heavy to lift. At the top of the stairs he turns right and heads toward me, and I have to jump out of the way. Granted, I'm sitting right in the middle of the hall, but it's unlike him not to step politely over me.

How rude! What is his problem?

I follow him into his bedroom, where Charlie is looking in Kevin's closet. "Oh, sorry," Charlie gushes. "I was just . . . Vicky and I were just talking about the Winter Ball, and I can't find one of my T-shirts. You know, the purple one? I thought maybe Mom stuck it in the wrong closet."

"What?"

It's funny, because Kevin is squinting at Charlie the way

Dad would. As if he's trying to decide who Charlie is, and what he's doing here.

"My purple—"

"What the hell is in your hair?"

"Oh!" Charlie's hand flutters up to feel what is on his head, as if he's already forgotten. "It's Vicky's headband. We were just trying it out because I might wear it to the dance."

Kevin takes a step toward Charlie, towering over him. "To the school dance? Where my friends can see you? You're going to wear that crap in your hair?"

Charlie flinches. "I don't know," he says tentatively, moving backward toward the closet. "Maybe not."

"Goddamn it, Charlie. It's one thing to humiliate me here in the house, but you have to drag your weirdness into school too? You don't think that affects me at all? You don't think that changes how people look at me? Jesus Christ."

And in one swift move, Kevin moves forward, overtakes Charlie, and twists his arm behind his back.

Kevin is bigger, taller, stronger.

He is the baby-faced, good older brother.

So what in the world—?

To my surprise, Charlie does not make a sound. He does not cry out. He does not even whimper. He just shuts his eyes as tight as he can and grits his teeth. And then he curses out Kevin with some very, very, very bad words muttered under his breath.

Ah! My Charlie is tougher than I thought he was.

I *yeow!* in protest.

"Knock it off. You're driving me CRAZY," Kevin growls. He hovers over Charlie, talking into his ear from behind, speaking softly but with a menace that I rarely hear from him. He keeps Charlie in a tight grip, sliding one arm around Charlie's neck, the other holding his arm behind his back. My eyes open wide. I can see Charlie can barely breathe, his face flushing, and I freeze in fear. "And you're driving Dad crazy. It's your fault

Dad is messed up. I have had it. SHUT IT DOWN. Right now. I don't want to see it again."

Where in the world is this coming from? I feel my heart beating hard.

I'm furious. I *hiss!*

Kevin startles, as if coming out of a trance. And then, in one move, he releases Charlie with a hard shove while ripping the headband off his head. He whips it out into the hallway.

Charlie stumbles forward and bangs his head against the doorframe. His hand flies to his forehead and his eyes fill with tears. Oh my goodness—Charlie will have a bruise that he will not be able to hide. But I suppose he'll come up with some excuse for it.

Charlie spins around. "Have you been drinking? Here?"

"So what if I am?"

"Why would you do that? Don't you see what it's doing to Dad? Don't you think Mom has enough to deal with right now?"

"Just get out." Kevin takes a step forward to give Charlie a final push with both hands. "Leave me alone."

I back away as Charlie staggers out into the bright light of the hall. He goes straight into his bedroom.

I hear him climb onto his bed and lie down. He doesn't bother to put a light on.

The house is silent for a moment.

And then my ears twitch as I hear the low sound of Aidan mumbling something, and Victoria's sharp laugh in response. I watch as Kevin appears in his doorway and listens. I am worried. He still looks angry. The hall light casts an eerie yellow glow over his face.

Something is seriously wrong.

We need help.

I give a sharp *rowr!* I want to cry out: *Help! Mom! Dad! Someone!* But Mom is not here, Dad has moved out, and there is no one to help.

Kevin ignores me and storms past, nearly stomping on my paw. When he bursts into Victoria's room, slamming her door open, I hear her cry out in surprise: "Hey!"

"YOU'RE NOT SUPPOSED TO BE UPSTAIRS."

"Dude." I pad over just in time to see Aidan getting up off the bed, moving deliberately and never taking his eyes off of Kevin. "Your mom's not here. Nobody cares. Why do *you* care?" He steps up and gets right in Kevin's face, so the two young men are chest to chest. "Why are you so concerned all of a sudden?"

For once, Kevin doesn't back down. "It's bad enough that guy Mark is always here. I'm sick of seeing your ugly face over here all the time. Okay?"

"Kevin," Victoria scolds him. "STOP." She shoves her brother in the shoulder. "Get out of here. You're not the boss around here."

"Maybe I am," he says, turning toward her. "Without Dad here, it seems like everyone just does whatever the hell they want. And Mom's not paying any attention."

Aidan folds his arms over his chest. "Hey. Kev. Back off my girl. You seriously want to fight me? *Me?*" He opens his eyes wider in mock surprise. "Because I'm not leaving unless your sister wants me to."

Kevin takes a quick step back and blinks. But he doesn't take his eyes off Aidan. "You're a jerk, you know that? What do you mean, *your girl*? I doubt you'll be saying that six weeks from now, when she realizes what a jackass you are."

ME-OWWW! I cry out as loud as I can.

And, just then, I hear the scratch of nails on wood and then the thumping of paws. Gretel comes bounding up the stairs at a gallop.

She heard me!

My hero!

Trotting in, Gretel gives a sharp *bark* that causes all of the humans to startle. She breaks into a long series of howls: *Roo roo roo roo roo roo roo roo roo!*

It's the sweetest sound I've heard all day. I know this will break everyone up.

"Gretel, knock it off," Kevin moans, but she won't stop.

Roo roo roo roo roo!

After a moment, Kevin shrugs and turns to Aidan. "Forget it. Just forget it. You're not worth it."

When he leaves the room, Gretel follows close behind, panting at Kevin's heels.

Victoria runs to Aidan and throws her arms around him as if to protect him from Kevin's words. "Ignore him." She kisses his cheek. "He's an idiot. Please. Don't go."

Aidan squeezes her back. "Nah. He's a pussy. He doesn't scare me. He's cranky though, isn't he?"

She giggles.

I pad back into the hallway. Gretel sits outside Kevin's bedroom door. He has shut her out, the door closed. When Gretel looks back at me, her brown eyes are deep and desolate as always. How can she comfort and protect humans who act unpredictably, and reject her help?

I walk up and touch my nose to her paw. Just to let her know I sympathize. I lick her paw until it is clean.

She allows it, and doesn't move away. This never happens. So I feel good about it.

What is going on? I try to ask her.

When she blinks, I can see she doesn't understand it either. And it is upsetting her.

When Gretel settles down to lie outside Kevin's door, I decide to go to curl up near Charlie's chest, to keep him warm. I jump up to his bed. He is still lying on his stomach, face turned toward the wall, one hand over his injured forehead. When I touch my wet nose to his hand, he throws his arm over me. I lick the salty tears that run silently down his cheek.

Now I know who the bully is. I am the only one in this family who knows. But I don't know how to tell someone. And I am not sure they would believe me if I could.

The truth is more terrible than I ever could have imagined.

It sounds like Charlie hasn't told Mom because he knows how fragile she is right now. He thinks he is protecting Mom. My poor Charlie. He is an innocent boy growing up fast, and he is starting to make the kinds of choices he shouldn't have to make.

I've been so worried about Charlie. And now the whole family is unraveling like a ball of yarn.

There must be a way Gretel and I could work together to repair this family. There is something worth saving in this family—a love that connects all of us and binds us together. I include Dad in this even though he has moved out, and Mark even though he is new. Like raindrops plunking onto the river, causing overlapping circles of waves, each member of our family impacts the next.

If only Gretel and I could talk! I won't give up yet.

Chapter 28
The Best, the Sweetest, and the Greatest

Charlie walks back and forth from his closet to his bed, over and over. I know he's had his outfit planned for some time in preparation for the school Winter Ball. Yet he has not put his clothes on. Wearing nothing but an old towel, he paces back and forth, staring at the outfit he has spread out on his bedspread. I watch him, confused. It's just a simple purple T-shirt, his jeans, underwear, socks, and sneakers.

What's the matter?

He picks up the shirt to look it over, but then puts it back down.

"Charlie!" I hear Victoria yell from across the hall. "Are you ready, or what? Aidan texted to say he'll be here in ten minutes."

Charlie takes in a deep breath and exhales in a dramatic sigh. He still stands there, as if he has all the time in the world. I catch his eye.

Get moving! Why are you standing around? For goodness sake.

"Okay, okay. Almost there," he calls out. Charlie springs into action all at once and pulls on his clothes. "I just have to dry my hair."

I go to check on Victoria while Charlie busies himself in the bathroom. Her dress is simple and black. Mom is helping her buckle up her fancy shoes. Victoria balances with one hand on the top of Mom's head while Mom squats down near her daughter's feet.

"Are you sure these shoes are comfortable?" Mom frowns, looking like she doesn't believe it.

"They're fine." Victoria tosses her hair and adjusts the dress around her hips. "I'll kick them off if they bother me."

"Aidan is driving?" Mom stands and folds her arms, staring at Victoria. "And you're taking Charlie there and bringing him right home afterward?"

"Yeah. And Ronaldo too. You know. The new kid at school. We're giving him a ride." Victoria checks herself again in her mirror before her eyes move to her mom's face. "It'll be fine, Mom. Not a late night."

"Okay." Mom glances down at the rug. "I'm sorry we didn't have time to go shopping for a new dress. You look nice."

"Yeah, this works. Good thing Paige and I are the same size. She's got a ton of dresses." Victoria flashes a grin at Mom to show her it's okay.

Charlie enters the room and stands in the doorway. Victoria squints at him.

"Is that what you're wearing?"

"Yeah." Charlie glances down at his outfit. "This is it. Why? What's wrong?"

"Aren't you forgetting something?"

"Um . . . no."

I walk up and rub my face against Charlie's ankle, to show him I think he looks just fine. Mom knits her brows together.

"Is he not dressed up enough?" Mom gestures toward his

jeans. "He doesn't need a button-up shirt or nicer pants, does he? Kevin used to dress up a little for school dances, but don't some kids go casual?"

"Yeah, some do. I just thought . . ." Victoria hesitates and glances up at Charlie's hair. "I just thought he was planning something else. That's all. But it's fine."

When Mom turns to head down the stairs, Victoria taps Charlie's elbow and then points to his head. They wait a beat in the hallway.

"Where's the headband?" she whispers, her mouth near his ear.

"I don't need it." Charlie doesn't meet her gaze, and pulls away. "It's not important, Vic. I'm not in the mood. Let's just go."

Victoria makes a face. But Charlie doesn't see it. He walks away and heads down the stairs.

Shaking her head, Victoria strides into Charlie's room, tottering in her high-heeled shoes. She flips on the light switch. After a minute she comes out gripping the silky purple headband in her fist, and shoves it into her small black purse.

I catch her eye. *Smart girl!*

She smiles.

Just as she's zipping her bag up, Kevin steps out of his bedroom.

"Hey, Kev. Why aren't you coming? You never miss the dance."

He shrugs. "I've been going every year since seventh grade. Been there, done that."

Victoria nods, assessing him. "Okay. But if you change your mind, just come over to the school. We'll give you a ride home."

"Who will? Aidan?" Kevin snorts. "No thanks. I'd rather walk." He pauses. "I'm going out with Phil anyway to get something to eat."

Victoria shrugs and carefully starts down the stairs, one foot at a time, a hand latched onto the railing. "Suit yourself," she calls over her shoulder. "I guess it'll just be you and Mom. I don't think Mark is coming over."

I watch Kevin's face fall as Victoria mentions Mark's name. His hands clench and his expression hardens. When Victoria reaches the bottom of the stairs, he pulls his phone out of his back pocket and punches the buttons.

"Dad," he says, his voice suddenly boyish. "Hey. What ... what are you doing tonight?"

He turns around in a circle, head bowed, as he listens.

"No, I don't have any. We have the Winter Ball tonight, so the teachers didn't give us any homework." He kicks his toe into the wooden floorboards. I watch dust particles disperse into the air. "Yeah, it's always on a Wednesday night. Every year. Don't you remember ... ? No, I'm not going. I've been four years in a row. I'm sick of it. So, you want to do something?"

Kevin spins around.

"Your stomach? Well, why don't you go to the doctor?" Kevin tips his head, and I can see the little boy he once was in his soft expression. "You should get medicine, Dad. Can't you get something for that?" He closes his eyes and leans one shoulder against the wall. "You don't need fewer pills, Dad, you need *more* pills if your stomach hurts." When he opens his eyes again, they are watering up. "Okay. I'm sorry. Yeah, get some rest. I just wish ... I just wish you were better already." His head drops. "Don't say that, Dad. You'll get better." He shakes his head. "Bye."

Kevin's shoulders slump. He sits down on the dirty, hard floor. I sit a few feet away from him and search his face. When he looks over at me, I blink, but I can see he isn't thinking about me. His mind is elsewhere.

I'm angry with Kevin, but I still feel bad when I see how miserable he is. We've lived together a long time.

Kevin is not a clever fox, like Aidan. I don't think he is capable of planned cruelty. He's always been a good boy. But there's certainly something wrong with him, and I don't know how to fix it. I don't know if Kevin has thought much about the pain he is inflicting on Charlie. I suspect he's trying to control his world, to manipulate what he can, to keep some things the same as everything else changes around him.

It's a battle he's going to lose.

Clearly, Dad has disappointed Kevin. I think Dad has disappointed Charlie too. I'm not sure the boys realize how much they have in common.

I leave Kevin and trot down the stairs to say good-bye to Charlie before he goes. He is sitting at the kitchen table with Mom, while Victoria repeatedly checks her phone. All is quiet. A small floor fan in the back room hums as it rotates.

Charlie. Look at me. Tell Mom. Tell Mom and Victoria about Kevin. Right now.

The fan swooshes and sighs. Moving right to left, and back again. Charlie's foot taps the floor. He runs a finger over his bottom lip. He looks like Kevin, preoccupied and staring into space. But he's anxious for a different reason. I suppose Charlie is nervous about the dance.

Charlie! It's a quiet moment. Tell Mom, so she can talk to Kevin privately while you are out. It will be perfect timing.

"Aidan's here," Victoria announces, standing. Her chair scrapes against the tile as she shoves it back. "He's waiting in the driveway. Let's go."

I jump out of the way. And then they're gone. The moment has passed.

Later that night, Victoria and Aidan open the front door quietly. Charlie and Ronaldo are right behind them, not speaking. They don't know that Mom is not asleep; she's watching TV in the back room.

"Mom!" Victoria startles as she enters the kitchen and hears the television. "I didn't know you were waiting up for us. Aidan was thirsty. I was going to give him a soda, and then he's going to take Ronaldo home."

Mother gets up off the couch and enters the kitchen. She's already in her pajamas, and looks sleepy. "Hi, Aidan. Nice to meet you, Ronaldo." She pulls the belt of her sweater to make sure the knot is tight.

"Hi, Mrs. Anderson," Aidan mutters, suddenly shy, standing behind Victoria.

"Hi," Ronaldo says, eyes bright, stepping forward to shake Mom's hand. "So nice to meet you too."

They all talk briefly in the kitchen. Victoria hands Aidan a cold soda from the refrigerator, which he chugs down. Victoria laughs and tells Mom a few stories about kids at the dance. Ronaldo joins in with a story of his own that gets Mom giggling. Charlie and Aidan stand to the side, listening. Charlie glances up once in a while. Aidan stares at the can he's holding.

"Okay, I'm heading to bed," Mom says with a yawn. "Don't stay up too late. It's a school night."

"Sure." Victoria gulps down a full glass of water. Her dark eye makeup is smudged, and her face is flushed. Charlie looks tired, dark circles under his eyes, his hair in disarray.

Once Mom is gone, Victoria nudges Charlie with an elbow. "It was fun, right? Aren't you glad you went?"

"Sure," he says. "It was good." He can barely manage a smile. He glances over at Ronaldo, who is also waiting to hear his answer.

"So? That's it? Good?"

"Yeah. It was good. Pretty fun. What do you want me to say?" Charlie turns his back to Victoria so he can reach up and grab his own glass out of the kitchen cabinet. He turns on the faucet to fill it with water.

Victoria shakes her head. "Nothing. Never mind." She grabs Aidan by the hand. "It's hot in here. We're going to talk by the

car for a minute. Ronaldo, just come out when you're ready."
She strides off, pulling Aidan in tow behind her, still full of energy.

When we're alone in the kitchen, Charlie hands the glass of water to Ronaldo. He leans back against the counter, but then startles. Reaching behind him, he pulls something out of his back pocket. It's the headband. So, then, perhaps Charlie did wear it! I watch as he slides it on his head. A perfect fit.

Ronaldo grins.

"You had fun, Charlie." He touches Charlie's shoulder gently. "Didn't you?"

Charlie's mouth hangs open a moment as he stares down at his shoulder, right where Ronaldo touched him. "Yeah," he says finally, in a soft voice.

Oh dear. Charlie drops his head to stare down at the small rug by the kitchen sink. He suddenly looks pale, like he might faint.

"Charlie," Ronaldo tries again, in a light voice.

Charlie doesn't respond. It's so quiet, I can hear the clock ticking in the back room. He is frozen to the spot.

A slight frown crosses over Ronaldo's face. "So. Do you think I'm okay to ride home alone with Aidan, or should I have my mom pick me up?"

Charlie's head snaps up. "Aidan? Oh . . . well, yeah. He's fine. He used to be kind of a jerk, but now I think he's okay. You'll be fine with him." Charlie's shoulders relax. "Everyone likes you. You know how to talk to people. You'll be good."

Ronaldo tips his head and smiles again. "Okay." He reaches up and touches the flower on Charlie's headband. "Oh my God, Charlie. Your hair looked so cool tonight."

"Thanks," Charlie says. Quiet. Thoughtful. Not breaking eye contact for once. A smile twitches at the corner of his mouth.

There's a long pause. But then Charlie's phone gives a *ping!* He grabs it off of the kitchen counter.

"Uh, yeah, that's Vicky. She says to come out. Aidan is ready to go."

Ronaldo nods. "All right. I'll see you tomorrow."

"Probably."

"Definitely."

We walk Ronaldo to the front door. Victoria comes inside and the children watch their guests drive away. Victoria is the first to bound up the stairs to get ready for bed.

Charlie reaches down with two hands and hefts me up onto his shoulder. "Hey, Lil," he sings softly. "Kissy, kissy." He smooches me a few times on the face.

Ewww. Not my favorite gesture of affection. But when he gives me a squeeze and leans his cheek against my shoulder, I feel the love and start to purr.

It is clear to me that Charlie had a wonderful time at the Winter Ball.

"Sweetie." He sighs again. He leans back to smile at me. "Sweet baby doll. Did you have a special night? You're the most beautiful cat in the world, have I told you that lately? You're the best, the sweetest, and the greatest. I hope I haven't forgotten to tell you. Your fur? So soft and stunning. Your personality? Amazing. Everyone loves you. You're so funny and nice."

Oh, boy. *Are you talking to me?*

I suspect he has someone else in mind.

Yes, I'm quite sure my Charlie had a good time. I keep purring as he heads toward the stairs to climb up to bed, clutching me against him with both arms. He forgets to turn off the kitchen light.

Chapter 29
Very Unkind

Mark hands a small cup to Charlie, who is wearing a red apron. Charlie digs the cup deep into a tall bag. When he slowly and cautiously lifts his arm, I see the cup is overflowing with white powder.

"Here." Mark hands him a knife. "Use this to even out the top."

Charlie slides the knife over the top to knock powder back into the bag. He glances up at Mark for approval, who nods.

I can see Charlie stands a little taller when he's next to Mark. He feels comfortable.

"Victoria is going to be so impressed when she hears you helped with the birthday cake," Mom gushes from her seat at the kitchen table. "You're making a red cake?"

"A blue cake with red frosting," Charlie answers with a grin. "Just like the one she asked for when she was in Kindergarten."

Mom laughs. When Mark walks over closer to her, she wraps her hands tighter around her mug and beams up at him.

"So, how was work today?" he asks. "How was little Emma?"

"Ohhhh." Mom sighs. "Not good. She spilled the glue again. And after lunch, one of the teachers caught her cutting up her dress with scissors."

Charlie gasps in horror, but Mark laughs heartily. "Ah. Good old Emma." He puts a hand on his stomach. "That kid is lucky she's got you to look after her."

Mom's cheeks redden, and she looks down at the table. I think she is pleased.

"How's the coffee?"

Mark made the coffee for Mom in a special new machine that he brought for her last week. At first, she eyeballed the machine suspiciously as he showed her how to use it. It sounded complicated.

Mom nods. "It's very good."

On different days, Mark has brought Mom a book, a painted dish, and a bracelet. She always smiles but puts these things quickly aside. To her, they are just *things*. Her needs are much more immediate. She wants to look at him, to hear his voice, to touch his hand.

"Stir the dry ingredients together, but not too fast or the flour will go everywhere," Mark says over his shoulder. Charlie nods and grabs a wooden spoon. Charlie holds the glass bowl handle with one hand while mixing with the other. Mark turns back to Mom. He pauses before blurting out: "Did your friends say anything about last night?"

Last night, two of Mom's friends showed up with a bottle of wine. It was their first time meeting Mark, and they all went out to the deck. The women cooed and clucked over him, and the later into the night it got, the more cooing and clucking they did. Mom did not drink the wine, preferring a glass of iced tea, so that is what Mark drank too. But he was very talkative, and by the end of the night everyone was in good spirits. Mark referred to them as his "new friends," which made the women laugh for some reason. As they were leaving, they patted his cheek and tapped his elbow and made him feel greatly admired. Mom had to practically shove them out the door to get them to leave.

"They liked you," Mom says, raising an eyebrow. "Of course."

Mark gives Mom his crooked smile. "Good."

"Yes, it's good. They approve. Well—it's not that I care if they approve. I should say: They understand."

Mark's smile fades. He scratches the back of his neck. When Mom doesn't say anything more, he walks over to her and takes her hand. "Katie. I know this must be hard for—"

"They understand. They do." Her eyes flicker over to Charlie, but he's busy pouring milk into a new cup.

Mark sighs. He suddenly looks tired. I know he didn't sleep well.

I heard Mark tell Mom that he woke up in a sweat in the dead of night. Mom listened with horror when he explained that he has nightmares, which always involve finding very sick babies in the strangest places, like under the kitchen sink. This is one way I know Mark is not yet at peace. His arms still feel empty from where he once held his warm baby.

Mom studies Mark's face and frowns. "Charlie," she calls, "We'll be right back, okay?"

"Yeah, sure. I've got it under control." Charlie pours a brown liquid into a spoon. Some splashes onto the kitchen counter, but he quickly mops it up with the edge of his apron.

Mom takes Mark just a few steps into the hallway, past where Charlie can see them. She puts her arms up around him and rests her head on his shoulder. One hand reaches up to play with his hair and she brushes her lips against his neck. Mark closes his eyes for a moment.

I think this is true: She wants Mark as her mate. Mom likes having a physical connection with him, and feels safe in his arms. She is learning to let go of Dad.

This is also true: Mark needs her.

Mark was brokenhearted, and then Mom came into his life unexpectedly. Now he is dedicated to her. He needs someone to talk to about his fears and disappointments. He tells her stories of his old life that make him laugh in disbelief, and to me, he sounds like he is describing someone else, instead of himself. He manages to say and express more in one conversation than Dad probably did in a month. He needs someone who will listen, and not judge. For him that person is Mom.

Mom wants Mark; he needs her. They are different things, want and need. *Want* can make humans do crazy things. Yet I think *need* may represent something deeper.

It is enough to draw them together.

Charlie looks over at me as I stare down the hall. He mouths: *What is going on over there?*

No worries. It's all good. Mom is fine. Keep mixing.

I think Mark overwhelms Mom sometimes. But when he leans back and smiles at her, she looks happy.

And when I finally hear her whisper, "I love you," while standing there in the dark hallway, there is nothing about it that feels wrong or forced or out of place.

If I were her, I would love him too. In fact, I believe I already do.

There is one day when Dad lets himself in the front door with his key, and wipes his feet on the mat. He tips his head and breathes in deeply. A serene look comes over his face. He is at peace. But I know it won't last long.

Mark is in the kitchen cooking strawberry muffins. I watched him take a tray out of the oven. When he bakes in our kitchen, the cakes create a smell that all of the humans love, and it is this scent that Dad responds to as he stands at the front door. It does not appeal to me personally, but the humans gravitate toward the kitchen when Mark is baking.

Right now, the children are in school. Mark is alone in the house.

Earlier, from a kitchen chair, I watched Mark carefully wash and trim the strawberries. He cut them thin, one at a time, and then fanned out the slices over the top of each muffin.

Mark takes his time when he is baking, and never appears flustered, the way Mom gets when she is rushing to cook dinner at the end of the day. He gave me a small piece of soft cheese once everything was in the oven.

Mark appears at the end of the hall to see who has entered the house. When he sees it is Dad, he slowly comes down the hall, a wary look on his face.

"Sorry," Mark says. "She's not here. She went for a run."

"A run? You mean running? Like, actual running? Around the block or something?"

"Yeah."

I don't blame Dad for being confused. Mom is usually at work, but today Mom took the day off, which is unusual for her. She also has never gone running in the past. It is something new she is trying out.

"So you live here now?"

"No." Mark seems reluctant to say more.

"It's okay," Dad says, squinting at him. "I understand. You're the rebound guy. That's how Kate and I are going to refer to you in six months, when you're gone. The rebound relationship. Whatever."

Mark seems skeptical. He raises an eyebrow. "Okay," he says carefully.

Dad stares at Mark, and the hostility seems to slowly seep out of him as he stands there, hanging his head and closing his eyes for a brief moment. "So, Mark." He stops, and wipes the back of his knuckles against his mouth. "Um, so. Okay. What has Kate said about me, exactly?"

Mark folds his arms across his chest and gives a disinterested shrug. He stares down at his work boots, which he tends to wear most days even when he isn't working on Mom's project. The ground is muddy now that the snow is melting and the spring rain keeps the dirt moist. And I can see he just doesn't put too much thought into what he wears. "I don't know. Not much, I guess. Nothing personal."

My whiskers twitch. I suppose it's true Mom doesn't talk too much about Dad with Mark.

Yet I have heard her say a few things.

I did hear her say she still loves Dad.

But that was a while ago. A full moon ago. Most of the work on the study is done. Yet Mark is still here.

Dad rolls his head back to stretch and take in a deep breath. "Yeah. Okay." I can see he doesn't believe that for a minute from the look on his face. He rubs the palms of his hands together, as if he's cold. "I'm trying, you know. It kills me to think that the kids are unhappy. I know I'm not their favorite person lately."

Mark holds himself tighter, and he nods, but doesn't respond.

"I wish there was more I could do. But I'm doing the best I can."

I *meow!* to let Dad know I appreciate what he is saying. He glances at me and looks amused. When he winks at me, I wink back at him.

When Dad is looking right at me—and really *seeing* me, not distracted, or in a fog—he has a very friendly look. I can imagine him looking at Mom in the same way, the way he used to before he went into the hospital, and I can see why she loved him and why she might *still* love him and why it's hard to let him go.

Mark clears his throat, which gets Dad's attention.

"Maybe you didn't really appreciate having a family," Mark finally says, quietly, almost to himself. He stares at the floor, lost in thought. "Until it was gone."

I listen to the words Mark has said, how they quietly hang in the air.

I know what Mark means. Mark had a family, and he lost it. He knows firsthand how quickly and easily everything is lost. His baby, his wife, his house—lost for good. It was a terrible shock to his system.

But watching Dad's face change, I think perhaps he is taking what Mark is saying in a different way. He feels Mark has made some kind of hostile accusation. His face goes blank.

"I see." Dad leans back on one foot and shoves his hands in his jeans pockets. "I see. Okay. That's interesting. So now, even though I've been a dad to three children for years, nursing them when they were ill, holding their hands when they were scared, drying their tears when they cried, working every day, putting my life on the line more times than I can count, getting injured in the line of duty, trying to recover, doing my best, suffering in silence, doing what the doctors ordered, this is all my fault. I did not appreciate my family. Hmm. That's an interesting theory." He rocks back on his heels. "And now, according to you, I have lost them. They're gone."

"No, what I—"

"Your words, not mine. 'I didn't appreciate them until they were gone.' That's what you said." Dad's voice gets louder and more aggressive. "I blew it. It's over for me. My life as I knew it is over. So now you're going to love and take care of my family for me. Is that it? Is that what you mean? You. A part-time contractor. To me, you look like a deadbeat trying to take advantage of my wife and her needy emotional state. Not to mention freeloading off her steady job, cozy home, and premade family."

Mark's mouth drops open. "No. No, that's not at all what I—"

"Did anyone mention to you that I got shot?"

Mark frowns and squints at Dad. "What?"

I don't understand. Dad got shot? What does he mean?

With a gun?

Dad lifts up his shirt to reveal a scar on his lower stomach. I've seen that scar before. I didn't know what it was from. I never thought much about it at all.

"Oh, yeah. On the job. While at work, so I could take care of *my family*, a drug dealer shot me. I was in the hospital for three days. I took the drugs they prescribed for me, and if I got hooked, well . . . That's just how it goes sometimes. You know. Tough luck, buddy. You're screwed. Better luck next time. Too bad you still have to get up for work every day and work through the pain." Dad drops the shirt. "Kate flushed my pills, and I'm glad she did because I don't want to be a loser drug addict like the guys I chase down every day. But now I sometimes need a drink. That's not against the law. Okay? It's not the end of the world. I'm sorry if she thinks that ruins life for everyone." He clears his throat. "But listen. Whenever you start thinking about how superior you are to me in taking care of a family, remember where I've been." He glares at Mark until the younger man must look away.

"Jeremy," Mark says to the floor, "I'm sorry. I didn't mean—"

"I have to go," Dad blurts out. He turns to slam open the screen door. He walks quickly down the front steps and out to his car.

"Wait," Mark calls after him, but Dad is already opening his car door.

"No, no. I'm leaving. You're right," Dad yells from the driveway. "You're the better man for the job. My turn is over. Good luck with it." He shakes his head, disgusted, and gets in the car.

Mark watches from the doorway, halfway in and halfway out, as Dad drives away. He takes in a deep breath and it comes out in a sigh.

Finally, Mom comes jogging up the street. Her cheeks are pink from the exertion.

She smiles at Mark until she sees the expression on his face.

"What's wrong?"

Mark opens the door wider, so I can step outside, and he follows me. He gently closes the screen door behind him. "Jeremy was here."

"What?" Her eyes open wider. "And? What happened?"

Mark takes a step out into the bright spring sunshine, and has to shield his eyes. From the top step, he looks down at Mom.

"I think I made a mistake. I said the wrong thing."

Mom swings around frantically to look back down the road, to check if she can still see Dad's car, but he is long gone. There is nothing to see but the canopy of trees overhanging the road on one side, the tall marsh grass that grows right up to the edge of the crumbling pavement from the other side, and a thin layer of dust hanging in the air. "What do you mean? You said something? You said some-thing?" Her voice gets higher as she asks more questions. "What did you say? Was he upset?"

Mark stands there, averting his gaze from the direct sun. He has his hands on his hips, and doesn't look at Mom. "Am I taking advantage of you?"

"What?" She runs right up to the bottom step and looks up at Mark, her hands outstretched toward him. "What are you talking about? What did you say to Jeremy?"

When Mark finally lifts his head to look at her, he is weary all over again. It's that flash of sadness I sometimes recognize. Most of the time, he hides it well. But right now the light washes him out, and the grief is plain to see.

"I love your house, and your family, and your life. I do. But that's only because I love you. I'm not trying to replace Jeremy. How could I possibly replace him? I didn't mean that he has no place here, or that your whole family has given up on him."

"Mark. Is that what you said to him?"

"No, but . . ." He brushes his hair off his forehead with his hand, but it just falls back down where it was. "I'm so stupid.

Vincent is right. I'm a walking disaster. I ruin everything I touch."

"That's not true." Mom stands as stiff as a board. Her voice is stern. "That is one hundred percent not true."

He looks at her, bewildered. "I don't get it, Katie. Why do you want to throw away one broken person for another? What's the point? You think I'm going to be any better than Jeremy? I'm starting to question if I ever could be better than him. There's a lot about him I didn't know or understand."

"Stop. Just stop it. Right now." Mom's hands are pink, and she squeezes them tight by her sides.

"I'm sorry. Maybe you should call him. Maybe you should take him back." Mark walks right by Mom without touching her. Mom's eyes follow him, but he doesn't look at her.

Oh! I don't like this one bit. Everyone is being very unkind.

Mom watches him go, and starts shivering in anger. I can tell she is upset, the way her pale face lights up in surprise.

"What is that supposed to mean?" Mom yells after him. "HEY. What is wrong with you?"

Mark, whose hand is already on the door handle of his truck, whirls around. His eyes flash, his nostrils flair, and he looks furious.

I don't like this at all. Both Mom and Mark seem to be itching for a fight, and I'm not sure why. I think Dad being here has made them both anxious.

"Let me go," he growls. "I just need to think."

"What do you mean, maybe I should take him back? Why in the world would you say that?"

Mark rubs his face with his hand, way too hard, like he is trying to wipe off his freckles. He looks tired. "Why do you think I would say that?" When Mark sees Mom has no reply, he goes on: "Why didn't you ever tell me Jeremy got shot at work? You never explained that part, how he got hooked on painkillers after getting shot in the stomach. That seems like something that could happen to anybody. Do you just . . . throw men out when you get tired of them?"

Mom's head jerks back slightly. "What?" She almost gasps in surprise. "Yes. Okay. He got shot. But that's not when Jeremy started drinking. That's just when it got SO MUCH WORSE." Her voice catches on these last words. "Why do you assume you know what I've been through? You don't. We've been struggling with this for a long time."

Mark turns, so he is not facing Mom anymore. For a moment he stands there looking sideways at her, as if weighing what he should or should not say. And, as he does, the anger in his face fades away. It is replaced with something worse. He looks disappointed.

"MARK," Mom persists. "Say something."

Now he finally looks away, toward the woods at the side of the house, and seems to fix on something between the trees. But I know he is seeing nothing. He chews on the inside of his mouth.

"You'll get tired of me too," he says quietly. "I'm the same as Jeremy. I mess everything up. Everything I touch falls apart. You just don't see it yet."

Mom doesn't know what to say. Before she can think of something, Mark opens the door and climbs into his truck. I am worried he is going to drive off with a dark look on his face, like Dad did.

I trot over to Mom and throw myself against her legs. She picks me up and holds me to her chest with two firm hands.

From how tightly she squeezes me in her arms, I can tell Mom is shaken. She is probably not sure whether she should be worried more about Dad or Mark. I am concerned about both of them.

I *mew!* Just a pitiful: *mew!*

"Lily," Mom coos soothingly to me.

I glance over, and sure enough, Mark is looking at me.

Mew! I try to make myself sound helpless.

Mark rolls down his window, and his eyes soften a bit. He hasn't started the truck engine yet. He is watching me and Mom.

MEW! I call out, louder. *Can't you see she's holding me all wrong? Won't you come and help me?* I squirm around and wiggle my butt to show him that I am uncomfortable.

"Lily, it's okay," Mom says.

And then I see: His eyes are tearing up.

And I think—

I am quite sure—

"Mark," Mom finally calls out. "Please. Don't leave."

Ah! He climbs down out of his truck and walks over to us.

"I'm sorry," he whispers to Mom, looking down at me with a concerned look on his face. I give him an innocent blink. He reaches out with two hands, and Mom stares at him, not understanding. When she finally realizes he wants to take me, Mom carefully hands me over. I am once again flipped upside down and nestled into the crook of his arm. Ah, much better. Mark gently rubs my tummy with his free hand, and I am content. I feel his body relax as I start to purr.

As Mom turns back toward the house, Mark gives me a quick shake of the head and raises an eyebrow. It is as if he is saying: *I know what you're up to, sweetheart.*

But we need you here! Mom needs you. Charlie needs you. I need you. You must stay.

I'm pleased with myself. I can't help it.

When he carries me inside and the screen door clicks shut behind us, I am overwhelmed with the scent of the muffins once again, and it smells wonderful. Like home. Thank goodness Mark came back!

This much is clear to me: Mark belongs here now. Mom and Mark must work this out. Our house would not be the same without him.

But also . . . I cannot deny the truth. I want Mark to stay for selfish reasons. I do think Mark may still help Charlie. But now that Charlie is getting older, and I realize how he feels about Ronaldo, I wonder how much longer I will be his best friend. And once Mom knows Charlie is being bullied, might she not send him away, the same way I was sent away when my leg was broken as a kitten? And then what will I have left? Will I be sent away too? Or if not, what will my life become without my sweet Charlie?

All of my fears, even ones I have been pushing out of my mind for a long time, surge to squeeze my heart in pain. I close my eyes and nuzzle my wet nose against Mark's soft shirt. He whispers into my ear, but I don't hear the words. The words don't matter. The arms matter. And they hold me tight.

Chapter 30
What Happened in the Garage

It is a few days later, and I am outside. I am angry at myself for not realizing sooner that Kevin is the one bullying Charlie. I wasn't paying enough attention to Kevin. And I still haven't figured out how to let my humans know what's going on.

The sun has started to fall from its highest position in the sky when a car pulls into the driveway, and then glides all the way into the garage. It is Dad's car.

This is odd. He rarely comes to the house during the day when everyone is out.

Before he moved away, there were a few times Dad came home at lunch. He rifled through drawers, all around the house, searching for his medicine. Checking in cabinets. Double-checking in closets. He would sometimes leave, frustrated.

Or if he found his medicine, he would sit and have a dose of it at the kitchen table. And then go back to work. But now he doesn't usually come by in the middle of the day.

Almost immediately, the garage door starts to go back down. I don't understand.

Why is Dad parking in the garage and shutting the door? He usually leaves his car in the driveway.

Is he here for some purpose?

And is he trying to hide the fact that he is here, for some reason?

With an impulsive jump, I make a mad dash into the garage, right past the back wheels of the car. I barely make it in as the heavy garage door comes cranking steadily down, brushing my tail. It's crazy, I know. But I want to go inside the garage with Dad and see what he's up to.

My action somehow seems to trigger the door to reverse course, and it starts to rise again with a loud grinding noise. I look back over my shoulder to see it lifting, letting the sunshine back in. I run to the stairs that lead to the house, to get away from all the noise.

I still miss Dad. Sometimes I find myself holding onto hope that Dad is making plans to move back home. But then I remember my friend Mark, and how much he needs Mom. And I realize that as long as Mark is around, Dad cannot come back. Mom will only have one mate in the end, whoever she chooses. Or maybe she will send them both away. I suppose that's possible too.

The car engine is very loud. I expect it to stop right away, but it does not.

I cower on the stairs. What's going on? The engine continues to grumble, pulsing with energy, and hurts my ears.

I see Dad look back over his shoulder, squinting in confusion. He shakes his head slightly. And then he reaches up toward the roof of the car to press a button.

The garage door begins to slide back down once again. Cutting off the sun. Leaving us in the cool, dark shadows. Sealing us in.

I feel my fur bristle in fright. *What's wrong?* I wonder. I sense that something is wrong. I don't know why Dad is taking so long to stop the car engine.

I decide to try and get high enough to see inside the car, climbing up to the top stair. I hear a whirring noise as the windows of the car slide down. I can see Dad. But he is not making a motion to turn off or get out of the car. He leans his head back against the seat and closes his eyes.

I sneeze as the air grows dense with the smell of chemicals. I don't feel very well.

This is not a good time for Dad to rest.

Wake up!

I now hear Gretel inside the house, scratching at the door. I believe she is trying to push open the door to the garage. She whines desperately, and suddenly I realize something truly is very wrong. What in the world is going on?

Perhaps Dad is very, very tired and cannot move. Or maybe he is ill and needs attention. The fumes in the garage will certainly make us both sick, if he is not sick already.

Dad!

It is no use. The temperature in the garage rises with the loud grinding of the engine. I realize I'm going to have to get Dad's attention. Maybe I can jump onto the car and walk on the windshield. From there I could *meow!* until he sees me.

I feel lightheaded. Perhaps this is a mistake. I might hurt myself. But Dad needs to wake up. Now. My ears can't take the noise any longer.

From my step, I take a leap toward the hood of the car. It is a long jump. Because I am so heavy, I land with a *wham!* on the metal, like a sack of cat food.

I thought I would land lightly on my paws. This is a little embarrassing.

But the good news is, Dad's eyes click open in surprise. It reminds me of a doll Victoria had when she was younger. The eyelids of the doll lifted when it was moved upright. But the eyes were glassy and you knew they couldn't see a thing. It was scary and unnatural.

This is the first thing that comes to mind when Dad opens his eyes.

Dad and I make eye contact. At first, I'm not sure he recognizes me, although he's looking at me.

Wake up!

He only hesitates a moment before stirring. He reaches forward in his seat and, thank goodness, he turns off the car engine. After he presses a button above him, the garage doors start to glide open, and—just in the nick of time—sunshine and fresh air come pouring in.

I stand frozen, on the car hood. Clumsily, I stagger to the edge of the car and jump with a *plop* down to the cement floor.

I hear the car's driver-side door open and shut. Dad comes over to stand next to me and lets me sniff his hand. I feel weak. He looks confused. "Lily? How'd you get in here?"

I let Dad lift me up with two strong hands and place me on his shoulder, the same way Charlie carries me. He holds me there, stroking my head and back, whispering apologies into my ear. I feel him slip one hand under my stomach with just the right amount of pressure, so that I'm comfortable and secure. His body slowly warms up and shakes gently.

Poor Dad. He needs help.

When I lift my head to look up at him, I see his eyes are just barely holding tears back. I don't understand what's wrong with Dad. Why he seems so sad, distracted, and lost.

What's wrong? I start to purr.

"I didn't know you were here," he tells me. "I'm sorry, Lily. I miss you, girl. I would never hurt you."

I purr louder to show him: no harm done. It's the best I can do, to be still and let him hold me.

"I won't do that again," he tells me. "I promise. I'm just really tired and my tummy hurts. I miss everyone. I don't know what I was thinking. That's not what I really want." He breathes in and out, a long sigh.

Dad finally puts me down, and I stretch. Gretel is still begging and clawing at the door. Dad lifts his head, as if just hearing it for the first time. He hurries over to open the door, to reassure and talk to her, to calm her down.

It is so strange. Dad's behavior has grown odd. He is worse than distracted—he is not paying attention at all.

I follow Dad inside, where the house is otherwise empty. He walks to the living room at the front of the house and lies right down on the rug to stare at the ceiling. This is strange behavior for Dad, but I understand he is very tired. Gretel lies on one side of him, and I lie on the other, tucked under his arm. It feels warm and wonderful. I hope we are comforting to him.

I think Gretel and I make a good team! I am starting to see that our goals are the same: to help this family. And we are stronger when we work together.

I wonder what Dad would do if he found out that Kevin is bullying Charlie. Dad is probably the perfect person to discipline bad behavior, because that is what he does at work. It would give Dad a purpose—a mission, of sorts—to correct Kevin when he does wrong.

In the meantime, I am glad I got Dad to wake up. The children would find it curious to come home and find Dad asleep in the garage. Gretel and I are going to have to keep a closer eye on Dad, every minute he is here. I start to think that it might be a good idea if Gretel went to live with Dad. He needs protection as much as anyone—perhaps even from himself. I would miss Gretel terribly, but sometimes we must make sacrifices for the good of the family.

I soon find out that Gretel agrees with me on this point.

Chapter 31
Better Offer

One afternoon just a few days later, I hear voices coming from the front room. I realize that Victoria is starting to shout. I believe she and Aidan are having a fight. Occasionally they bicker, but something about this is different. Victoria's voice strains with real anger.

When I round the corner, I see Victoria and Aidan standing in the center of the living room. Victoria is holding up her phone toward Aidan. He stands with his hands out in front of him and an expression of disbelief.

"Why?" Victoria's eyes shine with fury. "Why did she post this photo of the two of you at the party? Her arm is around you. She drew a heart on the photo around you two. It makes me sick. You guys look like . . . you look like you're *together*."

"Vicky. Listen." Aidan gestures wildly in front of him. "We had a conversation. She took a photo. Big deal. She probably had too much to drink. She was just being friendly."

"AIDAN." Victoria puts her hands on her head, as if to protect it from the ceiling caving in. "Why did you let her put her arm around you? What were you doing for her to think that might be okay? Julie said you were talking to Bunny for hours. Hours, Aidan. What did you have to say to her that was so important?"

"I don't remember." Aidan takes a step back, eyes wide, as if astonished at Victoria's line of attack. "Nothing. Nothing important. Maybe just . . . I don't even know."

"I think you do know. Liar."

"This isn't my fault, Vic. I didn't do anything wrong."

She wipes the air in front of her as if she might erase him, as if getting rid of him was as simple as performing a magic trick. "Asshole. You went to a party on the weekend when I was stuck with my dad, and you were probably drunk too, and you were talking to her in a cool-guy way where she thought: Yeah, I'm going to take a photo with Aidan, and draw a heart around it, and we're going to look really cute together, and he's going to love it. So how are you not at fault?" She puts her hands on her hips. "And why do you do this? This isn't the first time. What, are you secretly making plans for your next girlfriend?"

He grinds his teeth for a moment before answering in a dry, detached voice. "Yeah, Vic. That's exactly what I'm doing. Making my big plans for the future. Like the epic genius mastermind that I am."

Kevin comes down the stairs, cautiously, taking his time. He lets one hand slide on the smooth bannister as he hops down the last step.

Once Kevin stands in the entrance to the room, he says to Aidan, slowly and very clearly: "I think you should leave."

Victoria and Aidan both turn, surprised. I'm not sure they even noticed Kevin coming down the stairs.

I am surprised too. My whiskers bristle. Kevin seems too calm. He's moving in slow motion. It's strange. There is something off about him.

Aidan frowns at Kevin. "Back off, big man. We're busy."

Victoria shakes her head. "It's okay, Kev. We need to talk."

Kevin doesn't move. "But, Vicky—"

She spins around to face him. "GET LOST, KEVIN."

Kevin looks from his little sister to Aidan and back again. He swallows hard and winces, and I can see her reaction is painful to him. He turns and walks back up the stairs.

"Listen, Vic." Aidan steps toward Victoria, lowering his voice. "Maybe, yeah, maybe I *should* be thinking about my next girlfriend, okay? Because I know EXACTLY how this goes." His voice catches, but he presses on. "Like how your mom kicked out your dad for her new boyfriend. Like my mom throws over new guys constantly when she thinks she's found someone better. Except they're never better. They're always losers. But, yeah, I understand perfectly well. You're going to leave me the minute—THE MINUTE—you get a better offer, and I know that. I'm aware of how that works."

Victoria's face falls, and her mouth falls opens in shock. Her bottom lip trembles. "That's not how I work. That's not me at all. You're an asshole."

In a sudden motion, Victoria reaches out with two hands and shoves Aidan on the chest, with a hard snap of her elbows. He's not expecting to get hit with such force, and stumbles backward.

"WHAT THE HELL?"

"You said I don't trust you, Aidan, but I do. You're the one who doesn't trust me."

"I want to trust you, Vic." He rushes back and tries to take her hand, but she yanks it out of reach. "Victoria. I'm sorry. I didn't know Bunny was going to take a photo. It would have been rude to say no." When Victoria turns her back on him, he starts talking faster: "Okay. Look. Yeah, I probably talked to her a little too long. Okay? Are you happy now? I'm always surprised when someone likes me and actually wants to talk to me. But Bunny was just playing around. She probably posted that photo to get attention, to stir up drama just like this, to get people talking about her. Come on. She never even looked at me until I started going out with you. So put two and two together. This is all just a power trip for her."

Victoria sways while listening to him, anxious, glancing over her shoulder reluctantly now and then. "Aidan . . ."

"I don't like her. I don't care about her at all. I love you. Just you. You know that, Vic."

When she finally stops moving and they make eye contact, I know Victoria has already forgiven him. And he knows it too, because he relaxes and his whole face changes. He gives her that intimate look that says: *You're in this thing with me now, whether you like it or not.*

But Victoria isn't quite done. "I think you should text her and tell her to take the photo down."

Aidan reaches up to scratch the back of his neck. "Um . . . really? That would be awkward. I don't want to do that."

"I don't care. You're going to do it anyway."

Aidan pauses. "You know that if I text her, she and I will probably end up in a long conversation about what happened that night and why you're mad about the photo. You're okay with that?"

Victoria frowns again and her eyes flash with anger. "No, Aidan. I'm not okay with that. Why would you think—"

Kevin comes into our line of sight, and this time Victoria notices right away. He is like a cloud floating down the stairs. His baby face is blank, as emotionless as Dad gets, devoid of expression.

But there is one thing different about him than the last time he came downstairs: He has a gun in his hand.

And just as it is with Dad when he carries his gun, it is the only thing we all see. I scamper back under a chair. Gretel scrambles up onto her feet, ears alert.

Aidan startles, eyes open wide, and he looks to Victoria. She moves right in front of him, so she is standing between her brother and her boyfriend. Her hands move back to grab Aidan's hands, as if she needs to shield him completely.

"What—what are you doing, Kev?" she asks, suddenly sounding much younger.

"Nothing. I just want Aidan to leave." He walks into the room and blocks the exit, so Aidan would have to ask Kevin to move if he actually wanted to go out the front door.

"Why do you have a gun?" Aidan demands, speaking too fast and too loud. "That's not a great idea, dude. What is wrong with you? Even your crazy robot dad gave me a gun safety lecture."

Aidan shuts his mouth and swallows when Victoria starts tapping his hand lightly with her finger. *Tap tap tap tap tap.*

As if communicating: *stop stop stop stop stop.*

And then, out of the corner of my eye, I see Charlie. He has silently come down a few stairs, looking to see what is going on. I figure he was in his bedroom with his headphones on, but he heard the voices. I come out from under the chair, and my fur starts to stand on end. Charlie looks at me.

Don't move, Charlie. Don't speak. Stay hidden.

Charlie shrinks down and sits on a stair, watching through the slats of the stair railing.

Run, Charlie. Go back up the stairs.

But he does not move.

Gretel starts to pace. She has her eyes on Kevin. Back and forth, she stalks from one side of the room to the other.

At first, I think Gretel is just getting excited. I know she can read the tension in the room.

But the way she never takes her eyes off of Kevin, I start to realize she's not just getting worked up. I think she's getting ready to defend or attack. But Kevin isn't watching her. He's still glaring at Aidan.

I remember Dad saying that Gretel's main job was finding drugs. But he did also say she was sometimes asked to attack. Was that how she got injured? Who hurt her?

I watch Gretel, fascinated.

The way her fur bristles along her spine. The way she holds her head high. The way she pulls back her upper lip so a sharp tooth comes into view.

And then: a low growl.

Gretel would never hurt Kevin. Would she? She thinks he is second-in-command in this house, after Dad.

I wonder again: Who hurt Gretel? A bad person being investigated? A criminal being chased?

Or, perhaps, did Dad or someone on his team accidentally hurt Gretel? I suppose that's possible too. Maybe she was hurt by mistake.

Yet she trusts humans. For the most part. Most of the time.

Just not all of the time.

I listen carefully to her growl. She isn't scared. She is just eager to get to work.

Kevin finally glances down at Gretel. "Stop it, girl. Be a good girl. You're a good girl." He looks back up at Victoria. "I just want Aidan to leave. I'm sick of listening to the fighting." He doesn't sound angry. He speaks in a calm, even voice, but he is almost speaking too slow, like his mouth is having trouble saying the words. Kevin moves his hand, the one with the gun, to gesture toward them. "You can go too, Vic. Go with him."

"We have nowhere to go, Kev." Victoria's dark eyes glance down at the gun, then back up at her brother. "We can't go to Aidan's house. He's trying to avoid going there. We have to stay here."

"No, you don't. He has a car." Again, Kevin uses the hand with the gun to point toward the front door. "You can go anywhere you want. You just can't stay here. I want it quiet. I'm doing my homework."

I see Aidan starting to shake, his body quivering. He bites his lip and looks up at the ceiling. I am surprised at how quickly his eyes fill. One tear spills out and runs down his cheek. "God-

damn it. This whole family is crazier than mine. And that's saying something."

Victoria squeezes Aidan's hands tighter, and they turn white
with the effort. But she isn't able to stop Aidan when he rips his
hands out of hers and moves to slide past her, successfully getting around and in front of her. Kevin raises his arm.

"Are you leaving?" Kevin points the gun at Aidan.

"Aidan, don't." Victoria tries to wiggle and get in front of
Aidan again, but he holds her off with one arm. He has switched
positions with her, and now shields her body with his.

"JESUS CHRIST, KEVIN," Aidan begs, louder now, the
panic in his voice unmistakable, shaking one hand in front of him
and using the other hand to hold Victoria behind him. "Why
can't you just—"

Gretel looks at me with those big wet eyes. I tip my head, to
say: *yes*.

And no one sees it coming.

No one but me.

Chapter 32
Brave

Gretel is strong. And loyal. And brave. She is a wonderful family dog. These are all ways I could describe her, and I think she would agree.

Kevin has her all wrong.

I've explained it before.

Gretel does not think of herself as a "good girl."

Chapter 33
Tourniquet

There is a shriek. And moaning. Blood and torn flesh.

Kevin is on his hands and knees. And then he is lying on the ground.

"We should call 911," Victoria says, kneeling.

"No," says Aidan, crouching next to her. He is firm on this. "The cops might come. You want a bunch of hyped-up robots crawling around here, interviewing us for hours? No thanks. I'll just drive him to the hospital."

Kevin begs them to wrap up his arm but not take him anywhere. He says that if they report this, the police will make them send Gretel away. They will put her to sleep. It will kill Dad to lose his Gretel.

Victoria hesitates. I think what Kevin is saying must be true from the troubled look on her face.

His forearm is bleeding badly. His wrist looks torn. Victoria runs to fetch a full stack of white kitchen towels. Yet the blood keeps coming, drenching one towel and then the next.

Kevin cries out again and again in pain, thrashing his head back and forth, but forcing his body to lie still.

I look up to check on Charlie. He remains on the stairs, one hand over his mouth.

Don't move, Charlie. No one needs to know you're here.

"God, it hurts. Wrap it up tighter," Kevin demands. "TIGHTER. Make a tourniquet. Why doesn't anyone learn First Aid anymore?"

"Hide the gun," Aidan tells Vicky. "Stupid goddamn gun."

She grabs it and runs upstairs. When she sees Charlie, she freezes in surprise. But she doesn't say anything. She breezes past him, hopping up the final few steps.

Kevin winces and looks at Aidan. "Are you gonna tell your parents?"

Aidan snorts. "Am I going to tell my parents that you pulled a gun on me? Why would I do that? So my dirtbag dad can shake down my girlfriend's parents for money? Money that he would waste on total crap? No, thanks. That would be a no."

"Okay." Kevin rests his head back on the floor. His eyes flutter closed.

Aidan glances at Kevin's face. The color is quickly draining out of it. Aidan looks worried. He runs to the coat closet, and comes back with a black scarf. "Hey, man. I'll tie this real tight around your arm. You ready?"

Kevin opens his eyes again, but stares at the ceiling and seems to see nothing. "Go for it."

Victoria comes back downstairs and looks at her brother on the floor. We can all see how pale he is. She shakes her hands out, hard. "Kevin," she cries, "If it's you or the dog, I'm sorry, but you win. We're going to call 911. You're really bleeding."

But once Aidan ties the scarf tight and Victoria has arranged a bandage around and around and around Kevin's wrist, the bleeding slows. She brings ice, and over time, the emergency passes.

Thank goodness! I feel my legs start to wobble and relax, so I plop down on the edge of the rug.

Aidan sits with his legs crossed next to Kevin, who still lies on the floor. They have his arm propped up on a pillow. "So," Aidan says, "First your cat went psycho on me, and now your dog attacked you. You ever gonna trust that dog again?"

"Of course," Kevin states. "She's a trained police dog." He glances over at Gretel. "She was just helping out. She was doing what she was trained to do. Disarm the threat. Weren't you, girl?"

I think he's right. Gretel was never angry. She could have torn the muscle right off of the bone of his arm if she had wanted to with her powerful jaws. But when Kevin immediately dropped the gun and sunk to the floor, she let go.

Gretel trots right over and licks Kevin's hand. And then his face. It's sort of gross. But Kevin actually smiles. "Ew, Gretel. C'mon, stop."

It's the first time I've seen him smile in some time. I think he is tremendously relieved.

So are we all. Victoria reaches out to drag me over and hold me on her lap, and strokes me hard with both hands. I look up at her. Her eyes glisten with the shock of what's happened.

Aidan yawns, tired after all the excitement. When he and Victoria make eye contact, I can see the unspoken bond they share.

Victoria exhales and turns back to her brother. "I hid that gun where you will never find it."

"It's Dad's gun. He's going to look for it eventually."

"So tell him you lost it out in the woods." She scowls. "Or tell him the truth. I don't care. Either way. You're a TRAITOR." She leans down and gets right in his face, so I have to jump up out of her lap. "You threatened us WITH A GUN. You're out of your mind." Her nose scrunches up. "You smell like beer. Have you been drinking? Here, you've been drinking here in the house? Give me a break. You deserve whatever the hell you get for losing that gun."

Aidan puts a hand on her arm, as if to calm her down. "Hey. There's a ton of blood on this rug, Vic," he says.

She looks around and frowns. "Yeah. But it's a small rug. My mom could—"

"Don't tell Mom," Kevin begs. "Please. You've seen what she's going through. She can't handle it right now. Please don't say anything."

"Yeah, Vic," Aidan jumps in, "We don't need to tell your mom. It's okay. Let's just say you spilled your nail polish and roll the rug up and dump it somewhere. I don't want your mom to know we were fighting. I want . . . I want her to like me."

Oh! This is something new. Aidan wants Mom to like him? This is a good thing. A very good thing.

Victoria doesn't love the idea of throwing away the rug, but she finally agrees with the boys. They both don't seem eager to share their story.

Hmm. Maybe if Kevin and Aidan can somehow arrive at some sort of peace, there is hope for us all.

But there will never be peace as long as Charlie is being bullied. My stomach churns as I realize there is more work to be done here.

I walk over to the foot of the stairs. Charlie and I stare at each other. His face is sad. Tired. And very worried. He looks small, curled up in a ball on the stairs with his arms over his knees.

Perhaps . . . perhaps I've been taking the wrong approach all along. Maybe I don't need to identify, find, or confront the bully. I know who it is. And I won't be able to convince him to stop.

The person I need to get through to is Charlie.

I run up the stairs, and I follow him as we slink quietly into his room. When he sits on the bed, I climb into his lap.

"What am I going to do, Lil?" he whispers to me.

I push my head into arm.

You can see what's happening to Kevin. You know what you have to do. Or something horrible might happen to you.

He looks into my eyes. "I want this to be over. I can't stand it anymore."

I bat at his face with my paw. *Listen! You know what you must do, Charlie. It will only get worse if you don't make it stop. Right now.*

Charlie turns to bury his face in his pillow. He punches his pillow, and I understand. He's frustrated.

But when he turns over onto his back, Charlie finally sighs in agreement.

Later that night, I find Gretel in the kitchen. Gretel is the hero once again. This time, when I nuzzle my face into her paw, she allows it and even turns to lick my ear.

Hooray! Good job!

While I wish I'd been the hero today, I can't deny Gretel the glory in this case. When she looks at me, panting and satisfied, I give her a twitch of my nose.

I know a brave dog when I see one.

Chapter 34
Chalk

Charlie and I sit on the hot driveway. He is drawing with chalk. A bucket of chalk in many different colors sits at his feet. I watch him carefully sketch a picture while I doze on and off nearby.

The days are longer now, and the late afternoon sun is still at a high point, although closer to the river than the top of the sky. The air is heavy and sweet. The soil around us has thawed completely, and budding leaves on the trees emit a fresh scent. Beneath it there is still, as always, the sour stench of the marsh.

I breathe in the savory scent of meat being grilled. One of the neighbors must be cooking on a barbeque. It makes my stomach grumble. Yet I am not really hungry. The spring weather makes me want to run and hunt, but not eat. I am eager to shed my winter fat. Charlie is lean, as I can see when his T-shirt lifts off his torso as he reaches his arms to the sky to stretch.

I am surprised at how warm it is. First my wet nose, then my whiskers, and finally the pads of my paws on the stones all converge at once into the thought: The sun is powerful today. When I sit still, I feel it soak into my fur and right down to my skin.

While Charlie draws, I listen to the sound of the birds crying all around us. I watch squirrels leap from tree to tree, my ears tingling.

Charlie and I are both startled when we hear someone come out the front door. We cannot see who it is, because we are sitting on the other side of Mark's big truck, which is parked in the driveway. Charlie sits very still, as if hoping no one will notice him.

I, on the other hand, have no such concerns. I listen to the humans talk all the time, and they think nothing of it. So I haul myself up onto my paws and walk over to peek out from behind a big tire. Mom is standing on the front step. Mark follows her out and then turns, waiting for a moment until he is sure they have privacy as he shuts the front door behind him.

"Katie," Mark finally blurts out, "Just listen to me." He reaches forward to take her hand, but she retreats so he cannot touch her.

I turn my head to glance at Charlie. He has slid over so he is leaning back against the tire. He does not move or even seem to breathe. I suppose he wants to hear their conversation.

I don't know how much we will be able to hear, sitting in the driveway on the other side of the truck. My ears prick up, alert, to try and catch the words.

Rejected, Mark leans back against the railing and Mom stands just opposite him. He looks down at his feet, and from the movement of his eyes I know he is thinking about what to say. When he finally looks up at her, he does so with just his eyes, not lifting his head.

"I'm sorry about the other day," he finally says. "I didn't mean to get mad. Jeremy threw me for a loop."

Mark fell in love with Mom without really knowing too much about our family. I can't blame him for that. Love is unexpected sometimes. In this case, it seemingly came out of nowhere. And now the more Mark learns, the more he realizes how complicated things really are.

Mom has her hair pulled back into a ponytail, and when she shakes her head, the ponytail shimmies. Her face is free of makeup, her skin scrubbed clean. I think she is at the point where she needs Mark to see her exactly as she really is, with no pretense.

"I don't want you to take him back," he admits softly. "I don't know why I said that."

"Mark." She sighs. "It's fine. Look. I'm not taking Jeremy back. I'm not." She takes in a deep breath, and looks him over. "The problem is, we're all getting very attached to you. And I'm afraid you're going to wake up six months from now in a cold sweat, and wonder what you were thinking. You're going to look back on all this like it was a strange dream. You need to go find the right person—"

"Katie." He leans toward Mom, but keeps his hands in his pockets. I think if his hands were free he wouldn't be able to stop himself from reaching out and trying to touch her. "I don't understand why you keep telling me to go out and find the *right person*." He tips his head, and when the sun hits his face, he has to squint. "I already found her. You're her."

"I believe you when you say you think that right now," she says. "But you'll change your mind in six months. You're not thinking with your head."

"Is that what Jeremy is telling you? That I'll leave in six months?"

Mom just turns her head and does not answer.

"Remember, he doesn't know me, any more than I know him. Whatever you need me to do, I'll do. I want to stay here with you. Long-term."

Mom leans back against the railing, and taps her foot.

He is stubborn!

"So what's your plan, then? To get a job working for Vincent?" Mom asks. "Does he need permanent help?"

Mark rolls his eyes. "Um, let me think. No. That would be a definite no. Construction work is not in my future. I'm surprised I didn't shoot my foot with a nail gun. I'm horrible at it, remember?"

She nods. "Yes. I remember." Her body relaxes and she shifts her weight from one foot to the other. Mark must sense, as I do, that she is letting her guard down for a moment, because he takes a step closer to her.

"Katie. I don't need an elaborate plan. I like baking. The schedule's not bad. I could get up early to go to work, and then come home so we could be together in the afternoons. Or if we need the money, I could go back to law. I don't think the world needs more lawyers, but . . ."

Mom looks down at a ladybug that has landed on Mark's forearm. She reaches out as if she might gently wipe it off of him, but pulls her hand back. I think that she knows that if she touches him, she will lose her resolve.

"It would be worth it if you could help more people like Charlie."

"Yes." He nods slowly. "If I could help people like him, it might make sense to me."

Mom glances down and shakes her head. "You're still ignoring the obvious. You're avoiding the point." Her voice gets quieter. "One of these days you're going to want your own family. I have three older kids, and my home needs peace right now. I can't be . . ." She taps her foot, searching for the words. "I can't be a way station between the time you start to recover from your grief and the moment you realize you're ready to start your life over."

Mark frowns at this. I realize Mom is repeating language that he used with her when he was afraid she was going to take

Dad back. There is a pause, and I listen to the coo of an owl, calling from the woods just behind me.

"Katie. I don't want to start a new family all over again. I don't even know who that person is anymore, the person I used to be."

Mark crosses the front step and moves toward Mom so he can put his hands on her waist, and she allows it, putting her own hands lightly on top of his wrists and looking up at him. Her face is open, and I can see she's willing to hear him out.

"The person I used to be disappeared on the day that Hannah died. I was the one holding her, at the hospital, because Felicia couldn't do it anymore. It was four in the morning. And she took her last breath. It was—"

But he cannot continue. Maybe because there are no words. His face clouds over, distressed with the memory of it.

Goodness! The baby died in his arms. He has never talked about this in such detail before. He has talked about many things—but not this.

I remember every time Mark cradled and spoke to me. I see this man is still missing someone, craving someone, needing someone to hold.

He glances up at the sky, the blue expanse over the treetops, as if the answers he seeks are located just above him. Talking all in a rush, he explains: "When Hannah died, I was numb. I was empty. I had nothing left to give anyone. I didn't want a family, or my house, or my job. I really thought my life was over, that God had just decided that I wasn't meant to have those things. I didn't want anything." He drops his head to look at Mom. "Until now. It's been a surprise to me to see that a year later, I'm still here. I'm still alive. Things are still happening around me, and I actually care. I care about *you*."

Mom's grip on his hands tightens. "I'm sorry."

As I've said, Mom is always expressing how sorry she is for

something or other. It's funny, because the things that happen are never her fault.

"You're sorry to hear that I fell apart? That I quit my life?" He tries to smile, and seems exhausted. "Yeah, that's exactly how everyone felt. Including my friends. And my boss. And Felicia's parents. And my own parents. They're all still angry at me, for refusing to try again. But I didn't want another baby, and Felicia didn't either. Everyone thought we were running away. And we were. But I'm starting to think . . . Maybe starting over was the only thing I could do at the time."

"It's okay. You don't have to explain." Mom's nose twitches as if it itches, but she doesn't let go of Mark's hands to scratch it.

Mark tips his head to one side. "I'm not going to give up on us. Felicia and I loved each other. But I was a disappointment to her. I'm not going to be a disappointment to you too." He squeezes Mom's waist. "Who I am now is a lot different from who I was then. I want different things now. I just want to live my life. With you. Don't look so sad."

Mom frowns. She cannot stop *looking so sad*. That is just something she cannot do.

I glance back at Charlie, but he doesn't see me. He is staring down at the pavement, straining to listen.

Mom raises an eyebrow, and takes in a deep breath as if she's been holding her breath this whole time. She exhales slowly.

"So." Mom straightens up. "In a year, when you come crawling to me to say you made a terrible mistake, and you have to break up with me, and you're really sorry about it, do I then get to say I told you so? Because I hate being right all the time. I absolutely hate it."

"Not an option," he repeats, glancing down at her mouth, and then back up into her eyes. He has big brown eyes that lock on hers. He is so unlike Dad, who evades, and looks away, and closes himself off.

I can see this conversation is almost over.

"You also have to understand I have three kids," she goes on, desperately, voice shaking with disbelief, "They're part of the package too. So we'd have to take things slow. You'd have to show me that you care about them too."

"Are you kidding?" His eyes water up, and he tips his head quizzically. "Are you kidding me right now? I love kids. I haven't really had a chance to fully develop my dad skills yet, but . . ." He wrinkles his nose at her, and laughs. "I'm sure I have some wisdom to impart, of some kind. Right? Hopefully."

Mom throws her hands up in the air, and the relief on her face shows in the way her cheeks flush pink. "I give up. I seriously give up."

"Good." He swiftly moves to close the inches between them, until his body brushes up against hers and he can put his arms around her. "It's about time."

Resting her head on his shoulder, Mom sighs. She looks peaceful.

"Okay," she says. "I love it when you stay over. You're so warm." She squeezes him tight. "My feet get so cold at night. And Gretel refuses to come sleep on my bed."

What?

Gretel? Are they talking now about Gretel?

I'm startled, and it makes me sneeze. I shake my head. What about me? I sleep with Mom. She doesn't need Mark to warm her up. Honestly.

"Gretel is a bad dog," Mark says, but I can tell he's joking. "What kind of dog refuses to keep her master warm at night?"

Oh! First of all, Mom is not Gretel's master.

Second of all, Mark just called Gretel a bad dog. If only he knew!

Kevin told the adults that he cut his arm with his ax while chopping firewood with Phil in the woods. Mom asked to see the cut under the bandage, but Kevin wouldn't let her look at it. He told Mom that Victoria already did a good job cleaning it, under his expert instruction, and he didn't want to undo her fine work.

"You're right," Mom murmurs. "She's terrible, isn't she? Good thing I have you."

Oh, Mom! I realize she is kidding, but who speaks this way about Gretel? Good thing Gretel is not here to hear this.

Mark nuzzles his nose in Mom's hair and closes his eyes. I suppose I cannot deny he is good at warming Mom up.

I turn back to Charlie. At this point he has his hand over his mouth, as if he wants to call out but is stopping himself. He looks at me. When I walk to him and smash my face into his elbow, he scoops me up with two hands and presses me to his chest. I can tell he's excited. He must be happy that Mom and Mark are no longer fighting.

But it's time for action. It's time to let Mom know that we're here.

Charlie, now's the time to talk about Kevin. I hop up and smash my face into his jawbone. *Charlie, you must tell them now while we have a quiet moment.*

When he doesn't move, I scramble and scrape my way out of Charlie's arms. With a hop, I jump up to his bucket of chalk, place my front paws on the edge and stick my nose in. When I pull, my weight brings the whole bucket onto its side with a *crash!*

"What was that?" I hear Mom ask, turning to look.

Charlie freezes, his eyes wild with shock and panic. I'm sure he thinks I did that by accident. He would be angry if he knew it was on purpose. I'm sorry to expose him, but perhaps we shouldn't have been eavesdropping in the first place. Sometimes you need to know when to quit.

I catch Charlie's eye, and try to send him a shot of confidence. I tip my head and flick my tail.

Charlie! It's time to talk. No creature deserves to be hurt, Charlie, and I'm worried about Kevin. I'm worried that the next time you'll end up with a broken leg like I did. The damage to my leg can never be fixed, Charlie, and I don't want that to happen to you. Let's talk to them now.

Charlie looks at me and blinks. He stands up and dusts himself off with both hands. With a short nod, he moves forward.

"Hey, Charlie," Mark says when we walk out from behind the truck. He sounds amused.

"Oh. Hi."

"Charlie . . ." Mom puts her hands on her hips. "Have you been there this whole time? Have you been listening to our conversation?"

"Um. Well, no. I mean, I heard voices, but I wasn't really listening. I've been drawing. With chalk."

Charlie gestures down toward the driveway. Mom and Mark cannot possibly see what he's been drawing from where they're standing on the front step. But from where I'm sitting, I can see Charlie has drawn stars and moons, and hearts with letters in the middle.

Mom sighs. "Charlie . . ."

Charlie walks around in front of the truck and crosses the small front yard to stand at the bottom of the steps. I join him and sit at his feet. "I want to tell you guys something," he says quickly, perhaps trying to get it out before he changes his mind. I hope Mom's conversation with Mark has increased his confidence in the future. Charlie has gained a friend in Mark. He has someone on his side, someone who pays attention to what he says.

"Yes?" Mom asks slowly, curious.

"It's Kevin." Charlie takes in a shaky breath, and shrugs. When Mom and Mark just stare at him, not understanding, he lets his hands dangle by his sides as he shakes them out. "That's it. That's all. It isn't anyone in school. Or on the bus. So no one needs to call the school. It's Kevin. When we go to Dad's place on the weekends. He gets mad when I take up all of Dad's time.

Kevin drinks Dad's beer and he gets jealous, you know? Dad's always worried about me, that's all. He spends more time with me than he does with Kevin. And I'm getting hurt. I'm getting HURT."

Mom clearly has no idea what Charlie is talking about, or she is taking a minute to process what he is saying, because she just stares at him with a blank look on her face. But when Mark nods solemnly, and says in a low voice, "Thank you for telling us, Charlie," it suddenly hits her.

And the look on her face is one I hope to never see again.

Chapter 35
Going to Camp

The next day, Dad comes over. He and Mom sit on the back deck for a long time, talking. It is the longest conversation they've had in ages. When I walk by the glass door, I see Dad with his head in his hands, and it doesn't look good.

When Mom sticks her head in the door and yells for the boys to come down, Charlie and I are lying on his bed. Charlie gets up and carries me downstairs with him. I understand. He needs me for support.

Charlie walks out onto the back deck without bothering to put his shoes on. The weather has warmed up, and he has adopted Dad's habit of walking in bare feet around the house.

Kevin comes outside next, and he sits next to his mom. His face is pale, and he stares down at the wooden floor of the deck.

Instead of sitting in one of the chairs at the table like everyone else, Charlie sits a little farther away in a comfy lounge chair and plops me on his lap. We sink down into the cushion. Charlie rakes his fingers through my fur. I can sense that he's nervous.

Dad leans back in his chair and studies Charlie. "Your mom

and I have been talking." His voice is hoarse and raspy, as if he's been up all night. "We've decided that maybe the two of you need a break from each other." Dad rests his hands on the arms of his chair and speaks calmly, but with authority. "And I think my apartment over in Ipswich isn't working out. I can't live by myself right now. I've been . . ." He closes his eyes a moment. Then opens them. "I'm drinking too much and I'm going to check myself into a special program as soon as possible." He says this part quickly, speeding through it.

"A what?" Charlie asks.

Dad is going to a special program?

"It's like . . . it's like a camp," Dad says.

"Oh my God," Kevin mutters, bowing his head and dragging a hand across his forehead. "No it's not."

Dad clears his throat. "Okay, it's not like a camp. It's more like a hospital. It's a rehab facility." Dad looks sideways at his oldest son, who just rolls his eyes. "Anyway. I hope to be out soon, and after that I'm going to move in with Grandpa, right downtown. Charlie, would you like to come live with me and Grandpa for a while? Until Kevin goes to college next summer?"

Charlie's face transforms completely. He sits up straighter, his eyes lighting up. "What?"

Kevin's mouth drops open in surprise. He collects himself and interjects: "What? No. Dad. Why don't I come live with you, and Charlie can stay here?" He shakes his head, as if Dad has gotten everything backward.

Dad look steadily at his oldest son. "Sorry, Kev, but your mom needs you here. She's going to miss you when you go to college. More than you know. And I need you to stay here and keep an eye on your sister. I don't like that kid she's going out with. You're the man of the house now. And you could probably use a better role model. Someone who is sober. Your mom tells me that Mark doesn't drink much. That's not his thing. So this is the way your mom and I want it."

"Jesus, Dad." Kevin's eyes tear up. "I'm so . . . I can't even look at you." He buries his face in his hands.

"I know." Dad's face softens, and he nods. "I know you're angry with me. For everything. And I'm sorry. I'm really, really sorry. We can talk once I'm done talking to your brother. You can say to me whatever you want to say. But you can't take out your anger on your brother. Or Mark. Or anyone else." Dad's voice breaks, but he goes on: "You just can't. You need help."

"Help?" Kevin peeks up at his dad. "I don't need *help*."

"I'm sorry. I know how you feel. I don't want *help* either. But . . ." He glances at Mom. "We both need it. And there will have to be a serious punishment. Your mom and I will talk about it. Look. The alcohol has got to go, once and for all. Completely. You're a good kid, Kev. I know you are."

Kevin, sensing Dad's eyes on him, shrugs. "Okay." He folds over and rests his head on his knees.

The grief is clear on Dad's face, but he collects himself and turns back to Charlie. "So, buddy, what do you think?"

"Your dad and Grandpa would love to have you," Mom interjects. "You could help keep your dad in line. Make sure he gets to his AA meetings. But only if you want to. And if your dad is drinking, if he has even one drink, you have to move right back here. Same day. No kidding around. Grandpa is going to enforce the rules."

A smile plays on Charlie's mouth. He blinks, those long eyelashes feathering down and then back up.

"Me? Well, I guess so. Sure. I mean, as long as you're in town so I wouldn't have to change schools, then why not? Would I have my own room? Could I decorate my room any way I want? Can we paint it? Would I be allowed to walk to the beach this summer and go get pizza and go to the coffee shop and the docks and whatever?"

Dad nods, and he brightens too, giving Charlie a weary smile.

"Of course. Sure. Yeah. Why not. I mean, maybe. As long as you're careful."

"And I could have my friends over?"

"Yes. But let's not get carried aw—"

"And my friend Ronaldo. He can come over sometimes too? Like, you know, to watch a movie or something?" Charlie blurts this last part out in such a rush that it takes a moment for everyone to process.

Dad gives Charlie a look.

"Okay. Sometimes. But I'm not promising I'll like him. I might have to run a background check on him first."

Dad says this in a gruff manner, but Charlie just smiles back at him.

And then he laughs.

"Okay. Yeah, Dad. We could try it."

I'm happy for Charlie. I can tell he is very pleased. But . . .

Does this mean Charlie, my one true human companion, my very best friend, is moving out? Just as I feared?

He's leaving?

I look up to study Charlie's face, but he doesn't notice me. Has he forgotten about me already, when I am sitting right in his lap?

Kevin wrings his hands and squirms in his chair, looking terribly uncomfortable. I think he is unhappy with this outcome, but he accepts it. He is the good older boy, and he will do what Dad commands him to do.

Oh! These humans. I feel frustrated.

When Dad and I make eye contact, he frowns. "We should only take one pet," he says slowly. "I don't want to overwhelm your Grandpa. Besides, that wouldn't be fair to your mom, or Victoria and Kevin, to take both pets. So just one pet. The dog or the cat. It's up to you."

Charlie's mouth opens, and he finally looks down at me in dismay. We both glance over at Gretel. At her sad, wet eyes.

The way her ears stand alert. Her tail is not wagging. She looks forlorn.

Gretel only has eyes for Dad. She is so incredibly lost without him. He is her alpha, her true partner in life, her one and only. She would give up her life for him. Whereas I . . . I am a cat. I adapt. I adjust. Whoever feeds me earns my trust, and I certainly trust Mom.

I turn my head back to Charlie to say: *It's okay. I love you so much, Charlie, and I will miss you every moment of every day, but I think you should choose Gretel.*

He gently touches the fur right between my eyes. My whiskers stand alert.

I'm startled when Charlie suddenly bursts into tears. I am usually very aware of how he is feeling, but this catches me off guard. He cries out as emotion washes over him. While cats do not cry, I imagine what it feels like: hot, sharp, and terribly unfair.

Maybe Charlie is simply relieved to have everything out in the open, to have a resolution. But change can be scary too.

Mom is instantly at his side. Hands rubbing his back. Cooing reassurances in his ear.

"Oh, Charlie. It's okay," Mom says.

"We didn't mean to force a choice on you," Dad chimes in.

Charlie waves them off. "Dad needs Gretel," he insists, gulping for air. "We'll take Gretel. I'm sorry. This is my fault. Everything's my fault."

Dad scratches his ear. "What is?"

Charlie waves a hand at his father. "Your stress. Your problems. Kevin told me. I'm the reason you—"

"No," Dad cries out, visibly upset. "No, Charlie. Absolutely not."

Mom runs a hand through her son's hair. "No, Charlie. None of this is your fault. Please don't think that for one minute." She sits next to him on the lounge chair and rests a hand on his shoulder.

Charlie doubles over and crushes me, squeezing me against his chest. He sighs. "It's okay, Lil," he whispers, rubbing his face against my head, folding my ear back, his tears getting my fur wet. "I'm going to see you every weekend. Every time I visit. And it's not forever. Just until Kev leaves for college. Not very long. And then maybe Dad will be better." He wipes his eyes, and lifts his head to look around at his parents. "Dad will get better now, right?"

Mom shifts her weight, looking uncomfortable. "Maybe." She rubs her cheek with the back of a hand. "Maybe he'll be better. We don't know yet, honey." She glances at Dad and nods. "You'll have to let me know every day what's going on."

Dad gives Charlie a small smile. "Your mom's right. I don't know yet, buddy. I've been trying but I can try harder. I don't know what else I can do. We're gonna to have to take this one day at a time." The smile fades, and he taps a hand on the deck table. "Okay, Charlie. I hope to be in and out of the hospital in the next few weeks. So we'll make plans. But right now I need you to go inside so I can talk to your brother."

Kevin doesn't look up. He continues to stare down, hands folded between his legs.

"Um, okay." Charlie stands and hefts me up onto his shoulder. "Okay."

He nods, head up, back straight. With a last sniff, the tears are done. Finished. Complete. He gives his head a quick shake, as if tossing off cobwebs. And we walk inside.

My brave boy.

My best friend.

My Charlie.

Chapter 36
A Man Named Mark

These days, I worry most of all about the oldest boy.

But things are getting better.

The summer has started, and Mark comes over many times a week. He told Mom he'd be happy to sell what he had and move in here with us, but Mom told him they needed to take things slow. So he agreed. But I can tell he enjoys being here and always seems sorry to have to leave for his own apartment.

To me, it is as if he has been here all along. His scent is so familiar to me, his touch so soothing, I cannot imagine life without him.

Mom seems happier. More relaxed. She pays attention to little things. She takes flowers when Mark brings them and smells them carefully, touching the petals gently. She allows Mark to throw his sweatshirt on the couch, and lets him get away with cursing. She doesn't always rush to clear the dishes. I think she has decided that sometimes in life things are not always under our control, and maybe that's okay.

Dad seems better too, when he visits. He says a polite hello to Mark. He is awake and aware. There is more color in his face, and he looks around him sometimes as if he is seeing the world for the first time. I can tell he still misses Mom, from the way he gazes at her. But when she looks at him, he is able to look back with bright eyes and nod.

Mom wakes up early for work and Kevin and Victoria must get up too for their summer jobs, but when Mark stays over, he rises even earlier, before sunrise. He never went back to being a lawyer, as far as I can tell. He comes over in the afternoon smelling like food and spices, cheese and pepper and cinnamon and lemon.

Often he makes breakfast for everyone before he goes. He'll prepare some ingredients the night before, and then he is very quick about it as he pours muffin batter into a pan, and slides it into the oven to cook while he takes a brief shower.

The first time Kevin and Victoria came downstairs and saw muffins still warm and sitting on the counter, they were amazed. They did not believe the food could be for them, so they did not touch it. Later in the day, Mark just laughed and said, *Who did you think it was for?* Ever since, Kevin and Victoria have eaten what Mark leaves out ravenously and gratefully, grabbing their food in a napkin and hustling out the door.

Victoria whines and moans in the morning if Mark is not here to cook for her. She now feels entitled to her fresh breakfast. I have to scoff. It was not long ago that she was lucky to have time to grab an apple in the morning.

Sometimes Charlie comes home on the bus after school to hang out with Victoria, and Aidan gives him a ride to Dad's apartment on his way home at dinnertime. Charlie and Aidan get along much better than they used to. I think they recognize something in each other. They are both careful around other people. Neither one trusts people easily. But they have come to trust each other.

Kevin and Aidan seem to have reached some sort of understanding. I cannot say they are friends, but neither are they enemies who harbor resentments. No one is afraid to be here.

Now that the weather is nice, Aidan and Victoria lie on the lounge chairs out on the deck, so they don't bother Kevin very much. They are happy.

Mark keeps an eye on the teenagers for Mom when she is busy and distracted. He tells them to "knock it off" when they start bickering, and they listen. Usually. As I've said, Mark is comfortable with people and it's hard not to warm up to him eventually. Even Kevin talks to him once in a while. It turns out Mark knows a lot about colleges and writing "essays"—whatever those are—and Kevin starts to listen to his advice.

Kevin is the oldest boy, and a good boy. I can see he is sorry he hurt Charlie. He talks to Charlie cautiously when they are together. He keeps a respectful distance. He does not give Charlie orders or make mean comments. Rather, he asks how Dad is doing, and Charlie gives him frank and honest replies.

Perhaps the two brothers will never be best friends.

Or maybe, over time, they will grow close. They have been through a lot together. You never know.

As the days have passed by, the strangest thing has happened. Mark has become my new favorite human.

Charlie is no longer here all the time. I love when he comes to visit. But the rest of the time I miss him, to the point of grieving. I get sad and lonely. But at the same time, I'm a cat. I gravitate to the one who feeds me, who cuddles and sleeps with me, who understands my needs. Don't we all?

I find that with Gretel and Charlie gone most of the time, the dynamic in the house has changed. I think things have evened out, thanks to Mark's calm energy. I sprawl out on the kitchen tile and keep him company while he bakes. And when he's done, he picks me up with two hands and carries me over to the rocking chair.

We sit, and rock, and rest. When he flips me upside down to coo and call me his baby, I purr. He looks into my eyes to make sure I'm comfortable, or pulls me closer so he can kiss my head.

Other times, he closes his eyes and I watch his lips move as he talks silently. I don't know if he is talking to himself, or to me, or to someone else. No matter. I rub my head against his chest, and we are content.

Sometimes—not often, but once in a while—Mark gets upset. Even when we are just sitting and rocking. I can tell he's remembering something painful. His face falls, and his eyes water as he gazes at me. But the moment passes. It always passes. And life goes on.

When I get warm and sleepy, my eyes naturally begin to close. Mark takes in a deep breath, and I feel his whole body relax. But I know he will not fall asleep. He will hold me securely until he or I are ready to get up.

We all have an instinct to care for others, not just ourselves. We need to touch and hold and nurture and protect those we love.

Sometimes the one who receives our love is a very good baby who does not live very long. Sometimes, it is a strange man who shows up to build a bookshelf. And sometimes, it is an absolutely gorgeous cat with a funny limp who fits right into the crook of your arm.

I don't know if Mark and Mom will stay together as mates for a long time. I would like to imagine they will, but I realize that I will not live long enough to really find out.

Maybe someday Mark will have a new baby of his own. Maybe not.

Someday, I will pass away too. And then Mark will have another loss to deal with. But for now, for today, I am here. I am warm. And I am just the right size for cradling. Mark offers love, and I accept it unconditionally.

I am not a bad stand-in for the baby he lost. I may, in fact, be perfect for now.

SOMETHING WORTH SAVING

Sandi Ward

ABOUT THIS GUIDE

The suggested questions are included to enhance your group's reading of Sandi Ward's *Something Worth Saving*!

Discussion Questions

1. Were you surprised to find out who Charlie's bully was? Who did you think it was?

2. Are there any situations where you might have sympathy for a bully? Are there any reasons or excuses you think explain bullying behavior? How common do you think it is for a kid to be bullied by a sibling, or a friend of a sibling? Did that ever happen to you when you were a kid?

3. When trying to figure out what appeals to Victoria about Aidan, Lily speculates: ". . . perhaps she feels Aidan can take the place of Dad as a man who is devoted in whole to her best interests." Did you think Aidan would turn out to be someone Victoria could rely on? How did you feel about Aidan as the story progressed?

4. Did you think Jeremy's anxiety about Charlie was justified? Was it helpful or hurtful to Charlie that his father spent so much time and energy worrying about him?

5. When Lily realized that perhaps Kate felt scared by Jeremy's behavior, what was your reaction? Would you have felt scared in the same situation? What would you have done differently, if you were Kate?

6. Were you surprised that Charlie wanted to go live with his father after bonding with Mark? Would either man be a good role model for Charlie? Do you think Charlie and Jeremy will get along when they live together?

7. Were you surprised that Charlie chose Gretel to live with him and his dad? Is it symbolic of Charlie putting his childhood aside and accepting the changes happening in his family? Could you see Charlie begin to take on the role of "parenting" his father if Jeremy has problems in the future?

8. Do you think Jeremy is truly on the road to recovery, and will pull his life together? Why or why not? What about Mark? Does he seem to be coping with his loss?

9. Lily at first just sees Mark as a distraction for Kate, but over time, Lily begins to love him. What about Mark do you think appeals to Kate and Lily? Is it just that he is emotionally open, whereas some of the Anderson family members close themselves off when they are unhappy or stressed? Do you think Mark and Kate will stay together in the long run? Why or why not?

10. In the end, Lily and Mark have each lost a loved one (Charlie has moved out, and Mark is still grieving the loss of his baby). Lily and Mark seem to have found solace in each other. Do you know anyone who has found companionship in a pet after losing a loved one?

11. Have you ever had a big dog that your family depended on for protection? If a dog injures someone, do you think it's safe to keep the dog? How did you feel about the kids not telling the adults about the incident with Gretel and Kevin?

Author's Note

Thank you to my agent, Stacy Testa, of Writers House for her guidance, support, encouragement, and positive attitude. I couldn't do it without her!

Thank you to my editor, John Scognamiglio, and all the wonderful people at Kensington for their faith in my writing, and hard work in publishing and promoting the book.

Many thanks to Susan Breen, author of the Maggie Dove mystery series, for her insight and excellent suggestions on improving the manuscript.

Thanks to my family and friends for cheering me on as I keep writing stories. I appreciate it.

I am thankful for my fellow authors who are always generous in sharing ideas, inspiration, and critiques—and thanks for sending photos of your cats and books for my blog!

Last, but never least, a huge thank-you to my readers. I am one of you. I'm always looking for a great story that makes me feel and think and dream. I appreciate you taking the time out of your busy day to read my stories. Thanks for your notes, reviews, and positive thoughts.

Some of us suffer with pain every day, and blame ourselves for being a burden. Some of us grieve over someone we have loved and lost. Some of us live in fear, afraid of being punished if we express who we really are. But even when life is not perfect, life is worth living. Better days are around the corner. Sometimes the most courageous thing you can do is ask for help when you need it.

You can find me on Twitter, my Facebook author page, Instagram, or my web site.

www.sandiwardbooks.com
Twitter/FB/IG: @sandiwardbooks

Connect with Us

Visit us online at
KensingtonBooks.com
to read more from your favorite authors, see books
by series, view reading group guides, and more.

for sneak peeks, chances to win books and prize packs,
and to share your thoughts with other readers.

facebook.com/kensingtonpublishing
twitter.com/kensingtonbooks

Tell us what you think!

To share your thoughts, submit a review,
or sign up for our eNewsletters, please visit:
KensingtonBooks.com/TellUs.